MA. ✓

RETURN TO WHISPERING PINES

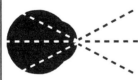

This Large Print Book carries the
Seal of Approval of N.A.V.H.

THE LANGTRY SISTERS

RETURN TO
WHISPERING PINES

SCARLETT DUNN

THORNDIKE PRESS
A part of Gale, a Cengage Company

GALE
A Cengage Company

Farmington Hills, Mich • San Francisco • New York • Waterville, Maine
Meriden, Conn • Mason, Ohio • Chicago

Copyright © 2018 by Barbara Scarlett Dunn.
The Langtry Sisters.
Thorndike Press, a part of Gale, a Cengage Company.

ALL RIGHTS RESERVED
Thorndike Press® Large Print Clean Reads.
The text of this Large Print edition is unabridged.
Other aspects of the book may vary from the original edition.
Set in 16 pt. Plantin.

LIBRARY OF CONGRESS CIP DATA ON FILE.
CATALOGUING IN PUBLICATION FOR THIS BOOK
IS AVAILABLE FROM THE LIBRARY OF CONGRESS

ISBN-13: 978-1-4328-5717-2 (hardcover)

Published in 2019 by arrangement with Zebra Books, an imprint of Kensington Publishing Corp.

Printed in the United States of America
1 2 3 4 5 6 7 23 22 21 20 19

*To those in the midst of
their darkest hour — keep believing.*

CHAPTER ONE

For He will command His angels concerning you to guard you in all your ways.
Psalms 91:11 (NIV)

1876
It was only the second day of September, but the air was crisp and falling leaves were floating on a gentle breeze, a sure indication summer would soon be saying good-bye. Adelaide Langtry was thankful the journey home to Whispering Pines, Colorado, had been much more pleasant than the trek east five years prior. She, along with her two sisters, had left Whispering Pines on a hot July day, and the entire trip had been one laden with dust, unbearable heat, and cranky, smelly passengers wedged elbow to elbow inside the coach. She couldn't imagine a more miserable experience, and she'd nearly jumped for joy when she'd learned there would be no additional passengers on

the last leg of this trip. Actually, it was a godsend; the three children she was taking home were able to stretch out and sleep, as they were at this moment.

After the children had worn her out with their many questions, she'd suggested they settle on the coach's bench seats while she read the story of David and Goliath. It was their favorite Bible story, and she'd read it to them so many times she knew it by heart. The children were quiet, listening intently, waiting for their favorite part of the story, David slaying the tormenting giant. Adelaide didn't make it that far this time; the rhythmic motion of the stagecoach lulled the children to sleep in minutes.

Adelaide's eyes flickered over their innocent faces as they slept. She smiled, thinking of their many questions about their new home and cowboys. Davey, who was twelve years old, going on twenty, wanted to be a cowboy, and to his utter dismay he had yet to see what he thought was an honest-to-goodness cowboy. Adelaide had all but promised him that a cowboy or two would be traveling with them, but it was not to be, and Davey was sorely disappointed.

In truth, Adelaide was as excited as the children to reach Whispering Pines. She couldn't wait to see her grandmother and her sister, Rose. She'd longed to return home for over a year, but she had promised to work for a period of time at the orphanage in Boston, and she had to see it through. It was always her plan to return home to teach, but when she started working with the children at the orphanage, she'd found her true purpose. Once she'd shared her desire to open an orphanage in Whispering Pines, the superintendent of the Boston orphanage lent his full support and plans quickly came together. Everything had fallen into place so perfectly, Adelaide's inner voice told her the orphanage was her destiny. She knew that as surely as she knew her name.

It wasn't without some regret that she was leaving some close friends behind, but Whispering Pines called to her soul. Her thoughts drifted to Prescott. Prescott Adler III and his parents were benefactors of the orphanage in Boston. They had donated the stately Colonial Revival–style home in Boston where the orphanage was located. She'd met Prescott the day she'd interviewed for a teaching position with the superintendent, and not long after their initial meeting, Prescott invited her to dine. Since that night, Prescott had been her escort to every social function he deemed worthy of his time and effort. Over the last few months he'd often hinted that one day he might make an offer of marriage, but it never materialized. She wondered if he missed her now that she was gone.

No doubt, Prescott's mother was overjoyed that Adelaide had left Boston. His mother never failed to remind her how fortunate she was to have caught her son's eye. Mrs. Adler had a way of looking down her patrician nose when she discussed Adelaide's inferior background, as though she'd had a choice in the matter of the family or circumstances into which she'd been born. The Adlers were one of Boston's wealthier families; old money, as Mrs. Adler would quietly discern when introducing her to Boston's elite. Frankly, Adelaide found it difficult to appreciate the difference between old money and new money. As Granny always said, *Money didn't determine a person's character.*

Pushing aside her thoughts of Prescott, and what might have been, Adelaide decided it was the perfect time to check her appearance while the children were sleeping. She opened her reticule to retrieve the elegant tortoiseshell compact that had been a Christmas gift from Prescott last year, and peeked at her reflection. She fiddled with her hair until she was satisfied her unruly curls were under control, then turned her attention on her pale face. As she pinched her cheeks to add a little color, she wondered what her sister Rose thought when she looked in a mirror. What would it be like to see the image of an uncommonly beautiful woman instead of an average face? She would never know; she had long ago accepted she would never have a face that would launch a thousand ships. Checking the mirror one last time, she muttered, "Not bad for an old maid."

She snapped the compact closed and glanced out over the passing landscape. No matter her accomplishments during the last five years, she worried her marital status would be the first thing everyone would mention when she arrived home. She'd told herself that twenty-six wasn't such an advanced age, yet she was well aware most women her age were married with children. Even her younger sister had recently wed the most handsome man in Whispering Pines, so Adelaide thought folks were bound to pity her all the more. It was generally considered unseemly for younger sisters to marry before the eldest married. Perhaps she wouldn't be subjected to as much salacious gossip, since her eldest sister, Emma, had never married.

It had occurred to her that once she told Prescott she was leaving, he might ask for her hand. But she hadn't made her decision to leave Boston to force his proposal. Even if he had asked her to marry, it wouldn't have made a difference in her decision to go home — at least that's what she told herself when he didn't profess his undying affection. She was fond of Prescott, but she'd always dreamed of marrying a man who took her breath away. Like her sister's husband, Morgan LeMasters. Not only was Morgan considered the most handsome man in the territory, he was also the most eligible, and there wasn't a woman in Whispering Pines who wouldn't have jumped at the chance to marry him. It came as no surprise Morgan had been smitten by Rose, and Addie couldn't wait to hear how he'd wooed her. Rose had had her choice of suitors in Boston, but she'd always kept them at arm's length, not encouraging their attentions. Adelaide sighed. If she were as comely as Rose, she wouldn't worry about being an old maid. Everyone would think she was just waiting for the right man. Sometimes the truth was more difficult to face, and more painful.

She told herself not to waste time worrying about what people might think. She was happy with her choices. Nothing would be as rewarding as opening an orphanage and providing children a home until they were adopted. Like the three children traveling with her now; they were starved for love and attention. Adelaide wanted to fulfill their emotional needs and provide them with some stability in their lives. *Faith, hope, love.* Isn't that what Granny taught were the most important things in life? What could be more important than loving children? She might die having never experienced the love of a man, but that didn't mean her life would have been meaningless.

Prescott often reminded her she shouldn't become so attached to the children since they would leave the orphanage one day. He'd said he couldn't imagine living on the premises of an orphanage as if the children were his own. Prescott was financially generous, giving the orphanage more support than she could imagine, but that was where his commitment ended. After spending a year with these three children in particular, she almost dreaded the day they would be adopted. If Prescott had asked her to marry and agreed to adopt the children,

13

she might have been tempted to stay in Boston.

She gave herself a mental shake. One couldn't live her life with what-ifs, one had to go forward. She glanced out the window once more and realized they were close to town. "Children, wake up. We are almost there."

Davey's eyes snapped open, and he slid across the bench to stick his head out the opening. "Really?"

Adelaide shook her head at his question. Davey reminded her of a doubting Thomas; he had to see everything with his own eyes to believe. "Yes, really." She leaned over and gently shook the girls. "Girls, time to get ready."

"Ready for what?" Jane asked as she slowly moved to a sitting position.

"Time to straighten your dresses. We are almost there." Adelaide watched as Jane's eyes moved to her younger sister, Claire. Jane was the middle child, and at ten years old, she'd taken on the responsibility of looking after her baby sister.

Jane stood and ran her hands over her blue dress, smoothing out the wrinkles before she squeezed beside her brother to look out the window.

Claire was only four years old, but she

understood they were going to a new place where they might find people who wanted to adopt them. She climbed in Adelaide's lap and focused her large, sky-blue eyes on Addie. "Are we going to find my papa now?"

Adelaide ran her fingers through Claire's blond curls and kissed her cheek. The question was asked with such yearning that Adelaide knew it was one Claire had long considered. "We are going to our new home. Right now, that is what is important. You will meet my grandmother, my sister, and her new husband. They will be part of your family too."

Claire scooted off her lap and tugged at her pink dress with her chubby little dimpled fingers. "Does it look good?"

Adelaide smiled at the beautiful child. "Perfect." She glanced at Davey and Jane as they craned their necks out the window. "Do you see anything?"

"No, ma'am, not yet," Jane said. "Miss Addie, do you think your grandmother will like us?"

Hearing that question brought a lump to Adelaide's throat. Sometimes the children would ask such questions so unexpectedly that it would catch her unaware. It never failed to sadden her that they thought no one would love them, or want them. "I *know*

15

Granny will love you, just as my sister Rose and her husband, Morgan, will love you."

"Are they as nice as you, Miss Addie?" Davey asked.

"I think they are, but you will see for yourself."

"Will we really learn to ride a horse?"

"You most certainly will. To live out here, riding is a necessity." Addie had wanted to teach them to ride in Boston, but the superintendent at the orphanage wouldn't hear of it.

"I think I see something," Jane said. "There aren't very many buildings. Are you sure this is the right place?"

Adelaide felt the coach slowing, and she leaned to look out over Jane's head. "It's a much smaller town than Boston."

"I want to see," Claire said, worming her way to the window.

The coach pulled to a halt in front of the hotel. Davey made a move to open the door, but Addie cautioned, "Wait for the driver."

The stagecoach driver, George, opened the door to see the two older children ready to jump to the ground. "I bet you children are happy to be here."

"Yes, sir," Davey said, leaping from the stagecoach. He looked around, and his eyes landed on two very large men and two

16

women walking toward the stagecoach.

Jane jumped to the ground next, and Adelaide was holding on to Claire's hand to help her out, but Claire pulled away and vaulted out the door.

"Claire!" Addie exclaimed in horror.

Sheriff Jack Roper had been talking with Granny, Rose, and Morgan when the stagecoach arrived, so he walked with them to greet Rose's sister. He was saying hello to George when he saw the little girl out of the corner of his eye. She was holding her arms out as though she expected someone would be waiting to catch her when she jumped. Reacting quickly, Jack took one step closer to the coach and scooped the child up before she hit the ground. His heart was in his throat when he looked down at the curly blond bundle in his hands. Her eyes were fixated on his face, and she didn't seem the least bit rattled by the incident. He couldn't help but smile at her trusting, impish face. He'd never seen such an adorable child. "Well, hello."

"Hello," Claire said, her blue eyes boring into his with more intensity than any outlaw Jack had ever faced.

"Claire! Don't you ever . . ." Addie stopped. Claire was safe and secure in the arms of a tall man who had his back to her.

Seeing Claire was not injured, Addie's heart rate settled.

"Addie!" Rose exclaimed when Addie appeared at the coach's door.

Jack turned, positioned Claire on his hip, and extended his hand to assist Addie to the ground. She didn't look a thing like Rose. Addie had auburn hair and blue eyes, and she was taller than her younger sister, not to mention she had a much fuller figure. While she might not be considered a heart-stopping beauty like Rose, she had a sweet, innocent look about her, and the bluest eyes Jack had ever seen.

As soon as the man holding Claire turned, Adelaide recognized Sheriff Roper. What she didn't remember, or perhaps she'd never noticed, was his ruggedly appealing face. His features were not as perfectly formed as Morgan LeMasters's, not handsome in the usual definition. More like strikingly dangerous looking. The slash of a thin scar running along the top of his cheekbone, along with his severely square jaw and penetrating silver-gray eyes, lent him a formidable appearance. "Sheriff," she said, placing her hand in his. As soon as her feet were on the ground, Rose and Granny converged on her and wrapped their arms around her.

"Oh, Addie, I'm so glad you're home," Granny choked out on a sob.

"I'm happy to be home." Addie was so overcome with emotion seeing her grandmother that she could barely speak. "It's so good to see you."

Granny pulled back, and seeing Addie's tears, she pulled her handkerchief from her sleeve and started dabbing at her granddaughter's cheeks. "Now, no crying. You're home and this is a happy day."

Addie wiped her tears away. "Of course it is. These are happy tears."

"Addie, you remember Sheriff Roper," Granny said.

Addie's eyes met the sheriff's. "Of course, nice to see you again."

Jack reached up and tipped his hat. "Miss Adelaide."

Addie thought his deep baritone voice matched his intimidating appearance. "Please call me Addie." She turned to Davey and Jane. "Let me introduce you to the children." She placed her arm around Davey's shoulders. "This is Davey, the eldest, and our protector on our journey." Jane was standing behind her, so Addie reached for her hand and urged her forward. "This is Jane, and I don't know what I would have done without her help." She pointed to the

19

young child in Jack's arms. "Claire is the youngest, and as you can see, a real handful." She gave Claire a stern look. "Claire, you shouldn't have jumped from the coach. You could have hurt yourself. Thank the sheriff for catching you."

Claire looked at the group of strangers before she turned somber eyes on Jack. "Thank you for catchin' me."

"Any time," Jack replied.

Running her tiny fingers over the scar on Jack's cheek, Claire frowned. "Hurt?"

The concern on her sweet face tugged at Jack's heart. "Not any longer, honey."

Claire smiled at his reply, and Jack returned her smile, flashing a row of perfectly aligned white teeth.

Like Claire, Addie couldn't seem to force her eyes from the sheriff's face. At first glance he appeared intimidating, but when he smiled, his face transformed from fearsome to remarkably handsome. She held her arms out to take Claire from him, but her eyes remained on Jack's mind-numbing smile.

Claire ignored Addie, shaking her head from side to side, silently conveying she was happy where she was. Jack just grinned at the child's refusal to leave his arms, leaving Addie speechless.

Claire placed her small hands on Jack's cheeks, turning his head until he was nose to nose with her. She studied his face, seriously appraising his every feature. "Are you my new papa?"

Jack was taken aback by her question. He didn't know how to respond to the darling little girl. He glanced Morgan's way, hoping his friend might help him out, but Morgan looked as flummoxed as he was.

Claire's question drew Addie's focus from Jack's smile.

Granny realized no one knew what to say to the child, so she spoke up. "Children, you can call me Granny if you like."

"Yes, ma'am," Davey and Jane said in unison.

Addie breathed a sigh of relief when Claire turned to stare at the older woman. "Granny?"

"Yes, Claire, you can call her Granny," Addie said. She wasn't certain, but she had a sinking feeling the child had already decided she now had a father and a grandmother.

Davey's eyes were bouncing from Jack to Morgan. The two men definitely fit his definition of cowboys: big and tall, wearing pistols and cowboy hats. He was enamored by them, and his curiosity was evident on his face.

Morgan saw Davey gaping at him and stuck his hand out. "Davey, nice to meet you. You can call me Morgan if you like."

Davey shook Morgan's hand and said, "Do you have horses?"

"Yes, I do. You'll be welcome to ride anytime on the ranch."

"I've never ridden a horse," Davey admitted.

Jack extended his hand to the young man. "We'll change that."

"Are you really the sheriff?" Davey asked when he took Jack's hand.

Jack pointed to the badge on his shirt. "Yes, I am."

"Are you really a cowboy?" Jane asked Morgan.

"Yes, ma'am," Morgan said.

"Can I ride a horse?" Claire asked Jack.

"You can ride in front of me until you are just a bit taller," Jack said.

That seemed to appease Claire. "Okay." She was running her small palm over Jack's cheek, feeling his afternoon stubble. "What's that?"

"That's my beard," Jack answered.

Addie was surprised at the sheriff's patience with Claire. She held her hands out again to Claire, saying, "Honey, we need to let the sheriff get back to work."

"But he's my new papa." Claire wrapped her arms around Jack's neck, hugging him as tightly as she could.

Addie had never seen Claire so taken with a man. She couldn't recall another man even holding Claire before, certainly not Prescott, nor the superintendent of the orphanage. She hated to disappoint Claire, but she couldn't allow her to think she had a new father and later have her hopes dashed. "No, honey, the sheriff isn't your papa, but you will see him often since he's the sheriff."

Jack's gut clenched when he saw tears welling in Claire's eyes. "I tell you what, honey, I'm riding to Granny's farm to do some work, so how would you like to ride on my horse with me?" He glanced at Addie and read the worried look on her face, and realized that he may have overstepped his bounds. "That is, if Miss Addie says it's okay."

Claire's lower lip started quivering, but she nodded before she buried her face in Jack's neck and sniffled.

"Are you sure it's not an imposition, Sheriff?" Addie asked. The sheriff hadn't given her much of a choice, lest she break Claire's heart the second time in a matter of minutes.

"No problem at all," Jack said.

"Addie, Jack is helping Morgan rebuild the farmhouse and there's more work to be done, so you will be staying at our ranch for a few days," Rose said.

Seeing the confused look on Addie's face, Granny took her hand. "We have a lot to tell you, but we'll explain everything later. We are having lunch at the ranch before Morgan and Jack leave for the farm." Granny hated to give Addie the sad news of her brother's death upon her return, but it wasn't something that could be avoided. Addie had already departed Boston when Stevie was killed in the fire at the farmhouse, and they'd had no way of contacting her.

Not wanting to be an imposition on Rose and her new husband, Addie said, "Perhaps it would be better if we stayed at the hotel. Adding four more to a household can certainly be daunting."

"We have the room, and we want you to stay with us," Morgan said. He picked up the valises that the stagecoach driver had placed beside them. "Let's get to the buckboard."

They reached the buckboard, and Addie approached the sheriff as he untied the reins of his horse. "Are you sure you will be okay with Claire?"

"We'll be fine." Jack couldn't stand the thought of the little girl crying, but he figured Addie was worried about Claire being on a horse for the first time. "We'll ride right beside you all the way."

"Claire, you listen to Sheriff Roper and do what he tells you," Addie said.

"Yes, ma'am."

Jack mounted his horse with Claire in his arms and situated her in front of him, telling her to hold on to the saddle horn. He wrapped his arms around her and backed his horse from the hitching rail.

"I gotta go," Claire said softly.

Jack chuckled, thinking she was anxious to be on her way. "We're pulling out, honey."

"I gotta goooo," Claire repeated, twisting around nervously.

When he understood what she was saying, he grabbed her around the waist and lifted her off his saddle, holding her in the air to the side of his horse. He held her at arm's length like a rock in a slingshot seeking his intended target — Addie. "Miss Addie," he said in a serious tone.

The women were chatting and not paying attention, but when they heard Morgan laughing they all turned to see what was so funny. Seeing Morgan's eyes were on Jack, Addie glanced his way. Jack was holding Claire away from him as if he'd just discovered she had the plague. Thinking he'd changed his mind about Claire riding in front of him, she arched her brows at him. "What is it?"

Panic was written all over the handsome sheriff's face. "She's got to go!"

CHAPTER TWO

During lunch at the LeMasters ranch, the children asked Jack and Morgan the many questions they'd been holding for real cowboys since they'd learned they would be traveling west with Addie. Addie had tried to pry Claire away from Jack while he ate, but the child insisted on sitting in his lap the entire time.

"I don't mind." Jack was enjoying the little sprite. He quickly learned she had more questions than he had answers.

"Jack, if your partner will let you leave, we'd best get to work," Morgan said.

Jack kissed Claire on the cheek before he passed her to Addie. "I'll see you later, sweetheart."

Addie stared into Jack's sparkling gray eyes as he waved to Claire, reminding herself that he was calling Claire *sweetheart,* not her. No one had ever called her sweetheart, not even Prescott. She glanced down at Claire, fully expecting her to cry when Jack left. But Claire surprised her when she kissed her palm and blew him a kiss, as Jane had taught her.

Jack pretended he caught her kiss and slapped it on his cheek, making Claire laugh. He stood to leave and when he passed Davey, he gripped his shoulder. "Son, how would you like to work on the farmhouse with us?"

Davey stared up at Jack. "Really? You mean it? I don't know anything about building a house."

"I mean it. Today is the perfect day to start learning how. You may want to build your own home someday. But you have to ask Miss Addie's permission."

Davey looked at Addie with such hope in his eyes, she couldn't refuse. "You will be back by dinnertime, won't you?"

"Sure thing." Jack thought the boy might enjoy some male company after traveling across country with three females.

Davey started to walk to the door, but he hesitated and glanced across the room at Jane. "Maybe I should stay here."

Addie knew what was troubling the boy. "Davey, Jane and Claire will be fine with us. Now go on and listen to the sheriff." On the way out the door, Addie heard Jack tell

Davey that tomorrow he would give them their first riding lesson after church.

Seeing Claire's eyes were getting heavy, Rose said, "Let me show you the bedroom where Jane and Claire will be staying."

They followed Rose upstairs, and Jane clutched Addie's hand. "Miss Addie, you don't look anything like your sister."

"No, honey, my sister Emma and I both have auburn hair and blue eyes. Rose looks like our great-grandmother. She had pale blond hair and blue eyes."

"But I look like Claire and Davey," Jane replied.

"But your eyes are different shades of blue."

"No one ever noticed that before," Jane said.

Addie wasn't surprised Jane thought no one noticed her. Claire garnered all the attention, partly because she was the youngest, and partly because her sweet face was irresistible. Jane was the middle child, and though she was pretty, she didn't attract as much attention. Addie understood what it was like to have a sister who received all the attention when she was in a room full of people.

Rose overheard their conversation. "Your eyes are a turquoise blue."

Jane blushed at the compliment. "Thank you. I've never seen turquoise."

"No? We'll make sure to show you some. Mr. Longbow has many pieces that he showed me when I was young."

"Miss Addie told us about Mr. Longbow."

"You will like him," Rose replied.

Addie smiled at Rose. She wasn't surprised her sister had already figured out that Jane needed some attention. That was the most amazing thing about Rose; her inner beauty far surpassed her outer beauty.

When they reached the upstairs bedroom where the girls were going to stay, Rose opened the door and led them inside. "I hope you don't mind sharing."

"No, ma'am." Jane's eyes widened in surprise when she saw the large, beautifully decorated room. The children had never had their own private room. At the orphanage there was only one room where all of the children slept, the beds lined in a row next to each other. Their belongings were placed in a chest at the foot of each bed. Jane turned in a complete circle in the middle of the room, taking note of the wardrobe, a large mirror, and a fireplace. "This is such a big room."

"Which bed would you like?"

Jane pointed to one of the beds covered

with a beautiful pink and white quilt. "Claire and I can take this one, and Davey can have the other one."

"Honey, this room is for you and Claire," Rose said.

Jane's smile vanished, replaced by a look of alarm. "But where will Davey sleep?"

"In the room right next door," Rose answered.

Addie understood Jane's concern that she might be separated from her brother. "Isn't it wonderful that Rose has thought of everything? When you want to talk to Davey, all you have to do is walk next door."

"Yes, ma'am."

Sensing Jane's uneasiness, Rose said, "Come with me and I'll show you Davey's room."

Jane looked at Addie. "Go ahead, Claire is asleep and I'll put her down for her nap."

Rose and Jane returned after seeing Davey's room, and Jane said, "If you don't mind, I'd like to take a nap with Claire."

Addie didn't think Jane was tired, but she knew she didn't want to leave Claire alone. It broke Addie's heart that Jane and Davey felt like they only had each other to depend on. Their lives had not been easy, but they had stayed together. "I don't mind at all, honey. Come downstairs whenever you want."

"When you've rested we will show you the ranch and some horses, Jane," Rose said.

"Yes, ma'am."

The women left the room and walked back to the kitchen. Granny had already washed the dishes, made some fresh coffee, and was sitting at the table waiting for them.

Rose poured the coffee and sat down beside Addie.

Addie caught the look that passed between Granny and Rose. "What are you two not telling me?"

"A lot has happened in the last few months, honey." Granny told Addie how her eldest brother, Frank, had become an outlaw. He was now a wanted man who had committed many crimes. He'd even set fire to their farmhouse and killed their youngest brother, Stevie.

It was difficult for Addie to believe the brother who'd always been her hero had turned to the life of an outlaw. "But why would Frankie do such a thing?"

"Honey, we don't know why. I stopped trying to understand Frank a long time ago. He doesn't have a sound mind," Granny said. "The fire happened before I received your letter saying you were on the way. I had no way of letting you know."

Addie sobbed as she listened to the details of Frank's many crimes. "What was his purpose in kidnapping Rose?"

"He hated me for marrying Morgan. But the truth is, he wanted me dead too. He said I betrayed him by marrying his enemy."

Rose understood what Addie was feeling. She'd had a difficult time accepting Frank's treachery. She'd never forget that day when Frank abducted her. "Frank had hatched the plan to ambush Morgan when he came for me. Frank shot him on the trail and left him for dead. One of Frank's men shot Jack, and he almost died. As soon as Jack finds out where he is hiding out, they will go after him."

Addie placed her hand over Granny's. "This is all so terrible. I'm so sorry he burned down our home."

"It's done, Addie. Morgan and Rose wanted me to live with them, so we had already moved my most meaningful possessions to the ranch. It has worked out for the best. Morgan and Jack are building a larger home to replace the farmhouse so there will be enough room for more children. Joseph Longbow has been working hard on building some furniture. God had a plan."

"Addie, why don't you tell us about the

children," Rose said.

"I'm afraid their story is a sad one, like most of the children in orphanages. Their father left their mother when Claire was born. Before Claire's first birthday, their mother dropped them off at the orphanage door. Davey, who was eight at the time, said his mother told him someone would come for them. She didn't say she would never see them again. There were attempts to find the mother, but she had disappeared. You can see how attached they are to each other. Davey has taken on the role of father, and Jane watches over Claire like a mother."

Rose couldn't imagine ever leaving the baby she was carrying. "That is terribly sad. Their mother must have been desperate to have done such a thing. No one would choose to leave their children behind."

Addie shook her head. "I used to think the same thing, but not all people should have children. Yes, there are many valid reasons children end up in orphanages. Many children have been orphaned due to diseases that wiped out entire families. When their parents die, these children roam the streets begging for scraps, trying to survive. Perhaps in this case, the mother had no means of support for the children. But we've also seen some cases where parents decide they don't want their children."

"Will they be adopted together?" Granny asked.

Addie had prayed for some family to want all three children. "That is my prayer. But I've been told I have to separate them if someone wants to adopt one of them."

"How dreadful it would be for them if they are forced to be separated. They are obviously devoted to each other," Rose said.

"Actually, I was worried about Claire being adopted first. To be honest, I'm surprised no one has adopted her yet. There were two families who wanted to adopt her in the last year, but she refused to speak to them. No matter how they urged her to talk, she simply would not utter a sound. I think both families didn't think she could talk, and that frightened them. I was hoping when we came here I would have a better chance of placing them in a home together."

"Perhaps she didn't speak so she wouldn't be adopted without her siblings," Granny said.

Addie had thought the children may have hatched that plan, though she never said as much to anyone. "Claire is a bright child."

It was evident to Granny that Addie had taken on the role of their mother. "You've grown quite fond of them."

"Yes, they are wonderful children. I wish I could adopt them, but the rules state that only married couples can adopt. They were very fortunate to be in the orphanage, or they may have ended up on one of the orphan trains. They would surely have been separated had that been the case."

"We heard about those trains," Rose said.

"I'm sure some of the children find a good home, but it is sad how they are treated. Many people are looking for workers, and the children are paraded about, like they are horses at an auction. Oftentimes, if the children don't live up to the standards of the people adopting them, they put them on the next train and off they go to another town."

"I can't imagine what they must go through," Rose said.

"The children certainly seem taken with Jack. It must be because he was an orphan, and he understands their need to feel wanted," Granny said.

Addie thought that might explain his tolerance with Claire's fascination for him.

"Jack rarely mentions his past, but he told Morgan he ran away from an orphanage and drifted from town to town when he was a young boy. I often think it must have been a sad, lonely childhood for him," Rose said.

"I wouldn't be surprised. If not for working at the orphanage, I may never have understood the hardships on these children." Addie thought Jack had successfully overcome his difficult past, and she hoped the children would be as fortunate.

Granny thought Addie could use some good news. She glanced at Rose, and said, "Have you given her your other news?"

"Not yet."

Addie looked from Granny to Rose. "What? You mean there is more bad news?"

Rose squeezed Addie's hand and smiled. "No more bad news. Morgan and I are going to have a baby."

Addie jumped up and wrapped her arms around her sister. "That is wonderful news."

"Now we need to find you a husband, Addie, so you can have some children of your own." Granny was determined to see all of her granddaughters married with children.

Just as she feared, her marital state would be the topic before long. "Granny, I think my life will be quite full with the children who will be coming to the orphanage."

"What about Prescott? Didn't he mention marriage?" Rose asked.

Addie shook her head. "I doubt his mother

would have approved if he had asked."

"Well, he doesn't need his mother's approval." Rose had met Mrs. Adler on several occasions, and she thought the woman was insufferable.

"It's for the best. If we had married, I'm certain he would have complained about how much time I spend with the children. I think once we had children of our own, he would have insisted I no longer work at the orphanage."

"Things have a way of working out as they should," Granny said. "Now what do you say we go upstairs and get you unpacked while the children are sleeping?"

When the girls awoke from their nap, the women took them to the stable to see some horses. The first person they saw was Joseph Longbow. "Girls, this is Joseph Longbow."

"Hi, Mr. Longbow. Miss Addie told us about you," Jane said.

Joseph nodded at the girls. "Hello."

"Joseph, how are you?" Addie didn't think Joseph had aged a day since she last saw him.

"Good. It is good that you are home," Joseph said.

Addie smiled at him. "Yes, it is good.

Granny tells me you have been making some furniture for the new house. I want to thank you for your help."

"It keeps an old man's hands busy." Joseph opened a stall to lead one of the horses out.

"Joseph, we are going to let the girls ride a horse to the farmhouse. Which one do you think would be best?" Rose asked.

"I'll get one saddled," Joseph said.

"We really get to ride on a horse?" Jane asked.

"I will hold the reins, and you and Claire can sit in the saddle. Would you like that?" Addie didn't need to ask the question; Jane was literally jumping up and down in anticipation.

"Yes, ma'am!" Jane grabbed Claire's hand and said, "We get to ride a horse."

"Ride with Papa," Claire said.

Addie kneeled in front of Claire. "Claire, the sheriff is not your papa. You need to call him Sheriff Roper. He's working at the farm where we are going, so please remember to call him Sheriff."

Claire stuck her lower lip out, but she remained silent.

Jane placed her arm around her little sister. "We are going right now to see Sheriff Roper."

Once Joseph tightened the girth on the gentlest horse in the stable, he lifted the girls in the saddle and passed the reins to Addie. "He is gentle."

"Thank you, Mr. Longbow," Jane said.

Joseph nodded.

"Now, Jane, put your arms around Claire and hold the pommel," Addie said, pointing to the pommel. "I will be on one side and Rose will be on the other, but we will go slowly."

Jane hadn't realized how far off the ground she would be once she was in the saddle. "I didn't know it was so high."

Addie remembered how hesitant she had been when she first learned to ride. "You won't think about that after a while."

"How did you learn to ride, Miss Addie?" Jane asked.

"My grandfather taught all of us to ride."

Addie and Rose walked beside the horse, leading it to the pine tree boundary between the ranch and the farm.

"I want to ride with Papa," Claire said.

Addie stopped the horse and looked up at Claire. "Claire, I know you understand me. Sheriff Roper is not your papa. We will not go see him if you refuse to call him Sheriff Roper."

Rose thought her sister was a little harsh

with the child, but she didn't want to intervene.

"She doesn't mean to be bad, Miss Addie. She just wants a papa real bad," Jane said.

Addie heard the fear in Jane's voice. The poor child always assumed if an adult corrected their behavior they would be sent away. "I know, honey. But we don't want to make Sheriff Roper uncomfortable. Let's just call him Sheriff, okay?"

"Okay." Jane was quick to agree, but Claire didn't respond.

Addie put her hand over Claire's. "Claire, what are you going to call Sheriff Roper when we see him?"

Claire had a mutinous look on her face, and Addie thought she wasn't going to answer. She'd hated to turn the horse around and go back to the stable, particularly since Jane wanted to ride so badly, but she thought it was important to make Claire understand she wasn't going to win this battle. She stepped a few feet in front of the horse, and was about to turn around when she heard Claire whisper, "Sherf."

Addie met her sister's eyes and saw she was trying not to laugh. To keep from bursting into laughter, she ignored Rose and looked up at Claire. "Good girl."

Chapter Three

"Davey, look, we're riding!" Jane exclaimed as soon as she saw her brother. "It only took us a few minutes to get here through those trees."

Jack was teaching Davey how to measure and cut a piece of wood on the sawhorse, but when he heard Jane, he dropped what he was doing and ran toward them. "I know, we went through there. I've never seen so many tall trees."

As soon as Addie tied the reins to the newly constructed rail, Jack was beside them. Claire held her arms out wide. "Pap . . ." She glanced at Addie and saw her frown, so she amended her words, saying softly, "Sherf."

Jack smiled as he lifted her from the saddle. "Did you come to see your new home?"

Claire shook her head back and forth. "I came to see you."

Morgan lifted Jane from the horse. "What about you? Did you come to see the house?"

"Yes, sir." Jane glanced behind her into the pine woods. "Where are the people who were laughing?"

"What people?" Davey asked.

"I heard people laughing in the trees," Jane said.

Addie looked at Rose, and they shared a smile.

"It was just the wind. It was really windy when we rode through there." Davey had heard the same thing, but the sheriff assured him the wind caused the unusual sounds in the trees.

Jack thought the girls would be as excited as Davey to see where they were going to live. "Davey, why don't you show Jane the house."

"Sure thing."

The adults followed behind, and before they walked into the house they heard Jane tell Davey that she'd met Mr. Longbow.

Jane could hardly believe this beautiful home was going to be where they lived. Even if no family adopted them, it would almost be like a real family living with Miss Addie. "Miss Addie, this is so pretty. It's nothing at all like an orphanage, it's like a real home. I can't believe we are going to live here."

Addie hadn't expected the home to be three times larger than the original farmhouse. "It's a lovely home." She turned her attention on Jack and Morgan, and her words were filled with gratitude. "You've done so much work. I never expected anything so grand."

"We didn't know how many would live here, but we can always add on if we need more room," Morgan said.

"This will mean so much to the children."

After they toured the entire house, Rose looked at her husband and said, "If you will look after the girls for a moment, Addie and I are going to walk to the cemetery."

"Of course." Morgan knew Rose wanted to take Addie to their brother's gravesite.

Addie looked at Jack, who once again had Claire's little arms wrapped around his neck. She reached out to take Claire from him, but he said, "She's fine with me. You ladies take your time. I will keep my partner entertained." Jack had never spent time with such a young child, and he was as mesmerized by her as she was taken with him.

Addie and Rose walked hand in hand to the serene site where their grandfather and brother were buried under a massive willow tree. A new cross marked Stevie's grave bearing his name and dates of birth and death. "Who made the cross?"

"Morgan," Rose said.

Addie started crying again. "Rose, I still find it hard to believe Frankie killed Stevie." Rose placed her arm around Addie's waist. "Frankie really is crazy. I don't know if he was always that way, but I know he is now." Rose explained how Frankie had treated her when he'd kidnapped her. "He tied me like an animal. After he shot Morgan, he told me he had killed him and laughed like someone insane. If not for Joseph Longbow, I would probably be dead."

Addie hugged Rose. "I'm so sorry for what you went through. Do you think Frankie will come back to Whispering Pines?"

"I know he will, particularly if he finds out Morgan is alive. That is why Jack is determined to find him first. Jack and Joseph found Morgan on the trail where Frank left him to die. They saved his life."

Addie shook her head. She didn't understand what had happened to her brother. "I do remember Frankie disliked Morgan when we were young, but I didn't know the depth of his resentment."

"I think he hated Morgan for everything he'd accomplished with his life. Morgan is

just a year older than Frankie. I didn't realize that when I was younger, I thought
Morgan was much older. But now that I
look back and remember everything Frankie
said about Morgan, I think he was eaten up
with jealousy. Frankie never worked for
anything, and Granny always took care of
him. Morgan is the man Frankie wanted to
be."

Addie kneeled beside her brother's grave.
"Poor Stevie. He worshipped Frankie."

They bowed their heads and Rose said a
prayer before they turned to walk back to
the house. It was the first time they'd been
alone, and Rose wanted to ask Addie about
Prescott while they had some privacy. "Tell
me, what happened with Prescott?"

"He hinted about marriage several times,
and he said he didn't want me to leave, but
obviously not enough to ask for my hand."

"Would you have accepted had he asked?"

Addie shook her head. "I tell myself that I
would have turned him down. I wanted to
come home. Yet, I can't say I don't want to
marry. Prescott might have been my only
chance."

"Prescott Adler will not be your only
chance. Selfishly, I'm happy he didn't ask
you. I wanted you to come home." Rose
didn't think Prescott was the man for her

sister, but she kept that thought to herself. "Do you love him?"

Addie hesitated. "I'm fond of him."

To Rose, that response was a *no*. Good. Addie deserved a man who appreciated what she had to offer.

Addie wrapped her arm around her sister's waist. "I'm so glad to be home, and I think the children will be happy here."

It was obvious Addie loved the children as her own, and she would be heartbroken if they were adopted. "It will be very difficult for you when they are adopted."

"Yes, but I will be happy for them. They deserve a family to love them."

"I think Claire has fallen in love with Jack," Rose said.

"I've never seen her act like that with a man. I don't know if she thought her father would be waiting when we arrived here, and Jack just happened to be the first man she saw. It's difficult for her to understand their circumstances. Davey, on the other hand, understands their situation all too clearly. He doesn't trust easily. He remembers his mother well, and he says he hates her. All of his anger is directed on his mother." Addie glanced at Rose, thinking she looked even more beautiful than normal. "I can tell by looking at you that you have a happy marriage. Morgan loves you dearly and he will be an excellent father."

Rose smiled at the thought of Morgan as a father to their babe. "I am so blessed. Morgan is the most wonderful husband, and he is so excited about the baby."

"I was surprised to hear you married Morgan. You were so afraid of him when we were younger. Who would have ever believed some woman hadn't snatched him up before you returned home?" Addie recalled how all the single women were vying for Morgan's attention before they'd left Whispering Pines to go east for their education. "Did you know right away that he was the one?"

"After we spent some time together, I realized he wasn't the terrible man Frankie had led me to believe for so many years. I can't imagine finding a more honorable man."

Addie hugged her sister. "I'm so happy for you."

"You will find the same happiness." Rose was confident the right man would sweep Addie off her feet.

Addie shook her head. "I think I'm destined to be an old maid."

"Nonsense. Whispering Pines is a growing town, and more and more eligible men are arriving daily. What about Jack? He's handsome, and judging by Claire's reaction to him, he has a way with children."

Addie thought about the sheriff's physical attributes. Tall and lean, with sandy blond hair, and the most unusual steel-gray eyes she'd ever seen. "A man as handsome as the sheriff would never give me a second look. I don't attract men like that."

"Don't be silly. You are beautiful," Rose countered.

"I'm passable. You are the beauty in the family. Emma and I always wished we could be as pretty as you." Addie may have been envious of her sister's beauty, but she wasn't jealous.

"You are both lovely. Remember, Granny says outer beauty fades, so your heart should reflect your beauty. And just look at Granny. She is old now, but even the younger men speak of her beauty. It comes from within."

Addie laughed. "Are you trying to tell me that there is hope for me?"

"Any man, including Jack Roper, would be fortunate to have you for a wife."

"Thank you, Rose, but you are my sister and you love me. All I can tell you is handsome men want beautiful women. I'm sure the sheriff has his choice of women, much like Morgan did before he found you."

"I don't think you give yourself enough credit, Addie."

"Prescott referred to me as a *handsome* woman."

Rose rolled her eyes. Leave it up to Prescott to give a back-handed compliment like that. They approached the house and saw a rider reining in at the porch. Rose recognized him and waved. "Well, speaking of handsome men. You are about to meet our new pastor, Clay Hunt."

Morgan and Jack greeted Clay, and introduced him to the children. When Addie and Rose joined them, Addie's first impression was Rose wasn't exaggerating; the pastor was an attractive man. Still, she didn't think he was as handsome as the enigmatic sheriff.

Rose gave Addie a look that only a sister would understand. It clearly said, *I told you so.* "Addie, this is our new pastor, Clay Hunt."

"I've heard a lot about you, Addie," Clay said. "I was hoping to meet you today. If you attend church with your family in the morning, I plan to make an announcement about the new orphanage. It would be a perfect time to introduce the children and the new schoolteacher to the congregation. I'll bet we will have some folks interested in adopting before you know it."

"Thank you, we will be there. School will be starting soon, and it would be nice to have the opportunity to meet the parents and children beforehand."

The pastor looked at the children and said, "It's a real pleasure to have you in Whispering Pines."

"Thank you," Jane said.

"I don't want to go to church. And don't think people will want to adopt us so soon. It don't happen that way," Davey said.

No one missed the heartbreak in Davey's voice. Jack understood better than most how the young man felt. He walked over to him and put his arm around his shoulders. "Sometimes we all get surprised. In the meantime, you and your sisters have a nice home here with Miss Addie."

"We'll pray for a new beginning for you, Davey," Clay said.

"I'm not much on prayer, either," Davey said and walked away.

"That boy is carrying a lot of weight on those shoulders," Jack said.

"Yes, he is." Addie turned to follow Davey, but Jack reached for her arm to stop her. "Take Claire, I'll go talk to him. He might need to talk to a man right now."

Addie started to object, but she thought perhaps Jack was right. It couldn't hurt for

Davey to have a man to talk to for a change, and Jack knew better than anyone what it was like for an orphan. "Thank you."

"I'm so sorry, I didn't mean to upset him," Clay said.

"It wasn't anything you said. The children have had so many disappointments," Addie explained.

Jack found Davey in one of the bedrooms sitting on the floor. "Mind if I join you?"

Davey shook his head.

Jack sat beside him and braced his arms on his knees. "You want to tell me what's bothering you?"

Davey remained silent.

Jack knew what was on Davey's mind. He'd been in Davey's position as a young man, and some things you just never forgot no matter how you tried to stuff them deep inside. When the children got off that stagecoach, his own childhood memories exploded to the surface like flowers popping through the earth during a spring thaw. When Claire touched the scar on his cheek, he recalled the day he'd received that ugly mark as clearly as if it had happened yesterday. In one of the many no-name towns he'd traveled through, a kindly cook in a restaurant had given him a freshly baked loaf of bread after he'd washed the dishes. He was twelve at the time, and though tall for his age, he was weak from hunger, having gone days without food. He'd left the restaurant through the back door and didn't see the knife-wielding man who wanted the bread as much as he did. They fought, but the man with the blade slashed his cheek to the bone, and won the battle. It was the only fight he'd ever lost. Life toughened him up, and what was left of any childhood innocence he may have had, was replaced with hopelessness and anger. Looking at Davey's despondent face was like seeing a reflection of his own image at that age. Other than Miss Addie, Davey and Jane no longer believed in the word of the adults they encountered. They'd lost their trust in the very people who should protect them. Claire was too young to be tainted by their bleak outlook, and Jack didn't want her to lose her innocent expectations. He wanted the children to know the love of a mother, and the strong, guiding hand of a father who would always protect them. He didn't know if he possessed the right words to assure Davey of the possibilities in life, but he wouldn't allow the young man to accept defeat. "You know, Davey, I was orphaned at a young age."

Davey's head snapped up and he stared intently at Jack. "Really?"

"Yep. I lived back East in an orphanage for a while, just like you and your sisters."

"No one ever adopted you?"

Jack shook his head. "I can't say I ever gave them the chance. I was a few years younger than you when I took off on my own."

"All alone? You didn't have sisters or brothers?"

"Nope, I didn't have anyone but myself. If I had sisters, like you, then I couldn't have left."

Davey nodded. "Yeah, it's hard with sisters."

"You've taken on a man-sized responsibility with your sisters. You know, Davey, even if you and your sisters aren't adopted, I think you will be happy here with Miss Addie."

"I wish we weren't going to be adopted. We'd be a lot happier if we knew we could stay here with Miss Addie. The girls love her so much."

Jack wished he could take Davey's burden from him. "I bet you've grown pretty attached to her too."

Davey nodded again. "We've talked about it, and the girls told me they want to stay with her."

Jack thought that explained why Davey didn't want to attend church. He didn't want anyone to see him, and take him away from his sisters. "I understand why you're worried. There's one thing I know that might help you though."

Davey looked at him. "What's that?"

"You shouldn't worry about something that hasn't happened. None of us know the future, and all we can do is make the best of the situation we're in at the moment. Does that make sense to you?"

Davey chewed on his lip as he considered Jack's suggestion. "I guess. But that preacher acting like someone would want to adopt us as soon as they meet us makes me mad. That's why I don't like going to church, they don't know what they are talking about. Most people say nice things, but they don't really mean them. God don't care about me and my sisters. No one will adopt all three of us. Maybe they would adopt me, or Claire, but Jane would be the one nobody will want. She's not strong like me, and can't do the work I can. Claire's young and so cute everybody wants her. Jane is the one who always gets hurt." He turned his sad eyes on Jack. "I don't think God cares if Jane gets hurt."

Jack's heart ached for Davey. He clearly understood why Davey was inclined to be angry with God. He'd had those same feelings when he was struggling to survive. "I used to feel the same way, Davey, particularly when God didn't answer my prayers to have a family."

"You know what I mean then," Davey said with grim satisfaction that his thoughts were finally confirmed by an adult.

"Yeah. I know what you mean. But you know what I realized?"

"What?"

"I realized that when it may seem like God isn't listening, He's preparing you for good things down the road. I knew I couldn't give up unless I wanted to go around feeling sorry for myself the rest of my life. I came to the conclusion that if no one adopted me, there had to be a reason. I may not understand the reason at the time, but one day I'd figure it out. That's what faith is all about; trusting when you don't see evidence at the moment that things will ever change."

"You go to church, Sheriff?"

"Yep, every Sunday."

"Miss Addie makes us go. I don't like going."

"Listen to Miss Addie. She always went to church as a young girl, and I guess you know her grandfather was a pastor. I'd say she's got a lot of pull with the Man upstairs."

"It hasn't done much good for us so far."

"Give the folks here a chance, Davey. Life is full of surprises."

Davey shrugged. "I don't want anyone taking Claire away from me and Jane."

Jack understood how difficult it would be to be separated from his sisters. He couldn't blame him for that. He didn't have all the answers, and he wouldn't fill Davey's head with possibilities that may never come true. He reached over and patted him on the back. "Keep trusting and believing, no matter what happens. You never know what tomorrow may bring."

Davey didn't say anything, but the way he studied Jack's face said he was searching for a reason to believe one more time.

Jack thought he'd let him think things over. "Are you ready to get back to work?"

"Yeah." Davey followed Jack's lead and stood. "Sheriff, what did you do when you left the orphanage?"

"I mostly roamed from place to place, didn't eat many good meals, and I took on odd jobs here and there. When I was fourteen, a sheriff in a small town took me under his wing. He gave me a cot to sleep on in the jail, made me go to school and church. I was eating regular, and not sleeping out in the weather, so I didn't argue about going. When I was old enough, he made me his deputy."

Davey didn't move; he stood there looking at the sheriff thoughtfully. "Maybe I could be a sheriff one day. How did you learn to shoot a gun?"

Jack didn't want to tell Davey about the many hours he'd spent practicing before he'd met that sheriff, preparing himself for a different kind of life. It was only by the grace of God that he didn't become an outlaw. "When I got older, I practiced with the sheriff."

"Would you teach me?"

"I'll teach you to shoot a rifle first. The most important thing is to be able to feed you and your family."

"You would really do that, Sheriff?"

Jack saw a hint of excitement in Davey's eyes. He reached out and clasped his shoulder. The boy definitely needed a man around. "Sure thing." He winked at him. "Let's keep this between the two of us right now. I'll need to get Miss Addie's permission, and we don't want to push things too fast."

Davey's smile faded. "I doubt she would

agree to that."

"I'll work on her. Now let's get to work."

Davey didn't move. "Can I ask you one more question?"

"Sure thing."

"Did you ever figure out the reason you weren't adopted?"

Jack hadn't thought about that question in a long time. "No, I can't say that I have."

"But you still think you will know one day?"

"That's two questions. But, yes, I still think one day I will know."

Addie saw Jack had his arm around Davey's shoulders as they walked from the house. Davey was looking at Jack with an expression Addie had never seen on his face; one of admiration. She knew something important had taken place between them. They reached the horse, and she said, "We're headed back to the ranch, Davey. We have some things to do before dinner."

Morgan lifted Jane on the horse, but Claire ran to Jack and held her arms up to him. When he swept her up in the air, she giggled.

Jack positioned her in the saddle in front of Jane. "Jane, I think you will make a fine rider. After church tomorrow, we'll all go riding."

Jane beamed at him. "Thank you."

He tapped Claire on the head, and said, "And you will ride with me, squirt."

"Davey, we will see you at dinner," Addie said.

"Yes, ma'am."

Addie smiled at Jack, and he nodded.

"Bye, Pa . . ." Claire said, and her eyes slid to Addie to see if she'd heard her. Seeing Addie's frown, she said loudly, "Sherf."

"Bye, honey. I'll see you tomorrow." Jack could barely keep himself from laughing at the way she said sheriff.

"Aren't you coming to dinner?" Addie asked.

"No, ma'am. I have to get back to town so my deputy can go home."

"Well, thank you for all of your work on the house." She tried to hide her disappointment that he wouldn't be joining them for dinner.

"It's been a pleasure. Doesn't hurt to sharpen my skills."

Morgan glanced at the pastor. "Can you join us for dinner, Clay?"

"I'm afraid not tonight. Addie, I will see you and the children tomorrow."

"We'll be there," Addie replied.

As they were riding away, Claire turned around and waved to Jack.

Jack knew she would turn around and he'd waited. He remembered being a little boy and knowing he wasn't important enough for anyone to go out of their way to wave good-bye. Whether they knew it or not, Davey and Jane bore the look of children who had been disappointed way too often. Maybe Claire could be spared the same heartache. Claire smiled wide when she saw him watching, and waved so enthusiastically that the women turned around to see who was waving to her. Everyone waved to Jack, and Jack didn't move until they disappeared into the pines.

CHAPTER FOUR

Frank Langtry and his gang had no trouble blending in with the other misfits in the small Mexican border town. They'd spent nearly a month in a drunken stupor, emptying their pockets of what cash they had managed to accumulate from rustling across the border. Low on money, and tired of the entertainment provided by the local women, Frank was ready to go back to Colorado. All he had to do was get his men to agree. They were sitting in their usual drinking hole when he broached the subject. "Why don't we head on back across the border tomorrow?"

"What for?" Deke Sullivan was afraid Frank wanted to return to Whispering Pines and create more havoc for Morgan LeMasters.

"Are we going rustling?" Corbin Jeffers asked.

"I think we should head back to Whispering Pines," Frank replied.

"Now why would we do a dang fool thing like that? I ain't had so much whiskey that I've forgotten we barely escaped the noose." Dutch Malloy was the only man in the gang Frank couldn't bully. He was a huge, hulking man, and Frank gave him a wide berth.

"I want to go back and take care of Joseph Longbow. You boys ain't forgot he's the only one who can identify us in court?" Frank wanted Joseph Longbow dead, but that wasn't his only reason for wanting to go back home. He'd heard from an outlaw who rode into Mexico from Las Vegas a week ago that Morgan LeMasters was still alive. Frank had shot him twice and left him for dead, but somehow he'd survived. He'd thought he was finished with Morgan once and for all, and he wasn't going to stop until Morgan LeMasters was dead.

"We ain't forgot nothing, but why don't we stay right here in Mexico? The law can't find us here." Deke wasn't buying that Joseph Longbow was the reason Frank wanted to go back. Frank wanted to kill Morgan LeMasters. Plain and simple, Frank wasn't going to be happy until LeMasters was six feet under.

"You want to stay down here forever? I say we take care of Longbow, and then they got nothing on us. We can go anywhere we want without looking over our shoulders for lawmen."

"Yeah? What about your sister? You kidnapped her, and I don't think a judge will take too kindly to that," Corbin reminded him.

Frank glared at Corbin. "It's her word against mine. I know you wouldn't doublecross me, Corbin, and tell what I did."

Corbin looked away from Frank's soulless eyes. He was scared to death of Frank. He'd wanted to ride off long ago and get as far away from Frank as possible, but after witnessing how he'd treated his sister, he knew he would never get away without a hole in his back.

"I ain't going back to Colorado. If you want to move on to another territory, then I'd be interested," Dutch said.

"I'm with Dutch," Deke said.

Corbin saw his opportunity to escape Frank's irrational schemes. He always thought Frank was afraid of Dutch, and he wasn't man enough to call him out. "I agree with Dutch and Deke."

Frank glanced at the last man in the gang, Reb Tucker. "What about you, Reb? You afraid to go back to Whispering Pines?"

Reb wasn't afraid of killing Joseph Longbow, but he wasn't keen on riding onto Whispering Pines ranch again. "After what happened last time we were in those trees, I'm not hankering to ride on that ranch again."

"All of you planning on staying right here? What about the Denver bank we were going to rob?" Frank asked.

"There's other banks, Frank," Dutch said. "We can ride to Kansas."

"That's true, but I don't have an inside man in Kansas. I have a friend who works in the Denver bank." Frank hadn't told his gang that he'd already robbed the Denver bank while they were waiting for him in Las Vegas. He'd robbed the bank with Walt, but Walt hadn't made it back to their designated meeting place. After the robbery, Frank ran from the bank first, carrying what he thought was his share of the loot. As he'd waited for Walt by the horses for a few minutes, he'd heard a shot. Seconds later, Walt emerged from the bank, saying he'd shot their inside man, Reuben. Frank didn't hang around, he'd ridden out of Denver fast, thinking Walt was right behind him. But Walt wasn't behind him, and he'd never showed at their meeting place. Frank didn't know if Walt was in jail or dead. Later, when Frank discovered that his saddlebag wasn't filled with his share of the loot, he realized he'd been swindled. Frank blamed the double-cross on Reuben, since he'd been the one to fill their saddlebags in the bank's vault. If Reuben wasn't dead, Frank planned to get information from him about Walt before he killed him. No one double-crossed him and lived to talk about it. Now that some time had passed, he began to wonder if Walt and Reuben were working together to cheat him out of his share of the money. Either way, if they weren't dead, they soon would be. "I know a place we can hide out in Denver, and no one will be the wiser."

"How do you know you can trust this fellow?" Deke asked.

"He was a friend of my brother. Stevie said I could trust him," Frank replied.

Corbin was tempted to remind Frank that Stevie was dead. Since Frank was most likely responsible for his death, he held his tongue. Frank's sister said Frank killed Stevie in a fire. Frank denied it, of course, saying he didn't know Stevie was inside the burning house, but Corbin was inclined to believe Frank's sister. Not only did he question Frank's story about Stevie's death, he wasn't so sure he hadn't killed Walt. He suspected Frank and Walt had robbed that bank in Denver, and something went amiss, but he couldn't prove it. All he knew was Walt never came back to their hideout after their trip to Denver.

"Since Stevie's dead, what makes you think that his friend will help you?" Deke asked.

Before Frank answered, Dutch said, "What makes you think he's still at that bank?"

"I figure we need to find out. It's not like we can get inside help on another job."

Dutch looked at Deke to get his take on Frank's plan. Deke shrugged, and Dutch took that to mean it was up to him to make the decision. "We'll meet you in Denver after you've taken care of business in Whispering Pines. You're the one who shot Longbow, so you can clean up that mess."

Frank didn't like that response, but he looked at Reb and Corbin. "What about you two? You going with Dutch and Deke, or coming with me?"

"I'm going with Dutch," Corbin said quickly.

Frank wasn't surprised over Corbin's decision. In his estimation, not only was Corbin dimwitted, he was also short on guts. "Reb?"

Reb was a lot like Frank; they both thrived

by living on the edge. "I'll ride with you as long as I don't have to go back on Whispering Pines ranch. We ain't seen Mason since we rode through those pines the last time we rustled. Do you remember those screams that morning?"

Frank didn't want to think about what they'd heard in those pines the last time they were there. "Yeah, I remember. Problem is, Joseph Longbow never leaves that ranch."

"I'll ride with you, but I ain't going through those pines again," Reb said adamantly. No one ever called Reb a coward; he wasn't afraid to do much of anything. Rustling or robbing a bank was fine by him. But the thought of riding in that pine tree range again scared him to death.

"Fair enough." Frank turned his eyes on Dutch. "Reb and I will meet you three in Denver at the end of the month." He told them how to find the house where he'd stayed with Walt before they'd robbed the bank. "You remember that place, don't you, Corbin?"

"I was pretty drunk when we were there, but I reckon I can find it again."

"Reb, what do you say we take off in the morning?" Frank asked.

"Sounds good to me. I'm tired of this place," Reb said.

"We'll be in Colorado City tonight," Frank said to Reb. They'd been on the trail for days, and both men were eager to have a good meal along with as much whiskey as they could handle.

"Good. Maybe we can spend the night in a real bed, and have ourselves some fun before we go on to Denver," Reb said. "I guess the boys stopped in Las Vegas. Hope they don't stay drunk so long that they forget to meet us in Denver."

"They'll show." There was one thing Frank knew he could count on and that was the greed of Dutch and Deke. They wouldn't miss a chance to rob a bank and share in the take. Frank didn't want to share the money, but he wasn't in a position to pull it off alone. If Reuben was dead, Frank would need more men this time. If Reuben wasn't dead, Frank might even rob the bank again on a Sunday morning, just like last time. He figured the town wouldn't expect the bank to be robbed twice within a few months, so they'd be complacent. The only difference would be, this time he'd kill Reuben before he left.

A few hours later, Frank and Reb left their

horses at the livery and walked to the Colorado City hotel. "Let's get cleaned up and have dinner in the hotel before we go to the saloon," Frank said.

"Yeah, I'd like to wash off some of this trail dust and have a rare steak," Reb said.

Frank chose a table at the back of the dining room so he could see everyone who walked in. When Reb joined him, he pointed to the chair at his side instead of across from him. He wanted an unobstructed view of the room. While they were waiting on their steaks, they had a cup of coffee and observed the other patrons. Frank immediately zeroed in on a lovely young woman in a fur-trimmed cloak, accompanied by a tall, distinguished-looking gentleman, as soon as they entered the room. He watched as the couple stopped to speak with several of the diners as they made their way to a table. Everything about the couple indicated they were of some means. Frank thought he heard one of the diners address the man as *Judge.*

When the waitress delivered their steaks, Frank said, "Who's that gray-haired man sitting over there with that pretty gal?"

The waitress turned to look where Frank was pointing. "Oh, that's Judge Robert

Stevens and his daughter, Charlotte."

Reb waited for the waitress to move out of earshot before he spoke. "Hope there's no wanted poster on you, Frank."

"Yeah." Frank couldn't take his eyes off of the judge's daughter. She was a petite woman, with long dark hair, and in Frank's estimation, she was as comely as his sister Rose. "She sure is a pretty thing."

"You'd best keep your distance from that one." Reb had never seen another man attract women like Frank. Frank could be charming when he wanted, and it seemed like women turned a blind eye to his darker side.

Frank smiled. "I could use a judge in my corner."

Reb wasn't about to bet against Frank when it came to women. If anyone could impress a judge's daughter, it would be Frank. "I reckon a judge's daughter could go a long way toward keeping our necks out of a noose."

Cutting into his steak, Frank was surprised Reb's thinking was in line with his own. "We might just have to stay here for a few days, Reb."

When they finished their meal, Reb was ready to go to the saloon, but Frank wanted to stay in the restaurant, hoping he could

71

find a way to meet Charlotte Stevens. "Just don't get drunk," he warned Reb.

"I'm going to have a couple of drinks and then I'll turn in," Reb said.

Frank handed him some bills. "Bring a bottle to my room when you come back." He wanted a drink too, but he had a feeling opportunity was knocking on his door. He asked the waitress to refill his cup while he waited for the judge and his daughter to finish their dinner. Before he finished his coffee, he saw the judge pay his bill. Now was his chance. He jumped up, threw some money on the table, grabbed his hat, and sauntered toward the judge's table. He timed it perfectly. Just as he approached their table, Charlotte stood and moved around her chair and Frank intentionally bumped into her from behind. Charlotte lurched forward, and Frank put his arm around her small waist to steady her. "I apologize, I wasn't paying attention to where I was going."

Flustered, Charlotte turned to look up at the man holding on to her waist. Beautiful blue eyes were staring back at her. "No harm done," she said softly as her gaze flicked over his handsome face.

Frank's eyes slid to the judge. "Sir, I'm

afraid I nearly knocked your wife over. I'm sorry."

The judge chuckled. "This is my daughter, Charlotte. Apology accepted, young man."

Frank stuck his hand out. "Sir," he said, without introducing himself.

The judge accepted his hand, and said, "I'm Judge Stevens." He pointed to Frank's arm around his daughter's waist. "And the young woman you are holding on to is my daughter, Charlotte."

Looking appropriately abashed, Frank quickly removed his arm. "I'm sorry." He gave the judge a disarming smile, and said, "You have a beautiful daughter, sir."

The judge beamed. "Yes, I think so."

"Do you folks live in Colorado City?" Frank asked.

"Yes, we do, and I don't believe I've seen you before," the judge responded.

"No, sir. I've been in Las Vegas."

The judge arched his brow. "New Mexico Territory? Quite a rough-and-tumble town."

"Yes, sir, that's why I left." Frank tried not to stare at Charlotte, but he could feel her eyes on him.

"Are you planning on staying here, or just passing through?" the judge asked politely as he started walking toward the door.

Frank was trying to think of a way to delay

their departure. "I'm headed to Denver. But from what I've seen, this is a nice town."

"It is a nice town," the judge replied. He glanced at his daughter and saw she couldn't seem to take her eyes off the handsome stranger. He was pleased his daughter was showing an interest in a man. He'd thought it was time she married and started a family of her own. Not to mention, he wanted some time alone to pursue a relationship with a particular woman he'd been seeing on the sly for months. Charlotte's mother had died when she was a young girl, and he rarely had time to spend with a woman. He'd just celebrated his fiftieth birthday, and he felt as though time was passing him by. It was time he got on with what was left of his life while there was still some life in him. Problem was, he couldn't get away from his daughter. Charlotte was very shy, and she found it difficult to engage men in conversation. Her lack of interest didn't encourage any man who may have been interested in courting her. If his daughter found this young man appealing, he thought he'd be wise to spend a few more minutes talking with him. He stopped in the lobby of the hotel. "My sister lives in Denver, and I am planning to purchase a home there. As a matter of fact, Charlotte is traveling to

Denver tomorrow to stay with my sister. We were planning on traveling together, but I have business here, so I will follow in a week." The judge did have business, but that wasn't what was keeping him in Colorado City. The truth was, he'd made plans to spend the entire week with his girlfriend. "I'm not certain it is wise to allow Charlotte to travel alone, but she is insistent."

They made their way to the door, and the judge looked back at Frank. "I'm sorry, but I didn't catch your name."

"Frank . . ." Frank didn't want to give the judge his last name, so he pretended to be distracted when he turned to offer Charlotte his hand as she stepped from the hotel to the sidewalk. "May I help you with your wrap, Miss Stevens?"

Charlotte held out her cloak to Frank. "Thank you."

The judge lit his pipe while he waited for Frank to wrap Charlotte's cloak around her shoulders.

"Judge, since your daughter and I are traveling in the same direction, I'd be honored to take the stagecoach tomorrow and look after her." Frank hoped he sounded helpful instead of excited to have time alone with Charlotte.

Judge Stevens looked hard at Frank. "That

is kind of you to offer." He glanced down at the pistol on his hip. "Are you capable with that gun, son?"

"I can be when I need to be."

"Hmm." The judge eyed Frank over the thin stream of smoke as he puffed on his pipe. The young man seemed to have gentlemanly manners which went a long way with the judge. He would rest easier knowing that someone was on that coach who could protect his daughter. He used his pipe to motion to Charlotte and asked, "What do you think, Charlotte? Would you like Frank to accompany you to Denver?"

Charlotte blushed. "It is very kind of him to offer."

Reb handed Frank the bottle of whiskey when he opened the door to the room at their hotel. "Are you alone?"

Frank motioned Reb inside. "It might be the last night I am." Frank opened the bottle and poured two glasses of whiskey.

Reb sat in the chair by the fireplace. "What do you mean?"

Frank handed Reb his whiskey, and downed the contents of his glass before pouring himself another shot. "You are going to Denver by yourself. I will be a few days behind."

"Yeah?"

Frank nodded. "I'll be traveling by stagecoach with the judge's daughter."

Reb laughed. "You're kidding?"

"Nope. Reb, by the time I get to Denver we won't need to worry about hanging."

"How are you going to manage that?"

Frank smiled at him. "As my dear grandmother used to say, *I think Providence just smiled on me.*"

CHAPTER FIVE

Before Pastor Clay said his final prayer, he made his weekly announcement. "As you know, we all have been waiting for our new schoolteacher to arrive. I'm delighted to say Miss Adelaide Langtry is here and prepared to meet your children." He waited while the clapping and excited whispers calmed down before he continued. "Folks, there is more news. Miss Adelaide is also starting an orphanage in Whispering Pines. The Langtry farm will be the new home for those children in need of adoption. We are very fortunate that Miss Adelaide brought three children with her to Whispering Pines. I'd like to introduce them to you this morning, and I know our congregation will welcome them with open arms." Clay motioned for Addie to stand with the three children as he introduced them.

Just like old times, Addie was sitting in the front row with her grandmother and sister. Morgan now joined them, along with the children. At the pastor's request, she stood and motioned for the children to stand as the pastor told the congregation their names.

"Miss Adelaide is hoping to find good homes for the children, and quite naturally, they would like to stay together. Until that time, they will be staying with Miss Adelaide at the Langtry farm. Please, everyone make them welcome, and anyone interested in adoption may speak with Miss Adelaide after the conclusion of our service. I know the heart of our church family, and I feel confident a good family will see their way to adopt those in need."

Addie was so thankful the pastor stressed she wanted the children to be adopted as a family, but suddenly facing the fact she could soon be losing them, filled her with dread. Her emotions were already running high because of the sad news of her brother's death, and learning about the misdeeds of her older brother. The joy she'd felt for months, anticipating returning home, was difficult to recall at the moment. It was fitting that the pastor's sermon this morning had been about standing up to life's challenges. It felt as though he had been speaking directly to her, and how her life had changed since leaving Boston. If the children were adopted soon, she would be facing new challenges.

Addie and the children took their seats for the closing benediction. Amen was barely out of the pastor's mouth when Claire scooted off the bench and ran down the aisle at full speed.

"Claire!" Addie hurried to the aisle to give chase, but people gathering at the end of the aisles made it difficult for her to see where Claire was headed. Claire had been squirming around during the entire sermon, and Addie had to give her *the look* several times. She didn't know why Claire had been so fidgety all morning, and she'd never taken off by herself. Standing on tiptoes, Addie tried to peer over the crowd. Finally, she thought she saw the top of Claire's light blond curls high in the air, and she had a pretty good idea who was holding her.

Standing at the door at the back of the church, Jack saw Addie and the children when he first walked in. He usually stayed near the door for easy departure should trouble erupt in town. After the prayer ended, he saw Claire bolt down the aisle, and he wondered if she had to *go* like she did yesterday. He wasn't surprised that when she reached him she held her arms out, letting him know she expected him to pick her up. He didn't disappoint her. "Hi, honey, how are you today?"

Claire hugged his neck and whispered in his ear, "Papa."

Before Jack could respond, Addie approached, her mouth set in a frown. "Young lady, don't you dare run away from me again!" She was going to have to speak with Claire about her fascination with the sheriff. So far, the sheriff had been nothing but tolerant of Claire's attention, but she feared he would get tired of her persistence if she didn't put a stop to it, once and for all. Not only that, but Claire would be totally confused when she was adopted by a family if she was emotionally attached to the sheriff.

Jack was blocking the door, and he saw the crowd coming his way. He spotted Clarissa Martin weaving her way through the throng of people, heading directly toward him with a wide smile on her face. If he was reading her right, she was about to latch on to his arm and cuddle up to him for the next fifteen minutes, or until he was able to escape. He'd been to her house for dinner several times over the years, and he'd even kissed her a time or two, but he'd backed off when she kept hinting about church bells ringing. He wasn't at that point in life when he was ready to wed. Uh-oh, she was just a few feet away, and he didn't know if he could get out of the church fast enough. He turned and said to Addie, "Let's go outside before the onslaught."

He'd barely made it outside when Clarissa appeared through the doorway and didn't stop until she was standing right beside him.

"Why, Jack, you sure look comfortable holding that little girl. I told you it was time for you to think about starting a family."

Jack thought if Clarissa took one small step closer she would be in his other arm. "Hello, Clarissa." He tried to outmaneuver Clarissa by taking a step back so he was standing next to Addie. He placed his free hand on the small of Addie's back when he introduced her. "Have you met Adelaide Langtry? And this pretty little girl is Claire." He glanced at Addie. "Addie, this is Clarissa Martin."

Eyeing Addie from head to toe, Clarissa said, "I don't believe we've met before."

Jack thought if he read Clarissa's expression accurately, she wasn't thrilled to be meeting Addie now.

"Pleased to meet you," Addie said politely, though the woman barely acknowledged her. She only had eyes for Jack. Since Rose had snagged Morgan LeMasters, Addie figured Jack was now the fish all the unattached women were trying to get on their hooks. Clarissa was an attractive young woman, with a neat and tidy trim figure, and long honey-colored hair. Addie figured she was just the type of woman Jack would find appealing. Old feelings of inadequacy threatened to surface. She would never be as thin or as pretty as this woman, but she reminded herself that did not give her cause to be envious.

"Addie is the new schoolteacher," Jack said.

Addie searched for something to say to the woman since she was obviously trying to ignore her. "Do you have children who will be attending school?"

Clarissa placed her hand on her chest as if she wasn't certain Addie was speaking to her. "Me? Why, heavens no. I'm not married." Clarissa stared pointedly at Jack.

Her comment was followed by an uncomfortable moment of silence. Jack felt Claire turn to look at Clarissa, but Clarissa didn't acknowledge her either. When Claire turned back to look at Jack, she rubbed her palm over his cheek, and said, "Papa."

"Papa!" Clarissa said the word loud enough to garner the attention of everyone filing from the church. "This is *your* child?" Her hazel eyes snapped from Jack to the woman beside him. The new schoolteacher. She looked her over once again, and curled her lip as if she'd just tasted something disgusting. She couldn't imagine how a mousy little schoolteacher could manage to make a man like Jack take notice. "You've had a child with *her*?"

"Oh, no, no!" Addie said quickly. She held out her hands to take Claire from Jack, and just to make sure the child didn't ignore her this time, she gave her one of her best *you'd better not shake your head at me* kind of looks. Claire grudgingly allowed Addie to take her from the sheriff. "I apologize for any confusion. I'm afraid Claire has taken a liking to the sheriff." She found it difficult to explain Claire's behavior to a complete stranger when she didn't understand it herself. Claire was an intelligent child, and Addie was confident she understood the sheriff wasn't her papa.

Clarissa gave an inelegant harrumph, loud enough to cause some of the church ladies who were eavesdropping to chuckle. "You should have a talk with that child and let her know the harm she can cause with loose lips."

Claire understood Addie was upset because she'd called the sheriff *papa,* but she didn't know why the other woman was making an angry face at her. Her lips started quivering, and she turned her watery blue eyes on Jack.

Jack placed his large hand on Claire's back, hoping to offer her some comfort. His eyes slid to Addie. "Don't be hard on her. There was no harm done, and these things happen."

"They most certainly do not just happen without some encouragement from adults," Clarissa snapped. She glared at Addie before adding, "Perhaps someone is prompting the child."

Addie was dumbfounded by the woman's rude behavior. She wasn't sure how to respond, and she didn't get the chance because Davey and Jane walked up and greeted Jack.

"Are these all of *your* kids?" Clarissa asked Addie. Addie took issue with her tone. "They —"

She was interrupted by Jack. "Weren't you listening to the pastor? These are the children who traveled with Addie from back East. They will be staying at the Langtry farm." He couldn't bring himself to say the children were orphans. He'd never liked the word; he'd thought it made children sound like they weren't valued.

Addie thought it prudent that she leave before she said something she shouldn't. "I do apologize for the misunderstanding. We will say good day." She turned to walk away with the children beside her, but she'd only taken one step when she was intercepted by a couple who introduced their son to her.

Clarissa's eyes were still fixated on Addie's backside when she said to Jack, "From the looks of her matronly figure, I just naturally assumed the children were hers. Women always become a bit round after two or three children." She turned her full attention on Jack and hooked her arm through his. "Where were you yesterday? I came by your office looking for you."

Jack's focus was on Claire, who was just a few feet away, staring at him over Addie's shoulder. She was opening and closing her little fingers in her special little wave. He'd heard Clarissa's catty remark, and he almost told her he liked Addie's figure just fine. He more than liked it. In his estimation, he should arrest her for being a danger to the public. The men in town would be tripping over their tongues every time they looked at her curves. He shook his head, trying to get his mind off of the schoolteacher's shapely figure. He was, after all, standing in the churchyard. He glanced back at Clarissa, who was now looking at him like she wanted to snap his neck like a chicken. *What did she ask me? Something about yesterday.* "I was at the Langtry farm yesterday. What did you want?"

"You seem to be spending a lot of time at the Langtry farm lately. I wanted to invite you to dinner today." Clarissa had invited Jack to Sunday supper several times over the last two years, hoping that he would eventually show more than a passing interest in her.

Jack didn't feel the need to explain to Clarissa where he was spending his time, but he tried to be polite. "I'm helping Morgan with the farmhouse. I won't be able to make it to dinner today. I'm having dinner at Morgan's."

Clarissa pressed closer to him. "Maybe you could stop later tonight for coffee and dessert."

"Sorry, I'm taking the children riding later, and then I'll need to get back to work so Webb can have some time off."

Clarissa pursed her lips in obvious disapproval. "I don't think it's wise to give so much attention to those children. You don't want them to become too attached, since they will be adopted."

Jack settled his hat on his head as he tried to think of a polite way to say *butt out of my business.* "Thank you kindly, but I think I'll seek my own counsel in this circumstance." Being the town sheriff had taught him to be diplomatic if nothing else. He tipped his hat, and walked toward Addie and the children. He hooked one arm around Jane and the other around Davey. "Are you two ready to learn to ride?"

"Yes, sir," Davey and Jane said together.

"Right after lunch," Addie reminded them.

"Let's hurry," Davey said, and took off at a full run to the buckboard. Jane was right behind him, and Claire squirmed in Addie's arms until she put her on the ground.

"You stay with your brother and sister, young lady," Addie said. "We'll talk about whether you get to ride when we get home."

When Claire was out of earshot, Jack said, "Don't be mad at her. They've all had a tough life. Now they've come to a totally new place, and Claire may be the only one not disillusioned with people. I just hope they won't be disappointed again."

She glanced up at him and saw his eyes were on the children. Addie thought there was a personal sadness in his words, along with a world of understanding. "You understand better than most. I just don't want her getting too attached, or making a pest of herself."

"I don't consider her a pest. She's a beautiful child."

"Yes, she is. It is nice of you to offer to teach them to ride, and I thank you for that. I've never seen them so excited. Actually, this is the first time I've seen Davey act his age. He's normally so serious that I worry he'll never have any fond memories of being a child. It meant more than you know that you included him yesterday building the house. He didn't even give me a hard time about attending church today. I have a feeling I have you to thank for that." After he'd been so kind to the children, Addie worried Claire may have caused a rift between him and Clarissa. "I'm sorry if Claire created a problem with your lady friend."

Jack appreciated her honesty. He looked down at her and grinned. "Don't worry about Clarissa, she'll invite me to supper again next week." Actually, he thought Clarissa would most likely pout for a few weeks, but it didn't bother him one way or the other. After the way she'd treated Addie and the children, he didn't care if he saw her again.

Addie admired his confidence. "I wouldn't

count on it. She seemed to be pretty angry."

"Don't you know, I'm like honey to a bee since Morgan married Rose," he teased. "There aren't many single men left in Whispering Pines. At least single men under fifty."

Addie thought he'd be handsome at fifty. "I think I figured that out as soon as I saw the women homing in on you after the service. I thought I might have to make a mad dash for the buckboard so I wouldn't be trampled." Addie wasn't teasing; she did notice other women keeping a sharp eye on him while he spoke to Clarissa.

Jack laughed. He liked her sense of humor. "Clarissa will be fine. It's these kids who have had too many people disappoint them. I don't intend to be one of them. Davey is a good boy who has too much responsibility for a youngster. They need to know that some adults will do what they promise. That's the reason they care about you. You're the one person who cares, and they love you for that."

His genuine concern for the children touched Addie. "I'm afraid I care a great deal about them. I will be filled with mixed emotions the day they are adopted."

Jack understood how she felt. He'd just spent a day with them, and he was already fond of them. They were good kids who'd been dealt a bad hand in life. "I just hope they will be adopted together. It'd be a shame for them to be forced apart."

"I know. That worries me more than anything."

Before they made it to the buckboard, several people stopped Addie to introduce their children who would be attending school. Addie kept an eye on the buckboard, and she could see the children watching her every move, silently telegraphing they wanted her to hurry the conversations.

After Addie met the last student, Jack said, "I think you met all of them."

"I counted eleven students, and it looks like there are some boys Davey's age, and a couple girls Jane's age. Are there any children Claire's age? She will be five soon." Addie expected to have a wide range in ages, but she'd hoped Claire would have at least one child her age.

"We have several younger children, but too young for school," Jack replied.

Granny, Rose, and Morgan joined them at the buckboard. "Addie, did Jack tell you that the farmhouse will be ready in a few days?" Morgan asked.

"That is wonderful news," Addie said. "It will be a fresh start in so many ways."

Jack didn't voice his opinion, but he wondered if she would be safe at the farm with three young children. He thought he was probably being overly cautious, but that came second nature to a lawman.

Once Jack and Morgan helped the women into the buckboard, Morgan pulled Jack aside.

"What did you say to Clarissa? She stormed across the yard as though the devil was snapping at her heels." Morgan had seen Clarissa corner Jack when he was with Addie and Claire, and he figured the woman would cause trouble. Clarissa was always looking for a reason to nettle someone.

"She said I shouldn't be spending so much time with the children, and I told her to mind her own business." Jack grinned when he added, "In a nice way, of course."

Morgan whistled. "She always was one to create problems where none existed."

Jack nudged Morgan with his shoulder. "You might have told me that before I started accepting her dinner invitations."

Morgan laughed as he walked toward the seat of the buckboard. "I didn't want to spoil all your fun."

Jack was still laughing when he untied his horse from the rail. Once he was in the saddle, he reined his horse beside the buckboard. Claire stood and held her arms out, a clear signal she wanted to ride with him.

"No, young lady, you are not riding with the sheriff," Addie said.

"Sherf," Claire pleaded.

Jack looked at Addie and the stern look on her face told him she would not relent. He couldn't bear to see Claire's sad face, so he rode ahead of the buckboard. He figured Addie was making her point right now, but she would allow Claire to join Jane and Davey on their first riding lesson. One thing was certain: Addie loved those children, and he felt certain it was difficult for her to scold them.

CHAPTER SIX

"Do you have a beau, Charlotte?" Frank wasted no time trying to get to know Charlotte once they were on their way to Denver. There were only two other passengers in the coach with them, and Frank was sitting close to Charlotte so he could speak to her in a hushed tone.

"Most men are too afraid of my father to call on me."

Frank leaned closer to her ear. "You mean to tell me you've never had a beau?"

Charlotte blushed. "I'm rather shy around most people."

Frank touched her ear with his lips and he felt her shiver. "You're beautiful. Have you ever been kissed?"

Charlotte glanced at the men across from them, and they were staring directly at her. "Shh, they will hear you."

Frank shot a glance at the men. He'd noticed them gawking at Charlotte before they boarded the stagecoach, as did Judge Stevens. The judge had pulled Frank aside and asked him if he was sure he could protect Charlotte's virtue if necessary. Frank assured him no one would lay a hand on his daughter unless it was over his dead body. The judge offered a handsome sum to escort his daughter to Denver, and while Frank needed the money, he needed something more important. He wanted the judge indebted to him, and he wasn't a man to kick a gift horse in the mouth. He refused the judge's offer, saying it was his pleasure to escort his daughter safely to Denver.

"You men might want to stop gawking at the young lady," Frank said.

Two sets of eyes slid from Charlotte to Frank. "She your woman?" one of the men asked.

Frank narrowed his eyes at him. "What difference does that make?"

"She don't act like no lady, allowing your hands on her," the other man commented.

"No harm in sharing," the other man said.

"Consider her my woman, and if you don't mind your own business, I'll stop the coach and we can settle this another way," Frank threatened. Frank prided himself on understanding how no-account drifters thought. They'd call your bluff until they realized you wouldn't back down.

Their eyes meandered down to Frank's pearl-handled Colt on his hip.

Frank smiled and leaned forward. "Yeah, I'm good with it." Since he'd started wearing his brother's gun, few men challenged him. There were two types of men who carried flashy guns: real gunslingers or aspiring gunslingers. Most men didn't want to chance gambling with their lives to find out which category he was in. He might not be as fast as his brother had been, but he could hold his own. Both men looked away, and Frank figured they weren't as interested in Charlotte if they thought they'd have to fight for her. He'd never fought over a woman, but there was always a first time. Gaining her father's trust was the goal.

Both men turned to look out the window. Frank knew he'd have to keep an eye on them, but he wasn't going to let them spoil his limited time with Charlotte. He slid back in the seat again and nuzzled Charlotte's neck. "Don't worry about them."

Charlotte nodded, but kept her eyes on the men. She thought the exchange between Frank and those two men was like watching a play. Frank was ready to defend her to the death. She was frightened and stimulated at the same time. Everything about Frank excited her. Unlike most men of her acquaintance, Frank was audacious and fearless. Most men kowtowed to her father, never uttering a word that might be considered disrespectful. Frank's brash and unconventional behavior attracted her more than his handsome face.

"What if I kissed you like you should be kissed right now?"

"Don't say such things. Father would never approve of your behavior."

"Honey, I can handle your father. He doesn't intimidate me."

"But the things you say are not appropriate." She was saying what was expected, but she wanted him to kiss her. The closeness of his body pressing against hers from hip to ankle created a flood of sensations she'd never experienced. She'd read about such feelings in the novels her father didn't know she read. He would have considered them scandalous. But those novels had educated her on affairs of the heart. She'd longed for the experiences of the heroines in those pages, and the intimacies no one in polite society discussed.

Frank barked a laugh. "Darlin', I'm not an appropriate kind of man." He cupped her chin and turned her face up to his. His lips were mere inches from hers, and he could see her pupils increasing in size. "Honey, when we get to the first stop, I'm going to find us a private spot and show you how to kiss."

Charlotte felt as though her skin was on fire. "You can't."

Frank put his arm around her and pulled her closer. "There's where you're wrong, sweetheart. I can and I will."

Over the next several hours Frank was relentless in his attack on Charlotte's delicate sensibilities. He'd made it his mission to know everything about her before they reached Denver. What he'd never expected was to like her as much as he did. He couldn't say he'd spent as much time talking to another woman before, but in the small confines of the coach, Charlotte was his sole focus. Initially, he'd planned on getting the judge in his corner through Charlotte, but surprisingly, Frank was attracted to her. He supposed it was her innocence that appealed to him. He couldn't say he'd ever spent time with an inexperienced woman, and he considered that a challenge. The combination of beauty and virtue made him think of his sister Rose. He'd thought she was innocent until she became involved with Morgan LeMasters. Now he hated his sister as much as he hated her husband.

True to his word, when the coach stopped so the passengers could get out and stretch, Frank took Charlotte by the hand. He led her to a private spot deep into some brush, far away from prying eyes.

Charlotte was breathless when Frank finally stopped behind a huge boulder. Frank had whispered his intentions for hours, and the anticipation of what he'd promised had been electrifying. When he took her in his arms, she was heady with anticipation of being kissed by him.

"Eighteen years old and never been kissed." Frank cupped her face in his hands and gently urged her mouth open with his thumbs. "Put your arms around my neck."

Charlotte did as he instructed, and when he lowered his lips to hers, she was startled by the warm softness of his mouth. Frank tightened his arms around her, and pressed her firmly against the rock. She stopped questioning the right or wrong of what he was doing, and succumbed to the demands of her youthful yearnings.

Minutes passed, and Frank was longing for more than kisses. When he heard the stagecoach driver whistle, he grudgingly pulled away from her. He smiled at her rosy cheeks, and the dazed look on her face. "I knew you would like to be kissed." He leaned in for another quick kiss before they walked back to the stagecoach.

Once inside the coach, Charlotte tried to appear composed, but she knew her face was flaming. By the smirk on the faces of the two male passengers, she knew the intimacy of what had passed between them was no secret. She questioned if all men kissed the way Frank kissed. It was probably wrong of her to want more, but when the stagecoach driver whistled, she didn't want to leave that secluded spot. She wanted to stay right there with Frank and learn the mysteries of what transpired between a man and a woman. Frank could teach her all of the things her father never discussed.

By the third night when they reached the way station, Frank had formulated his plan to marry Charlotte. It would be no hardship to have her for a wife; she was young and accommodating, and he'd already seen she hadn't resisted his advances. The more he thought about it, having a beautiful woman at his beck and call certainly had its appeal.

Charlotte was the only woman at the way station, and the owner gave her the one bedroom for the night. When the time came to say good night, Frank escorted Charlotte to her room and kissed her again. He lingered, giving serious consideration to joining her in the small bedroom, but he decided to stick to his plan. Once he walked back to the main room, he saw the two male passengers had spread their bedrolls on the floor and had settled in for the night. Frank grabbed a blanket and pulled a chair to the back of the room near the fireplace where he could see the men if they moved. Even though the two men had kept to themselves after that first encounter, he'd caught them eyeing Charlotte when they thought he wasn't watching. He understood these kinds of men, and he knew what was on their minds. He'd noticed Charlotte's bedroom door didn't have a bolt, so he needed to stay alert tonight. Covering himself with the blanket, he quietly pulled his pistol and cocked it before pulling his hat low over his eyes. He was certain he could have persuaded Charlotte to let him share her room tonight, but he was enjoying the pursuit. All things in due time. Wasn't that what Granny always said? His time was coming soon.

The silence of the room, along with the warmth of the fire, made it difficult for Frank to stay awake. He figured about two hours had passed, and no one had moved an inch, so he closed his eyes. His head bobbed up and down several times before he finally drifted off.

The two men waited for Frank to fall asleep before they quietly moved in their stocking feet to Charlotte's bedroom.

As was Charlotte's habit, she kept the oil lamp's flame low because dark rooms frightened her. But tonight it wasn't only the dark that disturbed her sleep. Thinking about Frank had her tossing and turning. He'd spent the entire day seducing her, and she hadn't had a chance to ask him personal questions. She knew very little about him, yet she thought she was falling in love with the handsome stranger. Hours later, she drifted off, thinking about a future with a man she barely knew.

The bedroom door squeaked when the men slowly cracked it open. They waited, listening for movement to let them know if anyone heard the noise. Silence. They peeked through the opening and saw Charlotte was sleeping, so they slipped inside the room.

Charlotte's eyes snapped open when someone covered her mouth. Before she could react, a strong hand trapped her arms above her head. The stench of the sweaty hand over her mouth made her nauseous. Fear gripped her when she realized she was staring into the evil eyes of one of the men from the coach. She had the presence of mind to try to fight him off, but when she tried twisting away from him, she realized the other man was sitting astride her legs. Still, she tried with all her might to fight them off with her limited movement. If only she could force the man's hand from her mouth, she could scream for Frank. Her struggles were in vain.

The man sitting on her legs flashed the large knife in his hand. "Stop moving or I'll cut you. You won't be so pretty then."

Her eyes locked on the gleaming long blade, and she stopped thrashing about. Realizing she was no match for this pair of vile miscreants, sheer terror paralyzed her.

The man holding her arms leaned closer to her face. "All we want is some of those kisses you were giving that other fellow."

The man with the knife snorted. "Yeah, we won't hurt you as long as you do what we want."

Charlotte tried to calm herself, hoping to hear someone — Frank — was coming to help her. But the only sound she heard was the pounding of her heart. Tears slipped from her eyes as she grasped her dire situation. No one was coming to help her. She was at their mercy.

"I don't think the lady invited you to her room," Frank said from the doorway.

Silence filled the room as both men turned to see Frank's pistol pointed in their direction.

The man with his hand over Charlotte's mouth released her. Charlotte gulped in a large breath of air as she tried to move, but she was held firm by the weight on top of her.

"Who wants to die first?" Frank's voice was deadly calm. He was going to kill them whether they drew on him or not. No one was going to take what was his.

The man who'd been holding Charlotte's mouth turned to draw his gun, but Frank shot him in the chest and he dropped to the floor. The man with the knife went for his gun, but only got it halfway out of the holster before Frank shot him in the head. His dead weight dropped on top of Charlotte and she started screaming.

Frank holstered his pistol, hurried to the bed, grabbed the dead man on top of Charlotte, and tossed him to the floor. Charlotte leaped into Frank's arms and buried her face in his chest. She didn't give a thought that she was wearing only her nightgown. Frank had saved her from a terrible fate, and the only place she wanted to be was in his arms.

The stagecoach driver and the owner of the station came rushing to the room.

"What happened here?" the station owner asked.

Frank nodded at the men on the floor. "They walked into the wrong room."

The two men pulled the dead bodies from the room, and Frank left Charlotte long enough to close the door. While he didn't think they would have another uninvited visitor, he pulled the bureau in front of the door for extra security. He walked back to the bed and pulled Charlotte on his lap and held her. "You're okay now, honey."

The next morning the stagecoach driver questioned Frank about the shooting. "I'll have to report this when we get to Denver."

"As I said, those men thought they were going to attack Miss Stevens and there'd be no consequences. I'm just glad I woke up when I did, or Judge Stevens would be wondering why you didn't protect his daughter."

The stagecoach driver believed Frank's version because the two men were in the bedroom, and there was a knife on the floor. When Charlotte joined them, he asked her if she could corroborate Frank's account of what happened.

After Charlotte related her account of the incident, she said, "Frank saved me from a terrible fate last night." Just thinking about what could have happened made her shiver. She knew it was wrong to allow Frank to stay with her all night, but she wasn't sorry. He made her feel safe, more so than her father ever had. "I don't know what I would have done without him."

"I'll tell the sheriff in Denver what happened, and he might want to talk to you. Seeing as the judge is your father, the sheriff will have no cause to doubt your word."

Once Frank and Charlotte were settled inside the coach, he pulled her into his arms. "We'll be alone now for the rest of the trip. When we get to Denver, we'll see the pastor and get married. After last night, it's the right thing to do."

"Do you want to marry me, or do you think it is your responsibility because you stayed in my room last night? We did nothing wrong, and I'm sure Father would understand." Frank had kissed away her fears, and they'd fallen asleep wrapped in each other's arms. To his credit, he hadn't taken advantage of the situation. Her father would not have approved of their sleeping arrangement, but he wasn't there.

"I want to marry you. Do you want to marry me? I didn't ask proper, but I'm asking now." While he never expected to hear those words from his lips, he meant them. Never before had he stayed with a woman overnight and just held her. His plan had worked.

Charlotte wrapped her arms around his neck. "Yes, I'll marry you."

Frank smiled. He couldn't have arranged a better outcome from this trip. When he'd offered to accompany Charlotte to Denver, he thought it was going to take some time to gain her trust and lay the groundwork before he asked for her hand. Now, here he was on the verge of having a judge as a father-in-law. All he had to do now was tell Charlotte about his past before they arrived in Denver. By the time he finished his tale of half-truths, Charlotte would be in his corner fighting for him, and she'd bring her papa along for the ride.

CHAPTER SEVEN

"Miss Addie, you sure are a good rider," Jane said. Addie rode with Claire in front of her so Jack could teach Jane and Davey how to ride.

"Thank you, Jane. I haven't been in the saddle for a long time, and I will probably be stiff tomorrow."

Jack thought she looked very comfortable in the saddle. "Jane's right, you'd never know you haven't ridden in a long time."

"This is fun," Davey said. They'd ridden around the paddock for an hour while Jack taught them the basics of riding. Once he was convinced they could handle the animals, he took them out on the range at a slow pace.

Addie was thrilled the children were having so much fun. Seeing the smiles on their faces made the pain she would feel tomorrow worthwhile. They'd listened intently to the sheriff's instructions, and he was wonderful with them. When they made a mistake, he didn't get upset; he'd focus on what they did right. Addie thought he'd make an excellent teacher. She found herself watching him instead of the children. "I don't think we could have found a better teacher than Sheriff Roper."

Jack pulled his horse close to hers. "Call me Jack."

Addie felt his eyes on her and she started to blush. "You are a very good teacher."

Smiling at her, Jack said, "I'll take that as high praise since it's coming from a teacher."

Every time she saw him smile, she'd lose her train of thought. She glanced at Jane and Davey and saw they had ridden a few yards ahead of them. "Don't get too far ahead of us."

"Yes, ma'am."

"And keep your heels down," Jack reminded them.

"Yes, sir."

"They really are good kids," Jack said.

Claire held her arms out for Jack to take her and let her ride in front of him.

"I fear this little one won't leave you alone."

"It's okay with me, if you don't mind." Jack waited for her okay before he lifted

Claire in front of him.

"Children are very comfortable with you."

Addie thought he was a unique man. His fearsome appearance probably served him well in his profession, but with the children she saw the gentleness beneath the surface. Looking at him, one would never have guessed he had such a tender heart. She always thought you could tell a lot about people by the way children responded to them. She'd never seen the children respond so positively to anyone before.

"I've never spent time with children, but I always thought I would like to have a family." He cast a glance her way. "How about you? Have you thought about marriage and children?"

"I think my time may have passed for marriage."

Jack was puzzled by her response. "What do you mean by that?"

"Well, I'm not as young as my sister. I'm afraid I'm not nearly as beautiful either."

"What does age have to do with marrying?" It took him a minute to decide what he should say about her appearance. He knew Rose was considered a real beauty, but Addie was pretty too. "You're every bit as pretty as Rose."

Addie laughed. "I believe you are a diplomat, Sheriff."

"You are —"

Addie held up her hand. "Please stop, I wasn't fishing for compliments. I was simply stating a fact."

"Well, I'd say your facts are wrong. You have the prettiest blue eyes I've ever seen." He felt Claire tip her head back and look at him. "That is, next to this little sweetheart in front of me." His eyes slid back to Addie. "You've got more curves than your sister."

She couldn't believe he'd noticed her figure, or commented on it. "Probably a few too many. I've never been as thin as Rose." Addie often lamented about her full figure to Granny. She'd developed early, and every year she seemed to be getting rounder.

"A man likes . . ." He didn't know how to say what he wanted to say. If he said he liked a woman with meat on her bones, she might not think that was very flattering. So he ended his sentence by saying, "a fine, shapely woman."

Addie knew he was staring at her, but she was too embarrassed to look his way. Prescott had never hinted that he preferred a woman with a fuller figure. As a matter of fact, when Prescott saw a woman who was trim, like Jack's friend Clarissa, he would mention how attractive they were. Addie always thought it was because his mother was nothing but skin and bones.

"Didn't you have a beau out East?"

"Beau . . ." Claire repeated.

Jack smiled. "Honey, that means a special fellow."

"Mr. Adler," Claire said, and made a face.

Claire's response stunned Addie. "Claire, do you know what beau means?"

Claire nodded. "He's not my papa."

Addie looked nervously at Jack. "I don't think she knows what it means."

"Uh-huh," Claire said softly.

Jack arched a brow at Addie. "So who is this Mr. Adler?"

"The Adlers are benefactors of the orphanage."

Addie said *Adlers*. Did that mean this Mr. Adler had a wife? Surely Addie wasn't in love with a married man. Was she being evasive? "So there is a Mrs. Adler?"

"Oh, yes, and their son. They are a very generous family. They provided the home for the orphanage in Boston."

"So the son was your beau?"

"Uh-huh," Claire said.

Addie expelled a loud breath. "He was my escort over the past year."

Yep, evasive, Jack thought. He'd dealt with enough people to know when someone didn't want to tell you the full story. He thought he might get more answers from Claire. "Did he mind you leaving Boston?"

"He thought I was making a mistake."

"Why did he think that?"

Addie didn't wish to say too much in front of Claire. "I suppose he thought I would miss Boston."

"Will you?"

"I will miss some friends, but I'm happy to be home."

Jack wondered if she was including Mr. Adler in the friend category. At least he wasn't a married man.

"Mr. Adler kisses."

At first, Addie wasn't sure if she'd heard Claire correctly, but she was almost afraid to ask her to repeat what she'd said. When she saw her lips puckered together as though she was imitating kissing, she wanted the ground to open up and swallow her.

Jack wasn't at all hesitant to ask Claire a few questions. "Who did this Mr. Adler kiss?"

"Miss Addie."

"Claire!" Addie searched her memory. She couldn't remember Prescott ever kissing her in front of the children. That didn't sound like something Prescott would do, so the children must have been spying on them when he would say good night at the door.

Jack chuckled. Now he was getting some truth. "And where did he kiss her?"

Claire reached up with her little pudgy finger and placed it on Jack's lips.

Jack kissed Claire's finger, causing her to giggle.

Addie watched him. It was such a tender moment. She wondered what it would be like to have a man like Jack kiss her. *Where did that thought come from?*

Jack looked at Addie, but she was trying to rein her horse away from him. "Miss Addie, I think your secret is out." So, she did have a beau who appreciated a woman with a lot of curves.

"I think it's time we ride back to the house," Addie said over her shoulder as she rode toward Jane and Davey. She planned to remind Claire what the Bible said about guarding your tongue to keep you out of trouble. When Addie told Jane and Davey it was time to return to the house, they begged to stay out longer.

"Do we have to, Sheriff?" Davey asked.

Jack smiled at him. "That's what Miss Addie said. But you can go with us to take some of the furniture to your new home, if Miss Addie approves."

"Can we?" Jane asked.

114

"May we?" Addie reminded Jane. "Perhaps we will all go along and help out." Addie told herself she was offering to help so the children could spend more time with Jack, and not because she enjoyed his company as much as they did. She just hoped Claire didn't talk about things best left unsaid.

At the farm, Addie ran her hands the length of the long table Joseph had built for the kitchen. She thought twenty people could comfortably sit at the table. "Joseph, this is the most beautiful table I have ever seen."

"More children may come here," Joseph replied.

Addie smiled at the thought of bringing more children to her home. "There will certainly be room for them at this table."

"Miss Addie, did you see our beds?" Jane asked.

"I did, and you should thank Mr. Longbow for his hard work," Addie said.

"Mr. Longbow, I've never had such a nice bed. Thank you so much," Jane said excitedly.

Joseph smiled at Jane. "You are welcome."

Addie thought she saw tears in the old man's eyes. "Look at our lovely table, Jane. Just think of all the people we can seat at this table."

Jane admired the table and glanced up at Joseph. "It's so pretty." Her eyes lit up when she said, "Miss Addie taught me how to bake a cake. I am going to make one for you, Mr. Longbow, if you come for dinner."

"I will come." Joseph nodded and walked out the door.

Addie hugged Jane to her. "Honey, I think you just did the impossible. Granny always told me that Mr. Longbow rarely eats dinner with anyone."

Granny walked in the kitchen and overheard Addie. "That's the truth of it. Joseph's a very private man." Granny took Jane by the hand. "I want you to see the quilts and feather mattresses Rose and I made while the men were building the house."

"Miss Addie has been teaching me to sew," Jane replied as they left the room hand in hand.

"Then you can help us make the pillows," Granny said.

Addie walked to the parlor just as Jack came through the front door carrying two chairs. Claire was right behind him carrying a cushion. Addie stopped and smiled at Claire, thinking it was a scene worthy of a painting: Jack and his mini shadow. Earlier when they'd been riding, Jack removed his hat, and Addie noticed the pale blond streaks in his dark blond hair. He could almost pass for Claire's father. She stopped her woolgathering and realized Jack was staring at her.

"This is my helper," Jack said, nodding at Claire.

"So I see." Addie hurried to him. "Let me take a chair."

"No need, just point to where you want them."

Jane ran down the steps and stopped midway. "Claire, come see our bedroom and our beds Mr. Longbow built."

Claire handed her cushion to Addie and followed Jane up the stairs.

"Put them in front of the fireplace," Addie said to Jack.

Jack placed the chairs where Addie was pointing. "How do you think you'll like your new home?"

"I think it's perfect. You all have done so much, I don't know how to thank you." She leaned over and plopped the cushion on one of the chairs.

With her back to him, Jack had a nice view of her ample figure. When she straightened and turned to face him, his eyes drifted from her eyes to her toes. Yep, she had curves packed in all the right places, soft and inviting. He thought she looked pretty standing there in the sunlight, her bright blue eyes shining with excitement. He was tempted to tell her she could thank him by giving him a kiss.

"Is there more in the buckboard?"

Jack's eyes were on her lips. He gave himself a mental shake. "Huh?"

Addie wondered what was wrong with him. "Is there more in the buckboard?"

"Morgan is grabbing the last chair." Jack started toward the door only to be halted by Morgan walking in with the chair in his hands.

"Where do you want this, Addie?" Morgan asked.

Addie pointed to the space for the chair. "The orphanage provided me with funds to set up a complete home, not to mention access to funds to buy a home. They will be pleased to know I will not need to purchase a home, or much furniture."

"You should charge Mr. Adler a monthly fee for the use of your property," Jack said.

Addie turned her eyes on him. "I can do that?"

"Of course. You should be reimbursed for the use of your home. And with this much property, if you have time, you can grow most of your food, which will save substantial money."

"Jack's right. The additional income will help you out since your earnings as a schoolteacher are fairly meager," Morgan added.

Addie was quickly learning all the things she didn't know. No doubt, Prescott's family were adept at financial matters, and they would probably agree to the idea. "Then I could repay you for your hard work."

Though he knew she didn't mean to insult them, her comment still irritated Jack. "We don't want payment. We did this for Granny and you girls."

"You keep the money for the orphanage," Morgan said.

"I'll send a telegram to Prescott and inform him of my arrangement," Addie said.

So, Prescott Adler was his name. The man Claire said had kissed Miss Addie. He wondered if a man named Prescott knew the first thing about kissing a woman. He almost laughed at the thought.

Chapter Eight

"Sir, you may kiss your bride," the pastor said to Frank Langtry.

Frank leaned over, took Charlotte in his arms, and kissed her. When the kiss ended, he whispered in her ear so the pastor couldn't hear what he had to say.

"We'll have to dine with Aunt Ruth first," Charlotte replied shyly.

"I don't want to wait, but I will for you." Frank took her hand, thanked the pastor, and headed out the door. He needed to meet his men, but tonight was going to be spent with his new bride. His men would have to wait until tomorrow.

Charlotte led the way to her aunt's home, and Frank could hardly believe his eyes. His bride had told him the judge and his sister had inherited some wealth, but Frank never expected she lived in the largest mansion in Denver. He figured there had to be at least twenty rooms in the massive brick structure.

"What did you say your aunt and uncle owned?"

"A mine."

"A silver mine?"

"No, a gold mine. My uncle died of a heart attack a few years ago, so poor Aunt Ruth lives in this monstrosity alone."

When Charlotte spoke of Aunt Ruth, Frank expected to meet an elderly woman. While Ruth was probably in her fifties, she was still a very attractive woman. He didn't know what to expect from the occupant of the lavish home, but he'd prepared himself for questions regarding his background and his potential to support his wife. Aunt Ruth surprised him by welcoming him with open arms, not asking one personal question. She told him she'd been praying for some time for Charlotte to marry and have children. According to Aunt Ruth, there was nothing more worthwhile in life than children, most likely because she and her dearly departed husband had never been blessed.

Frank charmed her through dinner with tales of famous outlaws he'd met in Las Vegas. Aunt Ruth was on the edge of her chair as he recounted gunfights he'd witnessed. He'd even amazed himself with his gift of storytelling. Who would ever believe Frank Langtry was sitting in the drawing room of the wealthiest woman in Denver, sipping a fine brandy, and married to the only heir of her wealth?

Before they'd retired for the night, Aunt Ruth hugged Frank. "I hope you won't object if I consider you the son I never had. Welcome to our family."

Frank kissed her cheek. "I'd consider it an honor."

After breakfast the next morning, Frank decided before he met up with his gang, he'd ride to the small house on the outskirts of town where the bank clerk, Reuben, lived. He'd waited for a few seconds after he knocked on the front door before he peeked inside the window. There was some furniture in the one-room house, but it didn't appear that anyone was living there. Frank thought the best place to find out some information would be at the restaurant in the hotel. Waitresses were always a good source for information about their small towns.

"Why, no, Reuben is no longer at the bank," the waitress told Frank.

"What happened to him?"

"Oh, we had a big bank robbery here one Sunday morning not long ago, and don't you know, Reuben got shot."

"You mean he's dead?"

"Nope. Reuben tried to stop one of the robbers and he got shot, but it wasn't serious. If you know Reuben, then you understand everyone could hardly believe Reuben had the nerve to face an armed man."

"Where did Reuben go?"

"No one knows. The other bank clerk said Reuben's nerves couldn't handle what happened and he went back East." The waitress nudged Frank's arm. "Reuben wasn't the kind of man who could handle being shot, even if it was just a graze."

Frank laughed at the thought. "No, he was a tenderfoot if I ever saw one."

She nodded at his apt description of the little bank clerk. "How did you know Reuben?"

"He helped me at the bank one day. Seemed like a nice enough fellow." Frank didn't lie; Reuben had helped him with the robbery. He'd been mighty helpful, right up to the very end when the little rat obviously double-crossed him. "Did they find the bank robbers?"

"No, Reuben said he winged one of them, but he got away. Can you believe Reuben even shot at a bank robber?" She didn't wait for a response. "The sheriff rounded up a posse, but they never found the men."

"What about the money?"

"Oh, they got away with the money," she replied.

"How much money did they get away with?"

She placed her hip on the table and leaned forward. "Well, you know they never actually said. I reckon they don't want to call attention to how much money they keep in the bank. But I heard tell that they got twenty thousand dollars. At least, that's what one of my customers who is a friend of the owner of the bank told me."

Frank figured that was as reliable as any information he might receive. He paid for his coffee and left the restaurant.

"Married? You?" Deke Sullivan couldn't believe his ears.

"Yep, and my new bride is the daughter of a judge."

"Dang, Reb told us you were coming by stagecoach with a judge's daughter, but we didn't know if he was pulling our leg or not," Corbin said.

"When did you get married, Frank?" Reb asked.

"Yesterday when we got off the stage."

"You didn't waste no time," Dutch said.

"Why should he? I told you how beautiful she is," Reb said.

"She is that. And now she is Mrs. Frank Langtry." Frank had to admit he felt some pride announcing his marriage to the boys. Charlotte was a beautiful woman and she was all his. And she came with a gold mine.

Deke grabbed a bottle of whiskey and some glasses. After he handed a glass to each man, he filled them to the brim. "Congratulations, Frank."

"Thanks."

They drank their whiskey, and Deke poured another round. "I guess you'll be settling down now."

Frank had to admit he hadn't considered settling down. "I don't know about that, but I think I've figured a way to get us out of this mess." Frank told them what he had on his mind so they would all have the same story, should he ever need them to back him up.

"All we have to remember is when Morgan accused us of rustling, we were together in Las Vegas, and just happened to be coming back home when the posse mistook us for the rustlers."

"You think that will work? What about Joseph Longbow?" Reb asked.

"Who will believe an Indian, if he even

testifies against us? I've already laid the groundwork with my wife." Frank had told Charlotte he'd been falsely accused and he was going home to clear his name. She'd believed every word he'd told her.

"Does she know we're guilty?" Dutch asked.

"No. I told her Morgan has had a lifelong vendetta against me, and that he is doing this to get to me."

"I don't know if a judge will buy that. He might listen to Longbow and believe him," Deke said.

"Then I'll just have to mention Longbow was being hunted by soldiers a few years back. Not only that, but a soldier went missing on LeMasters's land, never to be heard from again. Rumor had it Joseph Longbow shot him."

"I never heard that tale," Deke said.

"Well, you heard it now. We know for a fact several people have gone missing in those pines," Frank said. He didn't tell them that he'd been the one to start the rumor about a soldier being shot by Longbow.

"Just like Mason went missing," Reb said. Mason was one of the gang members who'd never ridden out of the trees on LeMasters's land when they last rustled.

Frank nodded. "Just like Mason. But I'll

tell the judge I heard Longbow killed that soldier. And everybody knows LeMasters hid Longbow from the soldiers."

Deke laughed. "I like the way you think, Frank."

"What judge would take the word of a Sioux over ours? We could contact the military and tell them LeMasters is harboring a murdering Sioux. They'd have soldiers combing that territory in no time." Frank rather liked the thought of the great Morgan LeMasters being arrested. "And after all this time with the wolves and coyotes, if they found some bones, who'd know if it was that soldier or not?"

The men looked at each other. "That might actually work," Dutch said.

"There's even one more thing in our favor," Frank said.

"What's that?" Deke asked.

"Not only is my beautiful wife the daughter of a judge, her family is a very wealthy one. I'd say they have more standing in the community than Morgan LeMasters has in Whispering Pines."

"You've thought of everything," Dutch said.

"Don't I always?" Frank countered.

The only man withholding his praise of Frank's plan was Corbin. "And what about your sister? She is the one who can testify against us. You kidnapped her."

Frank felt the surge of anger he always felt when someone challenged him. He narrowed his eyes at Corbin. "Like I told you before, you are the only one who was with me. It's her word against mine, and you already told me you wouldn't testify against me. Isn't that right, Corbin?"

Corbin felt a shiver run down his spine.

Frank stared long and hard at Corbin, and the other men glanced at each other, expecting Frank to pull his gun and shoot Corbin at any moment.

In an effort to relieve the tension in the small room, Deke asked, "What do we do now?"

"I still want to rob that bank." Frank knew he didn't necessarily need money now, but he wanted the judge to think he could provide for his daughter. He had a feeling Aunt Ruth would give him anything he wanted, including money. "That fellow Reuben doesn't work at the bank any longer though, so we'll have to come up with a new plan."

When Frank returned to Aunt Ruth's home, his wife was in the bedroom with a seamstress, being fitted for some new frocks, so

Aunt Ruth invited him to sit in the parlor for a chat.

"You know how long it takes women to make decisions. It may be a while. Why don't we go to the game room?" Aunt Ruth said.

"Game room?" Frank asked, following behind Ruth through the maze of long hallways.

"That's what I call it. Several times a week I play whist and bridge with some of the local ladies. Occasionally, we include the men in our games."

She opened the door to a cozy room with a fire already blazing in the hearth. There were several card tables in the center of the room, but Ruth headed for the settee in front of the fire.

"This is the warmest room in the house, and yet my poor old bones still feel the drafts."

"You're not old. You're a beautiful woman," Frank said.

Ruth smiled at him. "Thank you." She pointed to the long sideboard along one wall. "Would you pour me a brandy, Frank?"

Frank laughed. "You surprise me, Aunt Ruth."

She picked up a shawl from the arm of the settee and wrapped it around her shoulders. "Did you think ladies don't drink brandy?"

"I must admit I have never known a *lady* to partake," Frank teased. He'd seen plenty of women drink in every saloon he'd visited, but he'd never seen a lady drink hard spirits.

Aunt Ruth chuckled. "Just because one is a *lady,* doesn't mean one must be boring. I often think several of my lady friends who come for cards are really here to have their afternoon brandy. One lady of my acquaintance even smokes a cigar. We don't judge each other's peccadilloes."

Frank handed her the glass of brandy and winked at her. "Did your husband know of your vice?"

"Oh my, yes. He said spirits were good for calming the nerves."

"My granny wasn't against having a sip for medicinal purposes." Frank rarely revealed anything personal, but he felt comfortable with Ruth.

"So you have family here?"

"In Whispering Pines, but I guess you could say they have disowned me."

Ruth swirled the contents of her glass as she considered what she wanted to say. Her niece had told her that Frank had been seriously aggrieved, accused of things he hadn't done. Considering Frank had saved Charlotte from being savaged by two men at that way station, Ruth was inclined to give him the benefit of the doubt. "I hope you don't consider it a betrayal of a confidence, but my niece told me of your troubles and why you were going home. I want you to know if you need my support in any way, you shall have it. Charlotte fell in love with you rather quickly, but I daresay the incident at that way station had a lot to do with that." She saw Frank raise his eyebrows. "I assure you, she told me nothing untoward happened. She is full of praise for your gentlemanly conduct."

"I wouldn't have taken advantage of that situation," Frank said.

"Charlotte has been protected her whole life, it's all she's known. She wants a man who she feels can keep her safe since she is a very wealthy young woman. I'm afraid her father has done her a disservice cosseting her as he has. She is not prepared for the world. I must say I was rather surprised my brother allowed her to travel to Denver without being at her side." She flapped her hand back and forth as though she dismissed that thought, and continued on. "As you know, we don't have much family left. Charlotte will inherit the bulk of my estate when I die. I believe in giving while I'm still alive, so I provide her with a sizeable monthly stipend. Now that you are part of the family, I will increase the amount. I want Charlotte to be happy, and she told me you make her happy."

Once again, Aunt Ruth surprised him. "I don't know what to say."

"Frank, I'm not one to pry, but now that you are married to Charlotte, I feel it my duty to inquire if you have made plans. From our conversation last night, I have the feeling you are at loose ends right now." Without waiting for his response, she continued on. "Once you've settled what you came here to do, perhaps you should think about buying a ranch, or taking up a profession. I'm sure you'll want to do right by Charlotte, and I will help you both in any way I can. You might want to consider a position at my mine in Black Hawk. I'm sure we could work something out."

"You are being very generous, and I thank you. It's more than I deserve." Ruth was not judging him, not telling him what to do, and he respected that. She wasn't comparing him to Morgan LeMasters like his granny was wont to do his whole life. There was a small part of him that was tempted to try to turn his life around. But he couldn't fool himself into thinking that he would ever work a regular job. It was way too late for him to turn over a new leaf. He wasn't about to start breaking his back at ranch work after all these years. He'd schemed too much and lied too much. His past would eventually catch up to him. He couldn't run from that fact. The latest scheme he'd discussed with the boys would delay the reckoning for a few years if he was lucky. One thing was certain: Morgan Le-Masters would be in his grave before Frank left this earth. "As you say, once I have my business settled, then I'll be in a position to make a decision as to my future." To change the course of the conversation, Frank asked his own question. "What do you think Judge Stevens will say to our marriage?"

"I think he will be delighted. He wants Charlotte to be married and have children, and he was beginning to worry she would never marry. Don't get me wrong, he loves his daughter more than anything. But I know that he has been courting a woman — discreetly, I might add. Please don't mention that bit of information to anyone, not even Charlotte. My brother doesn't know I'm privy to his personal affairs."

Frank arched his brow in question. There were more sides to Aunt Ruth than met the eye.

Ruth smiled at his unasked question. "I have my ways of obtaining information, Frank. I'm not certain I approve of this particular courtship. More than likely it's simply a matter of feeling his own mortality."

Frank had wondered why the judge hadn't insisted Charlotte wait a week and travel with him to Denver. He couldn't say he was surprised a woman was involved in the judge's decision. Most likely, the judge was less interested in his mortality than he was in his baser thoughts. To hear Ruth talk, the judge had lived his life for Charlotte. Frank figured he was in no position to criticize the judge if he wanted to seek out a woman. After all, he'd pursued Charlotte for his own motives.

"I'm thinking of having a party for you and Charlotte after my brother arrives. What do you think?" Ruth asked.

Frank smiled. "I think Charlotte would love a party."

CHAPTER NINE

Over the next few days, Addie, Rose, Granny, and the children spent their time working on the interior of the new farm-house. The night before school was to begin, Addie invited everyone to the orphanage for dinner as a thank-you for their hard work.

Jack arrived for dinner before the other guests, and when Addie opened the door, she was once again struck by his striking features. He looked so handsome in his white shirt and black hat that he took her breath away.

Jack smiled at her as he removed his hat. "I don't know what you're cooking, but I smelled it a mile away."

Addie blinked at him, trying to focus on his words instead of his handsome face. "I hope it smelled good."

"Delicious."

Addie stepped aside. "Come in, please."

Jack glanced around, expecting to see the

children. "Where are the children?"

"They went to the ranch to make sure Joseph is coming. Jane baked an apple cake for him. I told her Joseph wouldn't miss a chance to have some cake."

"You don't mind them walking through the pines alone?" Jack asked.

A chill ran down Addie's spine. "I thought they would be safe. Am I wrong?"

"No. Some people don't like to go through there, but there's no reason the children won't be safe, as long as they know the way."

Addie smiled her relief. "They know the way. Davey would have made a great guide to the West. Before we left Boston, he'd memorized the map."

Jack thought she looked so pretty in her yellow dress that accentuated her generous curves. Her cheeks were rosy, just as he imagined they would be if he kissed her. *Where did that thought come from?* He couldn't say he was sorry he had a few minutes alone with her. "Can I help with anything?"

"Oh no, I don't put my guests to work. You can have a cup of coffee, or if you prefer, you can wait in here for everyone to arrive. I have a few more things to do in the kitchen." She realized she'd never been alone with Jack, and she didn't know quite what to do. She couldn't just stand there and stare at him.

"Coffee sounds good." In the kitchen, he hung his hat on one of the hooks he'd nailed near the back door.

Addie filled a cup for him, but when she turned to carry it to the table, Jack was walking toward her. He took the cup, hitched his hip on the counter by the stove, and glanced down at what she was cooking. "I thought I smelled chicken."

"Please tell me you like fried chicken."

"Yes, ma'am, as long as you have mashed potatoes too."

Addie pointed to one of the pots. "Right there. I was getting ready to mash them."

Jack spotted the wooden potato masher on the counter. "I can do that."

"Are you sure?" Addie couldn't believe he was willing to help in the kitchen.

"Sure thing. But you have to tell Granny I helped. She doesn't think I can cook. When I was shot, she brought me food every day for two weeks."

Addie was reminded that it was a man in her brother's gang who had ambushed him. "I was sorry to hear about what happened. We haven't had much of a chance to talk about Frank."

"What's done is done. Nothing we can do

about it now." Jack didn't really want to talk about her brother. He was going to have to go after Frank and bring him to justice. He didn't want his friendship with Addie to suffer when he arrested her brother.

She stopped turning the chicken and looked up at him. "I just want you to know I understand why you have to go after him. After what he did to Stevie and to Rose, he needs to be caught."

Jack nodded. "I'm glad you feel that way. Some people aren't so understanding when I have to lock up their kin." He started mashing the potatoes and glanced around the kitchen. A few days ago it had been just a room with four walls. But now, with all of her feminine touches, she'd made it warm and cozy. It felt like home. "You've made this kitchen real pretty."

"Thank you." She was surprised a man like him noticed such things. She leaned over his arm and reached for the butter.

Jack's hand stilled as her breast grazed his arm. *Mind on business,* he reminded himself.

Addie sliced off a good portion of butter and plopped it into the potatoes. She went to the ice box and grabbed the milk. After she added milk to the potatoes, she said, "Let me know if it needs more." She reached for the pan of biscuits and placed them in the oven. "This stove is wonderful."

"Morgan and I picked it up in Denver. Granny told us you love to cook, and she even cut a picture out of a catalogue to make sure we ordered the right one."

"Everyone has done so much, I don't know how to thank you," she said.

That was the second time she'd said that. The first time he was tempted to tell her he would take a kiss for a thank-you. He smiled to himself as he thought about saying it now that they were alone. "You could . . ."

She turned her big blue eyes on him, wondering what he was going to say.

His gaze started at her eyes and drifted to her pink lips. *Coward,* he thought. "Taste these potatoes."

Picking up a fork, Addie stuck it in the potatoes and took a small bite. She reached for another fork, dipped it into the potatoes, and held it to his mouth. His eyes met hers, and Addie thought her heart might leap out of her chest when those intense silver eyes slid down to her lips. She felt herself turning pink. "Salt and pepper?"

Jack grinned. He liked how he could fluster the schoolteacher just by looking at her. "Yes, ma'am."

Grease snapped in the skillet, causing

Addie to jump. She turned to check the chicken and grabbed the fork to turn the remaining pieces before they burned.

"That chicken smells as good as you, Miss Addie."

"Thank you . . . the only thing I have left to do is make some gravy." Suddenly the large room seemed to shrink around her. She couldn't seem to concentrate on anything other than the handsome man beside her.

"I love gravy." He knew he was making her nervous, so he moved closer and leaned down to her ear. "Do you have a bowl for the mashed potatoes?"

Addie shivered at his nearness. "Right on that shelf." She pointed to a shelf away from her. She removed the chicken from the pan, and reached for the flour to make some gravy. Thankfully, gravy required her full attention so it wouldn't burn. She picked up the milk and poured some into the skillet as she continued to stir.

Jack moved next to her again, so close that her skirt brushed against his pants. "I can stir for a while if you want to check the biscuits. They smell really good."

She relinquished the wooden spoon to him before she checked the biscuits.

"It's nice cooking with you." Jack had

never given a thought to how much fun it could be helping a woman in the kitchen. But being here with Addie, he couldn't think of another thing he'd rather be doing.

"Haven't you ever cooked with a woman before?" She tried to sound calm, though her heart was beating as fast as a Thoroughbred after a race. Then she made the mistake of looking up at him again.

Jack winked at her. "No, ma'am, I haven't. Generally, women have dinner cooked when I arrive." He didn't say he'd intentionally arrived early tonight so he could spend some time with her and the children before the other guests arrived. He'd told himself he liked spending time with the kids. Now, he realized it wasn't just the children he enjoyed. He liked being with Addie. He felt an easiness with her. It was like being home. A real home, where people talked to each other, ate together, teased each other, simply enjoyed being together. It was odd that he would feel that way, since he'd never really had a home.

When he winked at her and smiled that perfect smile of his, Addie realized she was in danger of becoming completely besotted with the devastatingly handsome sheriff. She thought he was teasing her, and not being flirtatious, but that thought didn't slow her heart rate. She reminded herself for the umpteenth time that a man like Jack wouldn't be interested in her. Trim and pretty Clarissa was his type of woman. "Perhaps next time you can help Clarissa with dinner. That might get you back into her good graces."

Jack cocked his head at her, his brows drawn together as if he was trying to figure out a complicated puzzle. He couldn't understand why she was thinking about Clarissa at this moment. Sometimes women could be downright confusing. She wouldn't look at him, so he said, "I don't think I have much to worry about on that score."

Addie interpreted his comment to mean he'd already mended fences with Clarissa. She wasn't surprised; a woman would be an idiot to stay mad at him. Actually, she was feeling a bit envious of Clarissa. She reminded herself that Granny would tell her envy was a sin. She handed him a bowl. "Would you put the potatoes in this bowl?"

Jack handed her the spoon so she could continue mixing the gravy. Addie was lost in thoughts, and stirring the gravy so vigorously that Jack reached over and placed his hand over hers. "Are you stirring or attacking?"

Her gaze was on his large hand covering

hers, and her heart started racing again. "Oh, I guess it is done." She glanced up at him and he was so close she could smell his scent.

His eyes were focused on her lips. "Addie . . ." He wanted to kiss her so badly he could almost taste her. He lowered his head to hers, but they were both startled by footsteps on the back porch. They turned together to see the kitchen door swing open and the children ran in. Claire ran right to Jack with arms stretched wide. He swept her off the ground, high in the air. "How's my girls and my best young man?"

Their faces lit up every time Jack spoke to them. He treated them as though they were the most important people in his life.

"We're good. School starts tomorrow," Jane said excitedly.

"Yeah, I wish it didn't start so soon," Davey said.

Jack heard from his tone that he wasn't as thrilled as Jane about school.

"I go to school too," Claire said.

"How about I take all of you to school in the morning?" Jack asked.

Claire responded by kissing him on the cheek and hugging his neck.

"Now, that's a fine thank-you." He glanced at Jane, and said, "What about you?

Does that earn a kiss on the cheek?"

Jane stood on her tiptoes and kissed his cheek.

Jack glanced at Davey and put his hand on his shoulder. "Don't worry, I won't make you give me a kiss."

Davey made a face at him, causing Jack to laugh. "You just wait, young man. One of these days you'll change your mind about getting kisses."

"That day is a long way off," Addie said.

Jack grinned at her as his eyes moved to her lips once again. "Well, he has something to look forward to, doesn't he?"

Addie thought Jack would know the answer to that question better than anyone.

"You'll really take us to school in the morning?" Jane asked.

"You don't have to come all this way just to drive us to school," Addie said.

"It's my pleasure." He winked at Claire. "Maybe Miss Addie should give me a kiss for taking her to school tomorrow. What do you think, Claire?"

Claire clapped her tiny hands together and said, "Un-huh."

Jack smiled at Addie. "Claire thinks you owe me a kiss."

Like Jane, Addie stood on her tiptoes and pressed her lips to Jack's cheek.

He was tempted to turn his head so her kiss would land on his lips, but the children were watching. He settled for tugging on a lock of her hair that had fallen over her shoulder. "For a kiss like that, I may have to take you to school every day, Miss Addie."

The remainder of the dinner party walked through the door, and everyone started talking at once. With Claire on his hip, Jack helped Addie carry the bowls to the table and Rose poured coffee.

Addie had added chairs at each end of the table and she placed Jack's cup at one end. "Jack, sit here." Jane and Davey quickly claimed the seats to the side of Jack.

Even if Addie hadn't considered the seating arrangement, he felt honored being placed at the head of the table. He looked around at everyone at the table, and for the first time, he had a sense of what it felt like to belong to a family. He felt the excitement of the children next to him, and their need to be loved by this family.

Addie looked at Claire sitting on Jack's lap. "Claire, sit on the bench by Jane so the sheriff can eat."

"I don't mind if she wants to sit on my lap." He kissed Claire's cheek. "I have to warn you, I may eat all of your potatoes."

Claire's face lit up. "Okay."

"She may leave more on your shirt than she does on the plate," Addie warned.

"It'll wash," Jack replied, unconcerned.

Addie lowered her eyes so no one could see she was about to cry. She'd never met a man like Jack. He was wonderful with the children, making them a part of everything he did, and she could see the small changes in their manner because of him. While she was thrilled they enjoyed being with Jack, she worried the day would come when they would be adopted and that relationship would change. No matter how much she wanted to protect them, she couldn't stop all of the heartaches they were sure to face in the future. She might as well allow them to enjoy today. As Granny always said, *Tomorrow will take care of itself.*

Morgan was the one who usually said grace, but she looked at Jack and asked, "Jack, would you give the blessing?"

At first, Jack stared at her blankly. He'd never said grace with a table full of people, but seeing all eyes were on him, he nodded. He almost choked up at the privilege, and he tried to keep his voice even when he said, "Claire, let's bow our heads so we can pray."

Claire interlocked her fingers, bowed her head, and squeezed her eyes shut.

Jack smiled, and when he glanced Addie's

way, he saw she was watching Claire and smiling too.

After Jack blessed the meal and said amen, he heard Claire say softly, "Thank you for my papa."

Jack felt a lump the size of Texas growing in his throat. He glanced at Addie to see if she'd heard Claire, but she was talking with Joseph and wasn't paying attention. When his gaze slid to Jane and Davey, he knew by their expressions that they'd heard Claire. He didn't want them to say anything to Addie that would upset her, so he simply shook his head, as if telling them it was their little secret. "Jane, Davey, I made the potatoes, so you'd better eat a lot of them."

"Did you really?" Davey asked.

"Ask Addie." He glanced her way and winked.

Addie blushed. She wished he would stop winking, it flustered her every time. "Yes, he did, and they taste wonderful."

"The sheriff is going to take us to school tomorrow," Jane said.

"That's nice of you, Jack," Morgan said. "But you don't have to come all the way out here. I was going to have one of my men take them to town."

"I don't mind," Jack said.

"We need supplies anyway," Morgan said.

147

Jack let the matter drop, but he'd tell Morgan later when they were alone that he wanted to take them. He didn't want Jane and Davey to think he'd changed his mind because it was inconvenient. Not to mention Claire would probably cry all the way to school.

Addie didn't let on that she'd been listening to every word exchanged between Jack and Morgan. She was disappointed Jack wouldn't be taking them, but it didn't make sense for him to ride from town only to turn around and go back.

Everyone finished their dinner, and Addie told Jane she could slice the cake.

"Mr. Longbow gets the first piece," Jane said, slicing him a large piece.

Joseph took a bite and told Jane her cake was about the best he'd ever eaten.

"Jane, are you asleep?" Davey asked.

"No, but be quiet, Claire's asleep," Jane replied.

Davey slipped into the room and quietly closed the door behind him.

Lifting her head from the pillow, Jane could see him in the moonlight. "Is something wrong?"

"No, I just couldn't sleep." Davey sat at the foot of her bed.

Jane sat up and propped the pillow at her back. "Me neither."

"Do you think Miss Addie likes the sheriff?"

Jane shrugged her shoulders. "I guess she likes him. Why?"

"Do you think she likes him as much as she does Mr. Adler?"

"I don't know. I don't know why she liked Mr. Adler in the first place," Jane said.

"Yeah. He never so much as said a word to us." Davey had never warmed to Mr. Adler, and he knew the girls didn't like him either.

Jane nodded her agreement. "Claire loves the sheriff. You heard what she said tonight. I wish . . ."

Davey interrupted her. "Don't go wishing for things that will never happen." He'd learned long ago that wishing for things didn't do a bit of good. "It was nice of the sheriff not to tell Miss Addie what Claire said at dinner."

"Miss Addie just doesn't want Claire to get too attached to the sheriff." They sat in silence for a moment, then Jane said, "Davey, do you think we will be adopted here?"

"I don't know. I just don't think most folks can take care of three kids. If we are adopted, I think we will be split up."

Jane tried not to cry. Davey always told her it didn't do any good to cry. "I don't want to be split up. Claire won't talk if someone tries to adopt her. I don't know how she thought of that on her own."

"I thought you told her not to talk," Davey said.

"No, I never thought of that."

"Well, it worked, but here everyone will know she can talk." Davey always worried every family would want a cute little girl like Claire.

"Yeah," Jane agreed gloomily.

"If one of us is adopted without the others, we'll run away like we always planned," Davey said.

"Where will we go?"

"I've been thinking about that. I heard the sheriff and Mr. LeMasters talking about all the abandoned homes out here. He said that's where outlaws are hiding out. Maybe we could find one and stay there."

"Is that where Miss Addie's brother is hiding out?"

"That's what the sheriff thinks," Davey replied.

"I can tell Miss Addie likes the sheriff. But the sheriff probably wouldn't want to marry the sister of an outlaw."

"Yeah. I heard the sheriff tell Mr. LeMasters that he was going after Miss Addie's brother." Davey stood and said, "We better go to sleep, we have to get up early. But don't forget our plan."

Addie was lying in bed looking up at the ceiling. It was difficult adjusting to the new sounds around her. She'd assured Granny she wasn't worried about staying alone with three children, but now that she was actually alone, she found herself on edge. She'd checked both doors twice to make sure they were securely bolted. Before Jack left, she'd noticed he'd ridden the perimeter of the property. She thought he was most likely doing it out of habit because he was a sheriff.

The more she tossed and turned, the more she worried. She tried to reassure herself that Morgan's ranch was just through the trees, it wouldn't take long for someone to get there. But if she needed immediate help, how would she notify them? She didn't even have a rifle to send an alert. Unlike in Boston, weapons were necessary out here. People taught their children to respect guns, but these children hadn't been around guns before. *Maybe I should get a dog.* The children would love that, and a dog would alert her if someone was about.

Addie thought she heard the children talking, but she didn't intervene. Jane and Davey often talked when they couldn't sleep. As long as they didn't stay up too late, she wouldn't say anything. It wasn't long before she heard Davey walking back to his room.

Her thoughts drifted to Jack. Each time she'd looked at him during dinner, holding Claire on his lap, she felt her heart might squeeze out of her chest. Every time Jack took a bite of food, he made sure Claire got a bite of food. She rarely heard Claire chatter as much as she did with Jack. They both smiled and laughed through the entire meal.

CHAPTER TEN

Unable to sleep, Jack crawled out of bed at three in the morning and made some coffee. Normally, he didn't have trouble sleeping, but he hadn't been able to stop worrying about Addie and the children being left alone at the farm. He was the last person to leave the farm after dinner, and while he'd made certain the house was locked and secure, he worried all the way back to town. He'd wanted to ask Addie if she had a rifle, but the children never left him alone with her. He didn't want to scare Addie or the children, but the West was no place for a woman alone. After what Frank had done to his brother, Jack feared he might be crazy enough to try to hurt all of his siblings. Frank wasn't his only concern. The town was growing and attracting some interesting characters. If men learned there was a woman alone, especially one as shapely as Addie, they might be tempted to make some unwanted visits. She had more curves than should be allowed on the female form, in his opinion, and she was certain to attract a lot of attention.

Sipping his coffee, Jack thought about the children at dinner. They hadn't stopped smiling the entire time, and he'd never enjoyed a dinner more. If he could, he would have had them all on his lap, along with Addie. She was just the kind of woman a man wanted to snuggle up to. He wondered how serious her relationship was with Prescott Adler. The man was dumb enough to let her take off alone with three children, so Jack didn't give him a whole lot of credit for having much common sense. In his estimation, Prescott Adler didn't deserve her. He couldn't imagine letting a woman he cared about make such a journey alone. He remembered Claire said Prescott kissed Addie. He wondered just how much kissing they'd done.

Addie wasn't expecting Jack when he pulled up in the buckboard the next morning. "I thought one of Morgan's men was taking us to school."

"I didn't want to disappoint the children," Jack said.

"You have time for a cup of coffee, if you

like," Addie said, motioning him to come in.

He followed her to the kitchen and something smelled so good it made his stomach growl. "I've had a few cups, but yours is better than mine."

"Did you eat breakfast?"

"Did you hear my stomach growling? I didn't cook this morning."

She did hear his stomach. She pointed to the same chair he'd sat in last night. "Sit down. I made some cinnamon rolls as a bribe to get the children going this morning."

Once he'd taken his first bite, he said, "Addie, you're a fine cook. If some men in town find out how good you are, they'll be lining up at your door."

"I may be a bit old for marriage, but I wouldn't want a man simply because he liked my cooking."

"Old for marriage?" Jack repeated, thinking she'd expressed the same sentiment before.

"I'm already twenty-six, and most men prefer younger women."

Jack shook his head. "You sure have funny notions about men and marriage."

"Well, you're about Morgan's age, and he married Rose. She's eleven years younger."

"I'm a year older than Morgan."

"And you like younger women," Addie said with finality.

Jack didn't wait until he swallowed his mouthful of cinnamon roll before he asked, "What are you talking about?"

"Clarissa. I'd say she's close to Rose's age."

"I like Granny too. Does that mean I want to marry an older woman?" He thought that was a pretty good comeback.

"You don't court Granny," Addie countered.

"What makes you think I court Clarissa?"

"You said she cooks you dinner." Addie had to think if he'd actually said he courted Clarissa. It didn't matter if he'd said as much or not. In her estimation if a woman cooked a man dinner, in her mind he was courting her.

"Granny cooks me dinner, same as Clarissa. So by your definition that counts as courting?"

Addie frowned at him, signaling that he knew what she meant.

"Why is it you are always bringing up Clarissa?" Twice in two days, he thought. There had to be a reason.

"I didn't know I shouldn't." Addie knew the reason she brought up Clarissa. Clarissa was the kind of woman men wanted to marry. Men like Jack, in particular.

"I'm not sure accepting a dinner invitation is the same as courting." Jack took the last bite of his roll.

"And I'm not sure Clarissa would feel the same way." She needed to put an end to this conversation. "But be that as it may, your relationship with Clarissa is none of my business."

"You cooked me dinner, so am I courting you now?"

Her eyes widened at him, and he smiled that smile that melted her heart. She'd walked right into that one. No wonder he was the sheriff — he certainly was adept at deductive reasoning. "That was a party. Not a private dinner." Addie gathered the children's plates from the table and carried them to the counter.

Jack carried his plate to the counter. He took his last sip of coffee and when he placed the cup on the counter, he leaned over and whispered in her ear. "Maybe you should cook me a private dinner."

Addie's skin felt like it might go up in flames when she looked into his silver eyes. Knowing he was teasing her didn't make her any less susceptible to his charms.

She didn't reply, so he leaned closer.

"Don't you want to know how I court a woman?"

She inched away from him. "As I said, I'm too old for you."

Jack chuckled. "Ah, yes, that's what started this conversation. But you never made your point."

"Yes, I did. Men want young, beautiful women, like my sister. Morgan was the perfect example. I'm sure he had the same women chasing after him who are now chasing after you, but he didn't ask one of them to marry. But when Rose came along, it was a different story."

"You don't give your sister much credit. Don't you think she has a lot more to offer besides a pretty face?"

"I didn't mean . . ." She stopped talking. Again, he had a good point. "Of course, she has a lot to offer."

"I asked Morgan how he knew Rose was the right one for him, and he said he thought God had a lot to do with it. He said when she stepped off that stagecoach, he knew his life had changed." Jack took a step closer to her again. "Of course, he liked the way she looked, but I know Morgan, and it took a whole lot more than that to get him to the altar." Actually, Morgan had told him he knew he had to marry Rose once he'd kissed her, because he didn't want another man to find out how good she kissed. But he wisely kept that tidbit to himself.

Addie hadn't intended to insult her sister, but that was exactly how it sounded. "Rose is a wonderful person."

Jack reached out and picked up a lock of her hair. "Miss Addie, I think you have a lot to learn when it comes to matters of what men want. Maybe I should cook you dinner."

His comment left her speechless, and before she formed a response, she heard the children coming down the stairs.

He leaned over and his lips touched her ear. "We aren't finished with this conversation."

Jack pulled the buckboard in front of the school and leaped out to help Addie to the ground.

"Who is that man at the front door?" Addie asked.

Jack saw the man when he pulled up, and wondered what he was doing at the school since he didn't have children. "That's Roy Coburn."

"I don't remember meeting him at church. Does he have children who will be attending school?"

"No." Jack had a bad feeling that he didn't really want to know why Coburn was there.

The children said good-bye to Jack, and Claire insisted he pick her up so she could give him a kiss on the cheek before he left.

"I'll see you later, honey," Jack said when she turned to wave.

When the children ran through the door, Jack walked toward the man. "Roy, what are you doing here?"

"I need to talk to Miss Langtry," Roy said.

Addie cast a concerned look at Jack. "Why do you need to speak with me?"

"I want to talk to you about adopting that boy," Roy said.

Addie heard the words she'd dreaded hearing. "Adopting . . ."

"Yeah, I want to adopt that boy," Roy repeated.

"But you must have a wife," Addie said.

"I got a wife. We want to adopt him."

Jack saw the color drain from Addie's face, and he thought she looked ready to faint. He placed his arm around her waist for support. "Addie, this is Roy Coburn. He and his wife, Sarah, own a farm a few miles from town. I don't think they lived here when you were a girl."

"The pastor said I was to see you about adopting him," Roy said.

While Jack talked, Addie had time to regain her composure. "Yes, you need to speak with me. Are you interested in adopting all three children together?"

"No, we just want the boy."

"We are trying to place them as a family," Addie said.

"Lady, are you supposed to put them up for adoption or not? We can't afford no three extra mouths to feed."

"Roy, she was just saying what she hoped was best for the children. There's no need to get riled up," Jack said.

"The pastor said to see her about adopting. He didn't say nothing about adopting all three together."

"Mr. Coburn, now is not the time to discuss this. School is getting ready to start. I will need to come by your home and speak to you and your wife together. It's my responsibility to ensure it is the right environment for a child."

"That sounds like a bunch of trouble, when I'm trying to help a boy," Roy said.

"You must understand it is incumbent on us to make the right decision for the welfare of the children. It wouldn't do for us to place a child only to find that it wasn't a good situation from the start."

"Well, come on out after school. I don't

have a lot of time to run back and forth. The pastor said there would be legal papers for me to sign, so bring those with you and we can get this done."

"We'll see how it goes when I come to your home. I'll need to speak with your wife also," Addie said.

"My wife don't have to sign nothing, it's all up to me," Roy said adamantly.

"All the same, I'll need to speak with her," Addie countered. "Now, I will say good morning. I have students waiting for me."

Roy jumped in his buckboard and rode away.

Addie watched him leave with a sinking heart. "Do you know him?"

Jack heard the misery in her question. "Not well. I see his wife in church every now and then. I've never heard her say more than two words at one time. I see Roy in town picking up supplies, but I've never seen him in the saloon. I guess I should talk to Clay. He probably knows them better than anyone."

Addie nodded. It had been a wonderful morning riding to town with Jack, and the children had been so excited he'd been the one taking them to school on their first day. Now, their whole world was about to be turned upside down.

"I'll stop by and talk to Clay to see what he can tell me about them."

"I can't take the children with me when I go see him tonight," Addie said.

"We'll drop the children off at Morgan's and I'll take you," Jack said.

"Thank you."

It broke Jack's heart to see how sad she looked as she walked inside the school. He didn't like the thought of the children being separated either, but he didn't know what choice Addie would have if Coburn only wanted Davey.

CHAPTER ELEVEN

"I guess I have no valid reason to deny Mr. Coburn's request, assuming his wife is in agreement," Addie said. Jack had told her the pastor said they seemed like good people, and Sarah was a God-fearing woman. Roy had never been in trouble with the law. Instead of enjoying the first day of school, Addie had been miserable knowing what she was going to be forced to do that night. She knew Davey didn't want to leave his siblings, but she'd been instructed she had to allow them to be adopted individually. "It may be a good opportunity for Davey."

Jack didn't want to sound discouraging, since she was trying to find the silver lining in the dreadful situation, but he didn't think the children would ever be happy without each other. All day, he'd been tempted to ride out to the Coburns' and tell them they should drop their request. No matter what he wanted to do, he knew it wasn't his place to interfere. As he'd learned early on in life, he didn't always understand the greater plan, and sometimes it was best not to meddle. Yet, he couldn't deny his inner voice was sounding an alarm. He tried to think Addie had the right attitude, believing it was possible this would be a good opportunity for Davey. Didn't he just tell Davey to keep trusting and believing? Maybe he should follow his own advice.

"Mrs. Coburn, your husband said you only want to adopt Davey. Had you thought about adopting the other two children?" Addie asked.

Sarah's eyes slid to her husband. "We can't afford that many children. We've wanted a child in the worst way." She sent Addie a pleading look, and whispered, "It's my fault I couldn't conceive."

Addie could see the visible anguish on the woman's face. "It's not our place to assign fault. Perhaps the Lord just had different plans for you."

"It's not that we wouldn't take more if we could," Sarah hastened to add.

"It was my desire not to separate them. You understand that they are very devoted to each other," Addie told her.

Roy Coburn stood, his jaw set, and his words were filled with annoyance, "Lady, we already talked about this. We want to adopt the one boy, and if you say we aren't able, then I reckon we need to talk to a judge."

"I didn't say you couldn't adopt. I just wanted your wife to understand what we prayed for. It was what we felt was in their best interest."

"Okay then, if we can adopt, where's the papers we are supposed to sign?" Roy asked.

"I'll have them at the sheriff's office tomorrow after school."

"We'll take the boy tomorrow," Roy said.

"I will bring him after school on Friday," Addie said in her best schoolteacher's no-nonsense tone. "That will give me time to prepare him for the move. We will have his belongings to pack, and there is no sense disrupting his first week at school. He will have the weekend to adjust to his new home."

Addie made it to the buckboard before tears started streaming down her cheeks. Other than her family, she'd never cried in front of anyone, but she couldn't hold back.

Once they were away from the Coburn farm, Jack pulled the horses to a halt, reached for Addie, and pulled her to his chest and let her cry.

"I'm sorry, I know I'm acting like a silly woman. I should be giving thanks for Davey to have a chance for a real family."

"I know." Her sobs were heartbreaking, and it was difficult for Jack to keep his emotions in check. He pulled his bandana from his back pocket and handed it to her. She dried her eyes, but tears continued to flow. Jack wrapped her in his arms again and held her, trying to soothe her the best he knew how.

Once he thought she was nearly cried out, he asked, "Are the children having dinner at Morgan's?"

Addie nodded. "I didn't know how long we would be at the Coburns'."

Keeping one arm around her, Jack picked up the reins with one hand. "We have to go through town to get to the farm, so I'm taking you to dinner."

She appreciated his kind gesture, but she wasn't in the mood to eat, not to mention her eyes were probably swollen from crying. "I don't think I would be very good company, and I'm really not looking my best."

"Then I'll take you home with me. I can fix us a sandwich. I don't think you should see the children until you've settled down." He thought if the children saw her upset about Davey being adopted, they might worry that he was going to a terrible place.

He was right, she was in no condition to see the children yet. But she didn't think being seen alone at the sheriff's home was a good idea. She was the schoolteacher, and she had to consider the impropriety of being alone with a single man in his home. "That's probably not wise for me to be alone at your home. If someone . . . if Clarissa saw me, the whole town would know by morning."

Clarissa. She'd brought her up again. Of course, Addie was right. Although the town was full of good-hearted people, they often jumped to the wrong conclusion. "I see your point."

"You can take me to the farm and I can get the children later."

"Does that mean you'll cook me dinner again?" Jack teased, trying to lighten the mood.

"You don't have to stay," Addie said, trying not to think of how alone it would feel at the house with no one there.

"You mean you won't feed a starving man? I haven't eaten since that roll you gave me for breakfast."

Addie was ashamed she hadn't even considered the amount of time he'd taken out of his day for her benefit. She didn't have to ask if that was the reason he hadn't eaten. "Of course, I will cook you dinner if you want to stay for a while."

Jack's eyes met hers. "I want to stay." Their gaze held for a few moments before Jack's eyes moved to her lips. He'd never wanted to kiss anyone like he wanted to kiss her at that very moment.

Jack unhitched the team, put the horses in the paddock, and washed up before he walked into the kitchen. Addie was at the counter rolling out some biscuits. "It already smells good in here."

"I'm warming some ham, and the biscuits will be ready soon." As she spoke, she slid the pan in the oven. Cooking dinner kept her mind busy, so she didn't dwell on how things changed in a day.

"I'll make the coffee. Do you mind it strong?" Having watched Addie in the kitchen last night, Jack knew where she kept everything.

"No, I don't mind."

As Jack was throwing beans into the pot, it occurred to him that his girls would be staying at the farm alone now. *His girls.* That was what he'd called them last night, and he remembered how their faces lit up. He realized he wasn't just thinking of Jane and Claire as his girls. He'd included Addie in that thought. He heard Addie sniffle and he glanced her way. He saw her wiping away tears again. He set the coffeepot over the flame and walked to her.

"It's going to be okay," he said, pulling her into his arms.

"I know. I truly am thankful for Davey's sake, but the girls are going to be heartbroken."

"He won't be that far away, and the girls will see him at school and at church. They can have him over for visits." Jack was trying his best to stay positive, and he hoped he sounded more convincing to her ears than he sounded to his own.

Addie looked up at him. "Thank you." She knew he was trying to make her feel better about the situation. "I haven't thanked you for everything you've done for me today."

Jack smiled at her. "You could thank me the way Claire thanks me." He was trying to make her smile by teasing her. At least he told himself he was only teasing.

Addie didn't think about what she was about to do. She placed her hand around his neck and pulled his head down and brushed his lips with a soft kiss. "Thank you."

Her bold move wiped the smile off his face. He stared into her eyes, and she didn't look away. "That's a fine thank-you."

Addie didn't know what had possessed her to do such a thing. It wasn't like her to make such a daring move. She was a reserved schoolteacher, not some shameless woman who threw caution to the wind. She didn't have an excuse. The plain truth was, she was attracted to him and had been from the moment she stepped off that stagecoach. He was the most handsome man she'd ever seen. But right now, as his eyes bore into hers, she was embarrassed by her behavior. He probably didn't enjoy being kissed by a frumpy old-maid schoolteacher. She felt the blush rising from her neck to her cheeks, and she lowered her eyes and started to turn away.

Jack wasn't about to let her go. He pulled her to a halt by cupping her face in his hands, urging her to face him. When she looked up at him, he lowered his lips to hers. It was a brief, gentle kiss, but one filled with a longing that surprised him. When she didn't pull away, his first thought was to deepen the kiss, but he reluctantly pulled back. She was vulnerable right now, and he wasn't a man to take advantage under the circumstances, no matter how much he was tempted. But his gentlemanly honor didn't prevent him from one more taste before he let her go. "That one was a better thank-you."

Flustered, Addie simply stared into his smoky eyes. She told herself he'd been teasing, and she shouldn't read more into the kiss, even if his eyes were telling her that he'd liked it as much as she had. She needed to put distance between them. "I think I smell the biscuits."

Dropping his hands from her face, Jack stood there rooted to the floor when she walked to the stove. *What in the heck just happened?* He hadn't really expected her to kiss him, but when she did, all he could think was he wanted to know what it would feel like to give her a real kiss. So he did. And he liked it. He more than liked it, he wanted more. Instead of standing there like an idiot and watching her move around the kitchen, he had to pull himself together. He grabbed two cups and filled them with steaming coffee as she placed the food on the table. He told himself to act natural, make casual conversation when they sat down. If he didn't get his mind off of that kiss, he might grab her and give her a kiss that she would never forget. Problem was, he wouldn't be able to forget it either, if the kiss they'd just shared was any indication. It had rocked him to his toes, and his brain was still in a fog.

They ate a few bites in silence, before Jack said, "I thought you had the legal papers with you when we went to the Coburns'." He tried hard not to let on that his world hadn't just been turned upside down in the span of a brief kiss.

Addie didn't know what to make of his kiss, and now he was sitting there acting as though nothing had happened between them. But she had bigger problems than trying to figure out why he had kissed her. "I had the papers, and I know Mr. Coburn was in a hurry, but I needed time to speak to the children."

He knew she would need as much time to adjust as the children would. "Yeah, he wanted to move pretty fast."

"I'm not sure how to tell them. They've been so excited to stay here together. Perhaps I should wait to tell them tomorrow after school. They can at least have a good night's rest tonight."

Jack leaned over and placed his hand over hers. "I don't think there is going to be a good time. But everything will be okay."

Addie looked at the large hand covering hers. He was warm, strong, and he made her feel safe and secure whenever he was around. He spoke with such conviction, she believed him. She looked up at him, nodded, and tried to smile, but tears were filling her eyes. Too much was happening at once: the adoption, her attraction to Jack, and that kiss.

Jack leaned over, wrapped his large hand around the back of her head, and gently urged her to him. His mouth covered hers and he kissed her soundly. Without leaving her lips, he stood and pulled her into his arms. It wasn't a chaste kiss like before, it was a soul-searching, mind-numbing kind of kiss. He didn't hold back, and neither did she. He held her so tightly he could feel her heart beat in rhythm with his own.

Addie was the first to pull away. "We should finish our dinner. I need to get the children soon."

Jack shook his head, trying desperately to make sense out of why he couldn't keep his hands off her. Not once, but twice. "Yes, we do."

"You don't have to stay. I can walk to get them."

He still had his arms around her. "I'm going with you."

Addie looked up at him. "Okay." She wanted him to stay. She wanted more of his kisses, even though common sense said she was playing with fire.

He released her and sat back down. "I'm staying the night."

Addie sat down and picked up her sandwich. "You can't do that. It's not proper."

"The children are here. What's not proper? I won't be in your bed." What was wrong with him? Why did he say that?

Addie opened her mouth to speak, but it took a moment before words actually came out. "It just wouldn't look right."

Jack didn't like her staying out here alone. He didn't know why he was feeling so protective, but he hadn't liked it last night when he left, and the feeling was stronger tonight.

"We'll ask Granny to come back with us. But I'm staying, even if I have to sleep in the barn."

"It's too cold, you can't sleep in the barn. It will be freezing tonight."

"I've been cold before. I'll live." He wouldn't mind sleeping in the barn if she warmed him up with her kisses in the morning.

"Are you expecting trouble? Is it Frankie?" Addie didn't understand why he was adamant about staying tonight.

"No, I'm not expecting trouble. I just

don't like you staying out here alone, without a man around."

"I'll get a rifle from Morgan," she replied.

"That doesn't make me feel a whole lot better. I'm staying."

"You can't stay every night. How would that look? And you have to return the buckboard to the livery."

"I don't care how it looks. I'm the sheriff, so it's not unusual for me to offer my protection when I think it is necessary."

"Why do you think it is necessary to protect me? Morgan is not that far away if I need help."

"Any woman alone needs protection. If something happened, it would take Morgan some time to get here, even if he knew you needed help. You have the children to consider."

"Do you stay at Clarissa's? Doesn't she live alone?"

Clarissa again. "She lives with her father. Besides, they don't live out of town in an isolated area."

"I appreciate your concern, but we will be fine." Addie didn't feel as confident about staying alone as she tried to make him believe. The thought of him being close in case of trouble was reassuring, but she couldn't count on him to stay every night for eternity.

"No arguing. Let's finish eating so we can get the kids and Granny." Jack's mind was made up, and no amount of arguing would change his plans.

"Granny went to bed not long after dinner," Rose said. "She'd been playing games with the children and I think she was worn out."

Addie passed a glance at Jack.

Rose noticed the look they'd exchanged. "Is something wrong?"

"No, nothing that I can talk about right now." Addie's eyes moved to the children who were putting on their coats. "We'll talk tomorrow."

Morgan handed Jack some extra blankets for the buckboard. "It's getting pretty cold out there."

Jack inclined his head, indicating that Morgan should follow him out the door. "I'm staying at Addie's tonight."

"What's going on?"

Jack quickly told him about Davey's adoption. "And I don't like Addie and the children staying alone."

"Word will get around," Morgan said.

"Like I told Addie, I'm the sheriff and I'm supposed to protect the people in our town."

Morgan arched his brow at Jack. "Is that all there is to it?"

Jack expelled a loud breath of air. "Yes. That's all there is to it."

"You plan on staying there forever?" Morgan didn't wait for a reply before he added, "This won't be good for her reputation."

"Why would anyone question a sheriff looking after a woman out here alone?" Jack knew the answer; he was choosing to be obstinate.

"I can have a couple of my men keep an eye on the place overnight," Morgan offered.

"You can't do that forever, either."

Morgan didn't have an answer. "I offered to let Addie and the kids stay here, but she wanted them to have their own place."

Their conversation ended when Addie and the children walked outside. Jack wrapped the children in blankets, and put one around Addie before they left for the farm. When they arrived back at the farmhouse, Jack carried a sleeping Claire inside.

After Jack gently laid Claire on her bed, Addie said, "I'll be down after they are all in bed."

He nodded, understanding she didn't want to have the conversation about him staying the night in front of the children.

Addie walked in the kitchen only to find it empty. She looked out the window and saw the buckboard was in front of the barn and the team had been unhitched. Thinking Jack was most likely caring for the horse, she walked to the front room to start a fire. She hated to make him drive all the way back to town as late as it was, but she didn't know if allowing him to stay was the right thing to do.

As soon as she entered the room, she saw a fire blazing in the hearth, and Jack was sitting on the settee with his eyes closed, sleeping peacefully. He'd removed his boots and placed them by the front door, along with his hat. She smiled, wondering if he placed them there for a quick getaway, or from habit. She stood there quietly and stared at his relaxed masculine features. She could almost envision how he must have looked as a young boy. In her estimation, he was a remarkable man, having overcome a difficult childhood to make something of himself. He could have easily become more like her brother Frank. Jack possessed an enviable strength of character, and yet he was remarkably tender.

He'd been so kind to the children since they'd arrived, giving up his own personal time to give them attention. After spending time with him, the children were smiling more, Davey seemed less jaded, Claire was always laughing. Jack did what most adults failed to do: he made the children feel important.

Her thoughts drifted to his kisses. She knew it was probably a mistake to kiss him, but he was irresistible. She thought she might never have another opportunity to kiss a man like Jack. So why not? What could it hurt? She sighed. Sadly, she knew the answer. She was on the verge of losing her heart to the man sleeping on her settee. She didn't want to be an old maid pining after a man who'd never consider more than a flirtation with her. It would be wise to rein in her longings, or she was bound to have her heart crushed. From now on, no more kissing.

She approached the settee, fully intending to wake him and suggest he return to Morgan's for the night. But seeing how soundly he was sleeping, she didn't have the heart to wake him. He had to be exhausted tonight, because she was, and his day had started long before hers. Thinking about all he'd done that day for her and the children, she decided to let him sleep. People would think what they wanted to think. They had done nothing wrong. She turned around and walked back upstairs to get some blankets. When she returned to the parlor, she placed a pillow beside his head and covered him with the blankets. After adding some logs to the fire, she lowered the lamp and left the room.

Jack didn't know what time it was when he woke, but the room was cold. He started to get up to stoke the fire, and he saw the blankets covering him. When he saw the pillow beside him, he smiled. She'd allowed him to spend the night. He thought she was going to give him a good argument, so he'd sat down after he'd built the fire to wait for her, but he'd obviously fallen asleep.

After he had a nice blaze going, he stretched out on the settee, stuffed the pillow beneath his head, covered himself with the blankets, and thought about Miss Addie's kisses. He liked the way her soft body felt in his arms. He'd kissed Clarissa before, and Addie was right, she was very slim and trim, but something was missing. Compared to Addie, Clarissa felt like a skeleton. It was difficult to explain, but he wasn't attracted to Clarissa in the way he was drawn to Addie. Clarissa was probably the type of woman he'd thought he was attracted to, but something had changed. His attraction to Addie was more instinctive, his desire for her more primitive. When he held Addie, she filled his arms, but it wasn't only a physical space, she filled a void in his being. He felt like she thawed his heart, much like the children.

He reminded himself attraction was one thing, but taking on all of the responsibility that came with her was another thing all together. He thought he'd be ready to marry by the time he found the right woman, but he wanted a relationship to develop over time, in a slow, orderly fashion. Like most men, he'd planned on finding a woman to court, marry, and make a home with before children came along. With Addie, it would be a package deal from the get-go, and that was a monumental leap from having a powerful attraction to a woman to making a permanent union with a ready-made family.

Chapter Twelve

After school ended, Addie and the children walked outside and saw Jack with Morgan and Rose.

"We came to take the children to the ranch," Rose said.

"Thank you." Addie had yet to tell the children about the adoption. She planned to talk to them tonight, and after school tomorrow they would take Davey to his new home.

"Miss Addie, why aren't you going home with us?" Davey asked.

"I have some business in town, and the sheriff will bring me home in a little while," Addie replied.

Claire had jumped into Jack's arms as soon as she saw him. "Can I go with you?"

"Not today, honey, but I'll see you in a little while," Jack replied, kissing her cheek and hoisting her inside Morgan's buckboard.

Jane walked over and grabbed Addie's hand. "Miss Addie, is something wrong? You've been sad all day."

Addie pulled Jane into her arms. "I'm fine, honey. I'll be home soon."

Jack heard Addie's voice tremble with emotion, so he hoisted Jane in to the buckboard. "Here you go, honey."

"I'll have dinner ready by the time you get there," Rose said. "You can eat with us before you leave."

Addie nodded. It would be easier if the children ate before she broke the news to them. She knew they would be too upset to eat if she told them beforehand.

"Jack, we expect you to have dinner with us," Rose said.

"Thanks, Rose." Jack was always thrilled when anyone cooked for him, but not today. He dreaded the thought of what was to come.

"I'll bring Davey to your farm tomorrow night." Addie indicated the line where Mr. Coburn's signature was required on the documents. She had looked around the farmhouse, and while it wasn't as nice as her new home, she couldn't object to the living quarters. "Davey's sisters will be with me so they can see where he will be living. I want them to see their brother often, and we will be inviting him to the farm frequently. Naturally, they will see him in school, but I want them to have some free time together." No matter how much she wanted to delay the adoption, she couldn't put off the inevitable.

"We're busy at the farm. As time allows, maybe the boy will visit, but it will be at my say-so," Coburn replied.

Addie was taken aback by his tone. "I'm sure you can understand how important it is for the children to stay in touch."

Coburn held up the papers he signed. "This means the boy's mine now, or am I wrong about that?"

Jack stood and moved closer to Roy. "Roy, we all want what's best for Davey. He's not chattel, and he has a right to stay in touch with his sisters. There's no harm being done, and it will help all of them as they adjust to this new arrangement. His sisters have been very dependent on him."

Roy looked at Jack, but didn't comment. He slammed his hat on his head and walked to the door. "I'll see you tomorrow night when you bring the boy."

When the door closed behind him, Addie slumped into the chair in front of Jack's desk. "He is not a pleasant person."

Jack wished he could disagree, but he didn't like Coburn's attitude. He walked to the door and saw Coburn was about to pull away in his buckboard, so he hurried outside. Reaching Coburn's horse, Jack grabbed hold of the bridle.

"What do you think you are doing?" Roy yelled.

"Roy, just so you know, I'll be out to your farm on a regular basis to check on Davey. Treat him right, or you'll answer to me."

Roy glared at him. "Are you threatening me because I did a good deed and adopted that boy?"

Jack leveled his steely eyes on him. "Take it any way you like. Just make sure you're good to him."

"What do you mean, Davey is being adopted without us?" Tears flowed from Jane's eyes as she sobbed the question.

"It means they didn't want all of us," Davey said.

Addie had told the children about the adoption as soon as they arrived home. She'd welcomed Jack's offer to stay while she told them, and she exchanged a look with him now.

"They wanted all of you, but times are hard, and they couldn't afford three children," Jack said.

Addie was thankful he'd known the right thing to say. "The Coburns don't live far away and Davey will come often for dinner. Of course, you will see him at school." Addie was trying her best to be positive, pointing out advantages of Davey staying in the same town. She prayed Mr. Coburn would be more agreeable than he was earlier today.

"I'll ride by and see Davey often." Jack wanted to assure the girls they didn't need to worry about their brother. He also wanted to let Davey know that they wouldn't forget about him.

Claire started crying and Addie pulled her onto her lap. "There's no reason to cry, honey, we will see Davey often." Even as she tried to reassure Claire, tears were forming in her own eyes. Jane jumped up, ran to Addie, and buried her head in her shoulder. "Miss Addie, I don't want Davey to go."

When Jack's gaze met Addie's, he saw the helplessness that she was feeling. Tears streamed down her cheeks. Jack felt powerless watching the three crying females. He left his seat and started to pace back and forth behind Addie's chair. He stopped suddenly, leaned over, and wrapped his arms around them. He glanced at Davey across the table. He was staring into space, as if he was in deep contemplation. Jack was worried about him. He was too quiet. "Addie, why don't you take the girls upstairs and get them ready for bed. I'll stay with Davey."

Addie couldn't speak, so she nodded. It might be good for Davey to have Jack there if he wanted to talk.

As soon as Addie and the girls walked away, Jack sat beside Davey. "How do you feel about being adopted?"

Davey shrugged. "I knew it would happen sometime. And we knew no one would want all of us."

"It's difficult for families to take on three children."

"But why would they want me instead of the girls? You'd think most folks would want a young kid like Claire."

"I reckon a lot of folks want boys to carry on the family name if they don't have sons of their own. Girls marry and take their husband's name." There were many reasons people chose boys, generally because the men wanted boys to help with the work, but Jack was reluctant to offer that explanation.

"Do you like Mr. Coburn?" Davey asked.

"I don't know him well." Jack didn't lie, he didn't know Coburn well, but he couldn't say he would be friends with him after his interaction with him today. "Pastor Clay says Sarah Coburn attends church frequently."

"That don't mean much to me." Davey had his own opinions about church people. From his limited experience, they didn't often live up to their words.

Jack put his arm around Davey's shoulders. "Davey, I know people have let you and your sisters down in the past, but I'm hopeful this time it will be different. I also know you don't want to leave your sisters, but I think we need to look at this in a positive light. You won't be far away, and if Coburn can't take you to see them, I will. That's a promise."

"Someone who don't live here could adopt Jane and Claire," Davey said.

Jack couldn't deny that fact, and he wouldn't lie to the boy. "That's possible, but I don't think it is very likely. You have to consider only locals will know about the orphanage."

"I wish someone like you and Miss Addie could adopt us. My sisters are crazy about both of you." Davey didn't see what harm it would do to let the sheriff know what his sisters really wanted.

"It has to be a married couple who adopts

children," Jack replied.

"Yeah."

Davey sounded so dejected it broke Jack's heart. "Davey, sometimes life doesn't go like we want, but remember our faith tells us God will see us through the tough times. Sometimes when things look the darkest is when the greatest blessings come."

Davey looked up at him, his eyes devoid of emotion. "I told you before, God don't care about me and my sisters. Never has. Just like my ma. She didn't care about us. She left us like we were nothing. Church-going people are no different, they just try to say the right things." Davey jumped up and ran out the back door.

Jack sat there a minute, debating whether he should go after him. Sometimes it was best to have some time alone to come to terms with the challenges ahead, yet he had a feeling Davey could use a man's perspective. He grabbed two apples from the bowl on the table, walked out the back door, and headed toward the stable. He knew he'd find Davey with the horses.

He walked to a stall where Davey was stroking the neck of the horse he'd ridden. Davey wouldn't look up and Jack knew he'd been crying. Jack stood beside him and started slicing the apples. "Here you go, he'll like this."

Davey took the apple slices from him and held one to the horse's mouth.

"Whoa," Jack said, pulling Davey's hand from the horse's mouth. He demonstrated how to hold the apple in his palm. "Hold it like this or he might take your fingers with the apple."

"Do all horses like apples?" Davey asked, holding the apple as Jack instructed and offering it to the horse.

"Most of them do. My horse seems to have a fondness for carrots." Jack braced his arm on the stall door and watched Davey feed the horse. "You know, Davey, I've been thinking about your mother."

Davey glanced up at him. "Why?"

"I can understand why you think she didn't care about you and your sisters because she left you at the orphanage."

"Yeah. She never cared. We never saw her again." Once the horse finished the apple, Davey started stroking his neck again.

"Well, I've been thinking your mother cared very much about you." Jack reached out to stroke the horse, and he could feel Davey's eyes on him.

"Why do you think that?"

"Because she named you after a king. I'd say she had big ideas about the boy you were, and the man you were going to become."

Davey's hand stilled on the horse. "A king?"

"Yeah, Miss Addie said your favorite Bible story is David and Goliath. Don't you know that that shepherd boy who killed that giant became a king?"

"Really?"

Jack looked at Davey and saw the doubt in his eyes. "Really. You can ask Miss Addie. And I have a feeling your mother named you after that shepherd boy. I think she knew you would face difficulties in your life, just like King David, but you would overcome them, just like he overcame his obstacles."

Davey's eyes filled with unshed tears and he turned back to the horse. "No one should leave their kids."

"No, they shouldn't," Jack agreed. "But we don't know the hardships they face, and they could have good reason. Maybe they think the best they can do is to make sure their children will have food and shelter. I'd say in some instances, it takes a powerful kind of love to leave your children if you think they can have a better life without you." Jack straightened and put his hand on Davey's shoulder. "Why don't you just try looking at the situation from a different point of view?"

"It don't make no difference anyhow," Davey replied.

Jack understood that at this moment, Davey might not be willing to give an inch. "It may not. Then again, it might make a man feel kind of special to be named after a king."

"Davey, this is Mr. and Mrs. Coburn." Addie's shaking hands were on Davey's shoulders as she introduced him to his new family. She then introduced the girls to the Coburns.

Sarah Coburn stepped forward and said softly, "It's nice to have you here, Davey." She greeted the girls, but Roy Coburn didn't say a word.

"We've brought Davey's things," Jack said as he climbed down from the buckboard. "I'll help you carry them in."

"Me and the boy can handle it," Roy said, walking to the back of the buckboard.

"I'd like the girls to see Davey's new home," Addie said. Her tone conveyed that she was going to have her way.

Roy pressed his lips in a disapproving frown, but he didn't comment as he grabbed a valise from the buckboard.

Jack picked up the second valise, and they all followed the Coburns inside. Sarah showed Davey a small space at the back of the cabin behind a curtain, where he would be sleeping.

Addie was disappointed that it wasn't a more private space, but she didn't comment.

Jane didn't hesitate to make her feelings known. "This isn't as nice as your room at home."

Davey and Jane looked at each other, and Addie knew they were communicating their thoughts in their own private way.

"This is his home now," Sarah Coburn said. "We may build more rooms at the back of the house soon, and he can have a larger room."

Jack placed the valise at the foot of the bed. "I'd be happy to help, Roy, when you start building."

"It won't be anytime soon," Roy replied. "Sarah's always wanting something done, but money don't grow on trees."

Jack had a response on the tip of his tongue, but it wasn't for polite company. He figured in this instance silence was golden.

"Boys need some privacy." Addie directed her comment to Sarah, since she seemed more cooperative than her husband.

Sarah nodded. "I'll keep that in mind."

They stood quietly for a few minutes, Jack and Addie dreading to leave Davey alone with the Coburns.

Claire wiggled out of Addie's arms, scrambled to Jack, and tugged on his hand. When he looked down at her, she said, "I want Davey to come home."

Jack picked her up and held her on his hip. "Honey, we have to think of this farm as Davey's second home now."

Claire buried her face in Jack's neck, and Jack's gaze slid to Addie's watery eyes. He knew he was in for another night of crying females, and darned if he knew how to solve the problem. "Davey, if you need anything, you come get me."

Davey nodded.

Jack squeezed Davey's shoulder before he turned and walked out the door with a tearful Claire.

Addie and Jane hugged Davey good-bye, but neither one could say the words they wanted to say.

CHAPTER THIRTEEN

"What are you doing here so early?" Morgan asked when he opened the door.

"I need to talk to you," Jack said.

"I was just about to have some coffee." It was Morgan's habit to have the coffee made before the women came downstairs.

"Sounds good. I haven't had any this morning." Jack removed his hat and hung it on the hook.

Morgan figured if Jack hadn't had coffee before he left town, he had to have something important on his mind. "Have a seat." He placed a cup of coffee on the table in front of him.

"It's cold out there." Jack took a sip of the steaming liquid, then said, "I heard early this morning that Frank Langtry is in Denver."

"Denver?"

"That's what I was told. My deputy heard it from a man in the saloon last night. The man told my deputy that Frank married Judge Stevens's daughter, and is living right in Denver with the judge's sister."

Morgan stared at him in disbelief. "The territorial judge? That Judge Stevens?"

"That's what the man told Webb. I haven't met the judge, but I heard he's a real hard case."

"It can't be Frank. How could he be married to a judge's daughter?"

"That's exactly what I thought, but Webb said the man knew Frank and assured him it was a true story. I'm going to ride to Denver to check it out. That's why I came over here first. I wanted to ask you to keep an eye on . . . the girls." Jack caught himself before he said *my girls.*

"Of course we will, but I'm riding with you to Denver. I'll have the men keep an eye on them."

"I don't think it's necessary for you to go. I doubt it's Frank."

"I don't think it's Frank either, but if it is, you know he's not riding alone. I'm going with you." Morgan stood and pulled a pan from the shelf and placed it on the stove. "We can take off right after breakfast."

After they arrived in Denver, Jack and Morgan stopped at the jail to speak with Sheriff

Trent and inform him of their mission. The sheriff had not heard that Frank Langtry was in town, but he had heard the judge's daughter recently married.

"As a matter of fact, Judge Stevens arrived yesterday. Apparently there's a big party planned to celebrate his daughter's marriage later today." Sheriff Trent pulled out his pocket watch and checked the time. "Have you men met Judge Stevens yet? He may be home for lunch if you time it right."

"Never met him," Jack said.

"Let me tell you, he's a no-nonsense man. I've only met him a few times, but he's not one to cross. I met his daughter, and she's a real pretty gal. I sure as blazes can't see the judge allowing her to marry an outlaw."

Jack looked at Morgan and raised his eyebrows. "I guess we might as well go by their home and find out if it is Frank." He glanced back at the sheriff and grinned. "I wonder if Frank's new father-in-law knows about Frank's history."

The sheriff chuckled. "Considering the judge's reputation, I wouldn't count on it." The sheriff told them where the judge's sister lived. "Her name is Ruth Butler. You won't miss her huge mansion high up on the hill. If I hear fireworks coming from that direction, I'll know things aren't going well." The sheriff was still chuckling as Jack and Morgan left his office.

"I'd think the sheriff would have heard if Frank Langtry was in town," Jack said as they rode down the street.

"Frank's not well-known in Denver. It's possible not many people would recognize him."

Deke Sullivan was walking out of the saloon carrying four bottles of whiskey when he saw Jack Roper and Morgan LeMasters ride by. He loaded the bottles of whiskey in his saddlebags as he watched them ride down the street toward the house where Frank was living. It was the same direction he needed to go to get back to the house where the gang was hiding out. He got on his horse and followed, keeping a safe distance between them. When he saw them turn and ride up the hill toward the big house, he had no doubt they were going after Frank. He reined his horse in next to a small house where he could watch what was going on without being seen.

An attractive older woman answered the door to the mansion, and Jack removed his hat before introducing himself. "Ma'am, I'm Jack Roper, the sheriff of Whispering

Pines." Jack inclined his head toward Morgan. "This is Morgan LeMasters."

Ruth smiled politely, and though she knew why these two men were at her door, she didn't let on. "Gentlemen. How may I help you?"

Jack wasn't sure how to proceed, so he said simply, "We are here for Frank Langtry."

"May I ask the purpose . . ." She was interrupted by a voice behind her.

"Aunt Ruth, will the judge be here for lunch?"

Jack and Morgan traded a glance, as if they couldn't believe their ears. They knew that voice belonged to Frank Langtry.

Frank walked behind Ruth and looked at the two men at the door. "I've been expecting you." He opened the door wide. "Come in."

"We're here to take you back to Whispering Pines," Jack said.

"You can't take him! We're having a party tonight to celebrate his marriage to my niece," Ruth said.

"Sorry, ma'am, but Frank is coming with us," Jack said.

"Let me tell my wife I'm leaving," Frank said.

"Ma'am, you can go get your niece. Frank

is not leaving my sight," Jack said.

Ruth looked at Frank like she was afraid to leave him alone.

Frank smiled at her. "Go ahead, Aunt Ruth. She's in the bedroom."

As soon as Ruth walked away, Frank looked at the men. "Bet you never expected to find me here, much less married."

Morgan stepped forward and slammed his massive fist into Frank's jaw, sending him flying through the air. He landed next to the stairway several feet from the door. Months of simmering anger over what Frank had done to his wife was behind that one punch. "That's for what you did to Rose. And I'd advise you to stay down, or I might break my promise to Rose and kill you."

It took a minute for Frank to regain his senses. He leaned on one elbow and rubbed his jaw. "You shouldn't have married my sister, LeMasters."

"Where's your horse, Frank?" Jack asked.

"The livery," Frank replied, getting to his feet when he saw his wife on the staircase.

"Frank?" Charlotte ran down the stairs to him. She was horrified when she saw his bleeding lip. "What happened? Look at your face!"

"Old score," Frank replied.

201

Jack glanced at Morgan. By the look on his face, he knew Morgan was thinking the same thing he was. The sheriff was right about one thing: Charlotte was a real looker. Jack wondered how she happened in the path of Frank Langtry. He'd never known Frank to stay with a woman overlong, and it came as a shock that he'd actually married. This one had to be something special, or was it her father who was special to Frank?

Charlotte turned her attention on Jack and Morgan. "My father will hear about this. Which one of you hit him?"

Jack ignored her question and asked his own. "Where is your father?" He wanted to explain the situation to the judge before he left town.

"He had business to attend to, but he will be back for the party," Charlotte said. "You can wait for him."

Jack didn't intend to wait; he wanted to get back to Whispering Pines so he could check on the girls. "If the judge has questions, he can speak to Sheriff Trent. We're going back to Whispering Pines, and I'm not inclined to wait around until dark to get waylaid by your husband's gang."

"Where are the boys, Frank?" Morgan asked.

"I haven't seen them in weeks. I imagine they are still in Mexico," Frank said.

"The judge is not going to like you taking my niece's husband from our home," Ruth warned.

"Tell the judge as far as I'm concerned you are harboring a criminal, if you knew he was a wanted man," Jack replied.

"I'm aware of what you have accused him of doing, but I also know that he is innocent."

"No, ma'am. Frank is many things, but I can assure you, innocent is not one of them," Jack countered.

Ruth wasn't inclined to believe the sheriff. "I'm sure this is all an unfortunate misunderstanding."

Jack turned his attention on Charlotte. "Get your husband a coat, unless you want him to freeze on the way to Whispering Pines."

Charlotte buried her head in Frank's chest. "Oh, Frank, what are we going to do?"

"Get my coat, honey. When your father shows up, tell him everything." He wanted a chance to speak to the judge and tell him the same story he'd told Charlotte, but the judge had left the house early that morning before he'd had the chance. He kissed Charlotte and whispered in her ear, "You remember everything I told you?"

Charlotte nodded, wiped her tears away and left to retrieve Frank's coat. When she returned, Jack took the coat from her and checked the pockets.

Frank grinned at him. "Do you think my wife was going to put my gun in the pocket?"

Jack glanced Charlotte's way. "Sorry, ma'am, no disrespect intended, but I don't think you know the man you married."

Charlotte turned her chin up at Jack. "I know exactly who my husband is, and you will not keep him in your jail. My father will have him released immediately."

Frank put his arm around his wife's shoulders. "Now, honey, don't take all of the fun out of this for them. I'm sorry about the party, but we'll have another one."

Jack didn't like the sound of that exchange, but he kept his thoughts to himself. "Let's go."

When they were on the porch, Morgan turned to Charlotte, who was standing in the doorway with tears in her eyes. "I was the one who hit your husband, and believe me, he got off easy. I don't know what stories he's made up for you, but this is not a man you want. You should tell your father to annul your marriage."

Deke's patience paid off. He didn't have long to wait before Sheriff Roper and Morgan left the big house with Frank. As soon as they turned for the livery, Deke got back on his horse and headed out of town. He had to get back to the boys and tell them what was going on. It looked like they'd be riding to Whispering Pines to get Frank out of jail. The bank robbery would have to wait.

"So how did you meet the judge's daughter?" Jack asked Frank once they were on their way back to Whispering Pines.

Frank laughed. "I'm just a blessed man. She's beautiful, don't you think?"

Jack thought she was beautiful, but he also knew Frank had an ulterior motive for marrying. "What I think is you married that young gal for a reason."

Frank just laughed. "How's my loving family?"

"Frank, you don't give one hoot about your family. You may have your new wife and her family fooled for now, but we know who you are," Morgan said. He was still tempted to pull him off his horse and beat him within an inch of his life. The only reason he didn't was he'd given his word to his wife, and to God.

Jack and Morgan picked up the pace so they didn't have to listen to Frank. The sooner they got him locked away, the better.

Once Deke told the gang he'd seen Jack and Morgan ride off with Frank, he said, "I reckon we need to go get him out of jail."

"What about the bank?" Corbin asked.

Deke glanced at each man. "Frank said he'd plan that robbery, so it will have to wait. We need to get him out of jail first."

"Don't you think his new father-in-law will get him out?" Reb asked.

"I don't think we should sit around and wait to find out. Now that they've got Frank, they probably think we are around Denver, so we should take off before the sheriff starts nosing around. I figure they won't be expecting us to find out about Frank's capture so fast, so we might be able to spring him before they know what is going on."

"I think Deke is right. Let's go," Dutch said.

Charlotte was in a terrible state when she met her father at the door. "Father, you need to go to Whispering Pines."

The judge had just returned from the hotel where he'd been visiting with his girlfriend, Leigh King. After spending the entire week with her in Colorado City, he couldn't bring himself to leave her behind. Leigh was the same age as his daughter, and she made him feel vibrant and alive for the first time in his life. He fully intended to marry her while he still had some good years left to show her a good time. He realized she might be marrying him for prestige and money, but he didn't care. He would provide a good life for her, and she could give him what he wanted.

Having left Leigh only minutes before, he was still riding high on a wave of ecstasy. But as soon as he walked through the door and saw Charlotte's distress, his lifelong responsibilities came crashing down on his shoulders. He tried to hide his annoyance when he said, "Let's go to the parlor, Charlotte, and start from the beginning." He thought a good stiff drink would make his daughter's rantings more palatable.

Charlotte told him everything Frank had told her about his past and his interaction with Morgan LeMasters. "This Mr. LeMasters has been out to ruin Frank for years. Frank said he's an important man in Whispering Pines, and that sheriff, Jack Roper, does his bidding because they are best friends."

The judge silently berated himself for not investigating Frank before he'd entrusted his daughter to him. But what was done, was done. Charlotte rushed into marriage of her own accord, but he told himself she must love Frank to have married him so quickly. It certainly came at an opportune time for him. He'd given Charlotte the best years of his life, and he wanted more. He wanted Leigh King, and the excitement that came with a younger woman.

"Father, please go to Whispering Pines to get him," Charlotte pleaded.

"Charlotte is right, Robert, you must get him back. I like this young man, and I believe his story," Ruth said.

"Give me a few minutes to think this through. You said he is accused of shooting a man on this Mr. LeMasters's property?"

"He said he didn't shoot anyone," Charlotte said.

"I will send a telegram to the sheriff in the morning demanding that he return to Denver with Frank and this LeMasters, and if he refuses, I will send Sheriff Trent to arrest him. When they get back to Denver, we can clear up this matter in no time." The judge wasn't inclined to ride to Whispering

Pines while Leigh was staying in Denver. He'd promised to take her on a picnic tomorrow, and he wasn't going to disappoint her. She was a lovely young widow with no children, and she could have her pick of younger men. If he didn't show her a good time, she might find a reason to take up with another man. He didn't know if she'd bewitched him, but from the first night together, he couldn't stay away from her. She'd only been married a month when her husband met with an unfortunate accident, so she was almost as innocent as his daughter. He feared an unscrupulous suitor might lead her astray.

The judge looked at Ruth. "You've heard his story and you say you believe him? Is it plausible he could be lying, wanting to use my position to free him?"

"I truly believe him, and I can tell he's crazy about Charlotte." Ruth wanted to believe Frank because he made her niece happy.

The judge wasn't as certain about Frank's story. It could be Frank had intended to meet him and his daughter in an effort to gain their trust. He'd seen and heard too much over the years from outlaws bent on escaping the gallows. He was no longer surprised at the lengths a man would go to evade the reckoning. Yet, he had his future planned, and he could well use his position to make things work out as he wanted. All his life he'd been a stickler for the law, honoring his profession with the seriousness it deserved, but now was *his* time. "Well then, I will do what I can to see he has justice on his side."

Charlotte kissed her father on the cheek. "Thank you, Father. I am confident Frank is telling the truth."

CHAPTER FOURTEEN

"What do you mean we are supposed to take Frank back to Denver?" Morgan asked when Jack showed up on his doorstep the very next morning.

Jack reached in his shirt pocket and pulled out the telegram. "I received this from the judge, informing me that I am to return to Denver with you and Frank, or he will have me arrested."

"I guess he didn't like us putting a halt to his party," Morgan said dryly, as he led the way to the kitchen.

"I'm sorry to take you away from the ranch again, Morgan, but I guess I don't have much of a choice."

Morgan arched his brow at Jack. "Guess I could just let you get arrested."

Jack shrugged. "It wouldn't be the first time."

Morgan laughed. "When are we supposed to have him back?"

"He said within the week, and I'm going to drag it out to the very last minute. Let Frank suffer in jail for a few days. What I can't figure out is why he wants you back in Denver."

"If I were a betting man I'd say Frank has told the judge he's innocent of all charges, and the judge wants to get to the bottom of it. I figure since Frank is his son-in-law, the judge will certainly take a personal interest. I was awake all night thinking about the reason Frank married a judge's daughter. Yeah, she's a beautiful woman, but I think old Frank had a deeper, darker motive when he said his *I do's.*"

Jack drank the coffee Morgan handed him. "The thing is, I had the feeling Frank might really care about her."

Morgan couldn't believe Frank had any redeeming motives. "If he does, it's the first person he ever cared about."

There was something nagging Jack, so he voiced his thoughts aloud. "I have a gut feeling we are not going to like this meeting. You know a man will do whatever he can to keep his daughter from being hurt. It's possible the judge won't hang him."

"It's more than possible, it's likely," Morgan agreed.

Jack finished his coffee and stood. "I guess

there's no sense in speculating until we know for sure what this is all about. I'm taking the girls to school, so I best head out."

Morgan got to his feet and walked Jack to the door. "Watch your back. I expect Frank's gang is going to be around before long."

"Yeah, but you can be sure they won't waylay me twice."

"What are you going to do about the girls staying alone?"

Jack shook his head. "Not much I can do if Addie refuses to stay here."

"You can't keep sleeping out there every night. At least, unless you don't care about ruining her reputation."

Jack turned to face Morgan. "How did you know I was?"

Morgan grinned at him. "Because I'm worried about them too, and I have men riding that way every night."

Jack frowned. "My horse is not there."

"No, but a buckboard is. Addie doesn't have a buckboard."

"Yeah." Jack could have kicked himself for not thinking of that.

The two men walked out on the porch. "Jack, it's none of my business, but you should consider how this would look if some of the women in town found out about your sleeping arrangements."

"I'm sleeping on the settee, and I can tell you it's darned uncomfortable."

"I didn't think otherwise, but I don't know if everyone would be as understanding if gossip started. Are you protecting a woman and children out of duty, or do you have more of a personal interest?"

Jack didn't say anything for a long time. He stood there twirling his hat in his hands, looking off in the distance. Finally, he said, "I'm not sure."

Morgan remembered how long it had taken him to come to terms with his feelings for Rose. He never expected to fall in love with Frank Langtry's sister. "It doesn't bother you that she's Frank's sister, does it?"

"Nope. The women can't help that fact, and now that they know Frank's ways, they both understand what we have to do."

"Do you mind if I ask what is holding you back?"

Jack understood Morgan was asking why he wasn't making some sort of declaration about his feelings for Addie. "She comes with a ready-made family, and I'm not certain how I feel about that."

Morgan had seen the way Jack interacted

with the children. Any fool could see he was crazy about them. "You're already taken with those kids."

"Yeah, I am. I'm just not certain I know how to be a father. I never had one to find out what makes a good one from a bad one."

His response surprised Morgan. "That's no way to look at it. I've never had a child, but I can't wait to be a father."

"You had a father, so you had an opportunity to see one in action. You know what he did wrong and what he did right. I'm not sure I have what it takes to be a good father."

Morgan couldn't argue that he'd learned many things from his own father. The most important thing his father had taught him was to be a good, honorable man. Jack had that covered. "You'll make a good father, Jack. You're honest, hardworking, God-fearing, and you'd be a good role model for those kids. That's what I learned from my father. It wasn't so much what he said as much as it was the way he lived his life."

"There is also the possibility someday either their mother or father could show up and take them back. How would I handle that?"

Morgan shook his head. "I see what you mean. That would be a tough one to handle.

Can they do that when they've been absent for so long?"

"It happens," Jack said on a shrug. "Not often, but it can happen."

"We can't live our lives thinking something may happen. What if it never happened?"

Jack chewed on his lip as he thought about Morgan's comment. He really liked kissing Addie, but they hadn't done much of that for a couple of days. That was probably a good thing, because kissing her seemed to fog his brain. Since Davey's adoption, he and Addie hadn't talked about anything else. He didn't think they knew each other well enough to think about a future together. But he'd never been so attracted to another woman. He didn't know how she felt about him, and there was the chance she still had feelings for Prescott Adler. There were too many unanswered questions right now for him to make a decision about his feelings, or a future with her. It was too soon. "I guess I'm not ready to make that kind of decision right now."

Morgan didn't push. "Since we don't know the whereabouts of Frank's gang, I'll have Rose make sure Addie stays here at the ranch for a while. That way her reputation won't be ruined, and you won't be exhausted running back and forth," Morgan said.

Jack nodded. "I think that's best."

"One of my men will be going to town for supplies later today, so I'll have him bring Addie and the girls back to the ranch after school."

Jack hated the thought of not seeing them tonight, but Morgan was right. A woman's reputation was not something to take lightly. He needed to put some distance between them before he lost his head. "Thanks, Morgan."

On the way to school, Addie thought Jack seemed preoccupied. She assumed it was because her brother was in his jail. "Jack, is everything okay? Are you concerned about Frank's gang?"

Jack had told her about the judge's telegram, and that he would be returning to Denver with Frank in a few days.

"Did you confirm the telegram? Could this be a ploy by Frank's gang?" Addie thought about the last time Jack had chased Frank's gang. He was shot and almost died. She couldn't entertain the thought of something happening to him again.

Jack hadn't thought the telegram could be a ploy. Addie was one smart woman. "I'll telegram the sheriff and tell him when we will be there."

"You're not leaving today, are you?"

"No, it'll be a few days. Why, did you need something?"

She shook her head. "No, I don't need anything."

They pulled in front of the school and Jack looked around to see if he saw Davey. "I don't think Davey is here yet."

The girls scampered from the buckboard to go in search of Davey. Addie turned to Jack and said, "The girls haven't slept at all since Davey left."

"I know it's a big change for them." Jack jumped from the buckboard to help her down.

Addie placed her hands on his shoulders as he lifted her to the ground. "Thank you for everything, Jack."

"Tell Davey hello for me."

"Maybe you'll get to see him after school."

"One of Morgan's men will be picking you up today." Jack had waited until the last minute to tell her about the arrangement.

Addie looked up at him, waiting for him to tell her why there had been a change of plans. When he didn't say anything, she said. "Oh . . . okay."

He tipped his hat, jumped back in the buckboard, and pulled away. He knew she'd wanted him to explain, but he didn't know how to tell her he just needed to put some distance between them. He'd miss seeing her and the children daily, but he'd decided this was the best way for him to handle the situation.

School ended, and Morgan's foreman was waiting for Addie and the girls. Addie asked him to take the children to Morgan's ranch, explaining that she had business in town. Davey hadn't been in school today, so she planned to ride out to the Coburn farm to find out the reason. She had little doubt that Mr. Coburn was trying to make his point that he was going to make the decisions regarding Davey's education. Addie was equally determined not to give up so easily. Davey's education was more important than Mr. Coburn's pride.

Before she made the trip to the Coburns' farm, she thought it was the perfect time to see Frank before Jack took him back to Denver. Now that she was aware of the terrible things Frank had done, she knew she couldn't rest until she'd faced him to ask him why.

As she approached the jail, she saw Jack on the sidewalk talking with Clarissa. Even in her heavy blue winter coat, Clarissa looked trim and lovely as usual. Addie instantly felt inadequate about her appearance. She thought with her fuller figure, she probably resembled a round bear in her drab brown coat. Just like a frumpy old school spinster. She'd bet Jack's hands could easily span Clarissa's tiny waist over her coat.

Addie came to a screeching halt when she saw Clarissa move closer to Jack, until there was just a hairsbreadth between their bodies. Clarissa slowly removed her glove and reached out to brush something from Jack's coat. Probably an imaginary piece of lint, Addie thought. Clarissa's small hand remained on his chest as she gazed up at him with a come-hither smile. Addie figured Clarissa was the reason Jack hadn't wanted to pick them up today after school. As much as she wanted to see what Clarissa would do next, Addie forced herself to keep moving. They were so absorbed in conversation, they probably wouldn't even notice her. When she was within a few feet of them, Clarissa stood on her tiptoes and kissed Jack's cheek, close to his lips. Her lips lingered on his skin as her hand glided seductively over his chest. "I'll see you tomorrow night. I'm cooking your favorite meal."

Addie saw the smile on Jack's face when she passed. He obviously liked the thought of Clarissa cooking for him. She had a strong urge to kick him in the shin as she passed, but she resisted.

Jack saw Addie out of the corner of his eye and whirled around. "What are you doing here?" He wondered if she'd seen Clarissa kiss him, or overheard her comment about dinner.

Addie ignored his question and glanced at Clarissa. Clarissa was looking her up and down, just as she had the first time they'd met. And just like the first time, the look on Clarissa's face telegraphed she didn't consider Addie a threat.

Jack glanced at Clarissa, and he thought she didn't look pleased to see Addie. "Clarissa, you remember Miss Langtry."

So, Jack was calling her Miss Langtry now. Addie smiled sweetly at Clarissa. It wasn't Clarissa's fault he was a scoundrel. She doubted Clarissa knew where he'd been spending his time. He'd been kissing her, and staying at her home, but now he was acting as though they weren't on a first-name basis. "Please call me Addie."

"Yes, I remember you. You are the one with all those children. I do believe at first I thought they were your offspring." Clarissa didn't bother to hide her scrutiny of Addie's figure again. "By looking at your . . . well, I was certain you'd given birth to those children. Your age . . . of course, I naturally assumed you were married by now."

Addie had to give Clarissa credit. She was trying to make it sound as if she didn't intend to say anything offensive. If Clarissa thought she was going to embarrass her over her age, figure, or marital status, she had a surprise in store for her. "No, they are not my children by birth, but by choice."

Clarissa arched her brow. "One would never know."

Addie had no intention of tolerating her snide comments. "As I always tell my students, one can never assume anything. Just like attractiveness and manners do not often go hand in hand."

Uh-oh. Jack thought he should put a halt to this conversation. He directed his attention to Addie. "What are you doing in town? Where are the girls?"

Addie was upset with him, and with the snooty woman he was planning on seeing tomorrow night. Her terse response reflected her emotions when she said, "I have business to attend to."

Yep, her frosty tone answered his questions. She obviously overheard Clarissa invite him to dinner, or saw the kiss, or both. He wasn't inclined to stand there on the street and explain that Clarissa had told him her father wanted to talk to him. He tipped his hat, and smiled at Clarissa. "I'd best get back to work. Clarissa, I'll see you tomorrow." He glanced at Addie, and added in an equally cool tenor, "I'll let you go about your business, Miss Langtry."

As soon as Jack walked away, Clarissa turned, without a word to Addie, and disappeared into the mercantile.

Addie stood on the sidewalk for a few minutes, trying to collect her scattering thoughts. What had she done to make him treat her like she had the plague while he was planning a night with Clarissa? *Miss Langtry, indeed.* She didn't even know what his favorite meal was. Well, he'd made his intentions perfectly clear when he'd smiled at Clarissa before he walked away. He certainly hadn't smiled at her. The bounder. She squared her shoulders, walked the few remaining feet to the jail, and opened the door.

Jack was talking to his deputy, but stopped in midsentence when Addie walked in.

"I'd like to see my brother," Addie said.

Her request took Jack by surprise. "Why?" He wondered why she didn't mention before that she wanted to see Frank.

"I don't think I need to give you a reason to see my brother. I didn't bring him a gun, if that is what concerns you. Shall I remove my coat so you can see for yourself?"

Jack thought about searching her just to be obstinate. Wouldn't that just set her back on her heels? "Where are the girls?"

"I sent them to Morgan's with his foreman. After I speak to Frank, I'm going to go check on Davey, since he didn't come to school today."

"What do you mean, he didn't come to school?"

She gave an exasperated sigh. "I mean Davey didn't come to school today." She thought she saw real concern on his face, but she ignored it. She wasn't in the mood to be generous or civil.

"How were you planning to get to the Coburns' farm?"

"Did you forget I can ride? I will get a horse at the livery."

"I'll take you."

"No, thank you. I'd rather go alone." She wasn't thrilled about going to see the Coburns alone, but after seeing him with Clarissa, she thought it best to stay away from him. She'd been in real danger of losing her heart to him, and she'd even imagined —

or hoped — he might be attracted to her after they'd kissed. But that dream had been dashed on the sidewalk. He'd probably been laughing the whole time at how easily she succumbed to his kisses. "Now, may I see my brother?"

Jack wasn't going to argue with her in front of his deputy. He didn't know why she wanted to see Frank, but he had no reason to stop her. "Webb, take her to see her brother, but don't open the cell."

Addie followed Webb through the door leading to the cells. There were only three cells, and Frank was the only occupant.

Webb stayed next to the door, trying to be as inconspicuous as possible, but he couldn't avoid hearing what they had to say.

Frank was lying on the bed with his hands behind his head when Addie approached. She waited a few seconds for him to look her way, but when he didn't move, she said, "Hello, Frank."

Frank slowly turned on his side and stared at her. "Well, if it ain't the schoolteacher."

Rose had told her Frank didn't resemble the brother they once knew, and staring at him now, Addie understood what she meant. Though his features hadn't changed much, she felt like she was looking into the eyes of a complete stranger. Granny had always said you could see a person's soul in their eyes. She couldn't recall what she'd seen in Frank's eyes when she was younger, but she didn't like what she saw now. She was staring into a cold, dark void.

"What do you want?" Frank asked.

Straight to the point, Addie thought. Well, she would give it to him straight. "I've heard about the things you've done, Frank, and I came here to ask you why. What happened to you?"

Frank smirked. "Nothing has happened to me. As you can see, I'm right here."

Addie stepped forward and gripped the bars. "You know what I mean, Frank. How could you kill your own brother? How could you kidnap Rose and try to kill Morgan?"

"Miss Addie, step back from the bars," Webb warned.

Addie didn't take her eyes off Frank, but she dropped her hands and took a step back.

"Yeah, Miss Addie, move away from the bars. Don't you know I'm a dangerous man?" Frank taunted.

She'd wanted to see Frank to get answers to her questions. She didn't understand what had led him on this path of destruction. After the death of their parents, their grandparents — Preacher and Granny — had welcomed them into their home without

226

hesitation. They may not have been rich in possessions, but they had a home filled with love. Granny and Preacher had nurtured them, taught them to care about family, how to live a righteous life, and the value of working hard for what you want. Considering their upbringing, it seemed impossible that one of her brothers would become an outlaw. "Talk to me, Frank. Tell me why you killed Stevie."

"They're lying to you. I didn't kill Stevie."

"You know Rose has never told a lie in her life."

Frank flopped on his back again and stared at the ceiling. "Rose ain't the sweet little thing she used to be. She's been different ever since she took up with LeMasters."

"Rose isn't the one who has changed. Are you going to tell me Stevie changed too? He worshipped the ground you walked on, and he would have done anything for you. If you didn't kill him, then you let him die in that fire. Did you set that fire?"

"I had nothing to do with Stevie dying in that fire."

"So you are innocent, and everyone else is lying? Rose, Granny, Morgan, and the sheriff . . . they're all lying about the things you've done?"

"Now you're getting at the truth. Morgan

LeMasters has always had it out for me. Granny even treated Morgan like he was her grandson, always believed him over me."

The hate in his voice was palpable. "Look at me, Frank."

Frank turned his head to look at her again. When their eyes met, Addie shivered. It wasn't her imagination — his eyes reflected the darkness within. In that moment, Addie knew he'd never admit he killed Stevie, or his many other crimes. She understood why Rose was petrified that Frank wouldn't be happy until he killed Morgan. He was filled with animosity toward Morgan. "I don't think the problem was how Granny treated Morgan. It was your own jealousy of Morgan that created the problems. Now, tell me the truth. Why did you kill Stevie?"

"Get out of here, Addie. I don't have anything to say to you. You go ahead and believe all their lies, but you will know the truth when the judge sets me free."

"Frank, Preacher and Granny loved you beyond measure. No grandparents could have done more for all of us. How could you disrespect Preacher's memory by turning your back on every moral law? How could you break Granny's heart? And have you forgotten what Morgan did for us? Morgan was a young man when he was building his ranch, but he found it in his heart to give Granny and Preacher beef every winter so we wouldn't starve. I'm sure he didn't have much to spare in those early days. You and Morgan are the same age, and while he was working long hours every day and night for his future, you were acting like a spoiled child. For some reason, you've always hated Morgan, and you thought you finally found a way to get to him by hurting Rose. Now I understand that your hate stemmed from jealousy."

"I said to get out!"

Her words were having no impact; there was no reasoning with him. No matter how much it hurt, she had to face the fact that Frank had set his course and there would be no turning back. Before she walked away, she had one more thing to say. "Leave Morgan and Rose alone. They have done nothing to you."

Frank jumped to his feet and grabbed the bars in a tight grip. "I don't need you telling me what to do. Like I told Granny and Rose, all of you make me sick. I hate the sight of you. You're no family to me."

Addie forced herself to look him in the eyes again. If you could see a person's soul in their eyes, then she was looking into the eyes of a soulless person. She understood she would never have the answers to her many questions. No matter how she tried to keep her emotions under control, tears filled her eyes. "You'd best ask for God's forgiveness for your many sins, Frank. He's the only one who can help you now."

"I don't need help," Frank replied, and threw his head back and laughed.

Rose had told her she thought Frank might be insane. Addie didn't know if he was insane, but without a doubt, he was evil to the bone. He felt no remorse for all the terrible things he'd done. She walked toward Webb without a backward glance, and wiped away the tears on her cheeks. Webb quickly opened the door and ushered her out. When she reached the outer office, she didn't notice Jack was still sitting behind his desk.

Jack could tell she'd been crying. He shot a quick glance at Webb before he jumped up and grabbed his coat and hat. "I'm going to take Miss Langtry to the Coburn farm."

Though she heard Jack, she didn't stop to look at him when she responded, "I'm going to the Coburns' by myself." She reached the front door and walked out without saying another word.

Jack stood there staring at the closed door

for a few seconds before he asked Webb, "What did Frank say to her?"

"She asked him why he'd killed their brother. Frank didn't admit to it, but he told her he hated his family. She told him he'd best ask forgiveness for his many sins." Webb shook his head. "Frank is plumb loco. All he did was laugh."

"Yeah." Jack looked at the door again, debating whether he should chase Addie down and insist on going with her to the Coburns'. She was miffed at him because Clarissa had kissed him, and he was inclined to think he should leave well enough alone since he'd decided to put some distance between them. Still, he didn't like the thought of her riding to the Coburns' with no means of protection, and he doubted she had a pistol stuffed into her reticule. He reached for his coat and hat. "I'll be back later, Webb."

Jack caught up with Addie before she reached the livery. "I don't think you should be riding off by yourself, considering it will be dark before you get to Morgan's."

Addie was emotionally spent. Not only was she worried about Davey, but after she'd happened on Jack and Clarissa conversing on the sidewalk, she realized that his relationship with Clarissa was more

231

involved than he'd led her to believe. Then there was her meeting with Frank. No matter that Rose had warned her what to expect from Frank, coming face-to-face with him shook her to the core. It was almost more than she could handle in one day, and she hadn't given a thought to riding home in the dark. Right now she didn't care if she had to ride to Denver alone in the pitch-black night. She certainly didn't want to be around Jack Roper. After seeing him with Clarissa, she knew he'd been trifling with her, and she was angry and hurt. The kindness he'd shown the children was the only reason she didn't say something she would later regret. "Thank you for your concern, but I'll be fine. I doubt that Frank's gang is anywhere near Whispering Pines."

"I wasn't thinking about Frank's gang. I don't think a woman should be riding alone in the dark. It's your choice; we can either get a buckboard, or if you insist on riding by yourself, I'll be riding right behind you all the way."

Addie glared at him. So it wasn't that he wanted to see *her* home, he just didn't think any woman would be safe after dark. Seeing the set of his jaw, she knew her wishes would be ignored. She threw her hands in the air and started walking, but stopped suddenly when she heard someone calling her name. She turned around and looked down the sidewalk. "I don't believe it!"

Jack turned to see a well-groomed man quickly approaching, wearing a three-piece suit, a bowler hat, and carrying a walking cane. Then it clicked. Prescott Adler. The man Addie left behind in Boston.

CHAPTER FIFTEEN

"Prescott?" Addie said his name as if she couldn't believe her own eyes. She took a step toward the man she thought she'd never see again.

Remaining stone-faced, Jack took measure of the man.

"Addie!" Prescott ran the last few steps separating them, pulled Addie into his arms, and kissed her right in front of Jack and every other person walking down the sidewalk.

Jack stared slack-jawed at the couple locked lip to lip. He glanced around and saw the wife of the mercantile owner sweeping the sidewalk in front of their store. She stopped midmotion when she glimpsed Prescott and Addie in their passionate embrace. Jack figured everyone in town would hear before nightfall that the new schoolteacher was having a tryst right in the middle of the street. Heck, he hadn't held

Addie as close when he kissed her. Jack's emotions quickly blossomed from fairly amused to furious in the span of a kiss. He was mulling over his choice of punching the man or just shooting him. Fortunately, he wasn't forced to decide before Addie pulled away from her ardent suitor. In his estimation, she sure waited long enough to disentangle herself from the dandy from Boston. She must have enjoyed his kiss.

Addie's face was flaming red. "Prescott! Remember where you are!" Her schoolteacher tone automatically surfaced as she glanced around to see who'd been watching. She spotted the woman in front of the mercantile with a scowl on her face. *Oh, heavens.* She knew her reputation would be in tatters if it wasn't already known that Jack had been sleeping at the farm. She didn't know what had possibly fostered Prescott's impassioned display. Not only had he held her much too close to his body to be deemed appropriate, his kiss was much too intimate.

Prescott reached out for her again and squeezed her to his chest. "I do apologize, my dear. You can hardly blame a man for his amorous attentions after having been separated from you for several weeks."

If Addie was stunned by his kiss, she

nearly fainted at his endearing words. He sounded more like a man returning from war than the man she left behind in Boston; the same man who'd barely remembered the day of her departure. During the time he'd squired her around Boston, he generally ended the evening with an innocuous peck, sometimes on the lips, but more often as not, he kissed her cheek. He'd certainly never kissed her with such unbridled passion. Perhaps he had missed her more than she'd imagined he would. "This is not the time, nor the place, for such demonstrations of affection."

Jack arched his brow, wondering if Addie was suggesting she would rather be in a room alone with this tenderfoot.

Extricating herself from Prescott's grip again, Addie's hand flew to her hair, making sure she wasn't disheveled. Her eyes darted to Jack, and registering his narrowed eyes and tightly clenched jaw, she said, "Prescott, this is Sheriff Roper. Sheriff, this is Prescott Adler."

Prescott extended his hand to Jack. When he'd seen Addie talking to the tall cowboy, he thought they seemed fairly engrossed in their conversation, and they were standing quite close to each other conveying a familiar relationship. "Sheriff." Prescott couldn't help but notice the sheriff's intimidating stare.

"Mr. Adler." Jack intentionally looked him over. Yep. Tenderfoot. He glanced back at Addie. "Didn't you tell me Mr. Adler is the benefactor of the orphanage?"

Pleased to find an opening to make sure this cowboy knew he'd already staked his claim, Prescott responded before Addie had the chance. "That's correct, Sheriff." He smiled affectionately at Addie. "We became quite close when she came to work for the orphanage."

Jack pushed his Stetson back on his head. "So I see." He pointed to the folks who had stopped to watch the sideshow. "Unfortunately, most folks out here are not accustomed to such displays in the street in the middle of the day. Maybe in the saloon, but not in polite society."

His comment rankled Addie. She waited for Prescott to defend her honor. Since her patience was running thin with Jack anyway, she wasn't inclined to wait long. Taking a step closer to Jack, she put her hands on her hips and glared at him. "Are you equating me with . . . with a common trollop?"

Jack raised his eyebrows at her. Point made. He almost said *If the shoe fits,* but refrained.

"I'm certain out here in this wild territory, even the unsophisticated would understand the unfettered affections of a suitor after a separation." Prescott pulled Addie back to his side, and away from the sheriff.

Jack really, really wanted to punch Prescott. "Out here in this *wild territory,* we unsophisticated folk are forced to overlook the unconventional behavior of big-city folk from time to time."

Addie saw the stare-down going on between the two men. Seeing Jack's eyes had turned a steely gray at the offense she was certain Prescott intended, she thought it prudent to redirect the conversation. "When did you arrive, Prescott?"

"On the noon stage. I just inquired about directions to your farm and was headed to the livery to hire a driver."

Jack almost snorted aloud. Didn't the man even know how to ride?

"I have much to tell you about the orphanage, but right now I was riding to Mr. Coburn's farm. Mr. Coburn and his wife adopted Davey. Davey wasn't in school today, and I want to make sure he is not ill."

"Do you think it is necessary to check on him after missing one day of school?" Prescott asked.

"Yes, I do. He was only adopted a few days ago, and I intend to make sure he is happy in his new home."

"I don't think it wise for you to interfere so soon. A new adoption can take time for all parties involved," Prescott countered.

It didn't go unnoticed that Prescott didn't inquire about the girls, or about the orphanage. "Wise or not, I'm going. You are welcome to accompany me, or you can come to the farm tomorrow after school as I won't be there until later tonight."

Prescott frowned at her, but he'd wait until later to express his displeasure that she elected to ignore his sound advice. "Very well. We shall hire a driver to transport us to where you need to go. I'd like to have time to chat."

"We can take a buggy," Addie said.

"We still need a driver," Prescott said. "Don't they have hired drivers here?"

Addie was getting testy that they were wasting time. She wanted to see about Davey and get home before midnight. "I can drive a buggy." Before Prescott voiced an objection, she spoke to Jack. "Sheriff Roper, now that I have an escort to the Coburns', it will not be necessary for you to accompany me."

"All the same, I think I'll ride along to

make sure Davey is doing okay." Jack wasn't about to let her go riding off with this dude who wouldn't know how to handle trouble if trouble came calling. He'd take bets that this character didn't even carry a sidearm, much less know how to use one. And he wanted to hear for himself why Davey wasn't in school. As far as he was concerned, Roy Coburn had yet to prove he could be a decent parent.

Addie figured if Jack came along she wouldn't be forced to talk to him because there wouldn't be enough room for him in the buggy. "Suit yourself." She turned and started walking toward the livery.

"I usually do," Jack retorted to her back. He found himself trailing the schoolteacher and the dandy down the sidewalk.

Addie spotted Mr. Coburn walking from the barn, so she pulled the buggy next to him. "Mr. Coburn, Mr. Adler has come all the way from Boston to check on the orphanage. Since Davey wasn't at school today, I thought he may be ill." Addie tried to mollify Roy Coburn because he'd definitely taken offense at Addie's appearance at the farm.

Jack didn't know what Addie had discussed with Adler in the buggy ride to the

240

Coburns', but he felt certain it wasn't the children.

"If he's our son now, I have a right to do as I see fit," Coburn said. "I've already told you we have a lot of work on the farm, and the boy don't have time for school."

"Mr. Coburn, it is imperative the children have an education. Davey was not adopted for free labor."

"He knows his numbers, he told me so himself. I reckon that's about all a man needs to know to be a farmer."

"Davey may not want to be a farmer. He needs an education until he decides what he wants to do with his life," Addie countered, her temper simmering on the edge.

Jack noticed Adler hadn't said a word. "Where is Davey?"

Coburn jerked a thumb over his shoulder. "He's out back. We've been building a shed. He told me you taught him some about building."

Without asking, Jack rode to the back of the house. Let Addie and Prescott deal with Coburn. When he spotted Davey, he dismounted and walked to him. "Davey, how come you missed school today?"

Davey glanced up at Jack, but he continued working. "Mr. Coburn needed my help."

"You could always help after school." Jack picked up the extra hammer and started nailing boards.

Davey shrugged. "I guess."

"How's it going out here?"

Another shrug. "Okay, I guess."

"Do you like it here?"

"It don't matter one way or the other."

"Of course it does." Jack stopped hammering. Davey reminded him of himself when he was a boy. Twelve going on one hundred, with a world of hurt on his shoulders. "Do they treat you good?"

Davey still didn't look at him. "I guess."

"Why didn't you go to church yesterday?"

"Mr. Coburn said he don't go all the time."

Jack tried to remember how often he'd seen Sarah Coburn at church, but he honestly couldn't recall.

"Addie's out front if you want to go say hello."

Davey stopped working. "What does she want?"

"She wanted to check to make sure you are okay."

"Is Jane and Claire with her?"

"No, they're at Morgan's."

"You can tell Miss Addie I'm fine."

"Why don't you tell her yourself? I'm sure

she wants to see you."

"I need to finish before dark." Mr. Coburn didn't like for him to slack off. He'd already gone to bed without his supper Sunday night for not moving fast enough when he'd told him to do something.

Jack hammered a few more nails, trying to think of a way to get Davey to start talking, but he heard someone walking behind them. He turned to see it was Addie and Prescott, with Coburn right behind them.

"Davey, how are you?" Addie asked.

"I'm fine. Just got to finish this work."

Addie stood beside Davey, but he continued working. "I don't want you to miss school. It's much too important for your future."

"I already told you, it's up to me when the boy goes to school," Coburn said.

Addie thought she might have more sway with Mrs. Coburn. "Where is your wife?"

"She's inside working. We don't have time to stand around here and gab all day. We're farmers with a lot of work to do."

Prescott wanted to leave. "Addie, I think Mr. Coburn has a point. It is up to him when the boy goes to school. After all, he is the new father, and he needs time to get acquainted."

She'd listened to Prescott's opinion on

the way to the farm, and her exasperation surfaced. "The boy's name is Davey, and he is accustomed to attending school. I should think you, of all people, would appreciate the value of an education."

"Of course, I do. But everyone needs time to settle in their new roles with adoptions. This isn't the first time I've seen these situations. You've only been doing this a year, but the superintendent of the Boston orphanage has told me of many adoptions that took some time for all to adjust."

Jack couldn't say that Prescott didn't have a point. Yet, he also noted Prescott hadn't even said hello to Davey, and he obviously knew him. "Why don't we compromise, Roy. Try to see to it that Davey gets to school three days a week right now. I was teaching him to ride, and he's a natural. He could take the horse to school."

"I got better things to do with my horse than ride back and forth to town."

That made two men in one day Jack wanted to punch. "Well then, if he can't take the horse, and you don't have time to take him, I'll ride out here and get him."

"I also want Davey to go to church every Sunday," Addie said.

Her tone angered Coburn. "I want you off my property right now. We go to church when we please, and I'll give the say-so when, and if, the boy goes to school."

"Addie, it's time to leave. We've pushed our good will too far," Prescott said.

"Now see here —" Addie started, but Prescott took her by the arm and whispered in her ear. "I believe you are too close to the situation, my dear. This is what I warned you about when you live with the children."

If Prescott hadn't been standing there, she'd have taken Davey home with her right then and there. Since Prescott was her employer, she had to listen to him whether she wanted to or not. "Davey, if you need anything, please let me know."

Davey didn't respond, so Addie turned to leave with Prescott.

Jack didn't move. "Coburn, Miss Addie didn't mean to offend you. I think you could be more accommodating to make sure Davey continues with his education and that he attends church. You know it's important for children to do both."

"Maybe you don't hear so good. He's my son now, and I'll make the decisions. So you can go with your friends. If I hear more from the lot of you, I'll talk to the judge about my rights."

"You can talk to the judge, but so can I. I'm certain the judge would appreciate the merits of an education."

Coburn stared hard at Jack. "We have nothing more to talk about."

Jack had never had any encounters with Roy Coburn before this, but he found him to be an unreasonable man. He remembered thinking one time when he saw Sarah Coburn in church that he'd never seen her smile. Judging by the way Coburn barked orders, Jack wondered if he did the same thing to Mrs. Coburn. Maybe he should get her alone and speak to her about her husband. She might have some sway with him, but Jack doubted it. Coburn seemed pretty set in his opinions. Jack decided it was best that he walk away before he lost his temper. "Davey, if you need anything, you know you can count on me."

Davey had stopped working to listen to the exchange between the two men. "Yes, sir."

"Get back to work, boy," Coburn instructed.

Davey resumed working at Coburn's command.

In Jack's estimation, Davey looked sad. As much as he hated to leave Davey behind, he didn't have a choice. "Davey, I'll come out from time to time, and we'll keep up with your riding lessons. I'm sure you'll have some free time."

"We'll let you know when there is time for foolishness. You ain't welcome to stop by anytime you want," Coburn said.

Jack was holding back his temper as he mounted his horse, but Coburn had pushed him too far. "Coburn, I'm the sheriff here, and I'll stop anywhere I darn well please, anytime I please. Not you, or anyone else, can say different."

"I wouldn't have adopted this boy if I knew I had to put up with all of this nonsense."

Jack really wanted to say he could void the adoption anytime he wanted. Problem was, he didn't want Davey to feel like he was being rejected because of something he did. "Davey, I'll see you in a few days."

CHAPTER SIXTEEN

"I'm sorry I don't have time for dinner, Prescott, I must get back to the farm." Addie was mentally exhausted from the events of the day, and she didn't feel like listening to more of Prescott's opinions about the situation with Davey. They'd argued all the way back to town about her interference with Coburn.

"Surely you can take another hour before you must leave," Prescott responded.

"It is almost dark and I have a long way to go." Addie was reminded Jack didn't want her to ride alone after dark.

Jack saw the buggy in front of the hotel and reined in behind them. He could over-hear their conversation before he dismounted.

"I don't like the idea of you riding all that way in the dark. Let me get my bag and I'll go with you and spend the night at the farm," Prescott said.

"I couldn't allow you to do that. No one will be there but the girls, and it wouldn't be proper for you to stay all night." Addie didn't dare mention that Jack had stayed at the farm. But the children didn't even realize he'd spent the night. Of course, she could ask Granny to come to the farm to act as chaperone. But she really wanted some time alone tonight.

"I'm afraid I must insist. The farm is now the orphanage, my dear. I have every right to stay there as I am responsible for the welfare of my employees. Besides, we have much more to discuss."

Jack dismounted and walked to the buggy. "I can see you home, Addie." He was silently delighting in the fact that Prescott Adler III needed a driver. The man was obviously out of his element out here in this *wild territory.*

"That won't be necessary, Sheriff. I was just about to tell Prescott I will ask Granny to stay at the farm since he does have a right to see the orphanage." She took some pleasure in letting Jack know that another man was interested in her. She might not find Prescott as physically appealing as Jack, but he was an attractive man, even if he was maddening.

Jack started seeing red. He couldn't believe she was going to allow this dandy to stay at the farm. She sure as heck didn't put up much of an argument to dissuade him.

Prescott climbed from the buggy. "My dear, I'll retrieve my valise and be back posthaste."

Addie ignored Jack after Prescott walked into the hotel.

Jack walked to her side of the buggy and braced his arm on the back of the seat. "How long is he staying?"

Addie smoothed her skirt as she considered her reply. "I have no idea."

"Why is he here?"

Addie leveled her gaze on him. "I imagine he's here to see me."

Jack leaned in until his face was inches from hers. "Tell me, are you going to kiss him like you did me?"

Addie thought he had a lot of nerve to bring that up. She gave him a mutinous glare. "Why not? What does a kiss mean? I believe you've recently had more than one woman kissing you."

So she had seen Clarissa kiss him today on the sidewalk. "You didn't see my lips on hers."

"She certainly seemed comfortable running her hands all over you."

Jack grinned at her. Clarissa did seem particularly interested in his chest today. "Men like to be touched. I guess Clarissa knows that."

Addie was so shocked by his admission that she had to search for an appropriate retort. "I'd say you got what you enjoyed today."

"You sound jealous."

"Ha! Why should I be jealous? What you do with Clarissa is of no concern to me. Just as what I do with Prescott is of no concern to you."

That wiped the smile off his face. "He doesn't seem very concerned about the children."

Addie couldn't deny that point. "That too is no concern of yours."

"I'm making it my concern. I care about what happens to Davey."

Addie wasn't willing to give an inch. "I'd say you have your hands full with your own child."

Jack frowned at her. "What the heck are you talking about? I don't have a child."

"Don't you? I'd say Clarissa is almost young enough to be your child."

He couldn't argue that Clarissa was fourteen years younger, but that wasn't young enough to be his child. "She's not that young. She's a full-grown woman."

"And I'm sure you've noticed," Addie snapped.

Yeah, he'd noticed. Clarissa had a nice trim figure, and she was very pretty. But he liked the way Addie felt in his arms. She was generously shaped, her curves soft and warm. It angered him that he couldn't forget how good she felt against his body. "She's a beautiful woman."

Addie knew Jack was comparing Clarissa's body to hers, and it wasn't unreasonable to think he found her lacking. She felt like crying, but she wouldn't dare in front of this cad. Thankfully, she spotted Prescott walking out of the hotel. "Well, I'm sure you two will have a fine date tomorrow. I'll be saying good night." She smiled at Prescott when he neared the buggy. "Are you ready to go?"

"Yes." He turned to the sheriff, who in his estimation, was much too close to Addie again.

Jack felt like grabbing Addie and kissing her on the lips right in front of Prescott.

"Are you accompanying us to the orphanage as well?" Prescott asked Jack.

Addie laughed. "Heaven's no. The sheriff must get his rest. He has a big date with a very young woman tomorrow."

Prescott was relieved to hear that news. Maybe he'd been misreading the sheriff's interest in Addie. "Be careful, Sheriff, young women can lead you astray."

"I'm counting on it. But as it turns out, I'm going to Morgan's for dinner tonight." Jack didn't say he was invited for dinner, but he knew he'd be welcome. He told himself he wanted to make sure they arrived at Morgan's safe and sound. If they were accosted on the trail, he couldn't depend on Adler to protect Addie. He also wanted to see how Adler treated the girls. He certainly wasn't prepared to admit that he was jealous. How could he be jealous of a dandy like Prescott Adler III?

Once they reached the ranch, Addie and Prescott walked inside the house as Jack saw to the horses. Morgan was in the stable, and Jack was relieved he'd have the chance to talk to him alone.

Jack told Morgan about Prescott Adler coming all the way from Boston to this *wild territory*. "Wait until you see this character. He doesn't even know how to handle a buggy."

Morgan stopped brushing down his horse and looked at Jack. "You're pulling my leg."

Jack held his hand in the air as if he were

swearing an oath. "He asked Addie if the livery had a man for hire to drive them."

Morgan shook his head. "I guess it follows he can't ride a horse."

"I don't know what she sees in a man like that."

"Why is he here?"

"By the way he kissed her right there on the sidewalk in front of God and everybody, my guess would be he is a lot more than the benefactor of the orphanage."

Morgan arched his brow at him. "Yeah?"

"It wasn't a brotherly kind of kiss, if you know what I mean."

Morgan thought he heard a hint of jealousy in Jack's voice. "How do you feel about that?"

"That's Addie's business. But it sure didn't do anything to help her reputation with the folks in town."

Morgan finished brushing his horse, and looked at his best friend. "I thought you were getting pretty friendly with her."

"I think we're friends, and I enjoy being with the children," Jack replied evasively.

That was a non-answer if Morgan ever heard one. "I got the feeling you enjoyed being around Addie too. You were spending your nights with her."

"I was spending my nights in her house,

not with her. There's a difference."

Morgan chuckled. "I guess there is."

"It would have been a whole lot more comfortable if I was spending the night *with* her instead of trying to sleep on that settee. That darn thing is so small I was eating my knees."

"The point is, you've been spending so much time with them, I can't figure out how you are getting any sleep."

"I don't like the thought of them spending nights alone on the farm without a man around."

"You think he's planning on staying here, or wanting her to go back to Boston?"

Jack hadn't even considered the possibility Addie might leave Whispering Pines. "I don't think he's here to see the orphanage. And a man like that wouldn't stay here long."

"Not likely."

"Anyway, I wanted to tell you I told them I was coming out here for dinner."

"You know you're welcome." They finished with the horses, and walked from the stable side by side. "Rose probably has dinner ready. Now why don't you tell me the real reason you came out here with them?"

Jack should have known Morgan would figure out there was more to the story.

"Adler is planning on spending the night at Addie's." He told Morgan about Addie seeing Clarissa kissing him. "It was nowhere near the kind of kiss Addie received from that dandy. She participated. I did not."

So, Morgan had his answer. Jack was interested in Addie. "Why don't you just admit it?"

"Admit what?"

"That you're in love with Addie."

"I'm not in love." Jack shrugged. "Sure, I like her, but I'm not talking love here. I just don't want folks to get the wrong idea about her."

"Are you in love with Clarissa?"

"Nope."

"Are you spending the night with Addie too?"

"She said she was going to ask Granny to stay at the farm tonight," Jack replied.

"Problem solved. Addie's reputation will remain intact."

"But Granny's room is at the far end of the hall. After the way Adler kissed her, and since she didn't object, he might be thinking of taking liberties."

Morgan looked at his friend. "You don't think Addie would let a man squire her around Boston knowing he couldn't be trusted with her virtue, do you?"

Jack shook his head. "No, but since she didn't mind him kissing her like he did, he might think she'd be more amenable to . . ."

"To what? Asking him to her room?"

Jack thought of Clarissa, and he had a feeling she wouldn't hesitate to invite him to her room. That was information he wasn't willing to share, not even with his best friend. "You never know what women are thinking when they want to get married."

"Even if Addie wanted to marry, I don't think she would do something foolish."

"And you didn't see that kiss."

"Jack, there is no reason for you to stay, since Prescott is here." Addie had finally wrangled the girls into bed, and she was exhausted. Whenever Jack was around they wanted to be with him as long as possible.

"You are going to need a buckboard in the morning to take the children to school. Not everyone is going to fit in that buggy. You can't drive them both."

Addie had thought the same thing. She couldn't believe Prescott had never driven a buggy. She was aware he couldn't ride, but heavens, who would have ever thought he'd always hired a driver. "I will have one of Morgan's men go with us."

"I told Morgan I would take you. That's why I brought Granny over in the buckboard tonight."

Granny overheard their conversation, and she didn't know why Addie was adamant Jack should leave. "Addie, Jack has had a long day, and I'm sure he's tired. Now that I'm here, there's no problem with him staying the night."

Jack smiled at Granny. "Thank you, Granny. I am tired."

Granny thought her granddaughter didn't appreciate everything Jack had done for her and the children, and she planned to speak with her about that very thing when they were alone. If Addie preferred Prescott Adler over Jack, well, the girl needed to have her head examined. Oh, she thought Prescott was a nice man, but he wasn't the kind of man that would make it in the West. He wasn't the kind of man who would make Addie happy either. "Jack, you can have my bedroom. I'm sure Addie won't mind if we share her room." Granny looked at Addie and smiled sweetly. "That is okay with you, isn't it, dear. Since Prescott has one bedroom, we are running out of rooms."

"Jack can take Davey's room," Addie said without enthusiasm.

Jack liked the sound of that. Davey's room

was between Addie's and the one where Prescott would be sleeping. He slept with one eye open, so he was bound to hear if Adler decided to take a midnight stroll.

"I'm going to warm some water for my bath." Addie was still angry with Jack, and she thought he had some nerve to be spending the night at her house when he was going to be with Clarissa tomorrow night. She was tired too, and with two men in the house, she was forced to carry water upstairs to bathe instead of pulling the tub into the kitchen, where it was more convenient.

"I'll carry the tub to your room," Jack said.

"I can manage." Addie left the room, leaving Granny and Jack alone.

"She seems out of sorts. I guess she's worried about Davey," Granny said, giving her granddaughter the benefit of the doubt.

"I'm worried about Davey too. He's not happy at the Coburns'."

"I was afraid of that. Sarah never talks much at church, but I think her husband is not the most pleasant person."

"That's the truth," Jack agreed. "He doesn't want Addie involved in Davey's life from now on."

"That would be difficult on the girls if they can't see their brother."

"I'm not through with Coburn yet. I hope

he'll begin to see things my way."

"If anyone can convince him, it will be you," Granny said. "I'll be saying good night."

"Good night, Granny." Jack heard the clank of the tub in the kitchen, so he walked in that direction. Addie had managed to pull it across the floor. "I'll carry it up for you."

"I can get it," Addie said, stubbornly refusing to accept his help.

Jack picked up the tub and hoisted it on his shoulder. "Warm your water and I'll carry that up."

It would have taken Addie twice as long to get the tub up the steps and carry the water, so she did appreciate his help, though she hated to admit it. "Thank you."

Later that night when Jack carried the tub back down the stairs, he thought a nice hot bath sounded good. Though he was exhausted and desperately needed some sleep, the thought of a hot bath was more enticing. It was well past midnight and he figured it made more sense to bathe in the kitchen so he wouldn't be carrying pails of water up and down the stairs and chance waking someone.

He placed the tub by the kitchen table, and once it was filled with hot water, he grabbed a towel from the closet under the staircase. As he was stripping out of his clothing, he placed his holster on the table within easy reach. He pulled a cigar and match from his shirt pocket and placed them on the table beside his holster before he climbed in the tub. The tub wasn't long enough to accommodate his long frame, but he leaned back, knees bent, and allowed the warmth to seep into his bones. It felt like heaven to him. He realized he'd left the kerosene lamp on the hall table, but the moonlight filtering through the kitchen window provided just enough light. He wasn't about to move to retrieve the lamp. He quickly washed his hair and dunked under the water before he soaped his body. Finished with his ablutions, he reached for his cigar, arranged the towel as a pillow, lit his cigar, and puffed away as he leaned back and closed his eyes. He figured he'd have a few minutes to relax before the water cooled.

Addie hadn't been able to sleep for worrying about Davey. Having Jack and Prescott both under her roof didn't help matters. The whole evening had been tense, and she hadn't wanted either man to stay at the farm. Prescott had made his displeasure known about Jack's presence when he'd said good night. She told him that with Granny staying, there was nothing improper. She tried to explain that it wasn't a rare occurrence for guests to spend the night so they didn't have to ride back to town in the dark. Of course, Prescott's next question was how many times before had Jack spent the night? Her response did not please him, but she wouldn't lie. Everything had been proper, and it angered her that he would imply otherwise.

She didn't know why Jack wanted to stay overnight, and she'd given him no indication that she wanted him there. She was still angry about Clarissa, and she stubbornly refused to be civil to him. But once Granny voiced her opinion, Addie knew she was outflanked. And she grudgingly had to admit Granny was right. Jack had been going since before dawn, and it wasn't fair to insist he ride all the way back to town. As tired as he was, he'd carried her tub upstairs, then back downstairs. She couldn't imagine Prescott carrying the tub. He would have gone into town to hire someone to do that kind of chore. Trying to be generous, she reminded herself that while Prescott might have some limitations in this environment, men from the West would be met with similar issues in the larger cities. She thought of Jack in a city like Boston. While she tried to think of something he wouldn't be able to handle, nothing came to mind. She thought of the places she would go with Prescott. Dinners and balls. Prescott could waltz, and she doubted Jack had ever waltzed in his life. She did miss the balls because she loved music and dancing. As much as it rankled her to admit, she figured Jack would be a coveted prize with the ladies in Boston. Even if he couldn't waltz, he was so manly, so physically appealing, women would jump at the chance to instruct him in the art of dancing. She grabbed her pillow from beneath her head, covered her face and groaned. She needed to stop thinking about Jack Roper.

Unable to calm her racing mind, Addie tossed the covers aside and swung her legs over the bed. She decided she would warm some milk, which was Granny's remedy for sleepless nights. At the bottom of the stairs, she saw the lamp on the table. Jack must have been really exhausted to forget to extinguish the lamp. That thought made her feel even guiltier for how she'd treated him tonight. She carried the lamp to the kitchen with her and placed it on the counter near the stove. After retrieving the milk from the ice box, she poured some in a pan. While waiting for the milk to warm, the memory of Clarissa running her hand over Jack's chest came to mind. Every time she replayed that scene in her mind, she'd get angry all over again. She didn't know why she couldn't stop thinking about that, because she had plenty of other worries. Determined to put Jack and Clarissa out of her mind, she glanced down at the pan and saw the milk starting to bubble. She reached for a glass and filled it with the warm milk. Just as she turned from the stove and took a drink of her milk, she noticed the tub in the kitchen. Then she realized someone was in the tub, and she let out a shriek. Her glass of milk crashed to the floor.

Mind foggy, Jack jumped up and reached for his gun on the table. When he turned with his pistol cocked, he quickly realized he was aiming directly at Addie. "What the . . ." He nearly dropped his Colt in the water when he remembered he was stark naked. He covered his lower region with his gun hand as he groped for the towel he'd used for a pillow. The towel had fallen in the tub, and he leaned over, searching the water with his free hand. He grabbed the soggy towel, held it in front of his lower half, and placed his gun back on the table. He was in the process of wrapping the wet towel around his midsection when Prescott ran into the kitchen.

The first thing Prescott saw was Jack standing in the tub holding on to a towel around his waist. "What the devil is going on in here?" Prescott's eyes darted from a nearly naked Jack to Addie standing there in her nightgown, with her eyes zeroed in on Jack.

Still in shock over seeing Jack in all his naked glory, she couldn't take her eyes off him. It was as if Michelangelo's statue of David had come to life in her kitchen. Except this man wasn't holding a slingshot, but a Colt.

"I asked what was going on," Prescott reminded them.

Jack gave Prescott a half grin and shrugged one shoulder. "Guess I fell asleep in the tub."

Finally, Addie was able to form a sentence, but her eyes remained fixed on Jack's chest. "I came down to warm some milk. I didn't know anyone was in here."

Prescott glared at Jack. "Do you normally bathe in people's kitchens?"

Jack stared hard at him. "At this late hour, I didn't expect anyone to be up."

Turning his attention back to Addie,

Prescott said, "How could you miss him with that lamp on?"

"I picked the lamp up off the table in the hall," Addie started to explain. Suddenly, she realized she didn't have to explain anything. Jack was in her kitchen, so he should be the one doing the explaining.

"This could easily be misconstrued as a planned assignation." Prescott's irritated tone said that was exactly what he was thinking.

"Are you saying that is what happened here, Prescott? Do you think I planned on finding the sheriff in the tub?" Addie asked, her own testiness surfacing.

Jack stepped out of the tub, still holding on to his towel. "If I were you, Adler, I'd think carefully how you answer that question." He wasn't going to stand there and let this dandy insult Addie. Granted, he wasn't thrilled Addie had seen him like the day he was born, but it was an accident.

"You've stayed very close to Addie all day, and I'd like to know what is going on between you two," Prescott said.

Jack thought he must not appear too threatening, soaking wet and holding a towel around his midsection, but he was on the verge of handing Prescott Adler III his head. He took one step toward Prescott.

"Don't insult the lady again."

"This is hardly good for Addie's reputation," Prescott said.

"It's mighty convenient that you are worried about her reputation now. You didn't seem so concerned when you planted a big kiss on her in the middle of the street in broad daylight," Jack countered.

"I am her fiancé," Prescott stated. "That gives me every right —"

"You're what?" Addie shrieked.

"I told you earlier I came here to ask you a very important question."

"You never said what you intended to ask," Addie said.

"Considering our exclusive relationship in Boston, I think it had to be obvious that a proposal would soon be made."

"I did not —" She stopped midsentence. There was no way she was going to have this discussion of a private matter in the presence of the half-naked Jack. She glanced at Jack, who was standing there taking in every word of their conversation.

Jack arched his brow at her. *Exclusive.* That sounded pretty serious to him. And she'd gotten all riled up because Clarissa kissed him on the cheek. This was turning out to be one heck of a day.

"Back to the matter at hand. Do you have

something you need to tell me regarding the relationship here?" Prescott flapped his hand back and forth, between Addie and Jack.

"No, there is nothing to tell. Prescott, this was an unfortunate accident. That is all it was. We all need to go to bed before we wake Granny and the children. Let's put this matter behind us." For the first time, she noticed Prescott was wearing a long green velvet robe, probably over a nightshirt. She wondered if Jack slept in a nightshirt. Why on earth was she even thinking of such things? Her eyes swept over Jack, from head to toe, as she bent to pick up the broken pieces of glass. The man was all muscle, with thighs the size of tree trunks. He was a sight to behold.

So, she has nothing to say to Prescott about our relationship, Jack thought. *I guess our kisses meant nothing to her.* "Addie, go on to bed, I'll clean it up," Jack said.

"I can get it," Addie said.

"Addie, you need to go to bed. The sheriff is not dressed for your eyes. And you are certainly not dressed for his." Prescott leaned over to take her by the elbow, urging her to leave the broken glass.

Addie wanted to tell him she'd already seen more of Jack than she'd ever seen of any man in her life, but she was afraid Prescott might fall into a dead faint. Just to make a point, Addie straightened and turned her gaze back on Jack. "Sorry I interrupted your bath."

Prescott nearly dragged her out of the room.

CHAPTER SEVENTEEN

The ride to town the next morning would have been quiet if not for the girls talking to Jack. He'd arranged several thick blankets in the buckboard so Addie and the girls would stay warm, and Prescott sat on the front seat beside him. Prescott was still upset over the situation last night, and didn't say one word all the way to town. Addie was relieved Jack didn't make an appearance in the kitchen that morning, since it was bound to be uncomfortable for all of them. Granny noticed Jack's absence at breakfast, and she carried a cup of coffee to him in the stable. Addie couldn't help but wonder if Jack would tell Granny what happened last night. If not, she was certain Granny would interrogate her at the very first opportunity.

Addie had been awake all night, unable to get the vision of Jack's naked body out of her mind. She tried and tried to stop thinking about him, but her traitorous thoughts would not cooperate. She couldn't have dreamed of a man so perfectly formed. She had no doubt a man who looked like that would surely want a woman who equaled his beauty. And that wasn't her. His body didn't have one ounce of fat, and her body was round and soft. Clarissa, with her thin figure and lovely face, was the perfect woman for Jack.

Addie tried to make sense out of Prescott's unannounced arrival, and his sudden interest in marriage. He'd certainly failed to mention his intentions before she left Boston. Maybe he did feel affection for her, but she didn't think it was true love. Now that she'd been away from Prescott, she'd come to realize she would never be happy with him as a husband. While Prescott had much to offer, he certainly didn't stir her blood like Jack Roper. And that was the problem.

Jack pulled in front of the hotel to drop Prescott off before he drove to the school. After Prescott's insinuations last night, Jack was intentionally provoking him. He could tell Prescott was still peeved, but he didn't really care. Last night, he'd waited to hear two doors close upstairs before he got dressed and cleaned up the kitchen. If he'd heard Prescott say one wrong word to Addie, he would have gladly knocked his teeth down his throat.

Once he finally crawled into bed in Davey's room, he'd stared at the ceiling the entire night. He was one dumb son-of-a-buck for falling asleep in the tub. He couldn't believe Addie had seen him in such a state. He must have looked pretty funny standing there holding his Colt over his privates before he got that towel wrapped around his waist. But being caught with his pants down wasn't the biggest surprise of the night. He'd never expected to hear that Addie was Prescott's fiancée. Funny, she failed to mention that to him when they were kissing. If she married Prescott, they would probably go back to Boston. There was no way he could see Prescott living out here in this *wild territory.* He wondered how the girls would handle returning to the orphanage in Boston, particularly since Davey would stay in Whispering Pines. In his estimation, none of the children seemed too thrilled to see Addie's fiancé.

Prescott jumped from the seat and walked to the back of the buckboard where Addie was sitting. "Addie, I'll hire a driver today, so come to the hotel after school."

"Did you forget Granny is taking the

buggy back to the livery, and one of Morgan's men will follow her to give us a ride home after school?" Addie was hoping to have a night of peace before she had to listen to what Prescott had to say.

"Then I'll invite myself out to dinner. I'll be there by five o'clock and I'll bring my valise."

Addie knew Prescott well enough that he would have his say, but she didn't want him staying another night at the farm. "It's not necessary to spend the night since Granny will be there."

"All the same, I'll be there." He leaned over and kissed her on the cheek just as Jack clicked the horse into moving. Prescott lurched backward, but the buckboard wheel missed his toes by inches.

Jack pulled in front of the school, set the brake, and jumped from the buckboard. He helped the girls to the ground before he reached for Addie.

As usual, Addie braced her hands on his shoulders when he held her by the waist to lift her from the buckboard, and the vision of his bare, muscled shoulders filled her thoughts. She could feel a blush rising over her cheeks.

"Fiancé, huh?"

"Bye, Sheriff. Please don't forget to tell

Davey hello," Jane said.

Jack turned to see the girls standing beside him. "Bye, sugar. I'll tell him." He leaned over and kissed Jane on the top of the head.

Claire tugged on Jack's pants. "Bye, Papa."

Jack kissed Claire in the same way. "Bye, honey."

Addie was so flustered at the memory of last night that she didn't even correct Claire. When the girls walked to the schoolhouse, she said, "I do not have a fiancé."

"Seems Prescott has a different opinion."

"He was upset." Addie wasn't in the mood to give an inch. "I fail to see how this concerns you," she said peevishly.

That comment really ticked him off. "I'm puzzled that you'd kiss one man while being the intended of another."

"That coming from a man who kisses one woman, and makes plans to dine with another," Addie snapped. She started to walk away, but Jack stopped her. He pulled a Bible from his coat pocket and held it out to her.

"I found this in Davey's room."

Addie stared at the Bible Davey had been faithfully reading. "I wonder why he didn't take it with him."

"I think we both know the answer to that.

I'm riding to Coburn's, so I'll see how he's doing."

"Ask him why he left this behind."

Jack nodded and stuffed the Bible back in his pocket. He thought about pulling her into his arms and giving her a kiss, but her next comment stopped him before he had the chance to act on his thoughts.

"Have a nice night with Clarissa." She didn't wait for a response; she turned and walked inside the school.

"Frank, can you hear me?" Corbin was standing under the small window at the back of the jail. The window was eight feet from the ground, and Corbin couldn't see inside.

"Yeah, I hear you. The deputy just left."

"I know, I waited for him to leave. You the only one in there?"

"Yeah."

"Me and the boys have it all planned out. We're at the old Conner place. Don't you worry none, but be ready."

"I don't need . . ." Frank heard someone opening the front door. "Shhh. Someone's coming."

"We'll be back soon." Corbin scurried away into the brush behind the jail.

Jack opened the door to the jail and Webb

followed him inside. "Webb, go on home and get some sleep. I'll be here all day."

"Sheriff, I slept in one of the cells last night. I figured I didn't have to worry about Frank's gang showing up, since you're taking him back to Denver tomorrow."

"Have you had some breakfast?"

"Yeah, Frank and I ate earlier. You can go on to the hotel for your breakfast if you want, I'll be right here."

Jack didn't even take off his coat. "I think I'll do that. I plan on riding back out to the Coburns' to check on Davey."

"What are you doing back out here?" Coburn asked as soon as Jack dismounted.

Jack pulled Davey's Bible from his pocket. "Davey forgot this and I wanted to see that he got it."

Coburn pointed to the back of the house. "He's back there working, but don't take up too much of his time."

As soon as Jack walked to the back of the house, he expected to see Davey working on the shed, but it was completely built. Jack looked it over before he spotted Davey on a ladder nailing boards on the barn.

"You did a fine job on that shed."

"Thanks." Like the last time Jack tried talking to him, Davey didn't stop working.

"Coburn wouldn't let you go to school this morning?"

"There's a lot of work to be done."

"You left this behind at the farm, and I thought you might want it." Jack extended the Bible to him.

"I don't have time to read," Davey said.

"You're starting to sound like Coburn. But school's important and so is church. There's not a better book to read than this one."

"Mr. Coburn says we got better things to do than read books."

"He's wrong. Everything you need to know is right here in this book."

"It's all just stories," Davey said. "I don't think none of it is true."

"What about the story of David?"

Davey looked down at Jack. "It's a story. What boy could really kill a giant?"

"You'd best finish that story."

Davey was quiet for a long time. "You really think a shepherd boy became a king?"

Jack leaned against the ladder. "I know he did. You know, Davey, that shepherd boy faced a lot of hardships. Even his own family laughed at him, thinking he wasn't going to be anything special. But he overcame every hardship that came his way. It wasn't easy, and for a while he made his share of mistakes and even gave up on himself. But God didn't forget about him, or give up on him."

The silence stretched out, and when Davey didn't respond, Jack said, "How are they treating you?"

Davey looked around as though he expected someone to be watching them.

Jack thought he saw fear in his eyes. "Davey, if you're having problems, you can tell me."

"He don't like you being here." Davey spoke quietly.

"Does he give you a hard time about it?"

"I gotta get to work, or he'll get real mad."

Jack didn't want to cause Davey trouble with Coburn. "I'll put your Bible right here." He pointed to a board beside the barn. "I'll see you when I get back from Denver." It troubled Jack that Davey was so unhappy, but he had no valid reason to remove him from the Coburns'. Still, he couldn't stand to see the forlorn look in Davey's eyes. Jack felt he'd let him down, and he couldn't live with that. He decided then and there he would talk to the judge tomorrow about having the adoption cancelled. Problem was, it was the same judge who was demanding Frank Langtry return to Denver. He wondered what his chances would be with that judge if he didn't offer a good reason to cancel the adoption. He didn't think the judge would be swayed by Jack's feelings. If he didn't have proof Coburn was a lousy father, what could he do?

On the way back to town, Jack saw some heavy smoke coming from the direction of town. Something was burning, and judging by the amount of smoke, it had to be a large fire. He kicked his horse into a run. In town, he quickly saw what was on fire. He jumped off his horse several yards from the burning shell of the jailhouse. The jail, his small house, and the hotel were in flames. Everyone in town had formed a line from the well to the fire, and were passing buckets of water as fast as they could to douse the burning structures. He spotted Addie in the line, with Prescott next to her. He saw his deputy, so he hurried to him, but stopped dead in his tracks when he saw Frank Langtry working by Webb's side. He joined the line next to his deputy. "What happened?"

"I don't know. It started at the back of the jail. I got Frank out, but he didn't run away, he started helping us."

Jack glanced at Frank, trying to figure out why he hadn't made a run for it. He didn't have more than a second to mull over that question before the hotel started collapsing. "Everyone get back!" The bank was separated from the hotel by a few feet, so Jack instructed everyone to redirect their efforts on the bank, seeing as the other buildings were a lost cause. While he worked, Jack looked at every face in the line, thinking some of Frank's gang might be in town. There were a few strange faces, which put him on high alert. He didn't know if the newcomers had been guests at the hotel, or were there to spring Frank from jail.

"I was able to get out some of your belongings before the house caught. I put them over by the mercantile," Webb said.

"Thanks, Webb."

Two hours later, the fire finally burned itself out. Most of the people dropped to the ground in sheer exhaustion. Jack walked to the back of the buildings to see if he could determine the cause of the fire. The hotel owner, Dwight Preston, joined Jack behind the remnants of his building.

"We always keep a couple bales of hay back here for people to sit on if they want some air, or have a smoke in peace and quiet."

Jack looked around for clues that the fire had been intentionally set, but he didn't see anything, or smell anything to lead him to that conclusion. "I reckon someone was just careless."

"This will do me in, with winter coming. I can't rebuild that quickly," Mr. Preston said.

"We'll all pitch in to help you rebuild. You won't have to do it alone."

"Thanks, Jack."

Jack joined Webb at the front of the smoldering jail. "Webb, take Frank to the boardinghouse and we'll stay there with him tonight." Even though Frank hadn't taken off, Jack wasn't going to take any chances. He was positive Frank had an ulterior motive for helping out with the fire, he just didn't know what it was yet. "Frank, are any of your friends in town?"

"I ain't seen anybody from that jail cell." Frank saw Reb standing a few feet from him. He figured Reb and Corbin set the fire in an effort to spring him from jail. No one in Whispering Pines knew Reb, and Frank wanted to send a message to his men, so he upped his volume so Reb could hear what he had to say. "If any of my boys were in town, I'm sure they'd know by now that we are going back to Denver tomorrow, thanks to my father-in-law. So you see, Sheriff, there'd be no need for them to break me out of jail. When we get to Denver I'm sure the judge will straighten everything out."

Jack glanced at the people in the street to see if anyone seemed interested in his conversation. He had a feeling Frank was sending a message when he loudly bragged about his father-in-law. "Just so you know, Frank, if we are ambushed, I'll shoot you first."

Frank laughed. "If my boys were here, Sheriff, I'd tell them to wait for me in Denver. I'll see them by tomorrow night, and I'll be free as a bird."

"Take him on to the boardinghouse, Webb." The mood he was in, Jack felt like punching Frank just for the heck of it. He whistled for his horse and led him to the mercantile, where Webb had placed his belongings. Next to his valise, Webb had stacked his rifles and pistols he'd managed to save. Addie approached him as he was loading the items on his horse.

"I'm sorry about your house."

Jack turned to look at her. "Webb saved a few things."

"Jack!"

Jack turned to see Clarissa hurrying down the sidewalk, and when she reached him she nearly vaulted into his arms. "I just heard your house burned down. You poor thing. You are going to stay with us, and I will hear no argument from you."

Addie wanted to scream at Clarissa's timing. She was like a homing pigeon where Jack was concerned, always landing in his arms. And naturally, she was perfectly groomed, looking as lovely as ever in her blue wool coat, while Addie's dress was covered with water and grime from her efforts in the water line. She hadn't even grabbed her coat when she'd hurriedly left the school to help with the fire. Now that the fire was out, she was shivering, but she didn't know if it was from anger or the cold.

Jack extricated himself from Clarissa's arms. "I have to stay at the boardinghouse with my prisoner."

"Webb can do that. I insist you stay the night with us."

Addie waited for Jack to refuse again, but he didn't say another word. She figured he was probably pondering the idea. She wondered if he'd bathed in Clarissa's kitchen.

Prescott walked up to stand beside Addie. "It looks like I'll be staying at the orphanage now that the hotel is gone."

Clarissa glanced at Prescott, and thinking he looked like a man of means, said, "I'm sorry, I don't believe we've met."

Before Addie introduced them, Jack spoke

up. "Clarissa, this is Miss Langtry's fiancé."

Clarissa's eyes darted to Addie. "I didn't realize *you* are engaged."

"We haven't formally announced it as yet," Prescott said before Addie thought of a civil response.

"No, we have not." Addie felt like saying there would be nothing to announce, but she didn't want to embarrass Prescott.

"Congratulations in advance," Clarissa said to Prescott. She turned back to Jack, and looped her arm through his. "You look exhausted. Why don't you come home with me now and you can relax before dinner."

"I have a lot to do here, Clarissa. Tell your father I will see him later." Jack wanted to cancel his dinner date, but since Addie was standing there with her fiancé, he wasn't about to change plans. She hadn't bothered to mention the true nature of her relationship with Prescott, so he took some pleasure in letting her stew about Clarissa.

"Jack, you know you would be welcome at Morgan's," Addie said sweetly. The thought that he might spend the night at Clarissa's made her see red. She didn't know why it was so upsetting to her, but it was.

Jack looked at her, trying to figure out what was going through her mind. He noticed she didn't invite him to stay at her house. Maybe she wanted to be alone with Prescott. He reminded himself that Granny would be there too. But last night Granny didn't hear the commotion going on in the kitchen, and he'd been as naked as a jaybird. Granny would have had a conniption fit if she'd walked in on that scene.

A frown passed over Clarissa's perfect features. "Jack has no reason to go all the way out there when he's welcome in our home. And he would be closer should there be trouble in town." Clarissa turned her attention on Prescott and smiled. "I'm certain your fiancée would like some time alone with you." She stood on her tiptoes and kissed Jack's cheek. "I must get home to get everything ready for you tonight. See you about six."

"I'll be there."

"Nice to meet you, Mr. Adler," Clarissa said before walking away.

Addie noticed Clarissa walked away without saying a word to her. That was just fine with her. Granted, Clarissa was pretty, but in her case Granny was right, beauty was skin deep. Rude went all the way to the bone.

"I saw Davey earlier," Jack said.

"Did you give him his Bible?"

"Yes. But he didn't seem to care one way

or the other. He's not happy."

"The boy will adjust. We need to give them time," Prescott said.

Addie felt like crying. It seemed like everything was falling apart since she'd returned to Whispering Pines. "I wish time would solve the problem." She had a feeling time wasn't what was needed. Davey and the girls needed love, and lots of it.

CHAPTER EIGHTEEN

As promised, Jack was at Clarissa's door exactly at six o'clock, totally exhausted. He hadn't slept the prior night, and his day had been nonstop. He hoped his head didn't drop in his plate during dinner. Knowing he was riding out early in the morning with Morgan to take Frank to Denver, his plan tonight was to find out what Clarissa's father wanted, have a meal, and get back to the boardinghouse as quickly as possible. With any luck, he might get a few hours of shut-eye.

Clarissa was smiling when she opened the door. "Right on time. Come on in the kitchen with me."

Jack removed his hat and walked inside. The house was filled with mouthwatering aromas from whatever she'd been cooking. "Something smells good."

"Please sit down, I was just finishing," Clarissa said, pointing to the chair where he usually sat when he dined at their home.

Jack sat and looked at the table. There were only two plates on the table. He had a bad feeling about that.

"Would you like some coffee?"

"That sounds good." Maybe a strong cup of coffee would keep him awake through dinner.

As Clarissa poured the coffee, she placed her hand on his shoulder and leaned into his arm.

Jack had a feeling he was in dangerous territory. "Where's your father?"

"He isn't here." She walked across the kitchen and picked up two large bowls from the counter and brought them back to the table. "We will be alone tonight."

"I thought he wanted to talk with me."

Clarissa sat next to him and picked up a platter of ham and passed it to him. "I wanted to be alone with you tonight."

Jack didn't know if he wanted to ask why she wanted to be alone. He had a feeling he knew what her answer would be. He slapped a ham steak on his plate.

"We are never alone," Clarissa said.

"Maybe because it's not proper and could ruin your reputation if people found out we were alone in your house. Does your father even know I'm here?"

"Yes, I told him we could never have a private conversation and we had things to discuss."

Uh-oh. Trouble was coming. He picked up the bowl of mashed potatoes and scooped out a considerable portion onto his plate. He was hungry and he wanted to eat, not talk. He especially didn't want to talk about what he knew she had on her mind. He shoveled a huge bite of food in his mouth.

"Don't you think it's time we had a serious conversation?"

Jack chewed — slowly.

Clarissa passed him a plate of cornbread. "We've seen each other for over two years now."

Jack took two pieces of cornbread and added them to his plate. He took another bite, since she didn't seem to care if he was engaged in the conversation.

She placed her hand on his arm. "I don't want to wait too long to get married, and be like that Langtry woman. Look at her, she's well past her prime, and I'll be surprised if that Mr. Adler really marries her. Can you blame me for thinking she'd given birth to those children? That's how women look after they've been married for years, given birth several times, and no longer care

289

about their appearance. Of course, I would never let myself go like that."

Jack gulped down his bite. He wasn't about to let her talk about Addie with such disrespect. "Addie's a beautiful woman, inside and out."

Clarissa laughed. "Beautiful? Surely you are teasing."

Jack gave her a steady look. "No, I'm not teasing. She's a beautiful woman, and she has the kindest heart I've ever seen."

"She's fat!" Clarissa's voice was near screeching level.

Jack raised his brow at her. "She's not fat — she has nice curves." He was reminded of how he liked the way Addie's curves felt when she was in his arms.

"Hmph, you may call it curves, I call it fat." Clarissa took a bite of food and was silent for a few minutes.

Jack had always thought Clarissa was a pretty woman, but the more he was around her, the less he liked her.

"As I was saying before, since we've been seeing each other for two years, I'd like to know what I can expect in the future. I haven't been accepting offers from other men."

Jack tried counting the number of times he'd actually had dinner at her home over the last two years. As best he could recall, it wasn't that many times. And he'd invited her and her father to dinner at the restaurant a few times so he wouldn't feel indebted to her. "I have never told you not to see other men."

"I just thought we had an agreement." Clarissa placed her hand on his arm. "Don't you think it's time we made plans?"

Suddenly, he lost his appetite and sat back in his chair. Dinner was over. In the past, he might have thought he would become more serious about Clarissa one day, but now he realized he would never feel that way about her. "What kind of plans do you have in mind?"

"Marriage plans."

Jack wasn't a man to beat around the bush. "Clarissa, I have no intention of marrying for a long time. I think you should accept other offers if that is what's on your mind."

"What are you waiting for? Do you think you will find someone more suitable than me?"

Jack thought she actually seemed stunned that he wasn't jumping at the chance to marry her. "I am not waiting for anything. I just don't want to get married right now."

"Is it that Langtry woman? Are you involved with her?"

"I think you heard she is engaged." Jack realized it wasn't by his choice that he wasn't involved with Addie. It was hers. When he'd kissed her he hadn't known she was taken.

"Then why have you wasted my time if you have no intention of marrying? There are many men who would appreciate what I have to offer, and I've spent my time waiting for you."

Jack wasn't going to insult her by saying he'd accepted the dinner invitations to have a chance to talk with her father. He really liked the man, and didn't often have a chance to spend time with him. "I had no intentions of wasting your time, nor did I intend to keep you from accepting other offers from men more inclined to marry." He stood, and said, "Thank you for dinner, but I think it's time I left."

Clarissa led him to the front door, and when Jack reached for his hat on the foyer table, she placed her hand over his. "I hope you take some time to think about this, Jack. I think you will realize what you are about to lose."

Jack settled his hat on his head and looked at her. He knew he wouldn't feel one ounce of regret when he walked out that door.

"You shouldn't wait around any longer for me." Once he was out the door, Clarissa slammed it behind him.

Addie was busy when they arrived at the farm, getting the tub in the house and carrying water so the girls could have their baths before dinner. Granny was in the kitchen preparing the meal, and she didn't know what Prescott was doing. When Jack stayed the night, he always pitched in and helped with the chores. She hadn't forgotten that he'd carried her tub and water for her. Prescott didn't offer to do a thing. He was too accustomed to servants doing everything for him. She was walking from the kitchen carrying a pail of water when Prescott came down the stairs.

"Addie, I'd like to speak with you."

"I'm afraid now is not a good time. I'm taking water upstairs so the girls can get their baths before dinner."

"After dinner then," he said to her back.

By the time dinner was over, Addie was tired, and she had yet to have a bath, which meant making numerous trips up and down the stairs again, emptying water and refilling the tub. No wonder Jack bathed in the kitchen. It made much more sense.

"Could I speak to you in the parlor?" Prescott said when dinner was over.

Addie had totally forgotten Prescott wanted to talk to her. "Of course." She had a feeling she knew what he wanted to discuss, and she was not enthusiastic to join him. "Let me help Granny with the dishes, and I'll be there in a few minutes."

Reaching the parlor, the first thing Addie noticed was the fire was about to go out. She grabbed a log and threw it in the hearth. One more thing Jack handled when he was there. Once the fire was flaming again, she pulled a chair closer to the fire to feel the warmth.

Prescott didn't sit; he paced back and forth beside her. "Addie, I think it's time we made our relationship official."

Addie didn't know what to say to him. The last thing she'd ever expected was for Prescott to show up in Whispering Pines, professing his affection for her and claiming her as his fiancée.

Prescott stopped pacing and turned to face her. "Don't you have anything to say?"

"By *official,* what exactly are you asking?"

"I mean become engaged."

"I'm wondering why you waited until I left Boston to declare your intentions. It seems to me you had sufficient time over the last year to ask for my hand if you were interested." There, she'd said exactly what was on her mind.

"I guess I wasn't ready to make my decision before you left." He walked over and sat on the settee.

No professions of undying love, or that he couldn't live without her. Not even close. Addie knew this was likely to be the only offer of engagement she might ever receive. For a man asking to spend his life with her, she didn't think Prescott seemed excited at the prospect. He almost seemed defiant. Was it because she wasn't jumping at the chance of becoming Mrs. Prescott Adler III? Had he expected her to throw herself at him when he arrived in Whispering Pines? "Why are you ready for marriage now?"

"Mother and Father have decided it is time I wed and have children to continue the family line. I know you care a great deal about children, and I think you would be a good mother."

She should have known his parents would be making the important decisions in his life. "Would we stay here at the orphanage if we married?"

A look of sheer horror passed over Prescott's face. "We most certainly would not. I have no intentions of staying out here in this uncivilized frontier any longer than necessary. We should become engaged now, and we will leave for Boston immediately. Mother may need several months to plan the wedding, and considering your age, we would not want to wait to start a family."

This time, the horror was on Addie's face. She couldn't imagine Mrs. Prescott planning her wedding. No doubt it would be the social event of the season, but that wasn't very appealing to Addie. "Would you adopt the girls and Davey?"

"Davey has been adopted. No, I wouldn't adopt children, we will have our own. The girls will return to the orphanage in Boston. I would permit you to continue seeing them until they are adopted."

Addie wanted to scream. He would permit her! The unmitigated gall of the man. As if he would have a say in the matter when she chose to see the children. She had no intention of returning the children to the orphanage in Boston. They were happy here, and for the first time they felt they were part of a family. Perhaps not a conventional family with a mother and father, but they had people surrounding them who loved them and cared about their happiness. It was a far cry from the orphanage in Boston. "Prescott, I'm sorry, but I don't think we suit for marriage."

Prescott stood again and walked toward her chair. His grim expression clearly conveyed that he hadn't expected that response. "Why not? We've already spent many hours together in Boston, and we seemed to get on very well."

"For one thing, now that I'm back home, I can't imagine leaving here again. I love it here, and I love having the children here."

"But I thought you liked Boston."

"I like Boston well enough, but I missed home. This is where I belong." Now that a man had finally said he wanted to marry her, Addie realized it wasn't as important as she'd once thought. Or was it because the wrong man was asking?

"Does this have anything to do with that sheriff?"

"You met his girlfriend in town. This has nothing to do with him." Addie told herself that was the truth, even though she knew she would take the memory of Jack's kisses to her grave.

"I think you should consider your options. If you stay here, you'll likely never receive another offer of marriage."

"That would be preferable to marrying and being unhappy."

"Why would you want to stay in this place

when you could live like a queen in Boston?" He didn't try to conceal his disdain for the West.

"My family, the children, the land . . . home. These are the things that make me happy."

"If not for the children, would you go back to Boston?"

"My family would still be here. I want to stay near my grandmother." Addie didn't know how she could be more transparent about her feelings without hurting him. Perhaps she should just tell him she didn't love him, but it wasn't in her nature to be cruel.

"I'm very disappointed in you, Addie. Perhaps after you sleep on this, you'll see things more clearly in the morning. Good night." He turned and walked out of the room.

Addie sat there for several minutes, staring into the fire. She thought of the many nights she'd prayed for a proposal of marriage. Prescott was right, another proposal was not likely to come again. She asked herself how she would feel if the girls were adopted and she was left alone at the farm. It would sadden her, but if the girls found two parents who would love them, she would be happy for them. The thought of living alone the remainder of her days wouldn't alter her decision. Nothing would change the fact that she would never love Prescott.

Granny walked into the parlor carrying two hot cups of tea. "I thought you might like a little treat."

"Thank you, Granny." Addie jumped up and pulled another chair close to the fire for Granny.

Granny sat in her chair and sipped her tea. "This is nice. It reminds me of when you were young. You were the only one who enjoyed drinking tea with me."

"Oh, Granny, I really miss those days."

"It is nice to reminisce. Sadly, things can never be the same." She reached over and patted Addie's hand. "You will have a lifetime to build new memories."

Addie nodded. She knew she had so many reasons to be thankful. She was home and surrounded by the people she loved most. "I am blessed."

"Did Prescott ask you to marry?" Granny figured Prescott had showed up in Whispering Pines for that purpose.

"He said we needed to make our relationship official, and return to Boston so his mother could plan the wedding."

"And you said no." It wasn't a question.

Granny knew Addie didn't love Prescott. Addie had fallen for Jack Roper, just as Granny had expected all along.

"I said no. He's angry with me. He said no one would ever ask me again. And he's right."

"Nonsense. You don't know that, and Prescott is just trying to have his way by making you think that."

"Oh, Granny, no one will ever want an old maid schoolteacher, at least not one who is . . ."

Granny frowned. "Not one who is what, honey?"

"Not trim and beautiful, like Rose."

"What in the world are you talking about? You are a beautiful young woman. You have curves that are the envy of many women."

Addie laughed. "Granny, if I had a big wart on my nose you would tell me I was beautiful."

Granny laughed with her. "I most certainly would not." She paused a moment, then said, "Although, I might ask Joseph for a concoction to remove it if it was very large."

Addie laughed. "Oh, Granny, I love you. But you have to admit most men would prefer someone pretty like Rose over me."

"And by someone, are you referring to Jack Roper?" When Addie glanced away,

Granny knew she'd gotten to the heart of the matter. "I've seen the way you two look at each other. And I don't think he stays here at night just because of the children."

"Jack is much too handsome for someone like me."

"As I said, that is nonsense. I've never met a man yet who didn't like a lady with curves."

"He might like a woman with curves, but he's having dinner tonight with a beautiful younger woman."

CHAPTER NINETEEN

"I can't tell you how happy I am that you made it back to Denver," Sheriff John Trent said to Jack when he walked into the Denver jail. "The judge said if you weren't back by tomorrow, I was to go to Whispering Pines to get Frank, and to place you under arrest for defying his order."

"Frank's outside with Morgan LeMasters. I'd like to put Frank in jail while I talk to the judge."

"The judge said if you showed, I should send you to his sister's home, and you are supposed to take Frank with you. He wants to see him first thing."

"Do you know what this is about?" Jack asked.

"The judge didn't discuss it with me, but I have a feeling that he's going to set Frank free. He was mighty upset that you took Frank to Whispering Pines." The sheriff grinned at him. "You ruined their party."

302

"I don't give a hoot if he was upset, or about his party. Frank's an outlaw, and I had every right to arrest him."

Sheriff Trent stuck his hand up in the air. "I agree with you. It doesn't make sense to me either, but we won't know until you take Frank down there."

Jack turned to walk out the door, but Sheriff Trent stopped him. "Hold on, I'll go with you. I'm mighty curious about this."

"Frank!" Charlotte ran to Frank as soon as she saw him walk through the front door.

"Where's your father, honey?" Frank asked his wife.

"He's in the study. I'll get him." Charlotte turned, but her father was walking toward the group standing in the entryway.

Sheriff Trent introduced Jack and Morgan to Judge Stevens.

"Charlotte, take the gentlemen to the parlor and offer them a drink. I want to speak with Frank for a few minutes."

"Judge, I'd like to stay with my prisoner."

"Frank is not going anywhere. Go into the parlor and have some whiskey. I'll be with you shortly." The judge put his hand on Frank's shoulder and led him down the hallway.

"Gentlemen, please come this way." Charlotte led the men to the parlor, where she poured them each a drink. "Please have a seat."

"Do you mind me asking, Miss Stevens, how you met Frank?" Jack said.

"Mrs. Langtry," Charlotte reminded him. "I don't mind at all." For the next ten minutes, Charlotte told them of her first meeting with Frank, and how he came to travel to Denver with her.

"That's some story. Frank was lucky to be in the right place at the right time," Morgan said. He thought it was more than luck; Charlotte and the judge were Frank's mark.

"You can say that again," Jack agreed.

"I'm afraid you have misjudged my husband," Charlotte said.

"Did he tell you he was wanted by the law when he met you?" Jack asked.

"Yes. He told me the circumstances, and I think Father will certainly correct this matter today." Charlotte stood and said, "Please excuse me, my seamstress is waiting for me upstairs."

When Charlotte was out of earshot, Sheriff Trent shook his head. "She's a pretty little thing, but I'd say she's a mite naïve. I wonder what story Frank gave her?"

"Frank's smooth. I'd bet he targeted her and the judge. I don't doubt he gave her some wild tale," Morgan said.

"That's what bothers me. If anyone could weasel his way out of a noose, it would be Frank," Jack said.

The men were still in the parlor twenty minutes later when Sheriff Trent got up and started to pace. "You don't think they all left, do you?"

"I'd hate to have to arrest the judge." Jack stood, walked to the door, and saw the judge coming his way.

"Where's my prisoner?" Jack asked when the judge entered the room.

"He is no longer your prisoner. He's upstairs with his wife," Judge Stevens replied. The judge poured himself a drink.

"Judge, I think it's time you told us what is going on," Jack prompted.

"First things first," the judge replied. "I want to know the circumstances that led to you and Mr. LeMasters to chase Frank all over the country."

Jack and Morgan summarized the trouble Frank had caused on Morgan's land, as well as his ensuing crimes.

"Frank has explained the situation to me a bit differently." He pointed to Morgan, and said, "Particularly the problems he's had with you, Mr. LeMasters. It appears to me this is a situation of your word against his."

"It's not only my word, Judge. He kidnapped his sister and set fire to their farmhouse, which resulted in the death of their younger brother. She's prepared to testify against him. And the man Frank shot on my ranch identified him as one of the rustlers." Morgan tried to keep his temper under control.

"I understand that his sister is now your wife," the judge said.

"Yes, she is."

The judge swallowed the contents of his glass. "In these familial issues, it's only natural that the wife would take the side of her husband."

"So you are saying my wife's word will be disregarded because she married me?"

The judge held up his hand to stop him. "Please allow me to finish. This family spat is not what concerns me."

Morgan jumped to his feet. "Family spat? That's what you call kidnapping and abusing his sister? What kind of judge are you?"

The judge puffed up like a ruffled hen. "Remember to whom you are speaking, sir. I am the kind of judge who is demanding to have this renegade Sioux who claims Frank shot him brought before me. It seems he is a fugitive from the law. Is that correct?"

"He is no fugitive," Morgan said.

"I understand that the military has been to your ranch to look for him, and that a soldier was shot in the process."

"That is incorrect," Morgan answered.

The judge leaned forward and glared at Morgan. "Which part is incorrect? Were the soldiers on your land searching for this Sioux, or were they not? Was a soldier killed while searching for said man? Did you hide this man from the soldiers?"

"The soldiers were there to search for him. But no one got shot on my land, or if they were, no one has found a body. Several people have gotten lost in those pines, but that's a far cry from accusing a man of shooting them."

"Does this Sioux reside on your ranch?" the judge asked.

"He is a native of that land. The way I see it, we are all just caretakers of the land." Morgan wasn't being evasive, he was simply stating what he believed.

"I will be sending a telegram to the military to find out the truth of what happened on your ranch when the soldiers searched for this Sioux. I have a problem with a citizen who would harbor Indians who were assigned to reservations. I will ask you again. Did you hide this man from the soldiers?"

Just as Morgan thought, Frank had found a way to twist the truth to his benefit. "I didn't hide anyone. The Sioux know the territory better than the white men who banished them from their homeland." Morgan told the truth. He didn't hide Joseph. Actually, Joseph had been the one to tell him the soldiers were on their way to look for him, and he left without Morgan's knowledge.

"Until I hear otherwise, I consider this Sioux a fugitive." The judge stared at Morgan for a few seconds before he turned to Jack. "Frank is in my custody. You have one week to bring this Sioux to Denver to give his testimony to me." He held his index finger in the air for emphasis and repeated, "One week. If he does not appear before me, I'm instructing you to arrest this man" — he pointed to Morgan — "for harboring a fugitive. I have heard from both parties, and I do not feel Mr. LeMasters's word is more credible than Frank's."

"Exactly how did Frank and his gang come by my horses they were riding when we caught up with them?" Morgan asked.

"He said he purchased them from another source."

"Now see here, Judge, Frank Langtry

produced no bill of sale, he shot Morgan and left him for dead, and his men ambushed me in Purgatory Canyon." Jack was just getting warmed up, but the judge stood before he'd finished.

"Enough. I've given my orders, and should they be ignored, or disobeyed, Sheriff Trent will come to Whispering Pines and arrest the lot of you."

"I'd be curious to know what Frank Langtry has on you," Morgan said.

The judge whirled around to face Morgan. "Careful, Mr. LeMasters, or you'll be spending the night in our jail."

Morgan took a step toward the judge, but Jack lurched from his chair and grabbed his arm before he did something as foolish as punching the man. It took a lot to rile Morgan, but the judge managed to get the job done. Jack didn't want his friend on the wrong side of the law.

Sheriff Trent couldn't believe what he was hearing. He thought the judge was being unreasonable. "Judge, don't you think —"

Again, the judge held his hand up, commanding silence. "If you do not obey my orders, then I will contact the U.S. Marshals' office and direct them to send a marshal to do the job for you. Now if you will excuse me, I have an important prior engagement. You can show yourselves out." The judge left the room, leaving the men in stunned silence.

Finally, Sheriff Trent glanced at Jack and Morgan. "Let's get out of here. We can go to the hotel restaurant for some coffee."

The three men rode to the hotel, and once inside they decided to order a meal with their coffee. After the waitress took their order, they tried to make sense of the judge's orders.

"I'd heard he was one tough son of a gun, but I never expected this," Sheriff Trent said.

"I know you won't bring Joseph here," Jack said to Morgan.

"No way. You might as well arrest me now. I don't like the thought of soldiers on my ranch again, but it looks like I won't have much of a choice."

Jack looked at Sheriff Trent. "Looks like you'll have to arrest Morgan and me. I won't arrest Morgan or Joseph Longbow."

"Tell me about this Joseph Longbow," Sheriff Trent said.

Morgan told the story of how he came to know Joseph. "All he wants to do is live free. The way I see it, he has that right. He's been an asset to our town, helping out with his doctoring skills after our doctor died. The only reason Frank has it out for Joseph is because of me. He sees Joseph as a way to get to me."

"Joseph's a fine man, and there's no way I would arrest him," Jack added.

The waitress reappeared to refill their cups. "Your dinner will be right out."

Sheriff Trent wasn't about to arrest either man, but he didn't know how he was going to keep his job once he disobeyed the judge. "Do you think the judge is willing to take Frank's word because he married his daughter? Maybe he's playing a tough hand to appease her, but when it comes down to it, he won't follow through."

"I don't read him that way. I think he will do exactly as he said," Jack said.

"He didn't seem inclined to listen to reason," Morgan said.

The waitress was placing their dinner on the table when Jack looked up and saw the judge walk into the restaurant with his arm around a very young, attractive woman.

"Look at that." Jack cocked his head toward the entryway of the restaurant. "That must be his important engagement."

Morgan and Sheriff Trent followed Jack's eyes. They watched as the judge helped the young woman out of her cloak. The dress she was wearing certainly displayed her voluptuous figure. Every diner in the room turned to look at her.

"Does he have another daughter?" Morgan asked.

Sheriff Trent glanced from Jack to Morgan. "She's not his daughter. Her name is Leigh King. Apparently, she traveled to Denver with him. The owner of the hotel told me he's been spending a lot of time in her room."

"She's a pretty gal," Jack said.

"She looks younger than his daughter," Morgan said. He noticed how the judge looked around the room, making certain everyone noticed his younger companion. He saw the three men at the back of the restaurant, but he didn't acknowledge their presence.

"Yeah, she's young and pretty. She's drawn some attention around town, showing off that fine figure. She's registered under the name Mrs. Leigh King, and when the clerk mistakenly addressed the judge as Mr. King, he wasted no time setting the young man straight. Mrs. King told the clerk that she is a widow. I've seen them together several times, but I've not seen his daughter with them."

"Well, looks like you might see them all together right now," Morgan said.

They watched as Charlotte and Frank walked into the restaurant.

"It galls me to see him walking around town a free man," Morgan said.

Charlotte saw her father and headed to his table. When she reached the table, the judge stood and introduced his companion to Charlotte and Frank.

"And how do you know my father, Mrs. King?" Charlotte asked pleasantly.

"Why, we are to be married soon."

Jack, Morgan, and Sheriff Trent could see Charlotte's face, and she didn't look pleased with whatever was being said. They couldn't hear what was going on, but the people at the neighboring tables told the story. The other diners stopped their conversations and gawked at the judge's table.

The judge's girlfriend jumped to her feet, and the entire room easily heard what she had to say. "I am not a gold digger! I am your father's fiancée." She thrust the large diamond ring on her finger in Charlotte's face.

Charlotte's eyes nearly popped from their sockets when she looked at the large, sparkling stone. "That's ridiculous," she screeched. She turned her angry eyes on her father. "Father, tell me this isn't so."

The judge's face was beet red as he

glanced around the room and saw everyone watching them. "This is neither the place nor the time for this discussion." He cursed himself for giving Leigh that ring last night. He'd intended to break the news to Charlotte first, but he didn't want to take the chance of Leigh losing her patience with him and moving on to younger, more robust pastures.

"I want an answer." Charlotte's eyes flicked over Leigh, noting her tasteless attire. "Are you marrying this" — Charlotte had never uttered such a word, but she said what was on her mind — "tart?"

"I am not a tart! I am a widow!" Leigh shrieked in a tone that equaled Charlotte's.

The judge stood and threw his napkin on the table. "Charlotte, apologize at once."

Jack was watching Frank during this little scene. It seemed as though Frank couldn't take his eyes off the judge's woman. "I think Frank likes what he sees."

"And I thought he was in love," Morgan said wryly.

"I guess you were right, it was opportune for him to be in love with a judge's daughter," Jack replied.

"I will most certainly not apologize," Charlotte told her father. On the chair beside Leigh, Charlotte saw the fur-collared cape, exactly like the one she was wearing. She pointed to the cape. "Where did you get that?"

Leigh realized Charlotte was wearing the same cape. "It was a gift from Robert."

Charlotte was aghast. She had selected the garment herself and it was very expensive. "Father, how could you buy her the same cape?"

"Charlotte, stop this nonsense! I said this is not the place for this discussion!" The judge was appalled that his daughter was behaving like a harpy in front of the other diners.

Charlotte was not to be deterred, and she hoped she shamed her father so he would end this foolishness. She eyed Leigh again. "Just how old are you?"

"I will soon be nineteen," Leigh replied.

Charlotte's sharp intake of breath could be heard over the totally silent room. "Father, you are marrying someone the age of your own daughter? Have you taken leave of your senses?" She didn't wait for a response; she turned and stormed out of the restaurant.

Frank didn't move. His eyes remained fixed on Leigh's lovely décolleté. He found the judge's woman very appealing indeed. But instead of standing there ogling the woman, he was smart enough to seize another opportunity to ingratiate himself with the judge. He leaned over and whispered to the judge.

"Thank you, Frank."

Frank smiled at the beautiful young woman, and said, "Nice to meet you, Mrs. King." He left the restaurant in search of his angry wife.

The judge took his seat and urged Leigh to sit down.

"I can't believe you didn't tell your daughter about us. When you straighten this out, I will be in my room, but don't come back until you do." Leigh grabbed her cape and walked away.

"Guess the judge's day just took a turn for the worse," Jack said.

"I'm tempted to arrest them for disturbing the peace," Sheriff Trent said.

"I'd pay to see that," Jack replied.

"I'd pay you to do it," Morgan said.

The three of them had their best laugh of the day.

Fifteen minutes later, Frank returned alone, and joined the judge at his table.

Jack, Morgan, and Sheriff Trent finished their meal, and Jack said, "I guess we'd best get back to Whispering Pines."

"I know a U.S. Marshal, and he's a reasonable man. I think I will contact him before the judge contacts someone. Once I explain to him what is going on, he might be inclined to see things our way," Sheriff Trent said.

"It can't hurt," Jack said.

After they paid for their meal, they were headed to the door when they saw the waitress deliver a tray of food to the judge's table. They heard the judge say to Frank, "I appreciate this, son." Frank stood and grabbed the tray of food.

Jack, Morgan, and Sheriff Trent lingered in the hotel lobby, waiting to see where Frank was going. Frank headed up the staircase with the food.

"You don't think he's taking dinner to the judge's girlfriend, do you?" Sheriff Trent asked.

"I wouldn't put anything past Frank," Morgan said.

"I can't believe the judge would trust Frank with his woman," Jack said.

They walked around the staircase and heard Frank knocking on a door. "Mrs. King, I have your dinner."

Sheriff Trent smiled. "I think things are going to get mighty interesting around here."

■ ■ ■ ■

On their way back to Whispering Pines, Jack and Morgan discussed the judge and Frank. No closer to understanding why the judge had made the decision he did, they were tired of trying to figure it out. Morgan needed to change the subject before he decided to turn his horse back toward Denver. "I'll meet you in town tomorrow morning and bring a few of my men to start work on the new jail and hotel."

"I'm sure Webb and some of the other men in town will have things cleaned up and be ready to start building," Jack said.

"I didn't even ask you how your dinner went last night with Clarissa," Morgan asked.

"Not so good."

Morgan eyed his friend. He suspected he had more on his mind than Frank. "I thought you liked Clarissa's cooking."

"I wasn't talking about her cooking. Her cooking is fine. But she said her father wanted to talk to me and he wasn't even there. She wanted to talk to me alone."

It was no secret that Clarissa had her sights set on Jack, so Morgan wasn't really surprised at her tactics to get him alone.

Jack glanced at him and arched his brow. "Clarissa wants to get married."

"Does she have a man in mind?" Morgan said, grinning.

"Very funny. Yeah. She wants to marry me."

"Aside from her very poor taste in grooms, did she say why she decided this now?"

Jack thought about Clarissa's reasoning. "Not really. She just said that we'd spent enough time together and it was time to marry."

"What'd you say?"

"I told her I wasn't ready to marry."

Morgan laughed. "That's not what Granny says."

"Granny had me married off the day she realized I wasn't going to die after she dug that slug out of me." Jack remembered Granny telling him all about Addie while he was recuperating. She'd insisted that Addie was the right woman for him.

"Granny told me I was ready for marriage before I had given it a thought. Her plans worked out pretty good for me," Morgan reminded him.

"Yeah, I'd say you've done well in your choice of a wife."

Morgan thought about the day he saw his wife get off that stagecoach just as he was about to hang her brother. "Jack, I don't think it was a choice. I think it was part of God's larger plan for my life. I never gave much thought to destiny, but it makes a man wonder. I think the way the children have taken to you is part of God's plan. Maybe it's your destiny to be involved in their lives. I think it's possible Granny knows something we don't. Maybe Addie is the one for you."

Jack didn't know how this conversation got sidetracked from Clarissa to Addie and the children. "You're starting to sound like Granny."

"I've learned not to dismiss some of Granny's more fanciful notions." If Granny was convinced Jack would marry Addie, he wasn't about to disagree with her. He figured she was more in tune to God's plans than anyone else he'd ever met.

"Clarissa's a pretty woman, and she's a good cook," Jack said, redirecting the conversation back to the matter at hand.

"Uh-huh." Morgan wondered if his friend was trying to talk himself into finding a reason to marry Clarissa.

"I like her father, he's a good man," Jack continued.

"Uh-huh."

"Maybe I should think about it," Jack mused.

"Think about what?"

"Marrying Clarissa."

"Do you love her?"

Jack knew the answer to that question without even thinking about it. "No."

"There's your answer."

Jack pulled his horse to a halt. "Did you know when Rose stepped off that stagecoach that she was the one for you?"

Morgan reined in his horse. "I knew there was something special about her. Don't get me wrong, I'm not saying I knew it was love right off, but I'd never seen anyone so beautiful. I never expected someone as pretty as her to have grit too. But she stood up to me and gave me the devil over trying to hang her brother."

Jack understood Morgan appreciated a person who stood for what they believed. "When did you realize you were in love with her?"

Morgan remembered the very moment he knew he was a goner. "The first time I kissed her. That girl could kiss. I knew I couldn't allow another man to find out how good she kissed."

Jack thought of Addie's kisses. He'd felt just like Morgan. Maybe all of the Langtry girls were good kissers. Prescott knew how good Addie kissed. He'd kissed her right in the middle of town, and Jack didn't like it. But it wasn't because he was in love, he just didn't want Addie's reputation ruined.

"What about Addie?"

Jack felt like Morgan was eavesdropping on his thoughts. "What about her?"

"Do you think you might love her?"

"It seems she's engaged to Prescott."

"What?"

"Yeah. She didn't mention that."

"She didn't mention an engagement to Rose." Morgan thought if Addie was engaged, she would have told her family.

"Beats me why she didn't tell anyone. Maybe she thought Prescott wouldn't come to Whispering Pines."

"Does he want her to go back to Boston?"

Jack had thought about that last night. If she went back to Boston, he'd never see her or the children again. "I don't know."

CHAPTER TWENTY

Frank knocked on Leigh's door, and when there was no response, he said again, "I brought your dinner."

"I didn't order dinner."

"I ordered dinner for you," Frank said.

Inching the door open, Leigh saw the judge's son-in-law holding a tray full of food. "Why did you bring me dinner?"

Frank could see she had been crying. "Thought you might be hungry."

Leigh stuck her head out the door and looked around. "Where's your nasty wife?"

"Charlotte's not so bad. She was just caught by surprise. Anyway, she's home. I'm alone." Frank thought she was even lovelier than he first thought. He was curious to know what she was doing with an old man. He smiled at her. "Aren't you going to invite me in?"

"Given the circumstances, I don't think that would be proper."

Frank gave her his charming smile. "Don't you think it's a little late to worry about being proper?"

Frank pushed the door wider with his shoulder, walked into the room and kicked the door shut with his boot. "The judge told me he'd been spending his nights in your room. I doubt you two are playing cards in the wee hours of the morning, so let's not start off our relationship by lying to each other." He walked across the room and placed the tray on a table.

Leigh didn't move. "What do you mean by that?"

Frank walked back to her and grinned. "I think you know."

Leigh took a step back to place some distance between them, but she backed into the wall.

Taking one step forward, Frank braced his arm on the wall beside her head. "I saw how you looked at me. You don't really want an old man for a husband, do you?"

Leigh's eyes flicked over his face. "Why would you ask such a question?"

Frank leaned in a little closer. "Your eyes gave you away."

When the judge introduced them, Leigh had thought the judge's daughter had certainly snagged a handsome husband. She stared into his blue eyes. His boldness appealed to that part of her that wanted to be just as daring.

Frank smiled when she didn't offer a denial. "You've been with an older man. Does he make you happy? You are a very young woman, and you will outlive him."

Averting her eyes from his, she said, "I have no choice in the matter."

Frank leaned down and covered her mouth with his. When she didn't pull away, he crushed her to him.

She wrapped her arms around his neck and kissed him with equal passion.

When Frank pulled away, he said, "That's what I mean. You want me and I want you. You don't have to marry the judge. There may be a way we can help each other out."

Leigh was clutching his shoulders, wanting to believe he might be offering her another way to survive, but it would be risky. "You're married."

"I married for a specific purpose. I think you are doing the same thing."

"What else am I supposed to do? I have no family, no way to make a living unless I want to work in a saloon."

"I understand your reasons. But there may be another way." He nibbled on her neck. "I like the way you taste."

Leigh placed her hands on his chest and was waiting when his lips met hers again. Within seconds, her pent-up desires were released on the promises of a complete stranger.

Later, Frank walked to the untouched tray of food and picked up a cold biscuit. He stuffed it in his mouth, walked to the bureau, and picked up the pitcher of water. After he poured himself a glass, he turned back to Leigh. "I'll give you a cut of the money we get from the bank. Once we are convinced they are not going to connect me with the robbery, you can tell the judge you've changed your mind and take the next stage back to Colorado City. I'll meet you there."

When Frank first met Charlotte, he thought he might really learn to love her and be faithful to her. Those feelings lasted right up to the moment he saw Leigh. Like his wife, Leigh was young, but when the judge introduced them, he could tell by the way she looked at him that she was not as naïve as Charlotte. She was more beautiful than his wife, and she knew how to dress to entice a man, showing off her mouthwatering curves. Frank appreciated what she had to offer and he wanted her. Charlotte provided him respectability, and he would benefit from that union as long as he needed the judge. He was attracted to his wife, but it was a different kind of attraction when he saw Leigh. She appealed to him on a primitive level. He had to have her.

"How do you know your plan will work?" Leigh asked.

"After that scene in the dining room, I don't think there is any question it will work." Men and women alike enjoy a catfight between two women.

"What will happen after the robbery?"

"As I said, I'll meet you in Colorado City."

"But you will still be a married man," Leigh reminded him.

"We will go somewhere and start over." Frank had no intention of leaving permanently, not as long as his marriage was serving his purpose. He had Morgan LeMasters where he wanted him, and he was going to see that through first.

"Why couldn't we go to Colorado City together?" Leigh asked.

"I have other business here, but I will be there as soon as I can."

"What happens to me if you don't show?"

"You could always tell the judge you changed your mind and want to marry him. Or, you sell that rock on your hand and take off to another city."

■ ■ ■ ■

The judge was in the parlor drinking when Frank returned home. Frank joined him and poured himself a drink.

The judge couldn't wait for Frank to sit before he asked. "What did she say?"

"You're going to have to give her some time. She's very upset because you didn't tell Charlotte."

"I didn't know how to tell Charlotte. You saw how she acted tonight, like a spoiled child. I knew she wouldn't understand."

"Leigh did agree to meet you for dinner tomorrow night."

The judge swiped his hand across his face. "Thank you, Frank. I've been so worried. I didn't know what I was going to do if she wouldn't forgive me."

"Have you talked with Charlotte?"

"I tried. She won't even answer her door. Ruth has already given me the devil over this. Charlotte went crying to her, and she is on Charlotte's side. Neither one is speaking to me right now."

"I'll talk to Charlotte and Ruth." Frank was definitely going to have the judge in his corner after tonight. "Mrs. King is a fine woman, and I can see why you want to marry her."

"She makes me feel young again." The judge didn't admit he was in love with Leigh. The truth was, he'd never loved Charlotte's mother as much as he loved Leigh. "Man to man, I can tell you she excites me like no other woman I've ever known."

Frank couldn't disagree with him there. His immediate attraction to the judge's girlfriend was inexplicable. "I understand."

"Charlotte's married now, and I don't want to spend the rest of my life alone. I want to take Leigh around the world and enjoy what time I have left."

"Sounds like you have it all planned out," Frank said.

"I've had a lot of time to think about it." Since he'd met Leigh, most of his time was spent thinking about his future with her. The judge stood and slapped Frank on the back. "I owe you, Frank. Let's go in the kitchen and see what we can find to eat. We didn't get to enjoy our dinner."

"I wish I'd known you were going to eat at the hotel. I would have told Charlotte I preferred eating at home." Frank was convinced he was going to be the judge's best friend before this was over. In return for

Frank's help, the judge would certainly keep him from the gallows.

"Honey, I understand why you are angry with your father. He should have told you about his girlfriend." Frank had no intention of asking Charlotte to work things out with the judge, at least not for a few days. He had his own plan, and the only way it was going to work was by stoking the flames of his wife's anger. "I don't think she's the type of woman a man in the judge's position should have for a wife. Just think of all the gossip. But, honey, I'm in no position to talk to the judge. You have to understand my future — our future — is in his hands. He could have the sheriff from Whispering Pines arrest me and I could be hanged."

"But, don't you see, she's not his girlfriend. Did you see that ring on her hand? She's his fiancée. That diamond cost thousands of dollars. And the cloak he purchased for her, I know how much that cost. He's spent a fortune on her already."

"I think all we can do is hope he tires of her." Frank knew his plan would put a halt to the judge's relationship once and for all, but he couldn't tell Charlotte.

"That woman could steal my inheritance."

"I think Aunt Ruth will have something to

say about that. I can't see her allowing him to do something so foolish."

"Did Father tell you how long he's been seeing her?"

"I think he's been seeing her for several months. She definitely has him under her spell." Frank was equally captivated by Leigh, but he would never dangle on a woman's hook like the judge.

"What does he see in that woman? While her dress was of fine quality, it was not one a lady would wear. I can't believe a man of his advanced years would embarrass himself parading around with a woman so young. Can you imagine what our friends would say if she became my stepmother?" Charlotte had never been angry with her father, but this newly discovered relationship was too much for her to tolerate. She'd been the center of her father's life, and she wasn't about to allow an opportunistic interloper to change that.

Frank almost smiled at the image of Leigh as his wife's stepmother. "Let's get some sleep." Frank was tired of hearing her whine, and he wanted a reprieve.

Early the next morning Frank rode to the small white clapboard house on the outskirts of Denver, where Reuben lived. He knocked on the door, and when no one responded, he opened the door and walked in.

"May I help you?" The owner of the house was riding by when he saw Frank at the door.

Frank turned to the man in the doorway. "I knew the fellow who lived here. Do you know what happened to him?"

"No, he left town rather suddenly after he'd been shot in a bank robbery. If you knew Reuben, then I'm sure you know he wasn't cut out for this kind of life."

Frank laughed. "You're right about that. And he didn't say where he was headed?"

"He said he didn't know, but I suspect he went back East."

Frank looked around the small, one-room house. He wondered if Reuben might have been careless enough to leave any clues behind. "Are you the owner of the house?"

"Yes, I'm Sam Drew, and the home is for rent if you're interested."

There were no homes nearby, so Frank assumed Sam just happened by. "Do you live near here?"

"No, I was riding into town and saw you at the door. I have a ranch a few miles east of town."

"Would you consider renting this house for a month?" Frank thought this was the perfect place for his assignations with Leigh. He didn't want to take her to the house where his boys were hiding out, and prying eyes would prevent him from going to her hotel room frequently.

"Only one month?"

"Yes, I'm afraid my business here will not take longer than that. I would stay at the hotel, but I prefer peace and quiet at night." He doubted he'd ever be at the house overnight, but it was the perfect place to meet Leigh during the day.

"I suppose one month would be fine. It's not like I have anyone else interested in the place. My wife keeps it clean, and as you can see, she does a good job."

The two men settled on a price for the entire month, and Frank paid him in advance.

"I'm sorry, I didn't catch your name," Mr. Drew said.

"Corbin Jeffers." Frank wasn't about to give him his real name.

"Mr. Jeffers, I hope you enjoy your stay."

Frank rode to the hotel and walked inside. There wasn't a clerk at the desk, and no one was in the lobby, so he ran up the stairs to Leigh's room. When Leigh opened the door, Frank stepped inside, closed and locked the door before giving her a kiss. "I have a place for us to go where it will be safe. We can't take a chance on people seeing us right now. I will meet you at the back of the hotel with a buggy in two hours."

"Are you sure no one will find us there?"

"It's on the outskirts of town and there are no neighbors. I'm going to see my boys right now, but I'll be back in two hours." He kissed her again before he opened the door and slipped out.

"I can't believe the judge let you go free." Reb had told the others that Frank was confident the judge would see that he was freed, but he'd had his doubts.

"I appreciate you trying to get me out of jail, but I knew the outcome, so I stayed to help put out the fire," Frank said. "I thought that act of kindness would go a long way with the judge."

"You were right all along, Frank. You said when you met the judge that he was going to be your ticket out of this mess," Reb said.

"Didn't I always tell you boys that these yokels won't ever hang me? The judge owes me now."

"What do you mean? He owes you for marrying his daughter? Reb said she is real pretty," Deke said.

"Well, in a way, he does owe me for marrying his daughter." Frank explained to the men about the judge's girlfriend, and how the judge trusted him to solve his problem with Leigh. When he told them what had transpired the prior evening with Leigh, they had a difficult time believing his luck.

"You mean to tell me you are involved with the judge's girlfriend when you have a fine-looking wife waiting on you at home?" Reb said.

Frank laughed. "You should see her. She's some woman." Frank told them about the judge demanding that Jack and Morgan bring Joseph Longbow to Denver. "Morgan won't bring Joseph, so that means we won't have to worry about having him identifying us on the stand. We'll go free, boys."

"I'm liking this judge already," Dutch said.

"But what happens when the judge finds out you're seeing his woman?" Reb asked.

"We won't be seen together. I've already taken care of that. She's going to help us out with the robbery. When it's done, she's going to head back to Colorado City. I'll meet up with her there."

"What about your wife? If you leave her, won't the judge put two and two together and figure out you are with his girlfriend?" Reb asked.

"I'm not leaving my wife for good," Frank said.

"How are you going to manage keeping two women?" Deke asked.

Frank grinned at him. "They won't be in the same city. I reckon I can keep up for a while until one or the other runs its course. I'm a lot younger than the judge, and look at the benefits."

"Dang, Frank, I don't know how you do it," Corbin said.

"Can I help it if women love me? You just have to have a good plan," Frank bragged.

"A plan is one thing, but women have a way of knowing when they're playing second fiddle to another one," Dutch said.

"You sound like a man speaking from experience," Frank said.

"Well, I ain't never married one," Dutch said. "But a long time ago I had two girlfriends at the same time. And I can tell you when they found out about each other, it was a sight to see. They brawled like two men, in the middle of the street."

The men laughed, and Frank said, "I'm counting on these two particular women not seeing eye to eye. Now, let's get down to business and plan this bank robbery."

CHAPTER TWENTY-ONE

Addie and Granny finished preparing breakfast, and they were still waiting on Prescott to make his appearance.

"Girls, go ahead and eat while it's warm. We won't be waiting on Mr. Adler any longer." Addie was irritated with Prescott for making them wait. He knew when they had to leave to get to school on time.

"I will be going into town later today to help out where I'm needed. I'm sure I can make sandwiches to keep the men filled while they're working on the buildings. You and the girls walk to the mercantile after school and we will ride home together," Granny said.

"Can we help after school? Maybe Davey will be there," Jane said.

"We can see Papa," Claire said.

Addie was pouring Granny some coffee, but she stopped long enough to give Claire *the look.* "Claire."

Claire hung her head, pretending to be very interested in one of her fingers.

"We will help if Claire remembers what I have told her about calling the sheriff papa," Addie said.

"Claire, remember what Miss Addie told you," Jane whispered to her sister. "You don't want to miss the chance to see Davey."

Claire's lower lip started to quiver. "I want Davey."

Jane jumped out of her seat and put her arm around her sister. "We might see him today."

Addie walked to Claire and Jane and gave them a hug. "We all have to remember to be happy for Davey."

Jane walked back to her seat. "How can we be happy? Davey's not happy without us."

Addie didn't have an answer. Jack had said the same thing. Near tears, Addie walked back to the stove.

"Maybe we should all pray for Davey's happiness," Granny said as she carried two more plates to the table.

Prescott walked into the room. "Good morning."

Addie and Granny greeted him, but the girls remained silent. Addie placed a cup of coffee in front of him.

"I trust you had time to think over what we discussed last night," Prescott said.

Addie had had another sleepless night thinking about Prescott's offer, but she hadn't changed her mind. She glanced at the girls and said, "Yes, I did, but I prefer to have this conversation alone."

"Have you changed your mind?" Prescott pressed.

Knowing her response was not going to please him, Addie tried to delay the conversation. "We will talk about this later."

Prescott reached for her hand. "I want an answer. Have you changed your mind?"

"No," Addie said softly.

Granny placed a plate of food in front of him. "Time to eat."

Addie took her seat and Granny said the prayer.

After the prayer, Prescott spoke first. "Addie, I don't think this home is going to work out for one of our orphanages. I want you to return the children to Boston immediately. If you want to continue your employment with the orphanage, you will have to do so from Boston."

Addie's fork dropped to her plate with a loud clang. The girls and Granny stopped eating, their eyes darting from Addie to

Prescott.

"You can't be serious," Addie said.

"I'm quite serious. I've had plenty of time to think this over. After seeing your inability to stop interfering with the boy's adoption, I have determined you are not the best person to manage an orphanage independently. If you choose to return to Boston, the superintendent will supervise you."

"What does that mean?" Jane asked.

Addie glanced at the girls. "Prescott, we should discuss this privately. Would you like to go into the parlor?"

"Why shouldn't they know? They will be going back to Boston, and it's best they know they will be returning as soon as possible. If you cannot accompany them to Boston, I will hire someone to do so. I plan to be on the next stage."

"We can't go back there. Davey is here," Jane said, on the verge of crying.

"The boy is no longer your family. He has a new family," Prescott said flatly.

Jane and Claire started crying.

"Prescott! How could you say such a thing?" Addie said, her voice faltering.

"Addie is right. You two go on in the parlor to have this discussion," Granny said sternly.

Addie stood, hoping Prescott would listen

to Granny. "Girls, it will be okay. We will work this out."

"It's time you and these children faced facts," Prescott said. "Once they are back in Boston, they will each most likely be adopted by different families. They will no longer have contact with each other." He glanced at Addie, and added, "I strongly suspect that you are the reason they have not been adopted to date."

"Mr. Adler, I'd suggest you keep your opinions to yourself at this table," Granny said. Granny wasn't one to lose her patience, but Prescott had angered her.

Addie fled the room, hoping he would stop talking if she wasn't there to listen. Prescott slammed his fork down on the plate and followed her from the room. Once they were in the parlor, Addie lit into him. "I can't believe you could be so cruel! What are you thinking, saying those things to the girls? You know they are crazy about their brother."

"As I said, Addie, you are too close to the children. You don't think any family will be good enough to adopt them. They will have a better chance of being adopted once they are back in Boston without your interference."

"Don't you understand their feelings? If

they are not adopted here, at least they are welcome to stay as long as they want. There is no reason for them to go back to Boston."

"We strive to have children adopted. That endeavor seems beyond your comprehension," Prescott countered peevishly.

"I understand perfectly that adoption is our purpose. What I do not understand is why children waiting to be adopted should be denied love and attention. Yes, I love these children, and I do not consider that a detriment to their well-being."

Prescott wasn't listening or didn't care about her opinion. "There's also the issue of your brother. You failed to mention to me that you had an outlaw brother. Had I known that in Boston, I wouldn't have allowed you to open the orphanage here."

"That's not fair. At the time, I didn't know Frank was an outlaw."

"Still, this is a fact that I can't ignore. I've made up my mind, and there is nothing further to discuss. The children are wards of the orphanage and as such, they will return to Boston."

Addie was so angry, she worried she might say something that would only make things worse. She took a deep breath before she spoke. "You made this decision because I refuse to marry you. If I had said yes, would you still be doing this?"

"You were perfectly clear. If we married, you would want to adopt these children. That led me to believe that you do not possess the professional objectivity needed for the position."

Addie wasn't going to deny the truth. If professional objectivity meant she shouldn't care about the children, then she wouldn't argue the point. "I can't get away until after the school year is complete to take the girls to Boston. And they need to finish this school year." She was hoping he would forget all about this situation by the end of the term.

"I told you I will make arrangements to see they are chaperoned back to Boston. It is not necessary for you to come with them. They will complete their school term in Boston."

"I never expected you to be so cruel, Prescott." She had another thought, but she wasn't certain it would make a difference if all he wanted to do was hurt her. "You don't have to give us financial support for the orphanage, we can make it without your money."

"This has nothing to do with finances." To indicate he was through discussing this subject, he said, "I shall be staying at the boardinghouse until the next stage out of here." Without another word, he walked out of the room.

Addie stood there staring at the doorway. What was she going to do? The girls would be devastated to leave Davey behind. Even if she had a husband, there was no way Prescott would allow her to adopt them. He was angry with her for rejecting him, and he was going to make sure she regretted her decision.

On the way to school, Morgan's foreman was driving the buckboard with Prescott sitting beside him. Addie and the girls were in the back, and the entire way to town no one said a word. Prescott was dropped off at the boardinghouse, and as soon as he walked through the door, the girls asked Addie their many questions.

"I'm not sure what we are going to do, but I will try to keep you here with me," Addie told them. "Let's go to school and try not to worry about this."

Addie had told Granny what Prescott said before they'd left home. Granny told her not to worry since she didn't think Prescott would be successful trying to find someone to accompany the girls to Boston. She was also confident that Prescott wouldn't travel alone with two girls. Addie hoped Granny was right.

"Why does Mr. Adler hate us?" Jane asked.

"Oh, honey, Mr. Adler doesn't hate you. He is doing what he thinks is best for you. He thinks you will have a better chance of being adopted in Boston."

"Then why did he want us to come here?"

"I don't think he understood how isolated some of the small towns are in the West." Addie tried to remain positive for their sake. "Don't ever think someone hates you, because it simply isn't true."

"He's never talked to us like the sheriff. He doesn't even act like he sees us. I don't even think he knows our names," Jane said.

Addie knew it was the truth. "He's a busy man with a lot on his mind." That was the kindest thing she could think to say at the moment. Granny always told her if you had nothing good to say about someone, say nothing.

When Granny returned to the ranch that morning, Morgan and Rose were in the kitchen. She told them that Prescott was insisting the girls return to Boston, and that the orphanage would be closed.

"Why would he do such a thing?" Rose asked.

"Because Addie refused to marry him. Addie thinks he will calm down, but I'm not so sure."

"He didn't take rejection well?" Rose asked.

"He did not," Granny said. "I'm beginning to wonder if Prescott thought the children would be adopted quickly, and then he could take Addie back to Boston. I think he's jealous of the attention she gives the children."

"I know Addie was surprised by his arrival," Rose said.

"If that's the reason he made this decision, I'd say that man doesn't know what he's missing. Those are good children, and any man should be proud to have them. Do you think I should talk to him when we get to town? Perhaps I can persuade him to change his mind," Morgan asked Granny.

"You can try, but judging by his attitude this morning, I doubt he'll want to be reasonable."

"What will he do if someone adopts the children before he leaves town?" Rose asked.

Granny looked at her and smiled. "I was thinking the same thing."

"Doesn't Addie need a husband in order to adopt?" Morgan asked.

"Yes," Granny replied. "But that's not

what Rose was thinking."

Morgan looked at his wife and arched his brow. "Oh?"

"We could adopt them for Addie. When Jack comes to his senses and marries Addie, they can adopt them legally from us."

Morgan wasn't opposed to the idea. "But what if Jack doesn't marry Addie?"

"Then we'd have two more children, and Addie can live here with them."

Morgan glanced from his wife to Granny. "You two seem to have this all worked out."

"Do you see something wrong with the plan?" Granny asked.

"Just one hitch. Clarissa made it clear to Jack the other night that she is interested in marrying him."

"Jack won't marry her, he doesn't love her." Granny knew if Jack loved Clarissa he'd have asked for her hand a long time ago.

Morgan laughed. "That's what he said." Morgan strolled to the back door and reached for his coat and hat. "I need to speak with Joseph, but I'll be back to pick you up."

"Give us enough time to put some sandwiches together for the workers today," Rose said.

"Okay." Morgan walked back and planted

347

a kiss on his wife. "If you are going today, you must promise me you won't be doing too much." He worried about his wife now that she was in the family way.

"Don't worry, Morgan, Rose will only be serving the sandwiches. I'll see to that," Granny said.

"Thanks, Granny. But don't you do too much either." Morgan didn't argue with them about going with him today. As long as Frank was roaming free, he felt more at ease if Rose and Granny were in his sight.

Morgan and Jack had worked on building the jail all day, but they hadn't had a chance to talk. They were working a few feet from each other as they nailed boards for the roof. Morgan hadn't realized it was already time for school to be dismissed until he saw Addie walking toward the mercantile with the girls. He worked his way toward Jack. "Stop working for a minute, I've got something to tell you."

Jack stopped hammering, swiped at the sweat dripping from his brow. "What's that?"

Morgan told Jack what he'd heard from Granny that morning. "Granny said when Addie turned down Prescott's proposal of marriage, he told her he was closing the orphanage and insisted the children be returned to Boston."

"What about Davey?" Jack asked.

"He said Davey was adopted and they wouldn't see him again."

Jack could hardly believe what he was hearing. "Did the girls hear him?"

Morgan nodded. "He said it in front of them during breakfast."

"Now why would he do a fool thing like that?"

"I guess he was angry with Addie."

Angry or not, it made no sense to Jack. "Why would he want to close the orphanage? There's no one better with children than Addie."

"I don't know. When I got to town, I went to the boardinghouse, hoping to talk to Prescott, but he wasn't there. Granny said she didn't think he would listen to reason."

"So Addie said she wasn't going to marry him?" Jack thought most women would jump at the chance to marry a rich man like Prescott Adler.

"That's what Granny said. He told Addie he was catching the next stage back to Boston."

"Too bad the stage won't be here for another three days." Jack wished there was a stage tomorrow to be rid of the scoundrel.

■ ■ ■ ■

Addie and the girls reached the mercantile, and she thought it looked as though the entire population of Whispering Pines had turned out to help. The framework on all three structures was nearly complete. Addie immediately spotted Jack and Morgan at the top of one structure, nailing boards. She looked around for Prescott, but she didn't see him. She thought about walking down to the boardinghouse to speak with him, but she wasn't prepared for another confrontation. Granny and Rose were in front of the mercantile, carrying cups of coffee to the men taking breaks.

Jack and Morgan were still talking when Jack glanced down and saw Claire standing on the sidewalk below, waving at him.

"Papa!"

Jane joined Claire, carrying two cups of coffee. "We brought coffee for you."

As soon as the men reached the ground, Claire wrapped her arms around Jack's legs and started crying.

Jack kneeled down and wrapped one arm around her. "Honey, what's wrong?" From what Morgan told him, he already knew, but he was stalling for time, trying to think of what he could say to calm her down.

Claire mumbled something through her tears, but Jack couldn't understand her. "What are you saying, honey?"

"She said we have to go back to Boston," Jane translated for him.

Jack picked Claire up, pulled his handkerchief from his pocket, and dried her face. "It's cold out here and you don't want your face to freeze."

Claire shook her head. "I won't see you and Davey again. Mr. Adler said so."

Jack looked at Jane, and he saw she was about to cry too. Morgan took the cups of coffee from her, and Jack pulled her to his side. "I'll have a talk with Mr. Adler." He wanted to do much more than talk to Prescott, but he wouldn't say that in front of the girls.

While the children were with Jack, Rose quickly told Addie about the plan to adopt the children. "You can live at the ranch with the children until you are married."

"As Prescott told me, I probably will never receive another offer," Addie said. "What happens then? I can't live with you and Morgan forever."

"Prescott isn't privy to God's plans," Granny said.

"My prospects are not good. Perhaps if I

were more comely —"

Granny placed her fingers to Addie's lips. "Shush. No more of that talk. Your words have power, and you have much more to offer than you are willing to recognize."

"Granny's right, Addie. You are a beautiful woman, and if you can't realize that, then how can you expect Jack to notice you?"

Addie turned to her sister. "Jack? Why did you bring him into this conversation?"

Rose placed her hands on her hips and gave her sister a look that silently conveyed she knew what was on her mind. "I think you know why."

"Rose is right," Granny said. "Addie, it's high time you stopped dressing like an old-maid schoolteacher and started showing off your curves."

"I'm expected to look like an old-maid schoolteacher."

"Nonsense," Granny said.

"The way I look is the least of my worries. I'm not certain Prescott would even let you and Morgan adopt the girls. He would see right through that plan."

"I can tell you one thing, Prescott will not find anyone in this town to take the girls to Boston. I've had all day to put the word out. If he wants them in Boston, he will have to take them with him," Granny said.

"He wouldn't want to be bothered with the children," Addie agreed.

Rose saw Jack and Morgan walking their way with the girls. "We'll talk about this later."

CHAPTER TWENTY-TWO

"We'll be wrapping things up here in the next hour," Morgan said to Rose.

"We'll finish up and be ready to go when you are."

"Jack and I will be back shortly," Morgan said.

"Can I go with you?" Claire asked Jack.

"Not this time. Stay here with Miss Addie." Jack kissed her on top of her head and passed her to Addie.

Jack and Morgan started to walk away, but stopped when they saw Roy Coburn and Davey riding toward the mercantile.

"Davey!" Jane hurried to greet her brother.

Claire squirmed out of Addie's arms and followed her sister.

Davey jumped from the buckboard and hugged his sisters. "I'm so glad to see you."

"We miss you, Davey. Do you like your new home?" Jane asked.

Davey glanced at Mr. Coburn and saw he was watching him. "Yeah."

Jane knew he wasn't telling her the truth.

Addie walked over to Davey and hugged him. "It's so good to see you. I've missed you."

Davey pulled away from her and leaned over to pick up Claire.

Jack noticed Davey's cool reception toward Addie. "How are you doing, Davey?"

"Fine."

"I was hoping you and Mr. Coburn would come into town earlier to help with the building of the hotel," Jack said.

Coburn jumped from the buckboard. "We got our own business to take care of."

"We want you to come home," Claire whispered.

"Boy, go on in the mercantile," Mr. Coburn said when he stepped on the sidewalk. He didn't acknowledge anyone as he passed them to enter the mercantile.

Jane walked in the store with Davey, but knowing Mr. Coburn was listening, she waited to talk to him. Coburn walked to the counter to hand his list of needed supplies to the clerk, and Jane leaned closer to Davey and lowered her voice. "Do you like it there?"

Davey shook his head.

"Mr. Adler is in town and he said we have to go back to Boston. He got mad at Miss Addie and now he's closing the orphanage."

"When do you leave?" Davey asked.

"I think in a few days. He won't wait until the term ends, and I heard Granny say the next stage will be here in three days."

Claire had her arms around Davey's neck and she whispered, "I don't want to go. I don't want to leave you and Miss Addie and Papa."

Jane saw Coburn glance their way. "Shh, Claire."

"This is all Miss Addie's fault," Davey said.

Jane was surprised at her brother for blaming Miss Addie. "No, it's not. Don't you see, Davey, she had no choice but to allow the Coburns to adopt you. And we heard her arguing with Mr. Adler, trying to talk him out of taking us back. I heard her crying all night. Please don't be mean to her."

"I guess you're right." Davey remembered what Jack told him about being angry with everyone when he'd been adopted. Davey knew he was taking his anger out on Miss Addie. Maybe it wasn't really her fault, but he still thought adults didn't really care what happened to them. "You remember what we talked about?" Davey whispered.

Jane looked at him and nodded. "When?"

Davey leaned in and whispered in Jane's ear.

"Boy, put that kid on the ground and carry some of this stuff to the buckboard," Coburn yelled across the room.

Davey put Claire on the ground and said good-bye to his sisters. "Be ready."

"Don't let it upset you," Jack said to Addie once the children walked inside the mercantile.

"Davey's so angry with me." Addie was on the verge of crying. She felt her life was spinning out of control. She wondered if she could have Davey's adoption voided. If the girls had to go back to Boston, at least Davey could go back with them.

"He's just missing everyone," Jack said. "Right now, he's blaming you for the adoption, but he will get over that in time."

Addie looked up at him. "Will he?"

On the way to the boardinghouse, Morgan told Jack about their plan to adopt the girls to keep them in Whispering Pines. "Addie can live at the ranch with them until she marries, and then she can adopt them."

"What did Addie think about this plan?"

Jack liked the idea of the girls staying close to Davey.

"Rose and Granny were going to speak with Addie tonight after the girls go to bed. I guess they'll be staying at the ranch, since Prescott won't be there."

Jack figured he could stay at the orphanage tonight. He no longer had a home or a jail where he could sleep. Of course, Addie might object. "Do you think Prescott would let you adopt them?"

"I don't see why not."

"Unless he's so angry with Addie that he'll use the girls to get back at her."

"Why don't you come to dinner tonight? I'm certain Addie would want to hear what you think about this situation."

Jack wasn't so sure that Addie would want him there, but he cared about the children's welfare. He didn't like the thought of them going back to Boston. He thought about how that would affect Davey. He felt certain Davey would find a way to follow the girls, because that is exactly what he would do if he were in Davey's position. "Dinner sounds good."

"You can spend the night too. Why don't you just plan on moving in until your home is finished?"

"Thanks, I will, because the boardinghouse is packed to the rafters."

As soon as they entered the boarding-house, Morgan spotted Prescott in a chair by the window, reading. "There he is."

They walked across the room and stood in front of him. Prescott looked up from his paper and said, "Gentlemen."

"We'd like to talk to you," Jack said.

Prescott figured Addie probably sent them over to try and persuade him to change his mind. "Unless you've come to tell me Addie has changed her mind, we have nothing to say to each other."

"Look, Prescott, it doesn't make any sense to close the orphanage. Addie is good to those children, and she cares about their welfare," Jack said.

"Jack is right. What happens personally between the two of you shouldn't influence the fate of the orphanage," Morgan said.

"Gentlemen, my business is no concern of yours. But as I told Addie, she is too close to those children, and I think that is the reason they have never been adopted. Not only that, but when I arrived in your town, I learned her brother is an outlaw. I can't see how that would be a positive influence on the children."

"You don't have to worry about that. The judge in Denver disagrees that her brother is an outlaw. He is now a free man," Jack said.

"That was just one of my reasons for closing the orphanage." Prescott snapped his paper as though he was eager to start reading. "Is that all, gentlemen?"

"Do you plan on taking the girls back with you on the next stage?" Morgan asked.

"I've tried to hire someone to accompany them to Boston, but have been unable to find someone suitable. If necessary I will send someone from Boston to come here and travel with them."

Jack knew this wasn't about the girls at all. Prescott wanted to hurt Addie. "This seems like a lot of trouble for two girls when you have too many children in Boston waiting for adoption. Or is your orphanage empty?"

"We take our charges interests to heart and want the best environment for them."

"You didn't seem to care much one way or the other about Davey's environment when you visited the Coburns," Jack countered.

Prescott threw his paper to the side table and stood. "Now see here . . ."

Morgan held up his hand to stall the impending confrontation. "What if a couple would be interested in adopting the two girls before you leave? Would you be agreeable to that?"

Prescott turned his attention on Morgan. "Do you have a respectable couple interested?"

"I believe I do," Morgan answered. "Would you have any objection, since this couple could provide them with a fine home?"

Prescott thought that might be the perfect solution. He could wash his hands of the matter, close the orphanage, and put this entire experience behind him. His parents were the reason he'd come in the first place. They wanted him to marry, and Addie was the only woman he knew that he thought he could control. She hadn't turned out to be as acquiescent as he'd thought. He still had a difficult time believing she'd turned him down. It gave him a sadistic kind of pleasure to close the orphanage, since that seemed to be what she wanted more than anything. "This would have to be done before I leave town." He wasn't going to take the chance Addie would interfere with the adoption once he was gone. He'd seen how she interfered with the boy's adoption.

"I'll get back to you tomorrow," Morgan replied.

■ ■ ■ ■

Addie, Rose, and Granny were loading the buckboard when Clarissa approached.

"It is a shame Jack's home burned down."

Addie turned and looked at her, wondering what she wanted since she was never civil to her.

"I asked Jack if he wanted to stay at my home, since he has no place to stay, but he was worried it wouldn't be appropriate. He's so thoughtful of my reputation."

Addie turned back to arranging the items in the buckboard without comment.

Granny heard what Clarissa had to say. She thought Clarissa was trying to get under Addie's skin. "Jack will be staying with us at the ranch."

"Well, hopefully it won't be for long. Jack and I discussed marriage last night."

"Does that mean we should offer our best wishes?" Rose asked.

Thank goodness for Rose. Addie couldn't have formed a sentence if her life depended on it. Hearing Jack discussed marriage with Clarissa was heartbreaking. Even though she'd suspected his relationship with Clarissa was more important than he'd admitted, it still hurt to have it confirmed.

Clarissa smiled. "After our evening together last night, I expect to be receiving best wishes very soon."

Addie told herself she should be happy for Jack. To really love a person meant you wanted what was best for them. But right now she wasn't feeling very loving. She wanted Clarissa to disappear.

"I was just going to do some shopping, perhaps buy a new dress for our next evening together," Clarissa said.

"That reminds me, I need to make a purchase before I leave. I'll be right back." Granny reached for Clarissa's arm. "I'll walk inside with you."

Later that night, Jack carried Claire to bed and tucked her in. She hadn't left his side since he'd arrived at the ranch. After he'd kissed both girls, he saw Addie standing in the doorway.

"You must be worn out. I'm afraid Claire didn't let you relax for five minutes tonight."

Jack walked to the door and together they walked down the hall. "They're worried about what is going to happen."

"I know. I am too."

Jack thought she sounded exhausted. He stopped walking and turned to face her. "Do you think Prescott is doing this because you turned him down? Or, do you think he really feels it is in the best interest of the children to return to Boston?"

Addie looked up at him. "Yes . . . no, oh, I don't know. Perhaps I am too involved with the children. I couldn't imagine that Prescott would be so cruel as to try to hurt me by using the children."

"Why didn't you agree to marry him?" Morgan told him earlier that she rejected Prescott's offer, and he'd wanted to know the reason.

"Many reasons," she said evasively.

"Like?"

"He wanted me to return to Boston and live there. Even if I married him, he wouldn't adopt the children." These were important reasons to her, but she had other reasons for turning down Prescott's proposal. The main reason was one she couldn't admit to him. Prescott wasn't Jack. No matter how much she tried to deny the fact, Rose was right, Jack was important to her. She told herself it wasn't love. She liked and admired him for so many reasons, and certainly for the kindness he'd shown the children. He didn't seem like the kind of man who'd share his feelings easily, but he'd shown his true heart to the children. She remembered what Clarissa had said that afternoon. Jack had obviously given his heart to her.

Jack noticed she didn't say she didn't love Prescott. "If he agreed to adopt the children, would you marry him?"

Addie turned away and proceeded down the hallway. "It doesn't matter, he'd never agree to that. Prescott wants children, but he wants his own children. We would always disagree over my close relationship with the children."

As they walked down the stairs, Jack said, "Morgan told me that he and Rose are thinking of adopting the children until you marry."

"Yes, but I told them they should consider that I may never marry."

Jack thought Prescott might come to his senses and agree to adopt the children if he really wanted Addie. "I'm sure you'll marry one day."

Addie didn't want to think about never finding a man to love her. "I saw Clarissa at the mercantile today. She said you had a lovely dinner last night."

That was a surprise to Jack. He hadn't seen Clarissa in town today, and in his estimation, their dinner was certainly not *lovely*. After he'd told her he wasn't ready for marriage, he couldn't get out of there fast enough. "Hmm."

Addie didn't think anything odd about his noncommittal response. "I'm sure she'll make a wonderful wife."

Jack didn't know why she was talking about Clarissa. She was the last person he wanted to talk about. "Yeah."

They walked into the kitchen and sat at the table with the others, and Morgan said, "Addie, have you decided you like our plan?"

"My only concern is you may have the children until they are grown."

"Nonsense," Granny said, dismissing the notion Addie wouldn't marry soon.

"Rose, I just want you to consider that possibility before you commit."

Rose leaned over and squeezed her hand. "We considered all possibilities. You and the children are welcome here forever."

"Then it's settled. I'll talk to Prescott and tell him our plans," Morgan said.

"I don't think Prescott thought you were talking about you and Rose adopting the girls," Jack said.

Addie's eyes widened. "You spoke to Prescott about this?"

"We saw him at the boardinghouse, and Morgan mentioned someone may be interested in adopting the girls, but he didn't mention names."

"What reason could he give for refusing us?" Morgan asked.

"None that I can see, but I'm still not convinced he will agree," Jack said.

Addie was of the same opinion. "I don't know what he will do. Prescott told me one reason he was closing the orphanage was because I didn't tell him I had an outlaw for a brother."

"If Prescott doesn't agree, we couldn't very well take it before Judge Stevens, given the circumstances with Frank," Jack said.

Morgan had already thought about that scenario. "Yeah. I can't see Stevens would agree to anything in our favor."

Granny thought she was the only one who was confident the children would stay in Whispering Pines. "One thing is certain; he won't find anyone in Whispering Pines to take the children to Boston. Given that, he may be more inclined to have the girls adopted now instead of waiting for the school term to end to have them returned to Boston."

CHAPTER TWENTY-THREE

Jack and Morgan dropped Addie and the girls off at school the next morning before they rode to the mercantile with Granny and Rose. Their next stop was the boarding-house, where they hoped to speak to Prescott again, but he wasn't there. They rode back to the new jail where they joined Jack's deputy working on the roof.

Webb reached in his pocket and pulled out a telegram. "Sheriff, this arrived a few minutes ago."

Jack read the telegram and looked at Morgan. "It's from Sheriff Trent. Marshal Holt arrived in Denver this morning. He said he'll be there until morning if we want to talk. Says he's chasing Joe Culpepper and Win Taggart."

Morgan thought he recognized the names. "The stagecoach bandits?"

"Yeah. He'll have his hands full if he catches up with them."

Morgan whistled low. "I'll say. They've killed their share." In addition to being robbers, Culpepper and Taggart were well-known cold-blooded killers.

"I guess I'd better ride that way and talk to Holt. I'd like to make sure he hears the story from us." Jack was thankful it was Holt he was going to see. Holt was a decent, honest man who would listen to facts, and the judge wouldn't buffalo him.

"I'll go with you. I want to get the situation with Joseph settled." Morgan didn't want Joseph to feel like he no longer had a home. Joseph was in his seventies, and Morgan didn't think he needed to be roaming the country at this stage in his life.

"What about Prescott?"

"We have a couple more days before he leaves." If Marshal Holt only heard the judge's and Frank's version of the story, Morgan figured he'd be forced to deal with soldiers on his ranch within a week.

"Webb, can you take the women back to the ranch tonight if we aren't back?" Jack asked.

"I sure will. Maybe I'll get a good meal."

"Let's go tell Granny and Rose where we're going," Morgan said.

Jack and Morgan arrived at the sheriff's office in Denver just before lunchtime. As soon as they entered the jail they were surprised to see Judge Stevens and Frank Langtry sitting there talking to Sheriff Trent and Marshal Holt.

Judge Stevens turned to see Jack and Morgan. Realizing they were alone, he slammed his fist on the sheriff's desk. "Where is that renegade I told you to bring to Denver?"

"I don't plan on bringing him to Denver," Morgan replied.

Stevens bristled at Morgan's blatant disregard for his authority. "Sheriff Trent, place this man under arrest."

Sheriff Trent's eyes darted from the judge to Marshal Holt. Trent thought Holt looked stunned by the judge's outburst. "Now, Judge, let's be reasonable."

"You gave us a week," Jack said. "I don't figure the week is up yet."

"Sheriff, you heard me. I've thrown out all charges against Frank. He's a free man." He flailed a finger in Morgan's direction. "This man is the one I want arrested. I want him held in contempt."

Marshal Holt stood and addressed Judge Stevens. "Wait a dang minute, Judge. I want to talk to these men before we do anything rash." Holt had heard of Morgan, and he wanted a chance to find out what was going on before Trent arrested him.

Judge Stevens was not to be second-guessed. "I'm the judge here, and I've instructed you to arrest him, Sheriff Trent."

"Judge, these two aren't going anywhere right now. I'm going to talk to them," Marshal Holt replied. "Now you and Frank go on about your business, and come back here in an hour or so."

"Marshal, if these two aren't here when we get back, I'll have you arrested." Judge Stevens glanced at Frank. "You go on and take Charlotte to lunch. Come by the house when you're done."

Frank grinned at Morgan and Jack as he walked out the door. "I'll see you two later." Frank tried to appear calm, but today was the day of the robbery, and like he was before all of his other robberies, he was twitchy. Knowing what was about to happen made him feel powerful. He knew his boys were already in town, but he'd never expected Jack and Morgan to appear this morning. He told himself it didn't matter, he couldn't call it off now. In his twisted logic, having Jack and Morgan in town made it all the more exciting. He was going to pull off a robbery right under their noses, and they'd never figure out that he was involved. He'd be in the clear.

Frank and the judge walked out of the jail, and Frank said, "Wonder what made them show up this morning?"

"It doesn't matter. You've told me the truth about everything, haven't you, Frank?"

"Yes, sir."

"Good. Now enjoy your lunch," the judge said.

Before Frank walked away, he said, "Judge, I saw Leigh earlier and she said she agreed to have dinner with you tonight."

The judge forgot all about Jack and Morgan. His eyes lit up like a young schoolboy. "Yes, she is, and I have you to thank for that. It looks like she is willing to forgive me. Now, all we need to do is get Charlotte to come around."

"I'm working on it, Judge." Frank felt like laughing. He'd done nothing but encourage Charlotte to harbor bitterness toward the judge's girlfriend. Charlotte's anger was going to be very useful today.

The judge put his arm around Frank's shoulder. "I know you are, my boy. And I won't forget what you have done. Leigh hasn't said as much, but I think you've talked her into forgiving me for not telling Charlotte about her. I plan on spending the night at the hotel. If you don't hear me come home, you know where to find me."

Frank laughed. He'd spent nearly two hours this morning at the little house on the outskirts of town with Leigh. He didn't think she'd let the judge anywhere near her hotel room tonight, or any other night ever again. "She is a beauty."

"I haven't been able to sleep for thinking about her."

"I understand." Frank had had the same problem. Once he split the take from the robbery with the boys, he planned to find a safe spot where he could hole up with Leigh for a few weeks. He'd think of some excuse for his wife and the judge. But, what did it really matter? The judge had dropped the charges against him. He was no longer a wanted man. He was untouchable.

Frank had timed it perfectly. He was escorting Charlotte to lunch, and they were passing the bank at exactly noon. Leigh walked from the bank and intentionally bumped into Charlotte, nearly knocking her to the ground. Charlotte clutched Frank's arm to keep from falling down.

"What do you think you are doing?" Charlotte said indignantly.

"I apologize, I'm afraid I was closing my reticule and wasn't paying attention," Leigh said.

Hat askew, Charlotte looked up to see who had nearly knocked her over. When she saw it was her father's girlfriend, she became enraged. Face now a blotchy red, she lit into her nemesis. "You did that on purpose!"

"I did no such thing. It was an accident. I was just going about my business," Leigh insisted.

"You are trying your best to intervene in my life. I want you to stay away from my father! What business could *you* have in a bank?"

Leigh's chin snapped up a notch and she smirked at the judge's daughter. "Depositing the money your father gives me. And you would be wise to mind your own business."

Charlotte looked her up and down. It enraged her all the more to see this trollop wearing the same cloak she was wearing. There was no way Charlotte was going to share her father, or what would be her rightful inheritance, with such a woman. "My father is my business, and I demand you stay out of his life."

"Your father is going to marry me whether you like it or not. You are just jealous because I'm prettier than you are."

Frank had told Leigh exactly what to wear, and what to say to Charlotte to set in motion a verbal spat guaranteed to create a scene in the middle of the street. And he'd been right, Charlotte was livid and she was losing her composure. Frank watched as people started gathering around the two screeching women, hoping to see a good catfight. He glanced inside the bank and saw Reb lower the shades on the front windows.

"My father will never marry the likes of you."

Leigh placed her hands on her hips and gave Charlotte a look of defiance. "Don't you think I have what your father wants? Or are you too blind? Maybe you can't see with that hat in your eyes." She reached up and snatched Charlotte's hat from her head and tossed it on the ground.

Charlotte's eyes widened at Leigh's insolence. "How dare you!" She slapped Leigh hard across the cheek. "You witch."

Leigh grabbed a handful of Charlotte's hair and tried to pull her to the ground. And the battle was on. The two women were squaring off like two bulls with their horns locked.

Frank didn't attempt to break them apart. His eyes were locked on the bank. He'd told the men how to enter through the back door, and to work fast once they were inside. Their horses were waiting in the trees for a quick getaway. He knew Charlotte and Leigh would draw a crowd when they started arguing, but he'd never expected a physical confrontation. It couldn't have worked out better. They'd been the talk of the town since that night in the restaurant, so he figured this little scene would distract the crowd for a good ten minutes, maybe more.

A shot rang out. Splintering glass crashed to the sidewalk. Frank shot a glance at the bank as he squatted down. Something was going wrong. He'd told them specifically not to fire their guns. "Get down." Frank reached for Leigh's hand to pull her to the ground behind him when another shot sounded like it exploded next to his ear. He glanced at Charlotte, and she was on her knees. Four loud bangs followed in rapid succession, causing people to scramble in all directions, hiding behind whatever they could find. Frank heard some commotion going on inside the bank. He pulled his gun and waited. Suddenly, there was complete silence from the bank, and Frank thought he heard horses in the distance. He waited, eyes on the door of the bank, for what seemed like an eternity.

Hearing footfalls on the wooden sidewalk,

Frank glanced around to see Jack, Morgan, Sheriff Trent, and Marshal Holt running toward him.

"What is going on here?" Sheriff Trent shouted as he approached.

"Shots were fired from the bank," Frank responded.

Jack and Sheriff Trent ran to Frank, and saw Charlotte lying on the ground. When she didn't move, Jack kneeled down and gently turned her over.

Unaware that his wife had been hit, Frank looked down to see what Jack was doing. Charlotte's eyes were closed, and there was blood at the corner of her mouth.

Jack held his forefinger to Charlotte's neck, hoping to feel a pulse. "She's dead." He moved to the judge's girlfriend, who was lying behind Frank. Frank turned around and watched in stunned silence as Jack placed his finger on Leigh's neck.

Frank had been focused on the bank door, and he hadn't realized that both women had been shot. "Leigh!" He dropped his gun, leaned over and shook her. "Leigh, wake up!"

"She's alive. Someone get the doctor," Jack called out. He glanced over at Morgan to see if he was watching Frank. Morgan's gaze met Jack's, silently communicating he was witnessing Frank's unusual behavior.

A clerk ran from the bank. "We've been robbed. Mr. Rivers has been shot."

Sheriff Trent and Marshal Holt ran into the bank.

Sheriff Trent saw the back door standing open. "How many?"

"There were three of them." The clerk pointed to the back door. "They ran out that way."

Sheriff Trent ran through the bank toward the back door. "Let's go!"

Jack and Morgan ran to the back of the bank and caught up with Trent and Holt. They stopped and listened, but they didn't hear anything other than the usual sounds of nature.

"They made a quick getaway," Sheriff Trent said. "Let's get our horses."

When they returned to the bank, they saw one of the clerks attending to the bank president, Mr. Rivers.

Sheriff Trent kneeled beside the clerk. "Can you tell me what they looked like? Did you recognize anyone?"

"No, all three wore masks, and their hats were pulled low. One man was really big."

"Did they get the money?" the sheriff asked.

"Yeah. That's when Mr. Rivers grabbed a

gun in the drawer and started firing."

Sheriff Trent stood and said, "I'm going after them."

"I'll go with you. I doubt this is the work of Culpepper and Taggart, but I've lost their trail anyway," the marshal said.

When they walked outside, they saw the doctor hovering over Leigh. Frank was still by her side, holding on to her hand.

"Did someone go for the judge?" Sheriff Trent asked.

"Yeah, here he comes now," someone in the crowd said.

The judge came running and dropped to his daughter's side. "Charlotte!"

Sheriff Trent placed his hand on the judge's shoulder. "I'm sorry, Judge."

The judge turned to Frank. "Leigh?"

Frank didn't respond, but the doc said, "She's in a bad way, Judge."

"Dear God." He pulled Charlotte into his arms. "My poor baby girl."

"Doc, Mr. Rivers has been shot," Sheriff Trent said.

The doc stood and spoke to some of the men. "Let's get both of them over to my office."

"We're going after them, Judge," Sheriff Trent said.

One of the clerks walked from the bank,

and the judge asked him what had happened. "When the robbers got the money, Mr. Rivers shot at them."

"Did he wound them?"

"I don't think he hit anyone."

"Who shot my daughter and Mrs. King? Did the robbers run out the front shooting?"

The clerk replayed the scene in his mind. "No, the robbers were standing in front of the window, and Mr. Rivers shot at them. He was facing the windows."

The judge could hardly believe what he was hearing. "Rivers shot my daughter?"

"Judge, it was an accident," Sheriff Trent said. "I'm sure Mr. Rivers didn't think where his shot might land in the heat of the moment."

Frank stood with Leigh in his arms. "I'll carry her to the doc's office."

"I'll go with you, Frank." If the judge thought something was odd about Frank carrying Leigh instead of caring for his own deceased wife, he didn't comment. One of the men standing nearby offered to carry Charlotte to the undertaker.

"Morgan, I know you need to get back to the ranch tonight, but I'll ride with them, at least for a few hours," Jack said.

"I'll ride with you to see what direction

they are going," Morgan said. "You know that clerk said one of the men was really big. That could be Dutch Malloy."

"You're thinking Frank has something to do with this," Jack said.

"Yep. You can bet he's neck deep in this."

"What do you make of that scene back there? Frank didn't seem at all concerned that he had a dead wife lying in the street."

Morgan had been as surprised as Jack about Frank's reaction. "I don't know what to think of that. Maybe the judge's girlfriend is Frank's girlfriend too."

"That's possible. Wonder if she knew Frank before she met Judge Stevens?"

"It wouldn't surprise me." Morgan had known Frank too many years to put anything past him.

"It'll be interesting to see what happens between the judge and Frank now that Charlotte is dead."

"The robbers seemed to have picked a bad time to rob this particular bank since there is a U.S. Marshal in town," Morgan said.

"What seems to be an odd coincidence is that Frank, his wife, and the judge's girlfriend were in front of the bank at the same time during the robbery," Jack said.

Morgan gave Jack a steady look. "That's no coincidence."

■ ■ ■ ■

The doc walked from the room where he'd been tending Mr. Rivers and sat beside the judge. "Rivers will be okay. He's awake and talking. He said those men got over forty thousand dollars. I haven't told him about Charlotte or Mrs. King. I don't see a purpose in doing that right now."

Judge Stevens nodded. "What about Leigh?"

"All we can do is wait and see." She'd lost a lot of blood, and the doc was worried she wouldn't survive the operation. Her prognosis was not a good one, but he couldn't bring himself to tell the judge that truth just yet. He didn't think the judge could emotionally handle losing two people in one day.

Frank hadn't left the room while the doc worked on Leigh. "Can she survive losing that much blood?"

"It's in God's hands," the doc replied.

Frank thought his comment sounded like Granny, and he wanted to scream in frustration. Like he'd always told Granny, God didn't care about him, and didn't expect him to care about those around him.

"I haven't told Ruth about Charlotte."

The judge didn't want to leave Leigh's side, but his sister needed to know what had happened.

"I'll go tell her. I'll get you something to eat on my way back," the doc said.

When the doc left, the judge turned to Frank. "Did you see what happened? How did Leigh come to be with you on the sidewalk?"

"I was taking Charlotte to lunch and we were walking by the bank when Leigh came out. The women had words, and I was trying to get Charlotte to leave, but she was angry. They continued to argue, and then the next thing I knew, shots were fired. I knew the shots came from the bank, so I yelled for everyone to get down. I had no idea either one of them had been shot."

"I can't believe my Charlotte is gone," the judge said.

Frank couldn't believe it either. Charlotte had been a convenient way for him to escape the noose, and though he wasn't faithful to her, he hadn't wanted anything to happen to her. Charlotte wasn't an exciting woman, she was safe and predictable. It was different with Leigh. She craved some excitement, and Frank was more than willing to provide all she needed. The risk of being found out by the judge seemed to heighten their passion. When it came right down to it, Frank had to admit that if he had to choose between the two women, Leigh was the one he didn't want to lose.

The judge leaned over and gripped Leigh's hand. "She must survive. I don't think I can go on without her."

Frank wanted her to survive too, but he also had to make some immediate decisions. He was supposed to meet his gang, and he was determined to get to the designated place. If he didn't show, he knew they would take off without him, along with his share of the money. There was no way he would forfeit that money. If the plan had worked out the way he'd intended, Leigh would have been on her way back to Colorado City. Frank planned to meet her there, and together they were going to find a safe place where he could hide out between robberies. Now that Charlotte was dead, he had no reason to come back to Denver other than to keep the judge on his side.

He had to think of a plausible reason to give the judge for leaving town. If Leigh survived, she wouldn't be ready to travel for days, so he'd come back to Denver and wait. Before he left to meet the boys, he knew he had to play the role of the grieving husband, and dutifully bury his wife.

The judge reached over and squeezed Frank's shoulder. "It's so kind of you to wait with me, Frank. I know you are devastated over Charlotte's death."

"I couldn't let you go through this alone, Judge."

Suddenly the door swung open, and Aunt Ruth stormed in. She didn't try to hide her anger when she reached her brother and shook her finger at him. "What are you doing here with this woman when you should be with your daughter?"

CHAPTER TWENTY-FOUR

"They've changed course, now they're headed west," Jack said when the men stopped to allow the horses to rest. Once they'd picked up the trail from the bank, it was obvious they were following four men, not three. "They are headed toward Whispering Pines, so we'll stay with you, Sheriff."

Sheriff Trent was grateful for their help. Four guns were always better than two when chasing outlaws. "Sounds good."

Jack glanced at Morgan. "You don't suppose . . ."

Morgan didn't need to hear the end of his sentence. "Yeah, this is Frank's gang, and it wouldn't surprise me if they were all headed to Purgatory Canyon again."

Jack nodded. That was exactly what he'd been thinking.

Jack explained to Holt and Trent about the last time he'd been in Purgatory Canyon. "That's where they ambushed me."

"I've never tracked anyone there, but I hear the terrain is impossible," Sheriff Trent said.

"You can say that again. There's no good way to get in there without getting picked off," Marshal Holt added.

Since the day he'd been shot in Purgatory Canyon, Jack had given a lot of thought about ways to successfully track outlaws in that widow's nest. He'd never figured out a viable solution. Even Joseph Longbow didn't know how they could enter that canyon without being seen. "I've thought about going in at night, but there are so many men hiding out in there, no route is safe. You can bet Frank Langtry and the other rustlers know that place like the backs of their hands."

"I wonder if Culpepper and Taggart are headed to the same place," Marshal Holt said.

"It wouldn't surprise me," Morgan replied. "It's the perfect place for outlaws to lay low."

"Culpepper and Taggart killed three people on their last hold-up, and two on the one before that. They'll definitely need a place to hide out. Every lawman is on the lookout for them."

Jack had another thought about where the

robbers were headed. In the past, Frank and his gang had used an abandoned cabin for their hideout. All he knew was the cabin was within a day's ride of Whispering Pines, but he'd never been able to pinpoint the exact location. "Frank and his gang hid out in one of the old abandoned homes near Whispering Pines, but I've not found the place."

Marshal Holt had chased outlaws long enough that he understood the difficulty of that undertaking. "There's so many of these old homesteads that it would take forever to find them all."

"Do you think Culpepper and Taggart are familiar with this territory?" Jack asked.

"I don't know, but outlaws have a way of finding like-minded men. I'm sure they've heard of the best places to hide," Marshal Holt said.

Sheriff Trent grabbed his reins. "Let's mount up and see where these hombres are headed. I figure they know they are being tailed by now."

The men followed the winding trail, sometimes heading back south before turning west again. They were about thirty minutes south of Whispering Pines when they rounded a bend and shots rang out. The horses reared at the onslaught of flying bullets. At the same moment, Jack and Marshal Holt fell from their horses. Morgan and Sheriff Trent dove from their horses and attempted to reach their friends as more shots slammed into the earth around them. The exploding melee scattered the frightened horses.

Morgan reached Jack and saw the hole in his coat. "Is Marshal Holt hit?" he yelled to Sheriff Trent.

"Yeah."

Morgan hoisted Jack over his shoulder, and the sheriff did the same with Holt, and they ran for the brush. Once they were out of sight, the shooting came to an abrupt halt. Morgan removed Jack's coat while Sheriff Trent tended the marshal.

"They're riding away," Sheriff Trent said.

"Yeah, sounds like two horses." Morgan found a hole in Jack's left shoulder.

"It hurts like a son of a gun," Jack muttered.

Morgan grimaced as he examined the wound. "I bet it does. I thought you were out." He held his bandana to the wound to staunch the bleeding.

"I was. I think I hit my head." Jack glanced over to see Marshal Holt beside him. "Is he okay?"

"Looks pretty close to his heart." Sheriff

Trent figured all he could do right now was stop the bleeding. He pulled his bandana out and pressed it to the wound.

Morgan stood and looked around to get his bearings. He pointed through the trees, and said, "We are about twenty or thirty minutes that way to the Langtry farm." He glanced at Sheriff Trent, and asked, "Can he make it?"

"He'll have a better chance if we get him to a doctor. I don't think I'm qualified to dig that bullet out." He inclined his head for Morgan to take a look at the marshal's wound.

Morgan agreed with the sheriff's assessment that it was going to take an expert hand to operate. "Granny can do the job." He glanced back at Jack. "Jack, can you make it to the Langtry farm?"

"Yep. Just help me on my horse."

Jack started to sit up, but Morgan held up his hand. "Hold on a minute. I've got to round up the horses."

Prescott made it a point to look for Addie in town after school that day. "I came to tell you that I've found someone who will accompany me and the girls to Boston. Please have them ready to depart in two days."

"What do you mean?"

"The girls will be leaving with me. I trust you will bring the girls to town in a timely manner."

The girls started crying, and Addie felt like smacking Prescott for his insensitivity. Addie gripped his arm and pulled him to the side so the girls couldn't hear her conversation. "Didn't Morgan mention someone may be interested in adopting?" She hadn't mentioned the adoption plan to the girls, just in case something went wrong.

"I've decided this is a scheme of your doing, and I want no part of that. The girls are going back to Boston. On my way over here I happened to see Mr. Coburn, and I told him there will be no further contact from you." Prescott had no intention of changing his mind.

"Prescott, I wish you would reconsider closing the orphanage." Addie was near tears, but she tried to maintain her poise because she knew the girls were watching her.

"I'm afraid that won't be possible."

Granny walked up at that moment to see the girls crying. "What's this? Why are you two crying?"

"Mr. Adler says we have to go back with him," Jane said.

Addie walked back to Granny and the

girls. "I'm afraid Prescott found someone to accompany him and the girls."

Granny turned her attention on Prescott. "Who is this person willing to travel with you?"

"I think you know her. Miss Clarissa Martin, a lovely young woman. I think the sheriff introduced us. When she came to see me last night she said she'd heard I was looking for a chaperone for the girls and offered her services for a fair price."

"I just bet she did," Granny said. She didn't understand why Clarissa would agree to do such a thing, but she intended to find out.

Addie could hardly believe her ears. Clarissa, of all people, was the one to do something so underhanded. But for what purpose? She was going to marry Jack. Certainly Jack had no hand in this. He was devastated at the thought of the girls returning to Boston.

"Mr. Adler, I'll tell you the same thing my mother always told me. Don't count your chickens before they hatch," Granny said.

Prescott tipped his hat. "Addie, have these girls here in two days."

Morgan opened the back door to the orphanage and eased Jack down on a kitchen chair. He walked back outside to help Sheriff Trent carry the marshal. They carried him to one of the bedrooms upstairs and Morgan came back downstairs to help Jack.

"I'll stay in the bedroom to the right," Jack said to Morgan after they made it to the top of the staircase.

Morgan held on to Jack as he opened the bedroom door. Once they were across the threshold, Morgan stopped and looked around the room. He grinned at Jack. "Guess you haven't lost as much blood as I thought."

"I didn't think I could make it any further," Jack said.

Morgan chuckled. "You can save the sympathy act for Addie. You might get a hole in your head when she gets home." Morgan helped Jack to the bed and removed his coat and boots. Jack may have been joking, but Morgan didn't like the way he looked. "I'll go get Granny."

Morgan walked to the bedroom where Sheriff Trent was removing the marshal's boots. "If you'll get some water boiling, I'll ride to the ranch to get Granny."

Morgan ran through the front door of his home and didn't stop until he was in the kitchen. "Granny, I need you to go to the farm with me. Jack's been shot, along with a U.S. Marshal." He realized the women and the girls were sitting at the table crying. "What's wrong?"

Addie jumped up. "Jack's been shot?"

With tears running down her cheeks, Claire looked at Morgan. "Papa's shot?"

Morgan lifted her into his arms. "Yes, honey, but he's going to be okay." He glanced at Granny. "The marshal is very serious, we need to leave now."

Granny hurried from the room to grab her medical bag. "Get Joseph."

Addie grabbed their coats and ran to Morgan's side to get Claire. "What happened?"

"I'll explain later." He headed for the back door. "Rose, get what you need to spend the night. I've got to hitch the buckboard."

"Where's Joseph?" Granny asked once they were all in the buckboard.

"No one knows. He may be in the woods, expecting the worst outcome from our trip to Denver." Morgan had been honest with Joseph, and while he didn't tell him to leave, they understood what he needed to do until this whole situation with Frank was at an end.

Within minutes Morgan pulled the buckboard to the farmhouse, and as soon as

Addie jumped from the buckboard, she said, "Where's Jack?"

"First room on the right." Morgan lifted Granny from the buckboard and picked up her medical bag. Once inside, he basically carried Granny up the staircase with Addie following him. Rose took the children to the kitchen to fetch the things Granny would need.

Addie reached her room and when she walked in, it jarred her to see Jack in her bed. The big, strong sheriff, with a gun on his hip, lying on top of her white eiderdown quilt with hand-embroidered pink cabbage roses. If ever anyone looked out of place, it was Jack. When she leaned over him, he stared at her with those dark silver eyes.

"Your bed is comfortable," he said, smiling at her.

She noticed his big body took up most of the bed.

Relief washed over her seeing him smile. "If you bleed on that quilt, I'll shoot you again."

Claire ran into the bedroom as fast as her little legs would carry her. She crawled beside Jack on the bed. "Papa, are you hurt?"

Removing his arm from behind his head, he pulled Claire to his side. "Nothing for you to worry about, honey."

Jane joined her sister on the bed. "Mr. Le-Masters said you were shot."

"Yep, I'm afraid I forgot to duck. Miss Addie is a little late if she wants to shoot me." Jack arched a brow at Addie. "Would you really shoot a man for bleeding on your bed?"

Addie felt like shooting him because she'd been scared out of her wits before she saw him. She'd imagined all sorts of horrible things, like seeing him near death when Morgan said he'd been shot. "Yes."

Jack gave her a lopsided grin. "Well, somebody beat you to it."

Like the girls, when Addie saw the blood on his shirt, she felt like crying. "Let me have a look."

"Morgan put his bandana over it to stop the bleeding."

Addie had a feeling Jack's wound was more serious than he was letting on. She didn't want the girls to see a gunshot wound and become more upset. "Girls, would you go back downstairs and tell Rose we need some water and bandages."

Claire held on to Jack, ignoring Jane's attempt to move her from the bed.

Jack winked at her. "Go ahead and do as Miss Addie says. I'll be right here waiting to see you later."

Claire crawled higher so she could kiss his cheek.

"Thank you, honey. That makes me feel a whole lot better."

"We have to leave," Jane said.

"Just for a little while. You can visit with me later." Jack wanted to assure them that he was going to be okay.

"I mean in two days we have to go with Mr. Adler," Jane clarified.

Jack's eyes snapped to Addie. "What does that mean?"

Addie shooed the children from the room. "I'll explain after we've taken care of you." Since his shirt was already unbuttoned, Addie gently pushed it aside and removed the bandana. It was the first time she'd seen a gunshot wound, and she thought she might pass out seeing the ugly bloody hole in his shoulder.

Jack was watching her face, and she visibly paled when she looked at his shoulder. "Miss Addie, remind me not to let you play a game of poker if my life depends on it."

She gave him a quizzical look. "What?"

"By the look on your face, I'd say I'm about to die, or you've never seen a gunshot wound before. Believe me, it's not as bad as the last time."

Taking a deep breath to calm her nerves, Addie made a mental note of everything she needed to do. "Let's get you out of your clothes."

Jack grinned. "Yes, ma'am."

Addie turned a nice shade of pink. "I mean your shirt." She leaned over to help him with his shirt, but Jack swung his legs over the side of the bed.

"Take off your pretty quilt. When Granny gets in here and starts digging on me, she'll have me bleeding out."

"I was only teasing about the quilt." Addie felt guilty that he was worrying about such minor things when he was obviously in a lot of pain.

"I'm not. Granny likes to make me suffer."

Taking a handful of the quilt, Addie jerked it from the bed and tossed it on a chair. "Now sit back down." She gently removed his shirt, fluffed two pillows, and stuffed them behind him before he leaned back.

Jack fumbled with his holster and Addie pushed his hands aside. "Let me do it." She'd never removed a holster before, and she thought it seemed almost too intimate a task for her to be doing. When she finished unfastening the holster, she glanced up at him and saw he was watching her every move. Their eyes held, and her fingers stilled.

"I'll lift my hips if you can pull it out."

Addie nodded.

Once she placed his holster aside, she held the bandana back over the wound. His darkly tanned face looked pale to her and she thought he might have a fever. She brushed a lock of blond hair from his forehead and felt his skin. She was so close she could see the darker silver streaks in his eyes. "You feel warm."

"Your hand feels cool." Jack fixed his eyes on hers. If he hadn't been in so much pain, he might have attempted to give her a kiss. "What was Jane talking about? Are you going back to Boston?"

"We'll talk about it later. Right now, I need to clean your wound."

She started to walk away, but Jack reached for her hand and held her in place. "Tell me now."

"Prescott told us today that he will not allow anyone to adopt them here. He's taking them with him to Boston."

"Granny said no one would go with him. Are you going with him?"

Addie looked away. "No, but he found someone."

"Who?" He couldn't imagine why anyone

would be willing to travel with Prescott.

Rose walked into the room with a bowl of water and some bandages. "Granny said to tell you she would be here in a few minutes." She glanced at Jack and saw he was holding Addie's hand. "Is something wrong?"

"No." Jack released her hand and Addie took the bowl of water from Rose and placed it on the bedside table.

"How's the marshal?" Jack asked.

"Granny got the slug out, but he's not regained consciousness." Rose gave Addie the bar of soap. "She said for us to get you ready."

"Where are the girls?" Addie asked.

"They are sitting in the hallway. I asked Jane to read to Claire to keep them from worrying."

Addie dipped the cloth in the water and started washing Jack's shoulder. "Is the water too warm?"

"No, it feels good." Jack was exhausted, but he didn't want to shut his eyes. He wanted to know what was going on, and he liked watching Addie take care of him.

Addie finished cleaning the wound before she started washing the blood from his chest hair. She'd never before washed a man's body and she found herself getting flustered under Jack's penetrating stare. "Am I hurting you?"

"No, ma'am." He found that her tender ministrations aroused sensations that made no sense under his present circumstances.

Rose left the room under the pretense of seeing if Granny needed her help, but she wanted to give them time alone. Watching them together, Rose thought there were some deep feelings between the two. She was equally sure neither one would admit as much.

"It feels good." At his statement, Addie looked at him, and saw him watching her hand on his chest.

It thrilled her to be caring for him instead of Clarissa. He might want Clarissa, but Clarissa wasn't here. She felt a pang of guilt thinking about her personal desires and not his. He might want Clarissa to know he'd been shot. Of course that would mean Clarissa would come to her home to see him, and that didn't sit well with Addie. It would have been difficult enough seeing Clarissa with Jack in her own home, but after hearing she'd agreed to take the girls to Boston, she didn't think she could tolerate having her there.

"Don't stop," Jack said when Addie's hand stopped moving. His mind was no longer on his pain, and he wanted more than anything to kiss her. He was just about ready to pull her to him, when she said, "Do you want me to send someone for Clarissa?"

Jack frowned at her question. "Clarissa? Why would I want you to do that?"

CHAPTER TWENTY-FIVE

"Jack Roper, can't you find something better to do than get shot?" Granny hurried across the room and placed her medical bag on the bed.

"It's the only way I can get you to feed me." Jack's eyes were still on Addie when Granny pulled out her instruments and started digging in his shoulder.

"Well, I'm glad no one has tried to pull this one out before I got my hands on you. It's not going to be as bad as the last time." Granny turned to Addie and said, "Honey, pull out that whiskey bottle from my bag and give Jack a glassful."

Addie quickly followed Granny's instructions and filled a glass to the brim for Jack.

"Drink it down and be quick about it. We need to get this out before it grows to you. I don't know why I bother digging these out, you'll just get shot again next week. I think you need to find yourself a new profession."

Remembering the last time she operated on Jack, Granny had been worried to death about him the whole time she was tending him.

"Aww, Granny, you know you like taking care of me." Jack finished the whiskey under Granny's watchful eye. "Is the marshal going to make it?"

"By the grace of God, he might."

Addie placed the bandages next to Jack's side, and Jack reached for her hand. "Will you hold my hand while Granny uses her instruments of torture on me?"

Granny looked at him and laughed. "You're a sorry case, Jack Roper. Who held your hand the last time?"

"You spent so long digging in my shoulder that I passed out. Don't you remember that? I thought doctoring was supposed to be a caring profession."

Addie sat beside Jack and intertwined her fingers with his. "Are you in a lot of pain now?"

Jack nodded.

Granny shook her head at him. She didn't doubt he was in some pain, but he was playing it to the hilt for Addie's sympathy. "Are you ready?"

Jack squeezed Addie's fingers. "Yep, I am now."

"Addie, there is going to be some more bleeding. You aren't squeamish, are you?" Granny didn't want to worry about Addie passing out while she was in the middle of her surgery.

Addie had always tried to stay calm in difficult situations, but her feelings for Jack were making it difficult to maintain her composure. She was the same way with the children. It broke her heart to see them in pain. She looked at the instrument in Granny's hand and shivered. "I'll be fine, Granny."

Granny cast her a glance and noticed she was paler than Jack. "If you feel faint, let me know."

Dabbing his wound one more time with a cloth, Granny got to work. To Addie's amazement, Jack didn't move a muscle as Granny dug into his shoulder. She was the one squeezing Jack's hand each time Granny pushed her device deeper into his flesh.

Jack couldn't take his eyes off of Addie's face. She was grimacing as though she was the one on the receiving end of Granny's surgical procedure. "You okay, Miss Addie?"

Addie looked at him and tears formed in her eyes. "Doesn't that hurt?"

Jack gave her a grin. "My fingers you're squeezing hurt worse than that hole in my shoulder."

Addie loosened her death grip on his hand. "I'm sorry."

"Miss Addie, I think you are my angel, sent to watch over me. Are you sure you're not going back to Boston?" Jack reached up with the intention of pulling Addie to him, but Granny slapped her hand on his chest.

"If you don't hold still, Jack Roper, I'll leave this slug in you. You're so full of nonsense, it'd serve you right."

"I think he's feeling the effects of the whiskey, Granny," Addie said in Jack's defense.

"Well, pour him another large glassful. Maybe it will knock him out. With him moving about, I can't get ahold of this thing."

Addie grabbed the bottle and poured another full glass and handed it to Jack.

"Maybe you need a shot, Granny, to steady your nerves," Jack said, noticeably slurring his words.

Granny glared at him. "There's nothing wrong with my nerves. I just need you to settle down."

"Stop giving me your evil eye, or I'll need more whiskey to settle down. I always thought you only carried the devil's tools in that little bag. I didn't know you had good whiskey in there."

Granny chuckled at his nonsense. "You're a sorry case, Jack Roper."

He placed the empty glass beside him on the bed and reached for Addie's hand. "Miss Addie, you're my pretty angel." Seconds later, he passed out.

"Thank the good Lord." Granny expelled a loud breath and went to work. She had the bullet out quickly, then stitched him up.

"Will he be okay, Granny?" Addie had been afraid to ask while Jack was awake. She knew he'd never tell her how badly he was hurting.

"He'll be fine, honey. Jack's a strong man, and I wish I could say this is the last time this will happen to him. I know you care for him, so you'll have to accept what he does."

Addie didn't deny her feelings. "He's a special man."

"Yes, he is. Now let's get him bandaged, then I'll have Morgan come in and take his pants off so he can get comfortable. He's going to be here for a few days, recuperating."

Morgan removed Jack's clothing and sat with him while Addie and Rose cooked dinner. Once the children were fed and bathed, Addie allowed them to see Jack, but she wouldn't allow them to wake him. She watched as they softly climbed on the bed and tenderly kissed his cheek.

Addie didn't scold Claire for calling him papa when she told him good night, but gave her a gentle reminder. "Sheriff Roper is going to be fine. He'll need a few days to recuperate, but he will be back to normal in no time."

Claire didn't respond. She climbed from the bed and walked to the door with her head hanging down.

"I'll read you a story before you go to sleep." By the time Addie returned to her bedroom to check on Jack, he was still sleeping. Granny was sitting in the chair, and Addie asked her again if she was certain he would recover.

"Now don't you worry about him, he's going to be fine. We all best be praying for the marshal tonight." She kissed Addie's cheek and said good night.

Jack awoke in the middle of the night to see Addie, wrapped in a blanket, sitting in a chair beside his bed. She was asleep, and while he wanted a drink of water, he didn't want to disturb her. She had dark circles under her eyes, and he knew she'd had an exhausting day. He saw a pitcher of water and a glass on the bedside table, so he leaned over, hoping he could reach the pitcher. He nearly fell out of the bed when two heads popped up beside the table. Jane and Claire.

"What are you two doing down there on the floor?" Jack whispered.

"Miss Addie was sleeping in here, and we wanted to make sure you were going to be okay," Jane answered.

Their concern touched Jack's heart, and it was a few moments before he could say anything for fear of becoming emotional. He noticed they were both wrapped in blankets, and he wondered if they were cold. "Jane, would you pour me a glass of water?"

Quietly, Jane untangled herself from her blanket and poured him a glass of water.

"Are you still hurt?" Claire whispered.

"I'm much better now. Why don't you girls jump in on the other side so you can stay warm?" He'd noticed someone had started a fire in the fireplace, but it was about to go out.

The girls quickly jumped in the bed beside him, and he motioned for Jane to pull one of the quilts over them. "You girls get some sleep. I'm just fine." He didn't have long to wait before the girls were sleeping soundly beside him. *All of my girls are sleeping.* He'd started thinking of Addie and the girls as *his girls* the first night he'd stayed all night with them. He'd often wondered how it would feel to be a father, and as he looked at their sweet, innocent faces, he couldn't imagine a more rewarding feeling. He had to find a way to keep Prescott from taking them back to Boston. But how in the devil was he going to do that?

Jack was still thinking about the situation with the children over an hour later when Addie opened her eyes. "Hello," he said softly.

Addie's eyes swept over the children lying beside him and she smiled. "Hello." She straightened in the chair and leaned closer to the bed. "How long have they been in here?"

"I don't know for sure. They were on the floor when I woke up, so I told them to climb in. I didn't want them getting cold."

"Can I get you anything?" Addie asked.

"Jane gave me a glass of water. That'll hold me over until breakfast."

"How do you feel?"

"Fine. You look tired."

"It's been a long day." Addie hadn't been able to sleep much the night before, and it had been an emotional day.

Jack glanced at the girls, then back at Addie. "You want to join us?"

Addie thought the girls looked very comfortable next to him, and she had to admit it was tempting. She imagined sleeping next to a man like Jack would be comforting. He had a way of making them feel safe and secure. She wondered what his fiancée would think about that. "I'd better not."

"I think it's time you told me who is going to Boston with Prescott."

She hated to say something that would upset him, but he had a right to know. "Your fiancée is going with him."

"Who?"

"Your fiancée, Clarissa."

Jack expelled a loud breath, and when Claire moved, he kept his eyes on her until she settled down again. He didn't know what was more infuriating: the fact that Addie wouldn't accept that Clarissa wasn't his fiancée, or that Clarissa would agree to take the girls back to Boston. What reason would she have for doing such a thing? He'd deal with both issues. "What do I have to say to make you believe me? Clarissa is not my fiancée."

Addie was puzzled. Clarissa had just told her that a wedding was imminent. "I don't understand. We saw Clarissa in front of the mercantile and she said you were getting married."

"She told you we were getting married?" Jack forgot to whisper the question and both girls moved.

Addie tried to remember Clarissa's exact words. She clearly recalled Clarissa intentionally wanted them to think she was marrying Jack. "I'm not sure of her exact words, but she definitely said you two discussed marriage and one would be forthcoming."

Jack reminded himself to keep his voice low. "We did discuss marriage, but I told her I wasn't interested."

"You aren't marrying Clarissa?"

"No."

"Are you sure she understood? I think she believes otherwise."

"She understood, all right." Jack had no question in his mind that Clarissa knew where he stood on that subject.

"Do you think she agreed to take the girls to Boston because she's angry with you?" Addie could think of no other reason Clarissa would do such a thing.

Jack had no doubt Clarissa made this decision to hurt him as much as Addie. He'd defended Addie on more than one occasion, and Clarissa didn't like it. "She was pretty upset with me."

In a way, Addie felt some sympathy for Clarissa. She had to be disappointed by Jack's refusal. Yet, she couldn't understand anyone who would try to hurt others over their own personal disappointments.

Jack certainly hadn't mentioned to Clarissa that Prescott was looking for someone to accompany him to Boston. "How did she even know Prescott was looking for someone to go to Boston?"

"I don't know. I'm going to try to talk to him again, and Morgan says he will try again. I just can't let him take the girls back. They are heartbroken over this. Prescott also talked to Mr. Coburn, so Davey has to know about the girls by now."

"Poor Davey. I know he feels everyone has deserted him right now." Jack knew Davey was having a hard enough time dealing with his new family, and this news would only make matters worse.

The girls seemed restless, so Jack and Addie stopped talking and they also fell back to sleep. When Jack awoke again, the girls were gone and Addie was placing a tray of food on the bed.

"Good morning." Jack tried to pull himself into a sitting position.

Addie hurried to the other side of the bed. "Let me help you." She grabbed the pillow from the chair and placed it behind him.

"You better stop taking such good care of me, or I may never get out of your bed." He was teasing her, but he had to admit he enjoyed being in her bedroom. He'd studied the room last night while Addie was sleeping. It was hard to believe how nice she'd made the room in such a short period of time. He'd been in women's bedrooms before, but this one seemed to tell the story of the woman who occupied the space. It was warm and inviting with the typical fussy feminine doodads; intricately embroidered pillows were on the bed and chairs, and lace curtains covered the windows. Multicolored little glass containers, along with two large oil lamps with half-moons and stars etched on the blue glass chimneys decorated the long bureau. The hand-hooked rug by the bed was designed with colorful butterflies and birds. But it was the handmade cross-stitch wall-hanging over the fireplace that he'd read over and over. *Home is where love begins.* He wondered if these things had been made for her trousseau. She'd said she didn't think she would ever marry, but it had been his experience all women had a trousseau ready and waiting for that special day. Addie had a lot of love to give, and if she ever married, her husband would be one lucky man.

"You're welcome to stay as long as you need," Addie said, pulling him from his daydreaming as she placed the tray of food on his lap. She glanced at his bare chest, and again, she couldn't get over his massive size.

"Don't let Granny hear you say that, she'll make me stay a month." He saw her staring at his chest. "Is something wrong?"

She looked up and realized by his grin that he'd caught her staring. "No. I was just thinking we'll need to change your bandage soon."

He didn't think she had it in her, but Miss Addie had just told a little white lie. "Is that what you were thinking?"

"Hmm." Addie wasn't going to respond to his question.

"I think you were liking the looks of me," Jack teased as he popped a freshly made biscuit in his mouth.

He was impossible with his teasing. "No, I was thinking that my bed is much too small for you. Your feet are hanging off the end of the bed."

"I guess if I stay here, I'll have to get a new one."

Addie, flustered by that comment, changed the subject. "Granny says you'll be up and around in a few days."

Jack turned serious. "I'll be leaving today. I want to talk to Prescott."

"Oh no you won't, Jack Roper," Granny

said, barging into the room. "I've already told Morgan if you try to leave, he has my permission to shoot you."

"I've got business to take care of." Jack wasn't going to let Prescott get on that stage tomorrow without talking to him first.

"Morgan will attend to your business for you. No arguing." Granny stood over him, all five feet, ninety pounds of her, puffed up like a mother goose. "I don't intend to waste my doctoring skills on a man who refuses to listen."

"How's the marshal?" Jack asked, ignoring her lecture.

"He made it through the night, and that is a blessing."

"Granny, I will be dismissing class early today. I intend to take the girls to see Davey." Addie would have cancelled school today if she'd had a way of giving the students advance notice. As it was, it might be the last chance for the girls to see their brother before they left for Boston. She didn't think anything she or Morgan said to Prescott would change his mind. She had no legal way to stop Prescott from taking them, but she could do this one last thing for them. They were so upset that they certainly wouldn't be able to concentrate in school. She wouldn't object if they wanted to spend the night beside Jack again. Tonight would be their night to do what they wanted.

"I'm glad you're taking them to see Davey. It's a sad day for everyone." Granny glanced at Jack, and said, "Sheriff Trent will be leaving this morning. He has to get back to Denver, and Morgan told him he'll send word about the marshal's progress." She turned to leave, and said, "I'll be back after you finish your breakfast so we can change that bandage." Before she left the room, she grabbed Jack's clothes from one of the chairs.

"Leave me my dang holster," Jack grumbled.

Granny carried the holster to the bed and hung it over the post. "I don't guess you'll be going anywhere in your present state."

"You're getting mean in your old age," Jack muttered as she walked out the door.

"I heard that."

Jack turned his attention back on Addie. "Is one of Morgan's men taking you to school?"

"Yes, Morgan is working on the hotel today and will bring me home when I'm ready."

Jack wanted to go with her, but Granny made certain he was staying put. "Make

417

sure he goes with you to Coburn's. And tell Davey when I can ride, I'll be over to see him."

Addie didn't respond because the girls came running into the room to say good-bye to Jack.

CHAPTER TWENTY-SIX

Frank, Judge Stevens, and Aunt Ruth stood side-by-side over Charlotte's grave after everyone had walked away. There was nothing left to say; nothing would change what had happened.

Aunt Ruth wiped her tears away and turned to leave. "You two come home for lunch."

Frank caught up with her and took her elbow in his hand. "Aunt Ruth, I'm going to leave for a day. I need some time to myself."

Aunt Ruth patted his hand. "I understand. You haven't had a moment alone since this happened." She looked at her brother. "You come home, Robert. You've been with *that woman* long enough. It's time you considered Charlotte's memory."

Judge Stevens was never one to take orders. "It's time you faced the fact that I intend to marry Leigh if she survives. And this morning the doctor said he is confident she will live."

"What are you thinking, Robert? You can't possibly marry that woman." Ruth thought her brother had taken leave of his senses. He was much too old to behave like a besotted fool over some young woman.

"Ruth, I've lived my life for everyone else. First for my wife, then Charlotte. I'm living for myself now. I've found happiness and I intend to enjoy the rest of my life. If you can't accept that, I'm sorry. But this is the last time I'm going to discuss this."

"Robert, you are going to have your heart broken. People will say you are trying to replace Charlotte."

"Do you think I care what people say? Like I said, I'm through discussing this. Now I'm going back to the doc's office."

Ruth turned to Frank when Robert walked away. "He was never one to listen to me." She placed her hand on his chest and softly patted him in a comforting gesture. "I know you need some time right now. But just remember you have a home here. If you are of a mind, you also have a job. I'd prefer family to run the mine, and you're family even if Charlotte is gone."

"I appreciate that, Aunt Ruth, but I don't know what I'm going to do right now. I need to do some thinking." Frank knew if he wanted to give up his outlaw ways, this was the perfect opportunity. But the kind of life Aunt Ruth was offering wasn't for him. He thought of Leigh. One of the reasons he was drawn to her was because of her need for excitement. Frank understood that need. Charlotte would have been happy with a husband and children, living a humdrum life. The thrill of his outlaw ways was as important to his survival as air.

"Take care, Frank. Oh, I forgot to mention, I told the bank to put some money in your account. It is in your name now that Charlotte is gone." She patted his hand again, and said, "I will see you later."

"Thank you, Aunt Ruth." He thought it was kind of her to put some money in the bank for him, but his share of the robbery was a nice tidy sum. He leaned down and kissed her on the cheek. "You are so good to me."

"Come back," Ruth said.

He hurried to the livery to get his horse. He was meeting his gang on the outskirts of Whispering Pines, but he couldn't take the trail, so that meant it would take twice as long to get there.

Reining in at one of the old abandoned

homes several miles south of Whispering Pines, Frank whistled to let the boys know he was there. All four men ambled from the brush with guns drawn.

"Who were you expecting?" Frank asked as he led his horse to the back of the shed.

"We were followed for hours, but I don't know what happened to them," Reb said.

"I saw Sheriff Trent riding into town as I was leaving." Frank had wondered why he'd returned alone. "Trent, that U.S. Marshal, Jack Roper, and LeMasters were the ones tailing you. But Trent came back without them."

"We figured we lost them sometime yesterday," Dutch said.

"Yeah, but we did hear some shots in the distance," Deke added.

"I didn't see anyone on the way here. I was off the trail, but I was careful." Frank was glad they found this old shack instead of returning to the old Conner place. He had a feeling Jack Roper may have already found that hideout.

"What happened inside that bank?" Frank listened to their side of the story as he unsaddled his horse.

"Reb shot that man in the bank," Deke said.

"He was shooting at me, I had no choice,"

Reb responded.

"He's not dead. But it looks like one of his bullets hit my wife," Frank told them.

"I'm sorry, Frank. Is she all right?" Reb felt bad about the shooting, but it was either shoot back or get shot.

"She's dead."

The men looked at each other. They didn't know how Frank was going to react.

"Frank, I'm real sorry about that. I knew his shots missed me, but I didn't know they hit anybody."

"Yeah. Those bullets hit my wife and Leigh," Frank said.

"Who's Leigh?" Deke asked.

"The judge's girlfriend."

Reb was more nervous hearing that he'd shot that woman. Frank seemed to care about her, at least more than his wife. "Is she dead too?"

"No, but she's in a bad way."

"I hope she'll be okay, Frank. I'm really sorry." Reb didn't want Frank to exact revenge on him over something that wasn't his fault.

"Me too." Frank turned to walk inside the house. "Let's go talk business."

Once inside, Frank reached into his saddlebags and pulled out some whiskey. "I thought you boys might be running low."

Corbin took one bottle and poured them all a healthy portion. "Here's to bank robbing."

After they downed their whiskey, Frank asked, "Now how much money did you get?"

Dutch walked across the room and picked up the bank bags. "Forty-three thousand two hundred dollars."

Frank was glad to hear they didn't try to cheat him. He already knew they had forty thousand dollars.

"How much do we get?" Corbin asked.

"Didn't you learn your numbers in school?" Reb had only made it to the ninth grade, but he'd already calculated his share.

"I didn't go to no school," Corbin said. "My pa kept us six kids at home to help on the farm."

Frank figured that explained many things about Corbin. "Corbin, that means you get a little over two thousand dollars."

Corbin smiled wide. "That'll buy me a lot of whiskey."

Frank slapped him on the back. "It sure will. Not bad for just holding on to the horses while the other men got shot at." Frank tossed the bags next to the table. "We'll count it out later." He looked around the room and said, "What do you have to eat?"

After they ate, Frank looked at Corbin and asked if he would stake the horses so they could graze. While Corbin was outside, Frank split the money, less Corbin's two thousand dollars.

"I hope Corbin never figures this out," Deke said.

"You don't have to worry about that. Corbin has never been too bright." Frank stuffed his share of the money in his saddlebags. "I'll be headed back to Denver in the morning."

"How come you're going back there? I thought you were coming with us," Reb asked.

"After what's happened, I think I need to stay there for a few weeks. I want to make sure they don't suspect I was involved."

Since they each had their money, it didn't matter if Frank returned to Denver. "You'll know where to find us," Dutch said.

"I'll be there. I don't know when yet, but I'll be there."

They drank whiskey and talked about how they were going to spend their money, until well past midnight. Finally, they all drifted off to sleep with the promise of good times ahead.

A few hours later the door to their cabin opened quietly.

"Well, I'll be, they're all sleeping like babies, Win." Joe Culpepper and Win Taggart were standing inside the cabin with their pistols drawn. The fire was barely flickering in the hearth, but there was enough light for them to see the five men sleeping on the floor. They'd waited outside for over an hour until they were confident the men inside were asleep.

Taggart saw a holster hanging over a chair, so he threw it over his shoulder. Culpepper collected three holsters lying beside the men and placed them on the table. That left one man who was still wearing his holster.

Culpepper picked up a whiskey bottle off the table, took a drink, and passed it to Taggart.

"From the looks of it, I think we're gonna have to wake these sweethearts up," Culpepper said.

Taggart kicked a chair and it skittered noisily across the plank floor. The men on the floor stirred, but were still so inebriated that it barely registered that they weren't alone.

Frank opened his eyes, wondering what had awakened him. He sat up and saw a chair on its side in the corner of the room.

He scrubbed his eyes and ran his palm over his face. "Who kicked that chair?"

"I did," Taggart answered.

Frank glanced up and saw the two strangers. He went for his gun, but it wasn't on his hip.

Culpepper grinned, and motioned to the stack of holsters on the table. "I think you forgot something."

The other men were slowly moving into a sitting position. Frank glanced at them and saw Reb was the only one still heeled.

"What's going on?" Dutch asked in a deep growl.

"We've got company," Frank replied.

Corbin squinted at the two men. "Who are you?"

"Win, maybe we should introduce ourselves," Culpepper said.

"First, I think they need to tell us why that U.S. Marshal was chasing them," Taggart said.

"Now that's a fine idea." Culpepper directed his pistol at Frank. "Why don't you start talking?"

"I don't know what you're talking about," Frank said.

"Want me to shoot him?" Taggart asked.

"Not yet. Maybe one of the other hombres

can tell us." Culpepper pointed his gun at Deke.

Deke didn't like the looks of these two, and he wasn't about to tell them about the robbery. "We didn't know anyone was following us. If they was, it's probably because we rustled some cattle."

Culpepper looked at Taggart. "We got ourselves some rustlers."

"You two bounty hunters?" Reb asked.

Culpepper and Taggart laughed. "Not hardly," Taggart said.

"I don't think you had the U.S. Marshal and three other men chasing you for rustling," Culpepper said.

Culpepper and Taggart had been riding off the trail toward Purgatory Canyon when they happened to spot the four riders moving fast on the trail. They found the perfect spot to wait and watch. The closer the four riders got to them, they recognized Marshal Holt and decided it was the perfect time to take him out.

"Maybe we rustled on the marshal's land," Deke said.

"What do you think, Win? Are they as dumb as they look?" Culpepper asked his partner.

Frank's head was clearing. The name Win was an unusual one. "Are you Win Taggart?"

Everyone had heard of the infamous stage-coach robbers.

"Are you Joe Culpepper?" Dutch asked the other man.

Culpepper smiled. "I guess they ain't as dumb as they look. Yeah, I'm Culpepper and this is my partner, Win Taggart. I'm sure you've heard of us, but I don't recognize none of you. Who are you?"

Frank got to his feet. He'd heard of these two killers, but he'd never seen them. "I'm Frank Langtry." He pointed to his men and introduced them. "We were cattle rustling near Denver and I guess we hit the wrong place."

Reb stood, and Culpepper waved his gun at the other men on the floor. "Stay where you are."

"I don't know if I believe them," Win said.

"That's why we're partners, Win. We think alike. I think these boys did something else to have the U.S. Marshal on their tail." Culpepper noticed their saddlebags were lying beside each man. "Win, grab those saddlebags."

"You ain't taking our saddlebags," Reb said.

Culpepper laughed. "I don't think I heard you right. Do you see who is holding the guns?"

Frank didn't know if Reb had heard of Culpepper and Taggart, but it was a fool's errand to challenge these two. Even though Reb was a fast draw, these two men had a lot of notches on their gun belts.

Reb glanced at Frank and realized Frank wasn't going to go against the two men. He didn't know if he could take both of them, but he wasn't letting them walk out of that cabin with the money in his saddlebag. "We need what food we have to get us to Purgatory Canyon."

Win grabbed Deke's and Dutch's saddlebags and threw them on the table. He placed his gun on the table, opened the first one, and glanced inside. "Well, lookie here, Cul."

Culpepper leaned over and looked inside the saddlebag, and Reb saw his chance. He went for his gun, and in the next instant, he was lying on the floor with a bullet through his skull. His pistol hadn't left the holster. It wasn't Culpepper who shot him. Taggart saw Reb go for his gun, and in one smooth move, he picked his gun off the table, turned, and shot Reb dead.

Corbin scrambled on his knees to check on Reb. "He's dead."

Frank had never seen anyone move so fast. He'd heard tales about these two, but most stories were often exaggerated. Not this time. He exchanged a look with his men. They were at the mercy of these two killers.

Culpepper stood over Reb's body, reached in his pocket and pulled out a playing card. It was the ace of spades with a bullet hole through the center. He threw it on Reb's body.

"What'd you do that for?" Corbin asked.

Culpepper laughed. "Ain't you heard? That's our calling card."

"Where did you get all this money?" Taggart asked.

"We found it," Frank said.

"You must be the luckiest sons-of-guns alive," Culpepper replied. "Get the rest of the saddlebags, Win."

Win gathered the rest of the saddlebags and looked inside all of them. "You're right, Cul, these boys are real lucky. We've hit pay dirt without lifting a finger."

Taggart trained his pistol on the men while Culpepper looked inside the saddlebags. He let out a whistle. "Where did you boys happen to *find* this loot?"

"Off the trail from Denver," Frank said.

"Langtry, other people might believe your lies, but don't count me as one of them." Culpepper glanced at his partner. "Win, will you get these on our horses? I'll keep an eye on these terrifying hombres. Maybe we should take them in. There might be a price on their heads." Culpepper wasn't about to go near a sheriff, because there was definitely a price on his head.

"You going to kill them, Cul?" Taggart asked.

Culpepper looked them over as though he was giving the question serious consideration. "Well now, that depends. If I let you boys go, do I have your word that you'll forget you saw us?"

Having no choice, Frank and his men nodded their agreement.

"We'll do the same. Win and I won't tell that you boys had all this cash on you. And judging from those bank bags over there in the corner, Marshal Holt happened to be in Denver at the right time."

Frank just stared at Culpepper. He knew they weren't about to go to the law. He figured that marshal was in Denver looking for them.

Win left the cabin with the saddlebags and the guns. He walked to the back of the cabin and took one of their horses and loaded their loot. When he returned, he said, "We're ready to go."

Culpepper narrowed his eyes at Frank. "I don't want to see you behind us. I don't know where you're going, but it better not be in our direction. Next time you rob a bank, I reckon you'd best do a better job of it."

After they heard Culpepper and Taggart riding away, Deke said, "Ain't we going after them?"

"With what?" Frank said, slamming his fist to the table.

"They took all our money, our guns, what food we had, and even our whiskey," Corbin moaned. "What are we going to do now?"

Frank was already formulating a plan. "We'll ride back to Denver. I'll get us some money and everything else we'll need. I'll meet you at that abandoned house and you can take off for Las Vegas. Stay there until the heat dies down, and I'll join you. We'll plan another rustle or robbery." Frank wanted to stay in Denver until Leigh recovered.

"Why don't we go after those two after we get some guns?" Dutch said.

"You know why we can't go after them in Purgatory Canyon. They'd kill us on sight," Frank responded. "Now if we see them somewhere else, we can take them on. At first light, we'll bury Reb, and we'll ride back to Denver." Frank wished he'd stopped at the bank to get the money Aunt Ruth had mentioned. He hoped it was enough to get the boys to Las Vegas.

CHAPTER TWENTY-SEVEN

Addie excused her students by noon, and she walked to the mercantile with the girls. She planned to find Prescott and try to persuade him one last time to leave the girls in Whispering Pines. Afterward, she would have Morgan's foreman drive her to the Coburn farm so the girls could see Davey. It would either be a visit filled with happiness, or a sorrowful good-bye.

Before they reached the boardinghouse, Prescott walked through the door with Clarissa on his arm. "Let's hurry, girls, and catch up to Mr. Adler."

"Prescott, I would like to speak with you."

Prescott and Clarissa turned together. "Addie, I think we've said everything we need to say."

Addie preferred to have this conversation without the girls around, so she reached into her reticule and pulled out a few pennies. "Girls, go to the mercantile and buy some candy. I will be there momentarily."

"I'll be going to Boston with those girls," Clarissa said.

Addie thought there was a gloating tone to Clarissa's words, so she responded in kind. "I'm surprised you have the time to go to Boston, since you are planning a wedding."

"Wedding?" Prescott echoed.

"Don't worry, Prescott, I have plenty of time to go to Boston," Clarissa assured him.

Addie glared at her, but she held her tongue. Clarissa was going to be with the children on a long trip and Addie wanted her to treat them well. "Prescott, I want you to leave the girls here. They are going to be adopted."

"I told you I will not leave them here. If they were adopted, I'm certain you would interfere just as you have interfered in the boy's adoption."

No matter how much she wanted to try to be civil, it proved difficult. "You are doing this to hurt me because I refused your proposal."

"One has nothing to do with the other. The orphanage has a reputation to uphold. As I told you, I was unaware you have an outlaw for a brother. There are many factors involved with my decision. The children

436

are the wards of the orphanage, and as such, it is my responsibility to consider what is best for them. Now, that is the end of the matter." He held out his arm to Clarissa. "Let us continue our walk."

"Don't worry, Miss Langtry, I'm certain one day you may find someone to marry you, and you will have your own children," Clarissa said.

Addie stared at her a moment, thinking of all the things she could say to her, but she remembered part of a Bible verse Granny often repeated: *A harsh word stirs up anger.* Still, she couldn't take back what she was thinking, and the words were harsh. "While you are busy interfering with the children's lives, I guess you haven't heard the man you say you are marrying was shot."

"What? What do you mean?" Clarissa looked as if she didn't believe her.

"He was shot while chasing bank robbers. I cared for him all night. He will be in bed for a few days, but he will be okay."

"Where is Jack?" Clarissa asked.

"He's at my home. Granny is caring for him today." Addie had said more than she intended, so she turned and walked away.

"What did he say, Miss Addie?" Jane asked as soon as Addie entered the mercantile.

"I'm afraid Mr. Adler's mind is made up."

Claire clung to Addie's skirt. "Are we going to see Davey?"

"Yes, honey, we'll go right now."

"We bought some candy for him," Jane said.

Morgan's foreman was waiting for them outside the mercantile. Addie dreaded another confrontation with Roy Coburn, but she hoped he would be more understanding, considering the circumstances. Her hopes were dashed when Mr. Coburn steadfastly refused to allow the girls to see Davey.

Morgan's foreman, Hank Murphy, didn't abide Coburn's unreasonable attitude. "Coburn, Miss Addie told you the reason for their visit, and it seems to me the least you can do is let the girls see Davey, since they may not see him again for a very long time."

Listening at the door to the conversation on the front porch, Sarah Coburn walked outside and said, "Davey's in the barn."

"Old woman, you'd best get inside and tend to your business," Roy said to his wife.

"Thank you, Mrs. Coburn." Addie felt sorry for Sarah Coburn. How any woman could put up with a man like her husband without shooting him deserved her admiration.

Sarah scurried back inside the house and closed the door.

Addie was tempted to give Coburn a piece of her mind, but she knew it would only make matters worse. She took the girls by the hand and walked to the barn. It was a tearful good-bye with Davey, and when they walked away, Addie thought it was one of the most difficult things she'd ever done in her life. They were halfway to the buckboard when Jane ran back and hugged Davey one last time.

On the way back to the farm, Addie thought about Davey's appearance. He'd lost weight, and the dark circles under his eyes worried her. He definitely wasn't the same vibrant, inquisitive young man who had arrived in Whispering Pines with her. Like the last time she saw Davey, he'd had very little to say to her. She hoped in time he would come to trust her again.

"Mr. Coburn is mean to Davey," Claire said.

"What do you mean, Claire?" Addie asked.

Addie didn't see Jane shake her head at her younger sister.

"Claire?"

"She means Mr. Coburn talks mean to him," Jane said.

"Mr. Coburn is not the most pleasant

man," Addie said.

There weren't as many tears on the way home as Addie expected after seeing Davey. Addie thought they were probably all cried out. It saddened her that they had faced so much emotional upheaval in their young lives. She was of the opinion that children brought into this world deserved to be children for as long as possible.

The girls ran to see Jack as soon as they arrived at the farm, and Addie told Morgan and Rose about her conversation with Prescott. "Morgan, I think it is a waste of your time to go talk to him. He won't change his mind."

"I'm going all the same. You know if I don't, Jack will go. Granny relented and gave him his clothes so he could get out of bed and walk to the chair. He's already been out of bed twice. I know he's just trying to figure out if he can make it to town without falling off his horse."

Addie didn't like the thought of Jack riding to town in his condition. Morgan was right, Jack would do anything for the children.

By the time Addie walked into her bedroom, Jack was sitting in a chair by the fire, and the girls were curled up in his lap sleeping.

It was a heartwarming scene: the big, handsome sheriff with the two girls sitting on his lap in front of the roaring fire in the hearth. Addie knew it was a picture she would carry in her mind forever.

Jack opened his eyes and saw her standing there gazing at them. "Hi."

Addie grabbed a quilt from the bed and covered the girls. "How are you feeling?"

"I'm fine. The girls told me what happened with Prescott. I think they're worn out. They fell asleep as soon as they crawled in my lap."

"Morgan has left for town to talk to him, but I don't think it likely Prescott will change his mind. Clarissa was with Prescott when I talked with him. She hadn't heard that you were shot, and I'm afraid I wasn't very pleasant to her."

"You have no reason to be pleasant to her." Jack thought of the many nasty things Clarissa had said about Addie. "I don't know why she agreed to do this for Prescott." He wondered if Clarissa was jealous of Addie, and that was the reason she'd joined forces with Prescott.

Addie thought she understood Clarissa's motives perfectly. Jack had hurt her and she was retaliating. "She seems set on this course."

"Maybe she should marry Prescott. They seem to have a lot in common." Jack had had a lot of time to think this morning about what to do if Prescott didn't change his mind. He thought he might have come up with a solution, but it might be too late. He'd discussed his plan with Morgan earlier, and if Morgan wasn't successful with Prescott, he would take matters into his own hands. It was a good thing Morgan was the one talking to Prescott, because right now, if he saw him, he knew he'd lose his temper. The children were too important to him to let them leave Whispering Pines.

Addie sat in the chair next to Jack's, leaned back and closed her eyes. Like the girls, she was asleep within minutes. Jack closed his eyes and thought about the night to come.

An hour later when Addie awoke there was a tray of food on the table.

"Granny said she didn't think you or the girls had lunch," Jack explained.

"No, we didn't. I'm afraid I indulged the girls with some candy today. Did you eat?"

"Yes, Granny believes in keeping me well fed." Jack glanced down at the girls. "Do you want me to wake them?"

"Yes, they won't sleep at all tonight if we don't."

442

Jack gently shook the girls. "It's time to have something to eat, girls."

"I'm not hungry," Claire said.

"I'm not either." Jane looked over at Addie. "I had a dream that we got to stay here with you, Miss Addie."

If only that were possible, Addie thought. She'd prayed and prayed, but as Granny always told her, sometimes prayers went unanswered for a long time. If what Granny said was true, the day would come when she would receive an answer, and she would know it was a gift from God.

"Why don't you two try to eat a little? Granny went to a lot of trouble to bring it to you." Addie handed the girls a half a sandwich each.

"How about giving me a bite of that sandwich," Jack said to the girls.

Claire and Jane stuck their sandwiches to his mouth. Jack laughed. "Tell you what, I'll take a bite of each one, if you take a bite."

"Okay," they said in unison.

"Hmm, that's good." Jack glanced at Addie and winked.

His expertise with the children always amazed Addie. He seemed to know exactly what to do in every situation. "Would you like some tea? Granny has four glasses on the tray."

"Yes, ma'am." Jack preferred coffee, but he'd drink the tea.

"I could go make some coffee," Addie offered as though she read his mind.

"I'll have coffee later." Jack had noticed the girls didn't mention Davey, so he was careful not to say anything that might upset them.

Rose came hurrying into the room. "Jack, Clarissa is downstairs."

Jack looked at Addie. "What does she want?"

"I'm sure she is here to see how you are doing," Addie replied. She rose from her chair and reached for the tray. "I'll take this to the kitchen. Girls, you can go with me so Jack can have some privacy."

"Stay where you are, Addie, I don't need privacy."

Rose took the tray from Addie. "I'll bring her up in a minute. Girls, come with me, I made some cookies."

When the girls hesitated to leave Jack, he said, "Bring me back a cookie."

When they were out of the room, he stood.

"What are you doing?" Addie asked.

"I was going to get my shirt from your wardrobe. Granny hung a clean one in there for me."

"Nonsense. Sit down." When he sat, Addie

draped a quilt around him. She wondered if Clarissa had ever seen him without his shirt. With that thought, she pulled the quilt together over his chest so not an inch of skin was showing. "Hasn't Clarissa seen you without your shirt before?" She couldn't believe she asked the very question she'd been thinking.

Jack grinned at her. "No, ma'am. She hasn't seen me in a tub either."

Addie's face turned pink. She couldn't believe he was teasing her about that night in her kitchen. "I see what Granny means when she says you are full of mischief."

"Miss Addie, you sure look pretty when you blush."

Addie shook her head at him. "I'll be back after your visitor leaves."

"I want you to stay. Please sit down." He indicated the chair where she'd been sitting. At least now he could prove to her once and for all that Clarissa was not his fiancée, and never had been.

Addie had just taken her seat when Clarissa walked through the door and hurried to Jack's side. She kneeled on the floor in front of him. "Oh, Jack, honey, I've been so worried since I heard you had been shot."

"I know Addie told you that I was fine," Jack said.

Clarissa reached up and placed her palm on his cheek. "I just had to see for myself."

"I have one question for you, Clarissa."

"What's that?"

"Why are you going with Adler to take the girls to Boston?"

Clarissa was surprised at his question. She jerked her hand away from his face. "I don't think we need to discuss this now."

"Yes, we do." Jack was determined to get an answer.

Clarissa glanced at Addie. "Perhaps we should discuss this in private."

"No, we can discuss it now."

"Prescott said he needed help. I've never seen Boston, and I had no reason not to go. He is paying me for my time."

"You know he's closing the orphanage, and taking those children from Addie."

"They are not her children." She smiled at him and tried to change the subject. "I came to see how you are. I'm thankful that you were not seriously injured."

"As you can see, I'm fine. Addie's taken good care of me."

Clarissa stood, leaned over and kissed his cheek and whispered, "Have you had time to think over our last conversation?"

Addie couldn't hear what Clarissa said, but Jack's expression said he wasn't pleased.

"Yes, and nothing has changed."

Clarissa pulled back, the smile erased from her face. "Perhaps you need more time."

Jack saw no way around making it clear to Clarissa he wasn't interested in marrying her, other than to be blunt. "Clarissa, I won't be changing my mind. You mentioned other men had interest in courting you, so I suggest you accept their attentions. I've never laid claim to you."

Clarissa glared down at him. She couldn't imagine a man who would refuse her. "I can see I've made a mistake in coming here."

"I thought we said everything we needed to say the last time we saw each other."

"I thought you had more sense. One of these days you're going to be stuck with the likes of her." Clarissa threw her hand in Addie's direction.

Jack's eyes settled on Addie. "I'd be honored if Miss Addie ever considered me husband material."

Addie's mouth dropped open at his comment. They stared at each other for what seemed like minutes. They didn't even notice Clarissa walking out the door.

Morgan returned from town and immediately ran upstairs to talk to Jack. "I couldn't get Prescott to budge. If we had a different judge in this territory I feel certain we could get an adoption approved over Prescott's objections. A decent judge would hear our case, and see Prescott is being unreasonable. I doubt Judge Stevens would do us any favors."

"Then I will try it my way. But it may be too late for the girls." Jack didn't think Prescott would agree to what he had in mind.

"Well, I've been thinking about that. If necessary, we'll go to Boston and go before a judge there. You're a respected man in this territory. You'll have me beside you to vouch for your character. I'm sure Clay will go with us. Having a pastor along could go a long way to sway opinion."

Jack grinned. "Wouldn't that beat all? An outlaw turned preacher swearing an oath for a sheriff."

Morgan chuckled. "There's a story for sure. Heck, we could do it up right and take Joseph Longbow with us."

"That would definitely have tongues wagging in Boston. Can't you see Prescott's face if that happened? Speaking of Joseph, have you seen him?" Jack knew Morgan was worried about Joseph.

"Nope. On the positive side, no soldiers

have shown up at the ranch. So maybe the judge was bluffing about that."

"I hope so, Morgan. Joseph doesn't deserve any trouble."

"No, he doesn't." Before Morgan left the room, he had one more question for Jack. "Are you going to go ahead with your plan tonight?"

"Yep, wish me luck."

"I'd like to hear you grovel. Good luck."

The girls were with Jack after dinner, but everyone was somber. Jane read a story to Claire, and Jack wasn't really listening, but Jane said, "Don't you like the story of David and Goliath?"

"Yes, honey, I like it very much." He'd told Davey to read about King David, hoping it would encourage him to stay strong through difficult situations. Jack thought about the events to come, and he felt he was the one who needed the strength.

"We don't have school tomorrow. Miss Addie told everyone to stay home," Jane told him when she finished her story.

Jack figured Addie would be too upset to teach once the girls left. "Girls, no matter what happens, no matter where you are, you know I will come to see you."

The girls nodded, but didn't respond. Claire crawled up beside him and pulled his face to hers. "I'll miss you, Papa."

Jack choked up, and it felt as if a vise was squeezing his heart. It was tearing him apart to have to say good-bye to them. "I'll miss both of you. But it won't be a forever good-bye, just a short good-bye." He remembered the day the children got off that stagecoach. When he'd caught Claire, and she'd called him papa from the start, he was definitely a goner. He'd fallen in love with them that day. He'd already made up his mind if he had to go to Boston and steal the girls, he was willing to do that.

Addie came into the room when it was time for the girls to go to bed. They kissed Jack's cheek one final time, and he hugged them. "Remember what I said, girls. I'll see you in the morning."

"Yes, sir," Jane replied.

Addie looked at him with tears in her eyes.

"Will you come back in here tonight?" Jack asked her.

"Of course. Can I bring you something?"

"You."

Later, when Addie returned, she handed Jack a fresh cup of coffee. "How do you feel?"

"Helpless at the moment." Jack took a sip of the coffee and shut his eyes. "Did Morgan tell you he had no luck with Prescott?"

Addie set her cup of coffee on the mantel and added some wood to the fire. "Yes, he told me."

"Addie, would you come here for a minute?"

Turning from the fire, Addie thought he needed some help, so she hurried to his bedside. "Do you need another pillow behind you?"

"Yes."

She reached for the pillow next to him, and when he leaned forward she placed it behind him. Before she moved away, he gripped her arm and held her close. "Addie . . ." He stopped talking and pressed his lips to hers.

Addie was still reeling from what he'd said earlier to Clarissa. She'd told herself so many times that a man as handsome as Jack would never be interested in her, and his comment to Clarissa was totally unexpected. And now, he was kissing her again. She gently pushed against his chest and said, "Jack, what are you doing?"

"Kissing you?"

"I mean, *why* are you kissing me?"

He met her eyes and grinned. "Why does a man usually kiss a woman?"

She raised her palms in the air and

shrugged as if to say she had no idea.

"If I remember correctly, Prescott kissed you in the middle of the street." That kiss still rankled Jack, and he'd come to realize it needled him because he cared about her. Lying in bed last night, watching her and the girls sleeping, forced him to face the fact that he cared more deeply about Addie than he'd been willing to admit. Who was he kidding? He loved her. He loved the children, and he didn't want to let them go. Since the first day they'd arrived, he'd found ways to spend time with them. He wanted to protect them, wanted to take care of them, wanted to show them the love they deserved, and wipe the pain of rejection from their souls. It touched him the way Claire called him *papa,* and he wanted to hear those same words from Jane and Davey.

He wanted to be a good husband to Addie. And right now, he wanted to know if she loved him. She'd kissed him without hesitation before, but they hadn't spent much time together since the last time they'd kissed. And when they were together, they were never alone. He'd thought she cared about Prescott, and she'd thought he was marrying Clarissa. He blamed himself for allowing Addie to believe he cared about

Clarissa. His only excuse was, he'd been a jealous fool over Prescott. He was angry with himself for taking so long to recognize he was in love with Addie. He prayed he hadn't waited too long. If she did care for him, he would do whatever was necessary to keep the girls from leaving on that stage-coach.

"Prescott kissed me because he hadn't see me in weeks. He said he missed me," Addie said, trying to explain Prescott's kiss one more time. She'd explained the situation before, and she didn't know why Jack kept bringing it up.

Jack took her hand and urged her closer. "Sit on the bed beside me. I want to talk to you."

"Maybe I should sit in the chair." Addie started to move away, but he held on to her.

"Please, sit beside me."

Addie sat at his side and Jack laced his fingers through hers. When he didn't say anything, she said, "What is it?"

"I don't want another man kissing you like that."

"Like what?"

Jack took a deep breath and prayed he didn't muck this up. "I don't want another man kissing you. Period."

Addie searched his face, trying to grasp

his meaning.

Jack reached up and threaded his fingers through her hair. "Kiss me, Addie."

Addie realized she was facing one of those moments in life that would change her future. Her heart was telling her one thing, and her head was throwing up a caution sign. Her mind was telling her, *You could have your heart broken.* Her heart was saying, *Take a chance on him.* She wanted to listen to her heart because she loved him. She leaned over, took his face in her hands, and kissed him.

Jack was so surprised she'd actually kissed him that it took him a second to respond. He hoped it never took him so long to react in a gunfight, or he'd be six feet under. Boy, could she kiss. No way was he ever going to allow another man to have the opportunity to find out just how good she could kiss. Hadn't Morgan told him he'd felt the same way after he kissed Rose the first time? Jack had thought his friend was crazy when he'd told him that. But not anymore. It made perfect sense.

Without his lips leaving hers, he used his good arm to pull her on his lap, and she wrapped her arms around his neck. Jack told himself he should end the kiss and have a talk with her, but he didn't want to stop.

She felt too good pressed against his chest. Her response to him said she wanted him just as much as he wanted her. Just a few minutes longer and he promised he would stop. But not right now. He ran his hand down her spine, from her neck to her waist, pressing her closer and closer. *Lord, give me strength to stop.* Finally, he pulled his lips from hers. "Marry me."

Addie blinked, trying to focus. She blinked again. His kiss rattled her brain. "What?"

Jack swallowed. "Marry me."

"Why?"

He tried to keep his eyes off of her lips. "I think we should marry."

Addie's mind began to clear. "You want to marry me to keep the girls here."

"Of course, I want to keep the girls here."

Addie tried to slide off his lap, but Jack kept his arm clamped around her waist. She looked into his eyes. It was wonderful of him to do anything he could to keep the girls in Whispering Pines, and her initial response was to accept because she wanted the same thing. But what would happen when it came time for the girls to leave home? Would he resent her because the reason he'd married her in the first place was now gone? "Jack, thank you for caring enough about the girls to sacrifice yourself.

I can't tell you how much that means to me. And as much as I am tempted to say yes, it wouldn't work. Even if we did marry, I can't see that would change Prescott's mind."

"Sacrifice myself? What in the devil do you mean by that? And why do you think it wouldn't work?"

She felt like crying, but she held it in. "You want to marry me for the girls. I appreciate that, but it is not the basis for a good marriage. When the girls leave home, you would no longer be happy, and —"

Jack held his hand up. "Now wait a minute. I love those girls, I love Davey, but I wouldn't marry a woman I didn't love to have them. I'd find another way."

Was he saying he did love her? "You aren't asking to marry me just so you can adopt the girls?"

Jack figured he might be working with half a brain after that kiss, but he got up to speed quickly. "I'm saying I've loved you since you got off that stagecoach. I want you and the children forever."

This time, her eyes filled with unshed tears. "But . . . but . . . I'm not . . ."

Jack squeezed her to him. "If you say you aren't pretty, I may never kiss you again." Like that would ever happen. "You are the most beautiful woman in the world."

Addie pulled back. "But I'm not like . . ."

Jack knew what she was about to say. He intentionally cast a glance over her round, soft figure. "If you don't marry me, I can guarantee you will never press those beautiful curves of yours next to another man. And you for darn sure won't be kissing another man."

"You like my curves?" Rose had told her time and time again, men loved women with curves, but she'd never believed her.

"Like them? I love them, and I get hot under the collar anytime I catch another man staring at them." He wasn't lying. He'd caught a few men staring at her breasts, and he felt like punching their eyeballs to the back of their skulls. As her husband, he'd let a man know if he was out of line, but he'd have to learn to control his temper when it came to men gawking at his wife.

"What about you? Do you love me?"

"I've loved you from the moment I saw Claire in your arms."

Jack arched his brow at her. "Say you'll marry me so I can kiss you again."

Addie did more than say yes. She kissed him again.

CHAPTER TWENTY-EIGHT

Frank parted company with his gang outside of Denver. He'd promised to meet Corbin later that night, at the little house he rented for his liaisons with Leigh. Arriving in Denver, his first stop was the doctor's office to check on Leigh.

Judge Stevens greeted him as soon as he walked in. "Doc said she's going to make it."

"That's great news. Has she awakened yet?"

"No, but she's moving around more, and the doc thinks she will today." The judge told Frank about the U.S. Marshal being shot. "The sheriff in Whispering Pines was shot too."

"You mean the bank robbers shot the marshal and sheriff?"

"Sheriff Trent said he wasn't certain it was the bank robbers. He said it could have been those two wanted men the marshal had been chasing. You may have heard of them before: Culpepper and Taggart."

Frank didn't respond because Leigh mumbled something. Both men moved to her side, but they couldn't understand what she was saying. The judge grasped her hand and brought it to his lips. "We're here, Leigh. Frank and I are right here."

"Leigh, can you hear me?" Frank asked.

"Frank?" Leigh mumbled.

Judge Stevens smiled. "Frank, I think she said your name."

Frank hoped Leigh had her wits about her when she awoke. He didn't want her to say something that would give away the nature of their relationship. It would be particularly difficult if the judge discovered the truth now that Frank didn't have the money to get them out of Denver.

They waited, but Leigh seemed to be sleeping soundly, so the judge asked Frank to join him for lunch. After lunch, Frank told the judge he was going to visit Aunt Ruth, and the judge headed back to the doctor's office.

Frank's first stop was the bank, and he found out Aunt Ruth had deposited two thousand dollars in his name. He didn't withdraw the entire amount, just enough to get the gang to Las Vegas and tide them over until he met them. His next stop was the mercantile, where he purchased some supplies and some guns. After he dropped his purchases off at the little house, he went to see Aunt Ruth.

"Did you think over my offer, Frank? I'd really like to have a member of the family running my mine. It'd be nice to have someone there I could trust."

"I don't know much about mining, Aunt Ruth." Frank had thought it over, and he'd come to the conclusion it might be the best way to come into some money fast. If he worked it right, he might come out on the winning end. Aunt Ruth already trusted him, and she was angry with her brother. He had a feeling he could worm his way into Aunt Ruth's will. And it was no secret the woman had a considerable amount of money.

"You're a smart one, you'd learn the business in no time. My husband delegated the menial tasks, but he stayed there to see to the day-to-day operations. It was difficult because he was away from home so much of the time, but he insisted he had to oversee the daily production. I'm sure you can see how easy it would be for those men to get the better of me. As an absentee owner, I don't know more than what they tell me. I get the reports weekly, and I have no way of knowing if they are telling me everything. It's a lucrative venture, and if you worked for me, I would make it worth your while."

Frank could see her point about trusting strangers. He'd bet they were robbing the woman blind. There might be unlimited potential for him to pocket a fortune in gold nuggets on the side. "For you, Aunt Ruth, I'll give it a try. I don't want anyone taking advantage of you."

Aunt Ruth hugged him. "Call me Ruth. It's a good decision, Frank. You'll be set for life and never have to worry about a thing. The mine is a two-day ride from here, and my husband built a small home there. Naturally, you are welcome to live there, and if possible, I'd like you to come to Denver at least once a month."

Ruth wanted to discuss another matter with him, so she said, "Let's go into the parlor for a brandy."

Entering the parlor, she took a seat in her favorite chair by the fireplace. Frank added a couple of logs to the fire before he walked to the sideboard. He'd quickly learned Ruth liked her brandy in the afternoon, so he poured her a healthy portion.

"Have a seat. There is something else I

want to discuss with you, and I want you to speak honestly. Before that young woman my brother is dallying with was shot, it's my understanding that you were spending some time with her."

"Yes, the judge wanted me to try to mend fences with her." Frank saw no reason to lie to her, particularly since he had a feeling she knew a lot more about what was going on than she let on.

"My niece thought she was out for his money. I'm interested to know what you think."

Frank saw an opening to further endear himself to her. "You're right, Charlotte didn't like her, but I'm not of the same opinion. She's a young widow who is lonely and scared. I don't think she has a means of support. The judge makes her feel safe. But, I have to agree with you, the judge looks foolish squiring such a young woman around town. For a man as prominent as the judge, it can't be helpful for his reputation. But he won't listen to reason."

"My point exactly. You understand the situation clearly. Robert seems to have forgotten our family name is well respected. Our father was a prominent judge, and Robert followed in his footsteps. I cannot allow him to taint his memory by behaving like a besotted fool." She leaned back in her chair and drank her bandy. "Frank, does the doctor think this young woman is going to recover?"

"Yes, she's doing much better."

"Can I count on you to keep this a private conversation?"

"Of course." Frank had a feeling he knew where this conversation was going.

"If, as you say, she is a nice young woman in a bad way, I am not without some sympathy for her and her questionable future. I would be prepared to offer a generous compensation if she were amenable to leaving Denver and never return. What would you think of that proposition?"

Just as he thought — a bribe. It was all he could do to keep from smiling. "I think that's an interesting plan. What do you have in mind?"

"I would think a young woman may find ten thousand dollars acceptable. Naturally, I would want a signed agreement that she would stay away from Robert. What do you think of that sum?"

Frank swirled the brandy in his glass as he thought of his response. "I think that is generous. Of course, it will take me some time to get to know her, and to find out if she would even consider this. How would I spend time with her without the judge knowing? He's staying pretty close to her."

"I've thought about that. Robert told me last night that he needs to go back to Colorado City. He needs to get back to work, but I think he's been waiting to make sure she will survive. While he is away, you could use that time to get to know her better. Robert said he may be gone two weeks, and that should be enough time to see if we could work out an arrangement. If she agrees, perhaps you could accompany her on your way to the mine and see that she is settled somewhere."

"It would be best to do this while he is away. If he got word that I was involved in this plan, he wouldn't like it."

"So you will handle this negotiation for me?"

"I would be happy to, Ruth." The more time he spent with Ruth, the more he liked her.

Frank arrived back at the doctor's office to find Leigh sitting up and talking with the judge.

The judge was overjoyed at her miraculous recovery. "Frank, Leigh was asking about you when she woke. She thought you were no longer here."

Frank walked to her side. "I'm glad to see you're awake. We've been mighty worried about you."

"Robert told me what happened." Leigh said very little when she awoke because she couldn't recall the shooting. The judge filled in the blank spaces for her, and she thought perhaps Frank had left without her.

"The judge hasn't left your side," Frank said.

"Frank was here with me too. He's been as concerned about you as I have been," the judge added.

Leigh looked at Frank, and said, "I'm sorry about your wife."

"Thank you. I'm just happy you are going to be okay." Frank stared into her eyes. He wanted to talk with her alone, but there was little chance of that happening with the judge hovering over her like a nursemaid.

The doctor walked into the room and said, "I think the patient better get some rest now."

"Yes, I am tired," Leigh said, and closed her eyes.

Frank looked at the judge. "Judge, you go ahead and get something to eat. I'll sit with Leigh."

"That's kind of you, Frank. I would like to have some coffee." He leaned over and kissed Leigh on the lips. "I will see you in a little while, my dear."

The judge left and Leigh opened her eyes. Frank held his finger to his lips, indicating for her not to speak until they heard the judge walk down the sidewalk. Frank pointed to the back of the doc's office, and whispered, "The doc is in the back." When Frank was certain it was safe, he leaned over and kissed her.

When Frank pulled back, she said, "I thought you left me."

"I had to leave for a day to meet the boys. Once you can travel, we will leave Denver. I have a plan." Frank kissed her again. "I've missed this." He'd never been possessive of a woman, but it was different with Leigh. He didn't even want an old man like the judge kissing her.

"Did they get the money?" Leigh asked.

"It's a long story, honey. I'll tell you about that later. Do you like that old man kissing you?"

"No, I hate it. Do you want me to tell him to stop?"

"Not yet, but you can tell him you are not up to his attentions. I don't want him getting suspicious about us right now."

"The doctor said I could go back to the hotel tomorrow to recuperate. He'll come by every day to see me."

"That's good. I'll just have to be careful coming and going." Frank told her the judge was going to go back to Colorado City. "Don't let him spend the night with you." Frank fully intended to be the one spending nights with her.

The judge left the restaurant and walked to the jail to see Sheriff Trent. "Sheriff, what have you heard about Marshal Holt?"

"Morgan LeMasters sent me a telegram earlier saying the marshal is doing much better. He thinks he's going to pull through."

"And the sheriff?"

"He's on the mend as well."

"Since Mr. LeMasters has been seeing to the needs of the marshal, I don't expect you to bring him in. Are you going back after those bank robbers?"

"I've contacted the U.S. Marshals' office and they are sending two marshals. Those boys are probably in Purgatory Canyon, and it'll take more than a few men to get them out of there. As a matter of fact, Sheriff Roper got shot in there a few months back, by one of Frank's boys."

The judge was adamant Frank was not involved with the ambush. "The sheriff was ambushed and didn't see the perpetrator. I still think you are wrong about Frank, Sheriff."

"Judge, I know you are wrong about Morgan LeMasters. That is a man of sterling character if I've ever met one. So is Sheriff Roper. I'd take their word any day over Frank Langtry's." He could see the judge was taking offense. "I know we are at an impasse on this issue, and I'm not certain how to solve it. But I won't bring either one of those men in on the word of Frank Langtry."

"I appreciate your honesty. I guess it's not necessary, seeing as how I've dropped all charges against Frank. It's a moot point right now. I'll tell Frank he needs to stay away from Whispering Pines, and let this situation settle down."

The judge's solution wasn't the outcome Sheriff Trent had wanted, but the judge had the upper hand. "Let's hope Frank Langtry walks the straight and narrow from now on."

The judge returned to the doctor's office and Frank left for a few hours. He grabbed some dinner, and walked to the little house to meet Corbin.

"Tell the boys I'll meet up with you in a month in Las Vegas." He handed Corbin cash and helped him load his horse.

468

"There's enough food to last until you get to the next town to buy more, and there are guns in that sack."

"You won't be there for a month? What if we run low on money?" Corbin asked.

"You can do some rustling if you run low." They were grown men, and Frank didn't consider it his responsibility to provide them with cash indefinitely. He wanted their loyalty, but there were times he felt like they depended on him too much. Deke and Dutch were smart enough to handle rustling, so they could get their hands on some cash if they needed it. "I'll see you in a month."

When Frank returned to the doctor's office, the judge was still there. "How's she doing?"

"She's been sleeping soundly." Frank wondered if Leigh was really sleeping, or pretending to be asleep.

"The doctor says she can be moved to the hotel tomorrow. If Ruth were more reasonable, I'd move her to the house."

"The important thing is she is getting well," Frank replied. He didn't want Leigh in Ruth's home.

"There's something else I wanted to talk to you about, Frank. I'm afraid I need to get back to Colorado City. I'm going to be gone for two weeks, and I'm asking you to look after Leigh for me while I'm away. I trust you to take care of her and get her whatever she needs."

"You know I'll do that for you, Judge." Granny often said life took strange turns. How much stranger could it get than having Leigh's lover giving him permission to look after her? He planned to do a very good job of looking after her.

CHAPTER TWENTY-NINE

Jack had Addie gather Granny, Morgan, and Rose in the bedroom to tell them the news.

"It took you long enough, Jack Roper," Granny said as she kissed him on the cheek. "I told you Addie was the one for you."

Morgan shook Jack's hand. "Congratulations. You should have known better than to argue with Granny."

"So when is the big day?" Rose asked.

"Soon. But we've decided not to tell the children until we speak with Prescott in the morning." Jack had already told Addie he was riding to town in the morning to speak with Prescott.

"I don't want him to go. I don't think he should ride yet," Addie said.

Jack reached for her hand and pulled her to sit beside him on the bed. "I'll be fine."

Morgan looked at his friend. He knew if he were in Jack's position, he'd do the same thing. "I don't think I can make him listen to reason on this issue."

Jack figured Morgan knew what he was thinking. "Morgan would do the same thing."

All heads turned to Morgan, and he threw his hands in the air. "Yep."

Granny looked from Jack to Morgan. "I don't know which one of you has the hardest head."

"You're right, Granny, I do have a hard head. If I'd listened to you and not waited so long to ask Addie to marry me, we wouldn't be in this situation with the children," Jack said.

"Jack, I'm old enough to know that *if* can be a troublesome word." She tapped Jack affectionately on top of the head. "You'd best be getting some sleep. Sounds like you're going to have an interesting day tomorrow."

Addie and Jack were left alone in her bedroom, and suddenly Addie felt insecure. "Jack, are you positive you are not asking me to marry as a way to adopt the girls?"

Jack blamed himself for not telling Addie after that first kiss that he cared for her. He'd even tried to make her jealous by seeing Clarissa. He placed his arm around her shoulders, urging her to lean on his chest. "Honey, you said yourself that Prescott probably won't change his mind. I'm not doing this for the girls. You love them, as do I, and I want us to adopt them, but if we can't, I still want you for my wife." He leaned over and kissed her, gently at first, but it quickly turned needy.

Addie didn't want the kiss to end, and it was difficult for her to pull away. "I think I need to sit in the chair."

Jack sighed loudly. "That might be a good idea. When you're this close to me, I can't seem to keep my hands off of you."

Addie attempted to scoot off the bed, but Jack wouldn't let her go. "I said it might be a good idea, I didn't say you should go. Stay put. I want to talk to you, so try to keep your hands to yourself."

Addie playfully smacked him on his uninjured shoulder. "I'll do my best."

After Addie settled next to him, he said, "You know, you don't need Prescott Adler to start an orphanage here. You don't need his financial assistance. We could expand the garden to supply more food, get some cattle, and while it may not be as large as some of the orphanages in the East, we could be a big help to some children."

While she didn't think it possible, Addie loved him even more in that moment. "It would be a lot of work. You would agree to do that?"

"I'm not afraid of a little work. If we need to add on to this house to accommodate more children, I can do the work. We can count on Morgan and Clay to help out."

"But do you think it will be too much when we start our own family?"

"We can handle it. I'm not saying we can adopt all the children, but they will have a home filled with love, and be well cared for until they are adopted."

"Some of these children can be a real handful," Addie said.

"Don't forget, I was one of those children. I'd say I fell into that category. But from what I've seen of some orphanages, children oftentimes have reason to be difficult."

"What if some of them ran away, like you did?"

"Addie, you're wonderful with the children, and they'd have no reason to leave. There's nothing we can't handle. We'll make sure they are adopted by good people." His thoughts went to Davey. On the surface, Coburn and his wife had seemed as though they would be good parents, but Davey wasn't happy.

"You're thinking about Davey, aren't you?" Addie knew Jack felt guilty about Davey.

"Yeah. I know he's not happy there, and I just don't know what to do about it."

"Jack!" Addie screamed from the hallway the next morning.

Jack's eyes snapped open at the urgency in her voice. He was sitting in the chair by the fire, but he jumped up and grabbed his gun. Before he took another step, Addie was already at the door. "What's wrong?"

"The girls! They're gone!" She ran to him and thrust a note at him. "Oh, Jack, they ran away."

Jack took the note from her shaking hand. Having heard the commotion, Rose, Granny, and Morgan had gathered at the doorway. Glancing at the group of concerned faces, Jack read the note aloud. *"Miss Addie, we are sorry, but we don't want to go with Mr. Adler. Don't worry about us, Davey is with us. Mr. Coburn hits him, and we want to be together. We will miss you and the sheriff and your family. Thank you for trying to help us. Jane and Claire."*

Jack put his arm around Addie's shoulders. "I'll find them."

"I was downstairs making breakfast and I noticed some biscuits missing that I had made last night, but I just thought someone got hungry in the middle of the night. When

I went into their room to wake them, the note was on Jane's pillow."

"They couldn't have gotten far." Jack released Addie to grab his shirt.

"I'll go, Jack," Morgan said.

"I'm going." Jack buttoned his shirt, fastened his holster around his waist, and grabbed his coat.

"I'll go with you. I'll have Murph stay here," Morgan said. "I'll saddle our horses."

"It's so cold outside," Addie said.

Jack held her for a minute before he kissed the top of her head. "Honey, I promise I'll find them."

"I want to go with you."

"No, you wait here. Morgan and I will move faster alone, and if Prescott comes, you'll need to explain the situation."

Addie swiped at the tears on her cheeks. "I should have known they were thinking of something like this because they weren't crying last night when I put them to bed. They'd cried every night before that."

"Honey, if anyone should have known what they would do, it was me." Jack remembered all too well the first night he'd run away from an orphanage. It was frightening, but he couldn't think of another way to change his circumstances. He'd had a different reason for running away. He was being abused, but these children ran away out of love for one another.

"I'll get some sandwiches together."

Jack took her by the hand and together they walked downstairs to the kitchen.

Ignoring the pain in his shoulder, Jack grabbed his rifle from the top of a high shelf in the kitchen. He'd placed it there when he'd spent nights on the settee. The women quickly prepared sandwiches for the men to take with them.

As soon as the bundles of food were ready, Jack kissed Addie good-bye. "We'll be back as soon as we find them."

Jack found Jane and Claire's footprints from the back door and followed them to the pines. A sense of foreboding threatened his confident determination. Those trees covered miles and miles of territory, and many men got lost, or captured by Indians, over the years. It was frightening to think of what could happen to young children vulnerable to the elements and other unseen forces.

When Morgan rode from the stable leading Jack's horse, he saw Jack at the pine tree boundary. He reached Jack and passed him the reins of his horse.

"They're in the trees." Jack braced himself against the pain as he hauled himself into the saddle. Jack pointed to an area by a large tree trunk where the pine needles were compressed, as if someone had been sitting there for some time. "Looks like Davey was waiting here for Jane and Claire. He had a long walk from Coburn's to the farm in the middle of the night." Just thinking about Davey out on the road overnight, in the cold, broke Jack's heart.

"If Davey left Coburn's right after dark, they could have at least three hours on us," Morgan said.

"Yeah, but I didn't want to say that to Addie."

Morgan understood Jack's reasoning. It didn't make sense to give the women more to worry about. "I've got to go to the ranch to get Murph. You go ahead, I'll catch up to you."

Morgan caught up with Jack in no time after he stopped by his ranch. "I wish Joseph was around, he could be a big help."

"Yeah, we're going to need all the help we can get. The kids are so light, their tracks are hard to see."

Two hours later, they no longer saw a trace of small footprints. But they found hoofprints.

"Unshod," Jack said.

"Yep." Morgan knew that meant it wasn't Joseph Longbow on one of those horses.

"It's not Joseph's," Jack said.

Morgan nodded. "No, his horse is shod."

They dismounted and searched for footprints. Jack tried to keep his mind off the many disastrous scenarios threatening to tear apart his control. "Whoever is riding those horses has the children."

"It looks that way," Morgan said.

Jack mounted his horse. "Let's follow them."

They followed the hoofprints west until the sun could no longer be seen through the trees. They'd been in the saddle all day, and when it became too dark to continue, they pulled to a halt.

"Jack, there's a spot a day's ride from here where I've left messages for Joseph."

"You mean you know how to find him?" Jack was surprised Morgan had never shared this information before.

"I've never told anyone, but years ago, Joseph told me of a spot where I could leave a message for him if I found the need. It looks as though these hoofprints lead in that general direction."

"Let's hope the men on these horses are friends of Joseph's," Jack said.

"Are you up to sleeping out in the cold?"

Morgan could tell Jack was in pain, and he was worried about him.

"I'm not going back without those children." Jack had already made up his mind to continue on until he found them, or die trying.

"I didn't expect you would." Morgan wasn't surprised at his decision. "Lucky for you, I put some extra blankets in my bedroll."

They dismounted and set about making camp. Once they cared for their horses, they started a fire, spread their bedrolls, and pulled out their food. They hadn't stopped to eat all day and they were both starving.

"Morgan, how come you never told me you had a way of contacting Joseph?"

"When the soldiers were on my land looking for Joseph, I figured the less you knew, the better. No one could ever accuse you of being party to harboring an Indian."

"Do you think there are many Indians hiding out in these pines?"

Morgan considered his response. He didn't want to worry Jack, but he couldn't lie to his friend. "Yep. And I'm afraid there are men a whole lot worse in here."

"Do you think the men that never come out of the pines are lost, or did they meet with some other end?"

"There's been so many that I think some are lost, but some weren't that lucky." Morgan recalled some of the stories Joseph had told him. Many men who didn't want to be found often hid out in the pines. It was every bit as deadly as Purgatory Canyon for anyone looking to find them.

Waiting for Jack and Morgan to come riding in with the children was agonizing for the women. They tried to keep themselves busy, but they kept running to the window, hoping to see the men ride in. Several hours later, they heard horses. Addie ran to the front door and looked out.

"Who is it?" Granny asked, hurrying to the door.

"It's a buggy, so my guess is Prescott."

Rose joined them, and they walked outside together.

The buggy driver reined in by the porch. Prescott didn't bother with pleasantries as he climbed from the buggy. "I told you to have those children in town early."

"The children ran away in the middle of the night," Addie said.

"I know you don't want to let them go, but this is ridiculous. I've had to waste my time coming here."

"Prescott, the children ran away. You're

welcome to look around, but they are not here. Jack and Morgan are out looking for them now."

"I have a difficult time believing . . ."

Prescott turned when he heard a horse riding in. Roy Coburn reined in at the porch.

Addie noticed Mr. Coburn's face reflected his usual look of annoyance.

Coburn didn't give her a chance to say hello. He bellowed out, "Where is he?"

At his question, Addie was confident Davey was with the girls. "I was just telling Mr. Adler, Jane left me a note saying they were running away. The sheriff and Mr. LeMasters are out looking for them." Addie pointed in the direction where Jack and Morgan disappeared into the trees. "They rode in that direction through the pines."

"Addie, have you hidden those children?" Prescott asked.

Granny stepped forward and waggled her finger in Prescott's face. "Don't you dare question my granddaughter's word. She told you the way of it, and the sheriff is out there looking for those children, after he's been shot. He has no business even being out of bed. You should be ashamed of yourself. You don't love those children, you only want to take them back because you want to hurt Addie."

Granny turned her attention on Coburn next. "Now, as for you, Roy Coburn. If it is true that you've been hitting that boy, then you best pray for forgiveness before the sheriff gets back."

"That's the problem with that boy, someone spared the rod. I've had it with that boy. Tell the sheriff if he finds him, don't bother bringing him back. I don't want him." With that said, Roy Coburn turned his horse around and rode off.

"I figured he wouldn't want to face Jack if he hurt Davey." Granny focused on Prescott again. "Now, if you care about those children, you can go out there and help look for them."

"I have a stage to catch," Prescott said. He walked from the porch and looked over his shoulder at Addie. "You can send them by the next stage."

Addie put her hands on her hips and glared at him. "I will do no such thing. Jack and I are to be married and we are going to adopt those children. I'm prepared to go to the judge in Denver and have this settled. Not only that, we fully intend to start our own orphanage right here. I don't need your support or permission. If you want to fight us on this, then you will have to come back to Whispering Pines."

"We'll see about that." Prescott climbed back into the buggy.

"Yes, we will," Addie replied testily. "Don't expect the children, they will be staying with us."

When Prescott and his driver rode away, Granny and Rose hugged Addie.

"Good for you. You stood up to that pompous . . ." Granny kept from saying the word on her mind so she wouldn't have to ask for forgiveness later. But since she'd thought it, she'd have to ask to be forgiven anyway. In this instance, she felt absolution would come easy.

"Jack couldn't have handled him better," Rose said.

Addie expelled a long breath. She'd been nervous standing up to Prescott, but she refused to allow him to use the children as pawns any longer. "I was tired of his manipulations, but I'm afraid I exaggerated about the judge in Denver. Jack doesn't think he will help us, but he told me he would find another judge if necessary."

"That judge may have a change of heart," Granny said. "The good Lord answers our prayers when we least expect it."

Chapter Thirty

The judge and Frank moved Leigh to her room at the hotel. After lunch, the judge informed Leigh of his plans to leave the next morning for Colorado City.

"I will spend the night with you tonight, my dear."

Leigh's eyes darted to Frank's. "Not tonight. I don't feel up to having company."

The judge didn't hesitate to discuss private matters in front of Frank. "I'm not expecting more than sleeping next to you."

"Robert!" Leigh was appalled by the judge's inelegant comment in front of Frank. "That is hardly the thing to say to a lady."

The judge laughed at her outrage. "Don't be prudish, my dear. Frank and I have no secrets. I can assure you, he has ascertained the nature of our relationship by now."

Even though Frank knew the judge had spent the night in her quarters before, she didn't want to have this discussion in front of him. Frank made it quite clear he didn't want the judge spending another night with her. She'd never turned the judge down before, and she had to make sure she did it in a way that would not arouse suspicion. "If you don't mind, I'm very tired and I would prefer to be alone tonight."

The judge looked as if he might argue with her, but Frank intervened. "Leigh may be more comfortable alone while she is healing."

The judge had no reason to suspect Frank had any motive other than considering the well-being of his love. He smiled at Frank. "I daresay I should bow to your expertise with the fairer sex. I've had little experience over the years." He walked to Leigh and started to kiss her on the lips, but she turned her cheek to him. The judge hesitated, then gave her a peck on the cheek. "Forgive me, my dear, for thinking only of myself. I've missed our evenings together."

"As have I, but I do need to recover." She glanced at Frank and said, "Isn't it time both of you had your dinner?"

The judge reached for his hat. "We'll leave you alone now. I'll return with your dinner."

"If you don't mind, I would rather rest.

I'm not hungry." She knew he meant well, but his hovering was tiring and making her tense.

"Well then, I'll say good night, my dear. I'll see you in the morning."

"The doctor said he would stop by before you go to sleep, Leigh," Frank said, subtly informing her when he planned to return tonight after the doctor's visit.

"Thank you, Frank."

As soon as they walked out of the room, the judge turned to Frank and said, "She seems testy. Do you think we moved her too soon from the doctor's office?"

"I think she will be fine. She probably needs some time alone. You know women, they like to have their private time." Frank slapped him on the back. "Let's have a drink."

They had a few drinks before dinner, and afterward they spent a good part of the evening in the saloon. The judge imbibed a bottle of whiskey, and Frank had to assist him home and help him into his bed. Ruth and the housekeeper had retired for the night, so Frank quietly entered his bedroom and tossed the bedclothes. If anyone looked in on him in the morning, they would think he'd slept there last night and got an early start.

"Did the doctor visit?" he asked as soon as he walked into Leigh's room.

"Yes, he changed my bandage again, and said he would see me tomorrow."

Frank walked to the bed, leaned over and kissed her.

"Do you think it's safe for you to spend the night?"

"The judge had so much to drink, he'll be lucky to wake up in the morning. I'll leave before dawn."

Frank was sitting at the dining table with Ruth when the judge joined them the next morning.

"Have a seat, I'll pour you some coffee." Frank grabbed the coffeepot from the sideboard and served the judge.

"Thanks, Frank, my head is pounding this morning."

"Were you in your cups last night, Robert?" Ruth asked.

Frank winked at Ruth. "I'm afraid it's my fault. I talked the judge into having a few drinks with me last night."

Under normal circumstances, Ruth would never approve of Robert drinking himself into a stupor at the saloon. She was much more forgiving knowing that he was with Frank, and not spending time with that young woman. Frank had agreed to try to talk some sense into the judge, and if that failed, she would rid her family of that young woman by paying her off.

After breakfast, Frank accompanied the judge to Leigh's room so he could say good-bye. "Frank will see to your needs until I return." He leaned over and kissed Leigh on the lips. "Get well quickly, my dear. I shouldn't be gone over two weeks, and if you are feeling well enough, we will take a trip when I return."

When the stagecoach arrived, the judge shook Frank's hand. "Take care of my girl, Frank."

"I'll see to it, Judge."

The stagecoach pulled away, and Frank returned to Leigh's room.

It was a long, discouraging night for Addie, Rose, and Granny. Though it went unspoken, they had expected Jack and Morgan to come riding in with the children before the night was over. As the hours passed, the more worried they became. They had a difficult time believing the children had walked so far that the men hadn't caught up to them. It meant the children were going to spend a full night out in the cold. Addie prayed the men had caught up with them but it was too dark to come home. If that was the case, at least the children would be warm and protected. Addie held on to that thought all night for her own sanity.

As worried as she was, Addie knew she wouldn't sleep, so she sent Granny to bed while she sat with the marshal through the night. The marshal was recovering nicely, but he still slept most of the time. Granny said it was God's way of allowing the body to heal. Addie wondered how a person healed from a broken heart. If something terrible befell the children, she couldn't imagine ever recovering.

Sitting in the quiet of the night, Addie thought about Jack and how he must have suffered as a young boy, to be on his own from a young age. It wouldn't have been a surprise if he'd become an angry adult, but he was far from that. She'd never seen the children laugh as much as they did around him. That first day, when Claire rode in front of him on his horse, she'd giggled so much, it was like she was a different child. The children always seemed on guard with most adults, but not with Jack. Addie knew it had a lot to do with trust. They trusted Jack, and she prayed Davey hadn't lost that trust now.

She thought about different ways she could insure children went to good homes, once she and Jack started their own orphanage. Even if it meant she had to visit the families every night for a while after children were adopted, she would do that. She never again wanted to feel helpless if a child was unhappy in a new home. Having a new family should be a time of joy for all parties, and she didn't want to see hopelessness in another child's eyes, as she'd seen in Davey's the last time she visited the Coburn farm.

"Now they're headed back west," Morgan said. It had been slow going as they'd wound their way through the trees for four hours. They'd been riding north, but they'd changed directions again. Morgan worried they might not ever find their way out of the forest if he didn't pick up some trail markers he'd left behind years ago.

"Do you think these men could be part of Joseph's tribe?" Jack asked.

"I hope they are the same braves that helped us out when Rose was abducted." Morgan had never felt as helpless in his life as that night he'd been shot and he'd had to rely on Joseph and two braves from his tribe to rescue Rose from her brother. But they'd done the job, and brought her back to him, safe and sound. They were good men, and he prayed to God they were the same men who had the children.

"I'm surprised they haven't figured out we are on their trail." Jack's previous encounters with Indians told him they seemed to have a sixth sense about being tailed.

"Yeah, I thought about that. Maybe they don't think anyone would be foolish enough to come in here."

"Except you." Jack was amazed Morgan knew his way around in these woods as well as he did. A man could easily lose his way, especially on an overcast day, or when dusk settled over the pines. Every direction looked the same. "A man could get lost forever in here."

"I expect many have. The first time I came out here, I had to mark a trail no one could find."

Last night, when it was too dark to go on, Jack wondered if the Indians had also stopped, or if they knew the terrain so well they would travel in the dark. If the Indians weren't friendly, Jack worried they wouldn't treat the children kindly. He wasn't one to take revenge; he believed in justice, and that was why he became a sheriff. But if anyone hurt those children, right or wrong, he wouldn't wait around to seek justice.

He knew Addie would be worried sick, and there was not a thing he could do about that. It never occurred to him to prepare her for the possibility they might not return for a couple of days. Just like he never expected the children might run away, and for that, he felt guilty. He should have seen the warning signs, especially from Davey.

Every time Addie heard a horse, her heart started pounding, but it was always Morgan's men coming and going. It seemed like the minutes were passing so slowly, as if time were at a standstill. The women went about their chores, silently, each lost in thoughts they didn't want to voice aloud. They came together at noon and prayed before their lunch, but they couldn't eat.

At dinnertime, the women carried their plates to Marshal Holt's room so he could have some company with his dinner. He'd been alert all day, and he had a lot of questions about Morgan and Joseph Longbow.

"Why are you so curious about Joseph Longbow?" Granny asked.

"As Sheriff Roper probably told you, Judge Stevens wanted Mr. Longbow in his court," Marshal Holt replied. "Jack and Morgan refused to take him to Denver. I guess I wanted to find out what is really going on."

"Marshal Holt, Frank Langtry is my grandson, and as much as it pains me to say this, you can't believe one word he says. What Jack and Morgan told you about Frank is the absolute truth. Joseph Longbow never killed anyone. You can tell that judge he has been duped."

The marshal didn't question Granny's word. "If you don't mind me asking, what caused the rift between your grandson and Morgan?"

Granny explained everything that had happened between Morgan and Frank over the years, and by the time she finished, the marshal was in agreement that the judge had made a mistake absolving Frank Langtry of his crimes. "When I get back to Denver, I will have a talk with the judge."

"Thank you, Marshal. I'm afraid Frank has disrupted all of our lives for much too long," Granny said.

"That's the least I can do for the family who saved my life. I certainly appreciate what all of you have done for me. It looks like I will be out of your hair before long."

"You won't be leaving before you are fully recovered, so don't be thinking otherwise," Granny said.

Marshal Holt chuckled. "Now I know what Jack meant when he said no one argued with you, Mrs. Langtry."

"You can call me Granny, and I hope your head is not as hard as Jack Roper's. He's out there in this cold right now, probably suffering in pain, but stubborn as a mule."

Marshal Holt exchanged a look with Addie and Rose. "I can't see a man worth his salt doing anything other than looking for those children, if he's able. Jack's a good man."

"Yes, he is," Addie agreed.

"Both of my granddaughters have chosen wisely. Preacher always said wisdom is more precious than gold."

"Preacher?" Marshal Holt asked.

"My dear late husband." Granny proceeded to tell the marshal about her deceased husband. She entertained them with humorous stories of her life with Preacher until their meal together came to an end.

When Granny left the room, Marshal Holt said, "She is a fine lady, with a way of making one forget their troubles."

Addie and Rose understood Granny's tactics as soon as she began talking about Preacher. She knew they loved to hear stories about their grandfather, and it would give them a few minutes of relief from their worries about the children.

"Granny always knows what everyone needs," Addie said.

"Why did she call her husband Preacher?" Marshal Holt asked.

Addie and Rose looked at each other and shrugged. They had never heard their grandfather called by his given name.

"He was a preacher, and everyone called him that," Addie said.

Their conversation stopped when Granny walked back into the room, and their eyes turned on her.

Seeing they were staring at her, Granny said, "Is something wrong?"

"Marshal Holt asked why you call our grandfather Preacher, and we didn't know the answer," Addie said.

Granny stopped, and stared off into space, her lips curving into a wistful smile as if a precious memory had taken hold. Finally, she blinked, and her thoughts returned to the present. "A week before my seventh birthday, we had a new visiting preacher who came to our small town. People gathered in our yard under a large weeping willow tree, where we held services in the summertime, to hear him speak. I can remember my mama and grandmother in a flutter that day because the preacher was having dinner at our home after the service. My father teased my mama about her head being turned by the handsome preacher. My mama was an uncommonly beautiful woman, and the ladies thought the preacher was as handsome as my mama was beautiful. Even though I was just a small child, I knew there was something special about him. But watching him that day I realized something very important. Mama was never one to flaunt her beauty, always saying beauty came from the inside. Just like Mama, the preacher didn't seem to set great store in his looks. Listening to him speak that day, I felt like I could almost see into his heart. His calling in life was to lead people to the Lord. Maybe some folks were drawn to him because of his handsome face, but everyone left knowing they'd met someone very special.

"On my birthday, my grandmother made me a doll. I named that old rag doll Preacher. Everyone told me it was a girl doll, and it should have a girl's name, but I wouldn't listen. I insisted on calling that doll Preacher. I told them that one day I would marry a man just like the handsome preacher. When I was thirteen years old, your grandfather moved to our town. He was sixteen years old, and his family called him Preacher. His mama told me he knew at twelve years of age he was going to be a preacher. And just like that preacher I met that day so long ago, your grandfather was just as special."

"Granny, I can't believe you have never told us that story," Addie said.

"Honey, I have so many wonderful stories of the old days, I sometimes forget what I've told you."

"Don't forget these stories, they are the ones passed down that connect the generations over the years," Marshal Holt said.

"Marshal Holt, I'm sure thankful you are still with us," Granny said.

"I'm the one thankful for you, Granny."

CHAPTER THIRTY-ONE

Jack and Morgan reached the area where Morgan had left a message for Joseph before. The tracks of the horses they were trailing crossed through the area.

"How will you know if Joseph was here?" Jack asked.

"He'll leave me a message." Morgan looked toward the sky, and said, "He's been here recently."

Jack glanced at him. "How do you know?"

"Be observant like the owl."

Jack frowned at him. "What?"

"That's what Joseph told me to do." Morgan pointed to one tall pine tree.

Jack looked up and saw the white owl feather hanging upside down from a limb. "Now what do we do?"

"We build a fire." Morgan unsaddled the horses while Jack built the fire.

As frustrating as it was to spend another night out here without finding the children,

Jack knew he had no choice.

They didn't have long to wait before Joseph came walking from the trees with two braves and the three children. Jack and Morgan immediately recognized the two braves who had helped them out a few months ago.

Claire ran to Jack. "Papa!"

Jane was right behind Claire, but Davey held back. Jack tried to fight back his tears as he kneeled and gathered the girls in his arms. "Thank God you are okay."

"We . . . just . . . wanted . . . to . . . be . . . together." Jane was crying so hard, it was difficult for Jack to understand what she said.

Jack looked at Davey standing apart from them. He stood and said, "Come here, Davey."

Davey took a tentative step toward Jack, fearing Jack was angry with him. When Davey reached him, Jack leaned over and wrapped him in his arms. "Don't you ever scare me like that again."

Davey had tears running down his cheeks as he hugged Jack tightly. "I won't go back to Mr. Coburn."

"If you want to run away again, you'll have to let me know so I can go with you." Jack dropped to his knees and held on to all three children. "Are you hurt?"

"No, sir. White Cloud and Little Elk found us and took us to Joseph," Davey said.

Jack turned to the braves and thanked them. "Didn't the braves scare you?"

"At first, the girls were afraid, but they were nice to us," Davey replied.

"Once you were in the trees, how did you know which direction to go?" Morgan asked.

"The angels told us," Jane replied.

Jack and Morgan exchanged a look. "They talked to you?" Morgan asked.

Jane nodded. "Didn't they tell you where we were?"

"I guess they did," Jack replied.

"White Cloud and Little Elk were hunting and found them," Joseph said.

Morgan motioned for everyone to sit down. "Did White Cloud and Little Elk find them before dark last night?"

Joseph nodded, and Jack breathed a sigh of relief they hadn't spent the night alone.

"They built a fire and gave us food," Davey said.

"You scared us all to death. Miss Addie is beside herself with worry."

Jane had calmed down enough to say, "We didn't want anyone to worry, but we didn't want to go back to Boston with Mr. Adler.

Davey couldn't stay with Mr. Coburn any longer because he hit him with a strap."

"Is that true, Davey? Did Coburn hit you?" Jack asked.

"Show him your back, Davey," Jane softly urged.

Davey didn't meet Jack's eyes. Jack didn't want to embarrass him in front of everyone by asking him to remove his shirt. "We'll talk about this later, Davey. You're not going back."

Joseph looked at Jack across the fire. "You are ill."

Morgan told Joseph about Jack being shot again, along with the U.S. Marshal.

"You are shot many times. You should wear the medicine pouch."

Jack didn't want to worry the children, but he thought he could use Joseph's medicine pouch right now.

Morgan handed Joseph and the braves some coffee. "It's safe for you to come home, Joseph. Tell Little Elk and White Cloud to come with us, and they can take two steers."

Joseph spoke to his braves, and they nodded their thanks to Morgan.

Claire climbed onto Jack's lap and leaned against his chest. Jane picked up a blanket and wrapped it around her sister. "Did you mean it when you said Davey didn't have to go back to Mr. Coburn's?"

"I meant it. And you girls aren't going to Boston." Jack hesitated, trying to decide if he should tell the children about his marriage. He thought they needed some reassurance, so he said, "Children, I don't want to get your hopes up, but Miss Addie and I are going to try to adopt you."

"But you have to be married," Jane said.

"Miss Addie is going to marry me."

"Really?" Jane asked.

"Yep. We're hoping you will want to be our children."

"Forever?" Davey asked.

Though Davey tried to mask his hopeful question, Jack saw it in his eyes. "Forever."

Claire pulled Jack's face down so she could stare into his eyes. "You're my papa."

Jack found himself tearing up again at the faith Claire had from the beginning that he was her papa. "That's right, honey. I'll be your papa for as long as you want me." Jack didn't know what kind of reaction he expected, but it wasn't the one he received. All three children started crying.

"I thought it would make you happy," Jack said.

"We are happy. We just never thought it would happen," Jane said. "We've always wanted Miss Addie as our mother, and when we met you, we prayed you would marry her before someone else adopted us."

"Your prayers were answered, as were mine. I always wanted a brave boy and two beautiful girls."

Addie ran out the door as soon as she saw Jack coming out of the woods with Claire sitting in front of him, and Jane behind him. Davey was riding behind Morgan. When they pulled their horses to a halt, Addie reached for Claire. Jane and Davey slid off the horses and ran to her. She hugged them tightly. "What were you children thinking? What if something had happened to you? What would I have done?"

"We're okay, Miss Addie," Davey said.

Addie's eyes sought Jack's and she noticed he was very pale and moving slowly. "Jack?"

"I'm okay."

Morgan took the reins of both horses. "He needs to be in bed."

"Children, help me get the sheriff inside." Addie placed her arm around Jack's waist and Davey moved to his other side.

"Can you make it upstairs?" Addie asked.

"Of course, I'm just a little stiff."

Davey and Addie got Jack to the bed, and Granny hurried into the room. After she hugged the children, she walked to the bed and scowled at Jack. "Tell me you didn't get shot again."

Jack gave her a grin. "I'm glad to see you too. And no, I didn't get shot again."

"Let's get you out of that coat so I can take a look at your shoulder." Granny and Addie helped him remove his coat and shirt. "You've bled through that bandage." Granny placed her hand on his forehead. "And you're burning up with fever. Just like the last time I tended you. I should shoot you myself."

"I love you too, Granny." Jack winked at the children, causing them to laugh.

"Oh, hush," Granny said, but she was smiling right along with the children. She turned to Addie and said, "Boil some water so we can clean this again. I'll have to put in a few new stitches."

Addie asked the children to go with her so Jack could have a minute to himself.

"Addie, I told the children we are getting married." Jack was trying to prepare her for all the questions they'd asked him on the way home.

"The sheriff said you are going to adopt us," Jane said.

"Yes, we are, and we are very excited about that." Addie turned to leave the bedroom, with the children right behind her asking their rapid-fire questions.

"Addie, I think you forgot something," Jack said.

She turned back to him. "What?"

"You didn't even kiss your soon-to-be husband."

Addie smiled at him and walked back to the bed and kissed him.

"Eww," Davey and Jane said together, and Claire clapped.

Jack laughed at their response. "You better get used to that, because I plan on kissing Miss Addie a hundred times a day."

After Jack's shoulder was sewn back together and bandaged, Granny took the children to get washed and ready for dinner while Addie spent a few minutes alone with Jack. Jack told Addie how the braves helped the children, so they hadn't been in the woods alone all night. "They said the angels told them which way to go."

"Emma and I always heard angels laughing, but Rose heard angels singing. She told me the day the house burned down, she was running through the woods toward the farm and she heard voices telling her to turn back, like someone was warning her of danger."

"Maybe Joseph is right when he says the Great Spirit watches what happens in those pines. It's definitely an unusual place."

Addie realized she'd never asked him what he heard when he rode through there. "What do you hear?"

"I always hear laughter too."

"Granny always told us that people hear different things. Just like Rose, Morgan hears singing."

"Would you mind getting Davey for me? I need to speak to him alone."

His serious tone worried Addie. "Is something wrong?"

"Nothing that I can't handle." Jack kissed her forehead.

Davey walked into the room and Jack asked him to close the door. "Come over and sit beside me."

When Davey sat down, Jack said, "I wanted to talk to you alone. Please tell me the truth, Davey. Did Mr. Coburn hit you?"

"Yes, sir."

Jack felt his anger rising, but he tried to keep his voice calm. "With a strap?"

Davey nodded.

"Will you show me?"

Davey slowly raised his shirt and turned so Jack could see his back.

The fading imprints of a strap were still visible on Davey's back. He'd been struck hard enough to leave marks, and more than once. The proof was there for Jack to see. Jack pulled Davey to his chest. "Aw, Davey, why didn't you tell me?"

"I didn't do something he wanted done fast enough. And I was afraid that you'd shoot him, and then you wouldn't be sheriff anymore. It wasn't the first time I've been hit."

Jack knew firsthand how a kid sometimes thought it was their fault if an adult hit them. "It may not have been the first time someone hit you, but it's the last time. I want you to know that I will never lay a hand on you in anger."

Davey had a hard time believing that nothing would make Jack angry enough to hit him. "What if I do something that makes you mad?"

"Even if you do something that makes me really angry, I will never hit you."

"What if I took your horse without permission?" Davey knew how Jack valued his horse.

"I might make you sit in your room for a while to think about things."

"What if you caught me smoking?" Davey remembered some of the older boys at the orphanage got caught smoking, and they received several lashes when the superintendent found out.

Jack chuckled. "I doubt I'd have to punish you for that. I imagine you'd be so sick, that would be punishment enough."

"What if —"

"No more what-if's, I gave you my word. So let's shake on it, man to man." Jack stuck his hand out to Davey.

Davey started to shake, but Jack pulled his hand back. "Wait a minute. You have to give me your word that you won't try to think of mischief just to test me."

Davey smiled at him. "I won't."

The two shook hands to seal their deal.

"Sheriff, do you think my ma really named me after King David?"

Without missing a beat, Jack said, "I sure do. It takes a brave man to walk through that forest with two young girls. I think your ma knew you were going to be a special man."

Davey didn't smile, but Jack could see in his eyes that he was pleased.

"You know, Davey, there is something else you need to think about. When you are faced with many burdens, instead of questioning why it happened to you, or blaming God, you should remember that blessings come with burdens. The Good Lord chooses those who can handle the burdens. Just like King David, you've handled your burdens well."

Davey's eyes met Jack's. "Would you mind calling me David from now on?"

"I think that is a fine idea."

The next morning Addie walked into the bedroom, but Jack wasn't there. She hurried downstairs to the kitchen and found a note on the table. "Coffee is made, and I will be back in a few hours. I love you, Miss Addie."

Morgan and Rose walked into the room, and Addie said, "Do you know where Jack went?"

"I didn't know he'd left." It worried Morgan that Jack had left without saying where he was going.

"He left me a note saying he'd be back in a few hours." Addie chewed on her lip. He'd told her last night he'd talked to Davey about Coburn. Davey had told him Mr. Coburn had hit him, but Jack told her not to worry, he'd promised Davey no one would ever hit him again. He also told her to start calling Davey, David, and not make a big deal out of it, and to ask the family to do the same thing.

Morgan thought it odd Jack didn't tell Addie where he was going.

Addie realized where Jack had gone. "Morgan, he talked to Davey about . . ."

Morgan didn't give her a chance to finish. As soon as Addie said Jack talked to Davey, he knew. He kissed Rose, grabbed his hat and coat off the hook by the back door, and ran out the door.

Addie and Rose stood there staring after him.

"What was that about?" Rose asked.

"Jack went to see Mr. Coburn."

Morgan pulled his horse to a halt in front of the sheriff's new office. Jack's deputy, Webb, walked outside to greet him.

"Hello, Morgan. What are you doing in town so early?"

Morgan didn't dismount, and didn't waste time on small talk. "Have you seen Jack?"

"Yeah, I was surprised to see him here so early this morning. Strangest thing happened; he gave me his badge and said I was acting sheriff right now. Said he'd let me know when he was up to taking over again."

Just as Morgan suspected, Jack was going to confront Coburn. "Thanks, Webb."

Morgan had already turned his horse when Webb called out.

"He didn't head back to the farm."

"I know."

Morgan made it to the Coburn farm in record time. Before he could get out of the saddle, Sarah Coburn came running from the back of the house.

"Stop him, Mr. LeMasters, he's going to kill him!" Sarah shrieked.

Morgan rode behind the house and saw Jack pulling Roy Coburn off the ground by the front of his shirt.

"Stand up, Coburn. You like to hit someone, well I'm right here. Try someone your own size for a change." As soon as Jack released Coburn's shirt, he dropped to the ground.

Morgan dismounted and walked to Jack. He looked down and saw Coburn's battered face. "That's enough, Jack."

Jack turned to look at Morgan. "You didn't see David's back."

"No, but look at him." Morgan pointed to Coburn splayed on the ground with his eyes closed, blood oozing from his nose. "I think he'll think twice about hitting anyone again."

Jack looked down at Coburn. "Miserable son of a . . ." He reached down and picked up his hat and smacked it against his thigh. "Let's go home."

Chapter Thirty-Two

Frank joined Ruth in the library to share in her late afternoon vice. While Frank was pouring the brandy, Ruth walked to the large mahogany desk and pulled a leather pouch from one of the drawers. She traded Frank the bag for her brandy. "There's ten thousand in gold in there. That's for Mrs. King."

"Why gold?"

"No record should Robert go snooping around."

"Smart." Frank liked the idea of gold. He figured Leigh wouldn't know how much the gold was worth, and he could keep some for himself.

"You've been spending a lot of time with that young woman. Will she be ready to leave soon?"

"I had to gain her trust, and she's well enough to travel now. We plan to leave in three days. I want to get out of here in case the judge decides to return early. What will you tell him when he finds out we are both gone?"

Aunt Ruth had already thought of that scenario. "I'll tell him you went to the mine to start work, and that I have no idea where she went." She drank some more of her brandy. "But it occurs to me if she goes back to Colorado City, Robert is certain to find her there. That's the first place he will look."

"I've thought about that." Frank had no plans to take Leigh near Colorado City. He'd fully intended to take her to Black Hawk with him. It seemed like the perfect hideout.

"I think it would be best if you take her to Black Hawk with you. There's room in that home, and Robert would never think to look for her there." She gave Frank a knowing smile. "And I suspect you would enjoy the companionship, at least for a while."

Frank arched his brow at her. "Ruth, you surprise me."

"I understand men. I wasn't fool enough to think my dear husband spent all his time alone in Black Hawk in that house. Men have their needs, and my husband was discreet." She spread her arms wide. "He gave me everything I wanted. You're a young

515

man, and I think you loved Charlotte in your own way, but men move on more quickly than women. You'll seek gratification where you can find it freely, and I don't judge you for that. I'm more pragmatic than most women. I'm grieved that Charlotte felt threatened by that woman. There was no need for her to worry about her father's money, she would have inherited everything I own. But I suspect it wasn't only her father's will that troubled Charlotte; she didn't want to share him with anyone. That was her true objection to that woman. Charlotte had Robert all to herself her entire life. And Robert was devoted to her. He wasn't trying to replace his daughter, he was, like you, seeking gratification. I do understand Robert's loneliness, but he should find a woman his own age. A respectable woman."

"You don't mind if I am with a disrespectable woman?" Frank teased.

"You're young. You'll be with many women before you settle down." Ruth pointed to the bag. "Just make sure she uses that money to resettle when you tire of her. It's hard for a woman to make it without a man. Once she's lived with you without benefit of marriage, her reputation will be in tatters. You'll be ready to let her go, but be kind."

Right now, Frank didn't think he would tire of Leigh. Of course, he'd felt that way a few times before, so Ruth might have a point. "Ruth, you are a wise woman who doesn't see things through rose-colored glasses."

"I take that as a compliment."

Frank lifted his glass in the air in salute. "You should." When Frank first met Ruth he thought she was a sweet woman. He'd quickly found out she was as shrewd as she was wise. Even though she was older, he found he was attracted to her.

"Will you be taking a buckboard to Black Hawk?"

"Yes, I figure I'll need some supplies. I plan to leave before dawn."

"Yes, that would be the best time to depart to avoid prying eyes." Pleased with their plans, Ruth settled back in her chair and sipped her brandy. Now all she had to do when Robert returned was convince him that she'd been right to warn him off that woman. Hadn't she been right, after all? It hadn't taken long for Mrs. King to take up with Frank. Perhaps Robert would come to realize he was being foolish, trying to relive a time that could not be resurrected. She understood the fleeting vigor of youth, and the remnants of what was left in its wake.

517

But it was her duty to encourage Robert to accept his future with the dignity their family name deserved.

Frank saw a problem with their plan. "If the judge asks the right questions, he's bound to find out we left Denver at the same time."

Arching her brow, Ruth said, "You're right. Perhaps I should tell him that the woman left town, and when you found out, you left to look for her."

"He'll ask how she left," Frank said.

"That would complicate matters." Ruth admired the way Frank thought through a plan.

"There's a stage tomorrow, headed east. I'll have Leigh go to the station and book passage."

Ruth smiled. "That should work. I'll tell Robert you found out she traveled east. If he makes inquiries, they'll be able to confirm they sold her the ticket. I doubt he would go to much trouble to find her if he thinks you are already looking for her. Of course, that plan would require you to return to Denver soon and tell him you couldn't find her."

"I can do that." Frank didn't think the judge was a stupid man, so he hoped Ruth could lie convincingly.

■ ■ ■ ■

"Do you have everything ready to leave early tomorrow?" Frank asked Leigh.

"Yes, I'm ready. When I purchased the stagecoach ticket this morning, I talked to the clerk for a long time. I know he won't forget me."

"Good." Frank had no doubt that the clerk would remember her. Leigh was beautiful and men noticed her whenever she walked into a room. It wasn't necessary for her to say a word. "I doubt the judge will ask around since Ruth is going to tell him I'm searching for you."

"Did she tell you about the home where we'll be living? Is it nice?"

"She said it had everything we'll need, and I'm certain it will be nice if her husband lived there. If you need anything in particular, I'll pick it up at the mercantile today." Frank hadn't given Leigh the money from Ruth yet. He decided he'd hold on to that money until he saw how things worked out. He didn't plan on staying at the mine longer than necessary. He'd find a way to pilfer some gold, hopefully enough to last a long time.

"You don't think she will tell the judge

519

about us?" Leigh was excited to be leaving with Frank, and she didn't want the judge to show up unexpectedly at their new home.

"She won't tell him." The judge might figure out the way of things on his own, but one thing was certain: Ruth wouldn't tell him. He wasn't sure he understood Ruth's motives, but she was adamant the judge should abide by appropriate social mores.

Leigh pulled Frank's face to her. "Frank, you wouldn't take me there and leave me, would you?" Leigh knew the judge would never leave her, but she wasn't as certain about Frank.

"No, I won't leave you." He kissed her, then he jumped up and walked across the room. He grabbed the whiskey bottle from the table and poured himself a good portion. He noticed her trunk in front of the wardrobe. "Get your trunk ready and I will load it on the buckboard tonight. In the morning, when you leave the hotel, walk in the direction of the livery. I'll be waiting for you."

"How long will it take us to get there?" Leigh asked.

"It will take a few days in a buckboard. We'll stop at a way station so we don't have to sleep out in the cold." He finished his drink and reached for his shirt on the chair by the bed. "I better get out of here."

The judge arrived three days after Frank and Leigh left Denver. He ran straight to Leigh's room in the hotel, and when he opened the door, she wasn't there. His first thought was to go in and wait for her, but he realized none of her personal belongings were lying about. Thinking she may have changed rooms, he hurried downstairs to see the clerk.

"Where is Mrs. King? Did she change rooms?"

"No, sir, she left a few days ago."

"Where did she go?"

"I don't know. I didn't see her leave. I just knocked on her door to see if she wanted some breakfast and no one answered. I waited until lunch to try to rouse her again, and when she didn't answer, I opened the door thinking she might be ill. I saw the room was empty, and all her things were gone."

"She didn't return the key, didn't check out?"

"You paid her bill for a month, and the key was on the bureau."

The judge suddenly had a thought that nearly made him ill. "She didn't have a setback, did she? Did the doctor see her?"

"She looked fine the last time I saw. She seemed to be doing very well. Mr. Langtry was spending a lot of time with her."

"She didn't leave a note for me, did she?" The judge was grasping for anything that would explain why she was no longer at the hotel.

"No, sir, her room was totally empty."

The judge left the hotel and headed to the doctor's office.

"Judge, it's good to see you again," the doctor said in greeting.

"Have you seen Leigh? Is she here?"

The doctor frowned. "No, I haven't seen her in several days. She was doing very well, and told me if she needed me she would stop by the office. Has something happened?"

"I'm not sure. She's not at the hotel." A million thoughts were swirling in the judge's head. Where could she be? Perhaps Ruth had had a change of heart and asked Frank to bring her to the house. "Thanks, Doc. If I need you, I'll let you know."

On the way to Ruth's, his mood lightened, certain that he was going to find Leigh there. Ruth was always a reasonable woman, and she'd probably come to realize how much Leigh meant to him. He'd thought if Ruth gave Leigh half a chance, she'd like her. Of course, she'd never love her as she did Charlotte, but he'd hoped they would at least be friends.

He ran through the house when he arrived, but no one was home, not even the housekeeper. After he searched the last bedroom, looking for any sign of Leigh, he hurried to the room where Frank had been staying, but it was empty.

Uncertain of his next move, he walked to the parlor and poured himself a drink. Perhaps Leigh decided she was tired of the hotel. Without finishing his drink, he grabbed his coat and hurried out the door. He inquired at the boardinghouse, but Mrs. Latimer assured him no one was staying in her home that she didn't know.

Dejected, the judge walked back to Ruth's. While he waited for someone to come home, he finished his drink. He made himself a second drink, built a fire, and sat down. Nursing his third whiskey, he heard the front door open and he hurried to the hallway.

"Where is she?"

Ruth hadn't expected him home for another week. "What are you doing home so soon?"

"Where is she?"

Ruth removed her coat and said, "Let's

go into the parlor. You can pour me a brandy."

In the parlor, the judge handed Ruth her brandy and sat across from her and waited.

Ruth had practiced her speech until she was certain she would sound believable. She took a deep breath. "Frank left home very early three mornings ago, said he was going to buy some supplies and check on Mrs. King. He told me she had recovered nicely, he was just checking in to see if she needed anything. But that morning he returned home an hour later. He told me she had left the hotel, and he'd already searched the town for her. He went to the stagecoach office, and was told she'd purchased a ticket on the stage headed east. Frank packed his things and took off to look for her. He said he couldn't face you without finding out why she left. He didn't want to let you down."

"But why would she leave? She couldn't have been up to traveling alone. Did you have a hand in this?" The judge couldn't believe that Leigh would voluntarily leave without telling him. It made no sense. They'd been so happy together.

"Of course not! I've never met the girl. I thought you said she was destitute. How did she get the money to travel on the stagecoach?"

"I left her some funds in the event of an emergency." He'd left her a considerable amount of money, but he didn't feel the need to mention that to Ruth.

"Obviously it was enough to purchase a ticket to wherever she wanted to go, and Frank said she was totally recovered from her injury." Ruth congratulated herself for playing her part beautifully. Frank would be impressed.

The judge slumped back in his chair and dropped his head in his hand. "I just don't understand why she would leave. She was happy, and we had plans to travel."

Ruth gave him some time to drone on about the loss of his love before she said, "Her reason may have been as simple as she realized you are too old for her. It's possible she met a younger man."

"When? We were together most of the time. Other than Frank, I was the only man around her."

"Robert, you know I may have been right. She was using you for your money. Tell me why you think a young woman would be interested in an old man? What could you give her that younger men couldn't?" She waited a second for him to respond and when he didn't, she said, "Money. She undoubtedly had never met a man of your means who showed an interest in her."

He jumped from his chair, walked to the sideboard, and filled his glass. "She said she loved me."

"Do you think she would be the first young woman to say those words to an older man, to ingratiate herself into his life? Don't be a bigger fool than you have already made of yourself."

The judge gulped his drink, and poured another. "Ruth, you don't know her. You don't know what we shared together."

"I know she's not here. She waited until you left to leave town. What else do I need to know? What proof do you need before you realize that young woman was using you because you are wealthy? And look at the result of her machinations. Charlotte is dead. She paid the price of that woman's schemes."

The judge was barely listening to his sister. His heart was breaking. "Thank God for Frank." He had faith Frank would catch up with Leigh and find out why she left.

Ruth smiled. "Yes, thank God for Frank. I imagine he'll come home and tell you that you've been crying over an opportunist."

The judge slammed his glass on the table.

"I can't sit here and wait. I've got to do something."

"You are sure you were speaking with Mrs. King?" Judge Stevens asked the clerk.

"Yes, sir. I asked her name. She's a real pretty lady. I wouldn't forget her."

"Did she mention her exact destination?"

"She said she was thinking of visiting family in New York."

That was the first he'd ever heard of family. Leigh had always told him she had no family. He thanked the clerk and left. After he arrived home, he walked back into the parlor and sat by the fire. Thankfully, he could hear Ruth talking to her housekeeper in another room. He needed some time alone to think, to relive his conversations with Leigh to see if she'd given any hints as to her whereabouts.

He only had a few minutes to himself before Ruth interrupted him. "Robert, you need to stop this nonsense of moaning over that young woman. Your health is suffering."

"I'm as healthy as a horse." To show his displeasure at her meddling, he jumped up and poured himself a drink.

"I'm worried about you. You are not looking well." Ruth had noticed before he left town that he was pale, but she thought he was just upset over leaving his girlfriend.

The judge jumped up. "Leave me alone, Ruth. I need some peace and quiet." He then took a step toward the door, clutched his chest, and collapsed.

CHAPTER THIRTY-THREE

Jack motioned for the marshal to take a seat at the table. Everyone came to the table carrying dishes, and Addie poured the coffee.

"I'll be going back to Denver tomorrow, and I want you all to know I appreciate everything you've done for me," Marshal Holt said.

"I'm happy to see you're feeling up to traveling, but you don't have to leave so soon," Jack said.

"You all treat me so good, if I stay longer, I may never leave." He looked at Granny and added, "Thank you for saving my life. I'm indebted to you."

"We are all indebted to Granny. She's saved my hide on more than one occasion," Jack said.

"I hope you will take care, Marshal Holt, unlike some people I know," Granny said, frowning at Jack.

"Granny, if not for me, your skills would

get rusty," Jack retorted.

"You're full of nonsense, Jack Roper. I don't know how Addie will put up with you." Granny tried not to, but she couldn't stop smiling at Jack. She loved him like a son, just as she loved Morgan.

Marshal Holt laughed at their banter. "I promise I'll be careful."

"I hope you'll come back for our wedding," Jack said.

"When's the big day?"

"Next Saturday. The pastor stopped by yesterday, and we made plans for noon. We're getting married at a special place in the pines." Jack looked at Addie and winked. "I don't want to give her a chance to change her mind."

Jane stopped eating and gave Addie a serious look. "You wouldn't change your mind, would you?"

Addie shook her head. "No, indeed. He is stuck with me, as are you children."

"We're happy to be stuck with you," David said.

Addie leaned over and kissed David's cheek. "That makes me so happy you feel that way, David."

"Will we have cake?" Jane asked.

"We most certainly will, a great big one," Rose said.

"Papa, can I have cake?" Claire asked.

"You can have all the cake your little tummy can hold on that special day," Jack said.

"Well, if we're having cake, I'll have to come back," Marshal Holt said.

"Bring Sheriff Trent with you," Jack said.

When Marshal Holt asked why they were marrying in the pines, Addie explained about the special place where the sisters had played when they were children. "Rose and Morgan were married there earlier this year."

"It sounds like a special place," Marshal Holt said.

"It may be a bit chilly, but it will be worth a few goose bumps," Addie said.

"Maybe I'll get married there one day," Jane said.

Jack hugged her. "I hope you stay my little girl for a while yet. Don't hurry to grow up."

"I can't believe we are going to be a real family," Jane said.

"You can believe it, honey. If anyone tries to take you children from us, they'll have to go through me. And that's a promise." Jack didn't make a promise he didn't intend to keep.

Granny shook her finger at Jack. "Your

new pa is not so easy to go through. But I'd rather not have to patch him up again."

"You children can rest easy, you have a whole family willing to fight for you," Morgan said.

"And you will have a new cousin in a few months, and we are going to need your help," Rose said.

"I hope we get another boy. We need more boys in our family," David said.

Jack smiled. It was heartwarming to hear David say *our family.* "I expect we will be blessed with many nieces, nephews, brothers, and sisters in the years to come."

The children started debating how many brothers and sisters they wanted, and the adults laughed as the numbers grew.

"Jack, I've been thinking you and Addie need to draw up those papers for your orphanage and your adoptions. I'll take them back to Denver with me, talk to the judge and explain the situation. It might not even be necessary for you to go to Denver." Marshal Holt had already made his mind up to help these folks out with the judge.

"I appreciate that. We'll have everything ready." Jack prayed the judge would listen to Marshal Holt, but if not, he was determined to find one who would.

On Saturday, Jack and Morgan were at the kitchen table at the farm having coffee, waiting for the women and the children to come downstairs. Pastor Hunt arrived with Jack's deputy, and Marshal Holt and Sheriff Trent were right behind them.

Jack met them at the door. "It's good to see you. Come on in and warm up while we are waiting for the women."

The children ran into the room, and Jack said, "Sheriff Trent, you remember my children, don't you?"

Sheriff Trent smiled. "I sure do. They were mighty helpful the last time I was here."

Each time Jack introduced the children as his children, they smiled wide.

"Papa, where is Mr. Joseph?" Claire asked.

"He's in the pines praying to the Great Spirit." Joseph had had a cup of coffee earlier with Jack, and he'd told him he was going to get prepared.

"Is his Great Spirit our God?" Jane asked.

"Well, Joseph describes him as the Creator of all, and that's how we describe God."

"Why doesn't Mr. Joseph go to church with us?" Jane asked.

"All of nature is Joseph's church," Morgan said. "His people were here long before us, and their church is where they are."

"Are the ladies ready?" Jack asked.

"Yes, we are," Granny said as she walked in with Rose.

"Children, get your coats," Rose said.

Addie walked into the kitchen and everyone immediately stopped talking. She was wearing a high-neck, creamy white satin-and-lace dress that skimmed enticingly over her voluptuous figure. It was gathered snugly at the waist and softly floated to her ankles. Her hair was styled in a loose bun on top of her head, secured by antique combs decorated with seed pearls. Wisps of curls fell seductively to her shoulders.

Jack had never seen a more beautiful woman. "Here's my lovely bride." He held his hand out to her, and when she placed her hand in his, he twirled her around so he could see her dress from every angle. He didn't care if the men admired her full curves — she was his.

Addie blushed as she twirled. "Granny made this dress."

Jack winked at Granny. "I expect she started sewing when she sat with me when I was shot back in the summer. She told me you were the one for me, and she was right. I'll never argue with her again."

"That'll be the day, Jack Roper. You'd argue with the devil himself." Granny held out Addie's coat to Jack. "Now quit ogling your bride and help her into her coat. If we don't get there soon, Joseph will be frozen."

"Yes, ma'am." Jack wrapped Addie in her coat and kissed her behind the ear. "You're the most beautiful woman in the world."

"I have the most handsome groom," she replied softly.

Jack didn't hesitate when the pastor told him he could kiss his bride. He held her close and gave her a kiss she would remember for the rest of their lives. "I love you," he said when he ended the kiss.

Breathlessly, Addie replied, "I love you."

After everyone kissed the bride and shook hands with the groom, Jack said, "Let's go home."

"Granny made punch," Jane said.

"You really are our Granny now," David said.

"I certainly am your Granny. I'm the luckiest granny in the world to have you as my great-grandchildren."

"We are lucky too," David said.

"I think I'm the most blessed man alive," Jack said.

"I will agree with that," Marshal Holt said

as they turned to walk through the pines back to the house. "I didn't get a chance to tell you earlier, but I saw Judge Stevens. I don't know if you heard, but he had a heart attack. He's going to survive, and I can tell you I think it scared the daylights out of him. I've never seen a man change so much. When I told him of your situation with the children, he didn't hesitate to sign all the papers. The children are now yours legally."

The children heard what Marshal Holt said and started jumping up and down.

"Can we call you pa now, and Miss Addie ma?" David asked.

Tears were in Jack's eyes when he responded. "I'd be honored if you called me pa."

Addie was so happy she couldn't stop her tears. "That would be wonderful."

Everyone was enjoying their cake and punch around the table when Granny inquired about the marital status of Sheriff Trent. "So you're a bachelor too. You may be interested to know that I have a third granddaughter coming to Denver in a few weeks. She's an opera singer."

"You mean Emma Langtry is your granddaughter?" Sheriff Trent asked.

"Yes, do you know her?" Granny asked.

"No, ma'am, but I saw her sing in New York a few years ago. Her pictures are all around Denver advertising her arrival next month."

"Now, Granny, I thought you told Clay that Emma was meant for him," Jack teased.

"She may well be, but that doesn't mean he won't have to win her hand. I'm not so sure the pastor wants to marry."

"When did that ever stop your matchmaking schemes?" Morgan asked.

"Are you complaining about my matchmaking, Morgan LeMasters?"

"No, ma'am." He grinned at Rose. "I'll never complain about that."

"You have beautiful granddaughters, Granny. Maybe I'll hang around Denver until she arrives to give the sheriff more competition," Marshal Holt said.

Granny liked the sound of that. "Good. We are all going to Denver to see her sing, and we'll meet you two there."

It was time for everyone to leave, and Morgan and Rose planned to take the children to the ranch with them so Jack and Addie could have the house to themselves on their wedding night.

The children were saying good-bye, and Jack pulled them into his arms along with Addie. They hugged each other for several minutes. "I have everything in life I ever wanted right here in my arms."

The children were almost out the door when Jack said, "David."

David stopped and turned to look at Jack. "Did you want me?"

"I finally figured out the reason."

David walked back to him. "You did?" He didn't need to ask what his new father was talking about.

"Yeah. I think He was saving the best family for me."

"Are you mad that it took so long?"

"Nope. I've been blessed beyond anything I could have imagined. I'd go through it all again for what I've gained."

David threw his arms around Jack's waist and hugged him fiercely. "Thanks, Pa. I think He saved the best for us too."

Addie and the others remained silent, knowing something momentous had just passed between father and son.

When Jack's gaze met Addie's, he saw she was on the verge of tears. He pulled her to his side and said, "Thank you for giving me this wonderful family."

Addie couldn't find the words to describe her happiness. Instead, she followed David's lead and wrapped her arms around her new husband.

Jane and Claire ran to them, and Jack wrapped his long arms around all of them.

When they said good-bye for the second time, Jack looked at Morgan and said, "Take good care of our children."

ABOUT THE AUTHOR

Scarlett Dunn lives in Kentucky surrounded by all manner of wildlife, and enjoys long "God walks" where most inspiration strikes. Possessing an adventurous spirit, and a love of history, particularly the pioneers of the West, she has a special place in her heart for all cowboys, past and present. Readers can visit her website: www.scarlettdunn.com.